Fires of Prophecy

Fires of Prophecy

Book Two
The Morcyth Saga

Brian S. Pratt

Fires of Prophecy
Book Two of The Morcyth Saga
Copyright 2006, 2008 by Brian S. Pratt

Books written by Brian S. Pratt can be obtained
either through the author's official website:
www.briansprattbooks.com
or through any online book retailer.

ISBN-10: 1438268459
EAN-13: 9781438268453

The Morcyth Saga

The Unsuspecting Mage
Fires of Prophecy
Warrior Priest of Dmon-Li
Trail of the Gods
The Star of Morcyth
Shades of the Past
The Mists of Sorrow*
*(Conclusion of The Morcyth Saga)

The Broken Key

#1- Shepherd's Quest
#2-Hunter of the Horde
#3-Quest's End

Qyaendri Adventures

Ring of the Or'tux

For my father. Even though we may not have spent as much time together through the years as I've wanted, he is still a very special person to me and always in my thoughts. A wonderful grandfather to my children, who love him dearly, as do I.

Prologue

"Find someplace to hide, I'll find you," he hears James say.

Miko glances back and sees him turning to confront the oncoming soldiers. His desire to stay to help his friend is strong, but he knows that he'll be more of a hindrance. His first duty is to help the kids get away. Turning back, he finds the fleeing children far ahead of him, turning down a side street. He hurries to follow, trying to catch them before they move too far ahead.

Rounding the corner where they fled, he sees the last few children turning another corner, even further ahead than before. Running as fast as he can, he comes to where they disappeared around the corner. Almost losing his balance from taking the corner too fast, he comes to a sudden stop. The kids are no where in sight.

Crumph!

The sound of a loud explosion comes from where he left James. "James!" he cries out, glancing back at the cloud of smoke and dust rising into the sky. Torn between his duty to the children whom he's lost and to his friend, he stands there a moment in indecision. Finally making up his mind to return to help his friend, he turns around and races back the way he had come.

As he rounds the second corner, a billowing cloud of dust engulfs him and he's unable to see anything. After a moment, the dust clears and a large pile of rubble is revealed blocking the street where several buildings have toppled over. Amidst the rubble are the bodies of Empire soldiers, lying there crushed to death under large sections of the toppled buildings.

"James!" he cries out, but receives no answer. Looking around frantically, he can't find James anywhere. Scared and alone, he races back again along the path he and the children originally took in an attempt to find some place to hole up until James finds him. Whenever he comes to an intersection, he stops before entering and carefully looks around the corner. Making sure no enemy soldiers are there before he enters the street, he then races toward the next intersection. Panic begins to take hold of him as enemy soldiers begin to appear as they move along the adjacent streets. *He's got to get off the streets!*

Hoping to find a place to hide, he tries opening one of the doors lining the street and is relieved when it actually opens. Pulling it open quickly he makes to enter when a vase smashes into the door next to his head. "Get out!" he hears a woman shrieking wildly and quickly ducks as he sees another pot come flying at him out of the corner of his eye. The pot strikes the door and ricochets into the street. "Out!" the woman screams again as she readies another projectile.

Slamming the door closed, he races down the street, panicking. From up ahead, a door opens and a man pokes his head out as he looks down the street. When the man notices him running, he opens the door wider and yells, "This way!" motioning for Miko to quickly come inside.

Seeing the man holding the door open and gesturing for him to hurry, Miko sprints forward, his panic subsiding. When he reaches the door, the man opens it further for him to be able to run inside. His anxiety decreases rapidly when he passes through the door and is safely inside.

Once he's inside, the man closes the door and Miko begins to say, "Thank you…" but stops suddenly when he realizes the man is advancing on him with a knife. A quick survey of the room reveals several men with bared knives and swords. Dread fills him when he sees a dozen or so people, both men and women along with a few children, sitting along one wall. To his astonishment, they are completely naked with their hands tied behind them.

"Strip!" the man from the door says. Miko, panic ready to consume him, remembers the slavers they fought on their way to the City of Light. Shaking his head in disbelief, he backs away from the man. Someone from behind grabs him and two of the men proceed to strip him naked, using their knives to cut the clothes off of him. He struggles to resist, but only gets socked in the eye for his efforts.

Shortly he finds himself sitting naked on the floor next to the others, his hands secured behind his back. Over to the side is a pile of clothing sitting in the corner, what's left of his clothes is tossed on top. The little boy sitting next to him starts to cry and the woman on the other side of the boy tries to comfort him but to no avail. The boy's cries grow louder and louder until one of the men comes over and strikes him on the head, knocking the boy unconscious.

"You bastard!" the woman yells at him.

The man turns to her and backhands her across the mouth. "Shut your mouth!" he yells at her. "Open it again and I'll slit your throat!" He draws his knife and menaces her with it, then sheaths it as he walks away, laughing.

The woman scoots closer to the boy and does her best to comfort the unconscious child. Miko can see tears streaming down her face.

"Here come some more," the man by the door tells the others. Opening the door partially, he sticks his head out and yells, "Over here!" while he waves to whoever is out there to come inside.

A man with a woman and two kids run inside. He begins to express their gratitude when the woman sees Miko with the other naked people sitting on the floor and screams. Realizing their danger, the couple grabs their kids protectively.

"Strip!" the man by the door commands.

The father pauses momentarily then launches himself at the man by the door. He throws a fist but is easily blocked. The slaver strikes back with the handle of his knife, clubbing him in the side of the head. The father stumbles backward from the blow, dazed. Two of the other slavers grab him and proceed to cut his clothes from him.

The woman screams as others grab her and the children, tearing them apart. Soon, all four are sitting naked against the wall with the others, arms securely tied behind their backs. They try to talk amongst themselves but are quickly silenced by the slavers.

Several times over the next hour or so, that scene is replayed as more people rush into the room seeking safety only to end up captured.

There finally comes a time when the man at the door turns to the other slavers and says, "I don't think there are anymore out there." To the naked people he says, "Alright, get up."

Miko finds it hard to rise with his arms tied behind his back. Using the wall for leverage, he makes it to his feet and stands there waiting while the rest of them get up.

One of the naked people remains seated against the wall. A slaver goes over to the man and kicks him, saying, "Get on your feet. Now!"

The man on the floor begins to topple over and falls to the ground, remaining motionless. The slaver checks him and then turns to the one by the door. "He's dead," he tells him. Then he glances over at one of the slavers and says accusingly, "You hit him too hard and cracked his skull."

The slaver being accused just shrugs and says, "Oh well, happens sometimes."

Giving him a dark look, the man by the door says, "Next one you kill, you're paying for. I don't intend to lose money because of a heavy handed thug."

"Thug?" the man asks, his face going red in anger.

"Yes, thug," he replies. "Now, let's get 'em lined up and back to camp." He stares down the man until he backs down and joins the others in tying the naked people together in a line.

Miko is tied in line between two children. Once they are all secured to the rope, the man takes the lead and they head out the door.

The sun is already beginning to rise above the horizon as they leave the building. Miko squints in the glare, eyes unaccustomed to the light after having been in a semi dark room for hours.

One of the women begins wailing and crying. A slaver comes over and uses a whip across her shoulders saying, "Silence!" When the whip strikes her she cries out with pain and shock. After two more blows of the whip she tries to muffle her cries and the whip stops.

Miko just looks on in shock at the red lines across her shoulders and back from where the whip struck her. He keeps his head down as he plods along, doing his best to not think about being paraded though town naked. The enemy soldiers they pass hardly even give them any attention, except for a few calls to the ladies in the group.

After moving down several streets, their group joins with another slave line and together they make their way to the southern wall. More and more of the enemy's soldiers can be seen. When they draw close to the gate, the head slaver brings them to a halt and has them wait while he talks with the guards. After a few words are exchanged, the slaver shows them a letter and they are allowed to pass through.

Outside the walls, Miko sees teams with carts filled with the dead as they take them over to a large, communal grave where they are deposited. Soldiers are everywhere, a veritable forest of tents covers the area outside of the gates for over a mile. When they pass a tent with several men standing in line outside, Miko can hear the cries of several women coming from within.

One of the smaller children asks, "Mama, what's that lady crying about?"

The woman, trying to hide the tears in her voice replies, "She's just sad," her voice beginning to crack. "That's all it is, don't worry about it."

Then a slaver comes and whips both of them saying, "No talking!" When they both remain silent, he goes back to his position next to the line.

Out away from the encampment of soldiers is a large area with many wagons and strings of people tied in lines just as they are. The only difference between those people and Miko's group, is that those people have clothes. The males all have a cloth wrapped around their loins while the women have a very short dress, all a drab brown in color.

When Miko's group arrives, they are taken to an open area nearby where they're told to stand and be still. The lead slaver moves to a nearby wagon and begins pulling out garb, similar to what the other slaves are wearing and begins handing them out to the other slavers. The slavers then take the garb and tie it around the men, and with the women they untie their hands before putting it on them. Miko feels somewhat better for having his privates covered. All the captured people visibly relax once they're dressed and covered.

Several of the slavers then move to another wagon where they remove crossbows which they hold ready to prevent anyone from trying to escape.

One of the slavers climbs onto the bed of a wagon and faces the newly arrived slaves. "Go ahead and sit down and rest," he tells them. "This may be the last chance you'll have for a while. No talking and anyone causing trouble will be dealt with." He glances around at the faces looking at him a moment then jumps off the wagon.

Miko does the best he can with his hands tied behind him and manages to make it to the ground without falling over. He sits there and rests, looking back to the City that's now securely in the hands of the Empire. All that keeps him from totally losing it is the belief that James will find him.

Over the next hour, several more slave lines are brought from the City and join with the rest. There are over a dozen different lines trailing behind several different wagons. With each line that comes, several of the guards that were guarding them grab crossbows and join their fellows in keeping watch.

At one point shortly after Miko arrives, a slaver begins moving down each line and unties the hands of the men and boys. Once they are all untied, another slaver mounts the wagon and addresses the people in the slave lines. "We will be passing out food and water shortly," he announces. "Don't waste any, it's the last you'll see until tonight. Your hands shall remain free, but if you make trouble, they will be secured again. If you try to escape, you will be shot. This is the only warning you'll be given."

Once the slaver is finished, other slavers begin passing down the lines, giving each captive a small cup of food and allowing them a single drink from a ladle, filled from a water bucket one of them carries. When Miko gets his, he eats the food ravenously, even though it tastes pretty bad. He drinks all the water and is about to ask for more when a girl of about sixteen in another line holds out her cup to a slaver and asks, "Can I have more?"

The slaver comes over to her and slaps her hard across the face, "Impertinent slave! You take what we give you and be happy that you were given anything at all."

The girl cries, "I'm not a slave!"

All the slavers standing within ear shot hear her and break out laughing. The slaver who had come over and slapped her says, "You are now," and laughs at her.

The girl starts crying hysterically and the man slaps her across the face again. "You shut up or it'll be worse for you." He grabs her by the hair and pulls her head back so her eyes stare right at him. "Do you understand?" he asks with an expression that says, 'The only answer better be yes'.

Tears streaming down her face, the girl just nods. The man releases her hair and walks away. She sits there and sobs to herself quietly.

Miko looks around and can see that until that moment, some of the people who were tied to the line hadn't come to that conclusion yet, that they were slaves. Some begin to murmur amongst themselves, others start crying. One of the slavers shouts, "Slaves only speak when spoken to, break this rule at your peril!" The people begin to quiet down until only muffled sobs can be heard. Several slavers come and collect the food cups that had been handed out.

An older slaver walks from the City and begins speaking with one of the others for a moment. After they are done talking, the older slaver returns to the City of Light. The one he was talking to turns to the slaves and shouts, "Everyone on their feet!"

Miko quickly gets up as do most of the people around him. Several others, either through stubbornness or not understanding, remain on the ground. Those that fail to stand quickly enough for the slavers are whipped until they are up and standing.

The one that ordered them to their feet announces, "When slaves are told to do something, they do it quickly and they don't ask questions. A slave who doesn't learn that rule fast, tends not to survive very long."

Miko begins to think that the man who's been giving them orders is the lead slaver for this group. He hadn't noticed it before, but the man's clothes look slightly superior to anything any of the others are wearing.

The lead slaver gets up on a wagon and with a nod of his head to the driver, it begins moving out, pulling the line of slaves behind it. Soon all the wagons are rolling, each with the lines of slaves walking along behind.

Marching under the hot sun soon has Miko exhausted and extremely thirsty. Only after they've been on the road for two hours does a slaver pass down the line, allowing each of them one cup of water while they're walking. No one dares to asks for more this time. This repeats every two hours until they stop for the night.

While Miko is sitting and eating the small amount of food they've given him, a voice is heard coming from within the group of slaves. "Where are you taking us?" a woman's voice asks.

"Who said that?" one of the slavers asks. With whip raised in his hands, the slaver rushes over to where the sound of the voice originated, looking from face to face in an attempt to determine who dared break the silence. Unable to find the source of the question, he looks around at them all and says, "The Slave Markets of Korazan." After a moment's pause to let that sink in, he adds, "Where you will be auctioned off to the highest bidder, to spend the rest of your lives as slaves." Laughing, the slaver goes back over by the fire and resumes eating his meal.

"Oh, James," Miko sighs quietly. "Find me!"

Chapter   One

James wakes to find the two boys are no longer there. The two girls are over in a corner huddled together, and talking in hushed voices. He stretches and sits up, asking, "Where are Jiron and Tinok?"

Startled, Delia and Cassie cease their conversation and look in his direction. "They're out looking for Jiron's sister," Delia explains.

"She was separated from us during the attack," adds Cassie, her yellow hair shimmering in the candle light.

Concerned, he asks, "Do you think it's wise for them to be about with all the soldiers in the city?"

"They'll be alright," Delia assures him. "Jiron knows how to keep hidden when he needs to."

Cassie nods her head in agreement.

Worried about the boys, but even more worried they may lead someone here, he tries to relax. Resting his back against the wall, he realizes there is nothing he can do about it now but wait.

He still feels weak and a little drained from the battle two days ago. Even though he's had two good nights of sleep and food, he still feels a little shaky. "Is there any more food?" he asks after his stomach growls loudly.

"Oh, yes," Cassie says. She gets up and goes over to a sack sitting against the wall. She pulls out some bread and cheese, bringing them over to him along with a bucket of water.

When she sets the bucket down next to him, she says, "Sorry, but there are no cups."

James smiles at her and replies, "That's okay." He takes the bread and cheese from her and removes his knife from its sheath, before slicing off a chunk of cheese. He only has to scrape a little bit of mold off with his knife.

While he eats, Cassie returns to Delia and resumes their conversation. Both occasionally stop talking and glance over at him, then when they realize he's noticed them staring, they quickly turn their heads away.

Sighing, James tries to ignore them. *Miko, what's happening to you?* he silently wonders. He's feeling better and stronger, but is still a little too shaky to attempt to go after him. Upset with his own weakness, he knows all he can do right now is try to regain strength quickly so he can go after him.

About that time, Jiron and Tinok come back in through the collapsed hallway. Earlier, he took a look and found it choked with stone and wood from when the building above had collapsed some time in the past. A small space has been cleared through the debris, wide enough to allow people to pass through in single file.

Several feet down the passage, a stone stairway extends up to the ground above, exiting in a corner of a park. From what Jiron told him, the opening is overgrown with bushes and grass, effectively hiding the entrance from anyone passing by.

Several years ago, when he was younger, Jiron had been playing in the area and stumbled upon the opening. Excited about finding a secret place, he decided to keep the knowledge of it to himself. Later, when he and Tinok became close friends he brought him here. Only because the Empire had showed up had they allowed Cassie and Delia to come.

Apparently, when Jiron had stumbled upon him during his battle with the soldiers, he was out trying to find his sister who had become separated from him earlier. When he saw James fighting the enemy and had actually driven them off, he decided to save him and bring him here. As far as Jiron knew, no one else has ever been down here in the years they've been using it for their secret clubhouse.

Delia sees them first and gets up asking, "Any luck?" Cassie stands up with her and they go over to them as they enter the room.

With a look of disappointment, Jiron replies, "No, and I looked everywhere."

"I'm sorry," Cassie says.

Jiron comes over to James and asks, "Can you help find her?"

Shaking his head, James replies, "Not unless you have something of hers I can use?" The look on Jiron's face tells him that he doesn't.

Feeling bad for the boy, but unable to help, he says, "She may still turn up."

"I doubt it," says Jiron, "I went to everyplace that she would've gone and she wasn't there. I can only assume that they found her and she's one of the thousands of slaves they captured."

"Slaves?" James suddenly interrupts. "Where are they being kept?"

"They had a big encampment outside of the walls for them," Tinok says, "but sometime yesterday, they started marching them south."

"South?" James asks.

"Yeah," Tinok replies. "Looks like they are taking them back to the Empire. Your friend is most likely with them." He looks over to Jiron and adds, "As Tersa may be as well."

"Can't we do anything?" asks Cassie.

"Like what?" asks Tinok, "Chase after and rescue them?" He looks at her incredulously, "They have hundreds of guards, not to mention their entire army occupying the city. It would be suicide!"

Jiron had been studying James' face while the others had been talking. When James glances over at him, he asks, "You're planning on going after your friend aren't you?"

"Yeah," James replies, nodding, "just as soon as I feel better. Miko is a smart kid, he knows I'll find him. He'll do what he needs to in order to survive until I get to him."

"You're crazy!" Tinok exclaims. "You're going to get yourself killed!"

"Perhaps," James says, "but I'll not leave him to his fate. He wouldn't be in this situation if it wasn't for me."

"What do you mean?" Delia asks.

"I came to the City of Light to find out all I could about Morcyth, a god that used to be popular around here a long time ago." He looks at them and asks, "You wouldn't by chance have ever heard of him, have you?"

They all four shake their heads no.

"Anyway," he continues, "Miko tagged along despite my attempts to warn him of the dangers. I had found out some info from Ollinearn, the Keeper of the Great Library here in the City. We were on our way out when the Empire's forces showed up and then things just went from bad to worse."

"The last thing I told him was, 'Find a place to hide, I'll find you.'" James finishes his bread and cheese then cups his hands together as he drinks water out of the bucket. Sitting back against the wall once more, he glances at the four faces staring at him.

"I'll go with you," Jiron states.

"What?" Tinok exclaims in disbelief. "You can't be serious."

"You'll be killed!" Cassie cries.

"How can I leave her in the hands of slavers?" Jiron replies. "I'm all she has left in this world and I'll not rest until either she's free, or I'm dead!" Turning to James he says, "So, when do we leave?"

James considers the request, and nods his head, "Alright, we'll go tonight." He turns his attention to Jiron and asks, "Can we get out of the City unobserved?"

"I don't know," he admits, "there are hundreds of troops stationed within the walls and thousands more on the outside. It looks like they plan to defend and hold the City against attacks from our soldiers. Both inside and out, there are many patrols and they've been doing routine sweeps of the houses, looking for anyone else still hiding."

Delia lays her hand on Jiron's arm and says softly, "So you truly intend to go after her?"

He looks into her eyes and says, "I have to."

"Then I'll go with you," she says, emerald eyes revealing the fear she's trying not to show.

"That wouldn't be wise," Jiron tells her. "You'll probably die or be taken as a slave if we fail."

"What chance do I have here?" she asks. "With all the Empire's forces occupying the town, what chance do any of us have if we stay? It's only a matter of time before they find us, we can't hide out indefinitely."

"I'm coming too!" Cassie says.

Tinok just looks at them like they are crazy, and then says, "Well, I'm not staying here by myself, better count me in as well."

James sits there thinking for a few seconds while they all stand there, staring at him. He looks at Jiron and asks, "Can you get us supplies? Like food?"

Jiron nods his head and replies, "Food's no problem, we have some stashed here as it is."

"We're all going to need packs to carry it with us," he says. "Can you get one for each of you?"

"Should be able to," he replies. "I'll go out now and get 'em."

Yawning, James says, "I've got to rest if we're going to do this tonight. I'm still not over the effects of the magic I used during the battle." He settles down on the ground and uses his backpack for a pillow.

The others go to the far side of the room and confer among themselves quietly, allowing him some quiet so he can fall asleep. Not long after James falls asleep, Jiron and Tinok leave through the passage to attempt to acquire four travel packs. Delia and Cassie remain behind.

A gentle shake awakens James and he opens his eyes to discover Delia kneeling beside him, shaking his shoulder. "James," she's saying, "wake up."

"What?" he asks, sitting up abruptly.

"It's night outside," she says, "and they haven't returned yet."

Coming awake quickly, he stands up and looks around, Jiron and Tinok are nowhere in the room. "How long have they been gone?" he asks worriedly.

"Several hours," Cassie replies from where she stands behind Delia. "He said they would be back before it got dark. I'm worried."

Concerned himself, James says, "Let me take a look outside and see if I can tell what's going on."

"Be careful," Cassie warns.

"I will," he assures her. "I'll just stick my head out and see what the situation is like outside."

The girls accompany him over to the passage and watch as he makes his way through the rubble to the stairway.

The passage is fairly choked with debris, he can't believe they managed to drag him through here unconscious after the battle. At the stairs, he has to step carefully so as not to dislodge any of the rocks and stones, the entire area seems very unstable.

Nearing the top, he begins to see the starlight being filtered through the bushes that have overgrown the entrance. He reaches the top of the stairs and slowly and cautiously, peers through the bushes to see what's going on outside.

He looks around and discovers that the bushes are located within a corner of a city park, that's wedged in among several buildings. It's not much more than a small grassy area with trees, where the people could take their ease from the worries of the day.

With only the stars above for light, James can't make out much more than vague shadows, but it doesn't look as if there's anyone around. He remains there scanning the area for several minutes before returning back down to the room.

"Didn't see them out there," he tells the girls as he leaves the passage.

"What are we going to do?" Cassie asks, fear in her eyes.

"I'm sure they're okay," Delia states with conviction. "They know the area and Jiron is good at evading people when he wants too. Besides, they may have had to take a longer route to get back, or hole up and wait until they can once again move without being seen."

"I hope so," Cassie replies.

"I doubt if we could make it out of here without him," says James. "We're going to have to wait until either he comes or we're sure that he isn't. So let's just settle down and get comfortable, it could be a while."

The girls go back to their usual place, with James accompanying them. They break out some of their supplies and have a little snack while they are waiting for the boys to return.

"So," begins James, "are you two their girlfriends?"

Delia laughs and Cassie blushes slightly. "I grew up with Jiron," Delia explains. "We are very good friends. When he realized the Empire's soldiers were within the walls, he came and found me. Cassie just happened to be there with me, and I wouldn't go unless she could come too. You see, she's my best friend. He tried to locate his sister, but there were just too many soldiers on the streets. So we headed here as quickly as we could, occasionally having to hide and wait until the enemy passed by. When we got here, Tinok had already arrived and we've been here together ever since."

"Do you think Jiron can actually lead us out of here?" James asks.

"If anyone can get us out," she says confidently, "he can. That boy knows every street and hideaway in the whole city."

"Let's just hope they make it back," he says wishfully.

"They will," Delia says, "you can count on it."

They sit and talk for a while until James begins to hear noises coming from the passage. All three look with both hope and trepidation to the entrance of the passage and hold their breath. Then, Jiron and Tinok step out into the room, carrying four backpacks filled with stuff.

"Told you," Delia says to James. Then to Jiron she asks, "What took you so long? You had us scared to death you weren't going to make it back!" She stares him down with hands on hip as he walks over to them.

"Sorry about that," Jiron apologizes, as he hands her a backpack.

"Yeah," Tinok says, "we had to lay low for a while. They brought in extra soldiers and are still in the process of searching houses." He hands his extra pack to Cassie.

"Seems they know there's a mage here somewhere, and they want him bad," Jiron comments as he looks toward James. "We overheard some talk between soldiers about it."

"Is this going to hamper our efforts to get out of here?" he asks.

"Shouldn't think so," Jiron explains. "I don't think they've blocked the way I was planning for us to take."

"And what way is that?" James asks.

"Can't really explain it," he says. "But trust me, the way should still be open."

When Cassie puts on her backpack, she says, "Just what is in here that makes it so heavy?"

"Some dried beef, water bottle, and other essentials," he explains. "There are also some extra clothes, just in case."

Once everyone has their backpack on, Jiron leads the way through the passage, with James right behind. Tinok is taking up rear guard with the girls in between.

They all wait at the bottom of the stairs while Jiron goes to make sure it's safe. "It's clear," he whispers back down after scanning the park, "come on up."

James begins to climb the stairs with the girls close behind. He reaches the top and joins Jiron outside while they wait for everyone to exit.

"Now where?" James asks once everyone has joined them up top.

"Just follow me and stay close," Jiron says. He has them hug the wall while they make their way toward the street at the end of the park. As they approach, marching feet can be heard coming toward them from further down the street.

"Now what?" James quietly asks.

Speaking to all of them, he whispers, "Stay silent and close to the wall, they should march right past us without even noticing we're here."

Standing still and quiet, they press themselves against the wall and wait. Soon the first soldiers appear from the left and continue marching down the street, past the park. Jiron's plan is working, not one soldier even bother's to look within the darkened park.

Aaachew!

They all look to Cassie in disbelief as a very loud sneeze escapes her.

Immediately the closest soldiers stop and turn at the sound. They see them there, partially illuminated by the few torches a couple of the soldiers hold. Both sides just stand and stare at one another for a brief second. Then James yells, "To the tunnel! Move!"

As if that is the catalyst everyone needed, all hell breaks loose. They turn and race back toward the stairs as the soldiers give chase.

As everyone reaches the stairs, James turns and lets loose the power, attempting to slow the soldiers' advance.

Crumph!

The ground explodes upward, tossing soldiers in the air and pelting them with dirt and other debris. Several soldiers had been in advance of the area that exploded and were now almost upon him.

In a panic, James pushes out with the power, literally tossing the onrushing soldiers backward, where they collide with their comrades.

"The mage!" he can hear coming from the street as more soldiers rush toward the park, starlight reflecting off their swords.

"James! Come on!" he hears behind him. Turning, he sees that everyone has already made it inside the tunnel and Jiron is there motioning for him to follow.

James runs over and enters, flying down the stairs. "What are we to do now?" he asks Jiron.

"We're trapped," Jiron explains. "There's no way out!"

When James enters the room, Cassie is there in tears. She looks to James and cries, "I'm sorry!"

"It's okay," he assures her, though in his own mind he's not nearly as forgiving.

Tinok is standing at the passage entrance, listening for pursuit. He turns and says, "They're coming." Suddenly two knives flash into his hands as he stands ready. Jiron takes up position next to him and two knives appear like magic in his hands as well, flashing in the reflected candle light.

He looks to Tinok and says, "You ready?"

"Yeah," Tinok replies with an evil grin. "Let's get it on!"

They stand there to either side of the doorway, James and the girls stand a little ways back from them.

Suddenly an enemy soldier comes into the room, sword out, and Tinok closes with him. The soldier sees him and strikes with his sword. Tinok easily deflects the blade with one knife while following through with a thrust with the other, piercing the man's chest and puncturing his heart. The soldier slides lifelessly off his blade to the floor as another soldier comes through the doorway, into the room.

Jiron takes this one and almost as fast as Tinok, dispatches him.

"You're getting slow, Jiron," Tinok says as he closes with the next one to come in. Knives flash and another body sinks to the floor.

The next soldier to come through is carrying a shield along with a sword and closes with Jiron. Jiron deflects the thrust of the sword with one knife as the shield comes and crashes into his chest, pushing him back further into the room. The soldier advances on him when all of a sudden one of his legs goes out and he crashes to the floor. Tinok had hamstrung him from behind as the soldier was closing in on Jiron. Jiron presses the soldier as he lies there on the ground, blocking a cut from the sword and avoiding the shield. He gets inside the man's defenses and slits his throat. He looks up to see Tinok battling another one.

"Don't need any help," Jiron says to Tinok with a grin.

"Sorry," Tinok replies, "I'll try not to save your life next time." His knives flash and another soldier falls to the floor.

Suddenly there's a pause as no more soldiers come through the opening. Tinok turns to James and says, "Alright Mr. Mage, you got any ideas?"

James suddenly realizes that he had been watching the fighting, awestruck at the relative ease in which they've been taking out the soldiers and not thinking about the situation at all. Red faced, he begins pondering the situation instead of wool gathering.

Another soldier enters, a veritable giant of a man. Standing easily a head taller than either Jiron or Tinok, covered in armor from head to toe, with a long shield on his left arm, he enters the room and immediately engages Jiron.

The man's sword is enormous and Jiron is unable to get inside his defense. The blows from his sword pack enormous power and when Jiron blocks a slash aimed at his midsection, his knife is knocked out of his hand, leaving it tingling.

Tinok is unable to go to his aid as he is fighting with another soldier, this one of a more regular size but carrying a shield. The soldier begins pushing Tinok back as another soldier enters the room.

James makes his mind up and releases the power. The ground begins to shake and from the passage leading from the room, they can hear a roar as the ceiling of the passage crashes down on those still within it. A cloud of dust fills the room as Tinok and Jiron battle the three soldiers that had made it in before the collapse.

The bull of a man is pressing Jiron, who now only has one knife and is reluctant to close with him. He's trying to stay just out of reach and stall for time, hoping that Tinok can finish with his two and come to his aid.

James scans the room but the only stones he can find to use are the ones near the collapsed passageway, and he is unable to reach them due to the fighting.

He tries to think of some sort of a spell he can use when he sees Jiron fall to the ground and the man raise his sword to finish him off. Cassie screams.

Seeing his chance, he releases the power and the man is picked up and thrown against the wall. Bones can be heard breaking as he connects with it. He slides to the ground, the tapestry that had once hung on the wall, falls with him, covering him as if it's his death shroud.

James looks to Tinok as one of his attackers falls to the ground, the man's tunic under his left arm, now red as his life's blood flows from him. Tinok easily parries a series of attacks from the remaining soldier, before slicing him across the forearm, causing him to drop his sword. He twists and with his other knife, comes in and thrusts between the ribs, piercing his heart.

As the last attacker falls, Tinok turns and looks at Jiron, "You okay?"

"Yeah," he replies, "my arm's a bit numb but it's beginning to get its feeling back. You?"

Shrugging, he says, "Got a couple cuts, but nothing major." He turns to James and says, "Now what? With the passage blocked we got nowhere to go."

"I don't know," he admits, "let me rest a second and we'll see what I can come up with."

They sit down while James considers the options. Jiron walks over to the large man, looking closely at him. "I've never seen someone so big," he says to the rest of the group.

"I thought he had you for a second there," Tinok says. He picks up Jiron's knife from the floor and hands it to him.

"Me too," agrees Jiron as he takes the knife. Turning to James he says, "That was sure some spell you used. Why did you wait so long?"

"I am new to this magic business and as long as you were in close contact with him, I couldn't do it without possibly hurting you as well."

Nodding, Jiron glances back at the giant. Then his eye catches something on the wall, behind where the tapestry had hung. "Look at this!" he says, waving everyone over.

On the wall is an indentation in the form of the Star of Morcyth. When James sees it, he unconsciously grabs the medallion through his shirt.

"Wonder what it is?" Cassie asks.

"I don't know," admits Jiron. "Strange how we never noticed it before."

"It's the Star of Morcyth," James explains.

They all turn toward him and Delia asks, "The star of what?"

"The Star of Morcyth," repeats James. He reaches in and takes out the medallion, showing it to them. Looking around as if for the first time, he says, "And this must be part of the High Temple of Morcyth that was destroyed centuries ago."

He removes the medallion from around his neck and goes over to the wall, placing it within the indentation. It's a perfect fit.

From behind them, they hear the sound of stone scraping on stone. Turning around, they are surprised to discover a section of the floor sliding over to reveal a staircase leading down.

"I'll be damned," Tinok says.

"Maybe it's a way out," suggests Cassie.

"Don't know," says James as his glowing orb appears in his hand. "But there's only one way to find out." He goes over and begins to descend the steps.

The rest glance at each other and then follow him down.

Chapter   Two

Fourteen steps take them down to a hallway that runs for a hundred feet before ending at a door. James can see another indentation, similar to the one found in the room above them, carved into the door. Taking the medallion, he places the face of it within the indentation and the door begins to silently swing open.

The first thing they notice when the door swings open is a four foot high white marble pedestal standing in the center of the room. Centered on top of it is a small, raised platform which looks to be made entirely of crystal.

James is the first to enter the room and a soft light springs to life, growing until it illuminates every corner. It seems to come from the very walls themselves. The room is octagonal in shape, with no discernible exit except the doorway he just passed through. The walls are unadorned, just plain ordinary stone, the floor is simply dirt. The only thing of interest in the room is the pedestal.

"James," Delia asks as she crosses into the room after him, "just what is this place?"

"I don't know," he replies. "I've never been here before."

When Cassie enters the room, she goes over and comes close to the pedestal, looking closely at the crystal platform on top of it. She runs a finger over it and says, "Remarkable."

"What?" Jiron asks as he comes over to her.

"Oh, just never saw such a large piece of solid crystal before," she replies, still fascinated by it.

Jiron turns to James and asks, "Do you think there may be another way out of here?"

Shrugging his shoulders, he says, "Maybe, after all the High Priest would have wanted a way to get out in emergencies." He starts to examine the walls and floor. Remembering the last time back in Merchant's Pass, the ceiling as well, but to no avail.

"It looks like something at one time rested upon this platform," she announces.

They all come over and she explains. "Here in the middle," she indicates the center of the crystal platform, "it looks as if something could have rested in there."

James closely inspects it and can see a place where something might have at one time rested upon it. There's an open space within its center in the shape of an inverted pyramid. "Wonder what it could have been," he wonders. Pressing down on the platform, he halfway expected something to happen and is disappointed when nothing does.

He turns away from the pedestal and once more resumes the search for a hidden door.

"What are we looking for?" Delia asks.

"Something that will trigger a release and open a secret door," explains James. "Of course, there's no guarantee that there will be one."

Cassie, still intrigued by the crystal platform, tries to lift it up and it easily lifts off the pedestal. "Look!" she cries excitedly.

Everyone turns at her cry and sees her there with the crystal platform in her hand. James rushes over and looks where the platform once rested. There again is the indentation in the shape of the Star of Morcyth. Removing his medallion once more, he sets the face of it within the indentation.

The pedestal begins to sink silently into the floor, while at the same time a section of the walls across the room from where they entered, begins to rise up into the ceiling. The opening reveals a crudely formed tunnel leading away into darkness.

To Cassie, James says, "Replace the platform." To everyone else he says, "Let's hurry, no way to know if it will close again on its own."

They all hurry toward the tunnel and when Cassie replaces the platform, the section of the wall begins to slide once more back down toward the floor as the pedestal begins rising. She runs quickly to get to the passageway before it closes completely and has to duck her head in order to clear it as she passes through.

Once the wall closes, leaving them in total darkness, James makes his glowing orb which gives them ample light to see their way down the passageway. Taking the lead, he follows it for several hundred feet, until it comes to an end. An old wooden ladder is there, leading up out of sight, into the darkness above.

Jiron says, "Let me check it out," as he elbows James aside and climbs the ladder. He disappears into the darkness above while everyone waits at the bottom of the ladder for his return. A minute passes and then from above they hear him say, "Come on up, it's safe."

James begins to climb the steps of the ladder, with the girls following and Tinok bringing up the rear. Upon reaching the top, James finds that they are now in another deserted basement. He looks around as the rest make their way up, and sees Jiron over at a door fiddling with the lock.

Coming over to him, he says, "Locked?"

Without halting what he is doing, Jiron says, "Yeah, but I should have it open in a sec."

James sees him using two small, thin, metal tools on the lock. Just after everyone gets up from the tunnel below, he hears a 'click', and Jiron opens the door as he turns to James with a satisfied smile on his face.

"Good job," congratulates James.

"Thanks," he replies. Opening the door, Jiron steps through, followed closely by James.

On the other side, they find themselves in a small, deserted alley, wedged in tightly between two buildings. "Do you know where we are?" James asks him.

"I think so," replies Jiron. "If I'm right, it isn't far to where we can get out of the city."

"I hope you're right," James says as he follows him down the alley.

Following the alley, they soon come to where it opens upon another, slightly larger one. Jiron holds up his hand for them to wait as he peers around the corner. He steps out into the larger alley and signals for them to follow.

He turns left down the new alley, hugging the side as they make their way carefully and quietly to where the alley intersects with a main thoroughfare. He has everyone stop and then motions for James to come closer. "Look down there," he whispers to him, pointing down the thoroughfare.

James looks where he's indicating and sees a gate. "Yeah?" he asks.

"Earlier when I was out, I saw some workmen trying to repair it," he explains. "I think they damaged it during their attack and may not have had the time to repair it. If we act quickly, we should be able to get through before anyone realizes we're no longer in our hideout back at the park."

"You may be right," James acknowledges. "Once they realize we're loose, we won't stand a chance of sneaking out." He looks down the road toward the gate and doesn't see any guards.

"They don't have any guards posted," Jiron says. "I think they're arrogant in their own superiority. They probably don't believe anyone would be foolhardy enough to try to sneak out with thousands of troops stationed around the city."

"What's on the other side of the gate?" he asks.

"A large courtyard that separates this gate from the one leading out of the city," he explains.

"What if that gate is shut and locked?" James asks.

"Last night they left it open," Jiron tells him. "I guess they see no reason to keep it closed because there is no one to keep out."

"Yeah, who would be stupid enough to come visit?" James reasons.

"Exactly," Jiron agrees. "Last night, there were horses picketed in the courtyard that we may be able to appropriate if they're still there."

"Alright," James says, "you sold me. Let's not spend the night here jabbering. Let's get the heck out of here!"

"Follow me," Jiron says as he takes one last look around and then cautiously makes his way over to the gate. The rest of them quickly follow until they're all huddled by the gate. Jiron pulls on the gate and it swings open, squeaking slightly on rusty hinges.

He pulls it open just far enough to allow them to squeeze through and holds it open until everyone else has made it to the other side. He follows the last person through and closes it again until it once more appears shut.

James looks around the courtyard but the horses that Jiron had mentioned are no longer there. The courtyard is not completely empty either, there are four cook fires spaced around the courtyard, each with several soldiers hanging around them. Pulling Jiron close, he points to the enemy soldiers and says, "There's no way we're going to make it across there without them seeing us."

"Maybe we need a distraction," he suggests.

"Like what?" James asks.

"I don't know," he shrugs, "what can you do?"

"How about a big explosion with lots of fire and noise?" offers James.

Jiron breaks out into a big smile and says, "I think that may do."

"All right, you guys wait here and I'll be right back." James slips back out the gate and runs up the street several blocks and enters a vacant building.

After several minutes, Jiron sees him coming back and holds open the gate for him. "You okay?" he asks when he sees how he's not walking quite straight.

"The spell took a lot out of me," he says, pausing before passing through the gate. "I should be okay in a little bit." He then passes through to the other side and Jiron once more shuts the gate.

They wait several minutes and nothing happens. They wait several more and still nothing happens.

Jiron looks to James and asks "Are you sure you..."

Crumph!!!!!

The concussion of the blast knocks them down and a giant plume of fire reaches toward the sky. Several buildings surrounding the explosion begin to collapse from the sheer force of the blast. The soldiers in the courtyard are knocked to the ground and James can hear their cries of shock as they see the sky light up with fire. Once they regain their feet, they race off toward the sound of the explosion, leaving the courtyard empty.

"Damn!" Tinok says as he looks at the fireball reaching to the sky.

"Let's go," James says in astonishment as he races to the gates leading to the outside of the city. His legs are a little shaky but are able to keep up the pace. Debris begins to hail down upon them as they make for the gates, dirt and stones falling from the sky pelt them as they cross the courtyard.

Delia cries out when a sizeable stone strikes her in the left shoulder, knocking her to the ground.

Tinok comes to her aid. "Are you okay?" he asks as he helps her to her feet.

"Not really, but I can make it," she says with determination as they hurry to follow after the others.

When they reach the gates, they discover that there's a section still missing, allowing easy access to the outside. They hurry quickly through to the other side, where they pause momentarily as they see men racing toward the city from all over the countryside in response to the blast.

Staying close to the wall, they hide in the shadows as they begin making their way away from the gates. Jiron grabs James' shoulder and says, "Look, over there." He points to a section of the enemy's camp off to the south.

Scanning the direction Jiron's indicating, James sees several horses tied to a tree near a group of tents. *Fortune!* They're all saddled. A large campfire is burning in a pit near them, bathing the entire area in light. They'll have to make their way through some of the camp in order to get to them.

"With everyone running to see what's up in the city," Jiron says, "we should be able to get the horses with little trouble."

"Let's hope so," James says apprehensively. "If anyone's looking when we enter the light, we could have problems."

"We've got little choice," Tinok says when he joins them. "We'll never get far on foot."

Turning to Tinok, James says, "Jiron and I will get the horses, you stay and protect the ladies until we return."

He waits for Tinok's nod and then he and Jiron run toward the horses. When they get close, James sees that there are a total of seven horses. They slow down and approach more cautiously when they're close to being illuminated by the fire. They edge around the fringe of the light, trying to get as close to the horses before entering the light and risk being seen.

When they're as close as possible, James looks around and sees that no one's in the vicinity. Signaling Jiron, they both hurry over and begin untying horses as fast as they can.

The horses begin making noises as they hurry about their work and all of a sudden, the flap of the closest tent opens up and a man peeks out. "What are you men doing with my horse?" he asks with an edge to his voice as he exits the tent and begins to approach them. He's wearing a plain cowled robe with the hood thrown back revealing shoulder length red hair. His eyes are dark and James can see anger smoldering behind those eyes.

James glances to Jiron and they both come to the same decision. Jiron's knives flash in the firelight as they spring to the ready. James takes a stone he had in his pocket and casting his spell, unleashes the magic as he throws it at the approaching man.

The instant before the stone leaves James' hand, the man flicks his wrist. When the stone nears him, it hits a barrier and ricochets away into the night.

Startled by the ineffectiveness of the stone, James hesitates a moment, trying to understand what had just happened.

"The mage!" the man cries out in shock, then his eyes get a calculating look.

Jiron launches himself at the man, knives flashing in a whirling pattern. As if he was dealing with an annoying fly, the man waves his hand toward him.

James feels a prickling along his skin as he watches Jiron being lifted off the ground and thrown a dozen feet away. Understanding comes, *He's a mage too!* James directs his magic to the ground under the mage's feet and lets it flow.

Crumph!!!!!

The ground explodes upward with incredible force. When the dust clears enough, James sees the man still standing there untouched. A three foot diameter of ground remains undisturbed beneath him.

"Is that all you have?" the man asks with contempt, words heavy in accent. He swirls his hand and it begins glowing red then he flicks it at James. A red light flashes toward him, striking him hard in the chest, knocking him backward onto the ground.

As the man makes his way through the crater that surrounds him, he says to James, "I was expecting more of a challenge, how disappointing."

James lays there unable to breathe, gasping as he tries to take in a breath. He sees a knife fly through the air out of the dark toward the mage, but it hits an invisible protective shield and bounces harmlessly away, landing on the ground.

Once the mage clears the crater, he gestures with both hands while staring intently at James. Suddenly, James' legs begin to cramp, he can feel their muscles knotting and twisting causing him great pain. He cries out from the pain and in desperation casts a spell, one he used many times back home, role playing. He feels it using up the remaining power within him, leaving him weak, barely able to move.

The approaching mage chuckles as he sees a clear, shimmering bubble appear between them, floating in the air. "What's that suppose to do?"

He casts another spell and the bubble begins sparkling as if fireflies were contained within. The mage's face loses its look of confidence and begins to exhibit worry. The sparkles begin increasing in luminosity as the man's face slowly turns to a look of confusion.

Jiron comes to James' side and asks, "You okay?"

Exhausted from the spell he just cast, he gasps, "Will be." The effect of the mage's earlier spell begins to dissipate and the pain in his legs subsides. Jiron turns to the mage and with knives ready, advances on him once more. James grabs his arm as he starts toward the mage, stopping him and warns, "Don't touch him or the bubble."

"Why?" Jiron asks.

Shaking his head, he replies, "No time to explain, we've got to get out of here. Now!" he shouts, then lapses into unconsciousness and sags to the ground.

Jiron looks to the mage who is shaking his head with a look of horror as he stares into the bubble, the sparks within gaining size and intensity. "No!" he cries in terror, suddenly dropping to the ground. The bubble is getting brighter and brighter by the second.

From out of the darkness, Tinok and the girls come running toward them. "Get the horses!" Jiron shouts as they approach. He begins to untie the remaining horses from the tree.

"What's that?" Cassie asks as she makes to approach the bubble.

"Get away from it!" Jiron yells at her. "James said not to touch it."

He hollers over to Tinok and says, "Help me get James on a horse." When he comes over, they lift him up and quickly secure him onto the horse with some rope.

Delia mounts a horse and then looks back over to the mage who is by now whimpering in terror. His hair, once a vivid red has now turned grey and he's beginning to shrivel in upon himself like a grape having spent too much time in the sun.

Jiron mounts and says, "Tinok, you stay next to James and make sure he doesn't fall off." He turns his horse toward the southwest, "Let's stay close together," he advises, "and maybe we can survive this." He glances over to the bubble; the sparks have grown until they now fill the entire bubble with a white light whose intensity is painful to look upon. The mage on the ground is no longer moving and appears dead.

Kicking his horse in the side, Jiron rides through the camp, the others close behind. Out of the darkness ahead of him, several men suddenly appear. Holding on tight, he rides straight through them, knocking them over. He looks back toward the bubble, and the light is now extremely bright, illuminating a large portion of the camp. He can see dozens of men running toward it, one of whom is wearing a cowled robe just like the other mage had. They race past the tents and reach the far side of the camp.

They pass numerous soldiers but none seem to notice them, all eyes are turned to the now brilliantly bright light. The guards at the fringe of the camp take notice of them approaching and command them to stop. A crossbow bolt flies past, nearly striking Tinok as they race through. They flee into the dark grasslands to the southwest of town, leaving the guards behind. They don't get too far before...

Schtk!

They look back at the sound from the backs of their horses, everyone holds their breath in anticipation of what may happen. Then…

Booooooom!

A giant explosion, ten times the force of what they experienced when that building blew earlier. They feel the concussion wave as it washes over them, luckily they're far enough away that it doesn't hit them with enough force to knock them over, just causes their horses to miss a step. They stop and look back at the camp.

Reaching toward the sky is a tower of flame, the roar from which can be heard even though they're now far away from it. The base of the fire extends throughout the camp in every direction, burning everything within.

They sit there in awe as the flame punches through the clouds and then slowly dissipates, appearing as if it's sinking back down to the ground.

"Dear god!" Cassie exclaims.

They all glance at the unconscious James and then look to each other. Tinok asks, "Just what have we gotten ourselves into?"

"I don't know," Jiron replies, shaking his head as he glances again at James. "I don't know." Kicking his horse, he leads them out into the grasslands.

Chapter   Three

James awakens in the morning light. Sitting up suddenly, his head begins to spin and starts aching as if a hundred little hammers are pounding away on it. He holds his head until the pain has subsided to a more tolerable level and then looks around as he takes in his surroundings. The others are still asleep and five horses are picketed a little ways away from the camp, the saddles had been left on for a quick getaway.

A moment of panic sets in when he can't locate his backpack, then he realizes he had been using it as a pillow. Opening it up, he reaches in and removes some food along with his water bottle.

Deciding not to wake the others, he sits there and eats while he contemplates the events of the day before. *The Empire's mage almost had me,* he thinks to himself. *I'm just a rookie compared to them, they've probably been doing this for a long time. My spells seemed to be rather ineffective against him, too. Going to have to work on better, more innovative spells, gotta surprise them next time or I'm toast.* He remembers his last spell and smiles, *I bet he never saw that coming!*

Hearing one of the sleepers stirring, he looks over and sees Cassie as she leans up on one arm and looks over in his direction. He holds up some of his food, silently offering it to her, but she just shakes her head no. She grabs her pack and gets up, coming over to sit next to him.

She opens her backpack and takes out some of her own rations and then asks as she begins eating, "You okay?"

"Better," he replies through a mouthful of food. "The more powerful the spell, the more it takes out of you. Sleeping last night has helped a lot. After I'm done eating, I should be fine, if a little fatigued."

"That's good," she says. "We were all worried about you last night, after you passed out."

"It's what happens sometimes," he tells her. "Just how long did we ride last night?"

"Several hours, I think," she guesses. "It seemed like a long time. Everyone was getting too tired to stay in the saddle so we stopped here and made camp."

"We probably shouldn't stay here too much longer, the Empire will want to find us in a bad way," he says.

During their conversation, everyone else awakens and joins them for breakfast.

"What was that thing you did last night?" Tinok asks when he settles down next to him.

"You mean the bubble?" James asks.

"Yeah," he answers. "When it went off, it must've taken half their camp with it."

"Really?" James asks, surprised. "I wasn't sure what was going to happen to tell you the truth. I've never actually done that one before. What happened, exactly?"

He sits there and finishes eating while Tinok relates to him the events after he passed out. When he gets to the description of the explosion, James is quite astonished.

"You see," he explains when Tinok is done telling him, "I designed the bubble to do two things. One is to absorb the power from any magic spells currently active in the area, and the other is a little more complicated. You see, when a mage casts a spell, he opens a conduit from his core of power, usually only enough to accomplish whatever spell he intends to do. My bubble grabs that flow, pulling the power into itself, while at the same time preventing the mage from closing the conduit. The result is that all the mage's power is sucked out of him and absorbed into the bubble. That must've been what was giving the bubble the light, the mage's power that it had absorbed."

"Now here's the part I've never been able to really test before," he explains. "What happens when the bubble is filled to capacity and reaches critical mass?"

"Critical mass?" Delia asks, confused. "What's that?"

"Critical mass is when something is filled to capacity and ready to 'pop', for lack of a better term," he explains. "In this instance, it could no longer hold the power, so it exploded. I would guess the size of the bubble and the amount of power it had absorbed would determine the intensity of the explosion."

"You could wipe out an entire army with one of those!" Tinok exclaims.

Shaking his head, James says, "Not necessarily, after all it would only work if there was a mage present. Also, if everyone ran away before it exploded, it wouldn't be doing too much harm."

"I see your point," he says, somewhat disappointed.

"Now," Jiron interjects, "what are we going to do about rescuing my sister and your friend?"

"Well, first of all, where are we exactly? Which way did we go when we left the City?" he asks.

"We headed southwest," Jiron answered.

"So it's safe to assume that we are currently in enemy territory," James concludes, "and will continue to be for a long time."

"Yeah," agrees Tinok.

"I propose we continue to head south and try to find out where the slavers intend to take them," he suggests. "Once we know that, we'll have a better idea of what we can do."

"Let's get going then," Jiron says, anxious to get started.

"I agree," James says, shouldering his backpack as he stands up. He goes over to one of the horses and swings up, head spinning from the exertion. When it calms down he scans the surrounding countryside and is relieved to find nothing moving across the grassland, except for the tall grass, waving in the breeze. The southerly breeze feels good as the summer sun begins to warm the day.

He notices that Delia needs Tinok's help in climbing into the saddle and that she is favoring her left arm. He walks his horse over to her and asks, "Are you okay?"

"A stone hit me when the building exploded last night," she explains. "It hurts, but I don't think it's broken, just bruised."

Feeling guilty at being the cause of her pain, he says, "I'm sorry."

She smiles at him and says, "Hey, don't worry about it. We got out didn't we? This is pretty minor compared to the fate I would've had if we hadn't." She pats him on the arm with her right hand and gives him a reassuring smile, then continues, "So don't feel bad. I don't, okay?"

He smiles back at her and says, "Alright, I won't" Glancing around to see that everyone has already mounted and is ready to go, he turns his horse to the south and breaks into a canter. The others follow along behind.

He takes the lead with Jiron next to him, the girls in the middle, and Tinok eating their dust at the rear. After they've traveled a ways, he asks Jiron, "Just where did you and Tinok learn to fight so well?"

"Fight clubs," he replies.

"Fight clubs?" James asks.

"Yeah," he says, as he continues riding. "They're not altogether legal, but many of the wealthy pay to have people fight one another with weapons for their amusement. It pays pretty well, but you usually don't survive long."

"I always did the knives, so did Tinok. We both rose up through the ranks quickly, you see we both kind of have a knack for this sort of thing. We never were set against each other and were able to become friends. Friendship with another in the fight clubs is rare, because often you have to face them in the pit, many don't even bother. But we got along well, even though we knew a day would come when we would be set against one another."

"Finally, the day came when we were set to face off in the pit. You never know who you will be facing until your name is called. When our names were called, we both marched out into the pit and by this time, our friendship had grown very strong. We both could see that the other's heart was not in this. When the order was given, Tinok opened himself up to me, didn't even try to defend himself, he was willing to sacrifice himself rather than strike me. The crowd was not happy, they had come to see blood spilled. They began calling for me to kill him, but I couldn't."

"I came and stood next to him and cried to the gathered people, 'We will not fight each other.' You can imagine what happened next, they sent in the bruisers, the ones who deal with problems in the pits. Two came in, wielding clubs. We stood our ground and in no time at all, they were dead at our feet. We stood defiant before the crowd, side by side."

"Next, they brought in two armored guards with swords, and to the shock of everyone there, they soon laid dead at our feet too. After that the crowd began to realize what they were seeing, and started applauding us. Two upstarts, who wouldn't play their game, ended up playing their game." He breaks out into a laugh. "So from then on, they paired us up. They would send two, three, sometimes four against us at a time, but none could match us."

"Incredible," James says.

"Yeah," agrees Jiron, "it was."

"What made you start in the first place?" James asks.

"My sister and I used to live on the streets," he explains. "And one day, a man came to me and told me about the clubs and that he thought I might have some talent at it. He offered me a silver if I came and at least tried some sparring with him. I did and found I actually did have some talent for it. I'm pretty good with any weapon as it turns out, but with the knives, I'm very deadly."

"The man trained me for six months and then I had my first fight. They put me against another knifer and I took him relatively fast and received coins for winning. After several fights, I was able to get a small place where my sister and I could live, a place she would be safe until she could hopefully find a good man. She never wanted me fighting, but you gotta do what it takes to survive."

"I understand that," he says.

From behind them, Cassie interrupts and asks, "Do you think they're going to follow us?"

James turns into his saddle and says, "Most assuredly, it's only a matter of time. I'm just hoping they won't think that we're escaping further into their territory. Most likely they'll think we've already headed north or due west toward the Silver Mountains and Cardri. That's where I would think to look if I was them. I doubt if anyone will remember which way, exactly, we were heading. They were a little preoccupied at the time."

Next to him, Jiron breaks out into a laugh and nods his head.

They ride on for another hour before they begin to see a town appearing on the horizon. They keep an eye out for movement but the place appears to be abandoned. As they approach they can see why, buildings stand empty, gutted with flame and dead bodies are scattered around the area. A road passes through the center of town going from east to west, though there appears to be no one upon it.

"Do you think the Empire did this?" Cassie asks, as they stop well away from the town.

James says over his shoulder, "Most likely they did it on their way to the City."

"Shall we go see if anyone is alive?" Delia asks.

"I think anyone who's alive would've gotten away before now," James replies. "Besides, we can't take the chance that we will be discovered here."

"But someone there could need our help!" she insists as she points toward the town.

"Sometimes," he begins to explain, "you have to think of…"

She gives him a dirty look and kicks her horse, galloping toward the town before he even has a chance to finish.

"Damn!" Jiron exclaims as he races after her.

The rest hurry after, attempting to catch up with Jiron and Delia.

"Are you crazy?" Jiron yells at Delia when he catches up with her.

Getting down from her horse, she goes over to one of the bodies lying on the ground to see if they're still alive. Not paying Jiron any attention, she moves on to the next.

He dismounts and goes over to her, grabbing her by the arm and turns her to face him. "We cannot stay here! The Empire will use this road and it's only a matter of time before they get here."

Staring him in the eye, she says, "Let go of my arm!" and continues staring him down until he does. When he lets go, she says, "Then help me, but I'm not leaving until I know there is no one here to help." She turns her back on him and continues on to the next person.

James rides up and says, "We gotta get out of here."

Jiron looks at him and says, "She won't leave until she's sure there's no one to help."

"Damn!" James curses, and then looks up and down the road, making sure no one is approaching. "Alright, everyone fan out and search for survivors. Cassie," he says to her, "you keep a lookout and if anyone comes from either direction, you let us know, fast."

She nods her head and then finds a position where she can keep both directions of the road in view. It's not too hard as this is a rather small town with only a dozen or so buildings.

The others move from body to body but are only finding dead ones. Jiron goes through the buildings, but again, no one alive is found.

"Someone's coming!" Cassie yells as she hurries back toward them.

"Where?" yells Jiron and James simultaneously.

She points off toward the west and says, "There."

James looks and asks, "Did you see how many?"

"More than one," she replies. "But I didn't count, I felt you needed to know as soon as possible."

"Delia!" James hollers over to her. When he has her attention, he points to the west and says, "We've got company!"

She looks west and sees the rider coming and runs over to where the others are. Tinok has already gathered the horses and they all enter one of the larger buildings, bringing the horses inside. James and Jiron take position by the window and watch. The others hold the horses, trying to keep them as quiet as possible.

It's not long before they hear the approaching riders. James watches as perhaps a score of riders make their way through the center of town, passing right in front of where they're hiding.

"...the dead? Seems wrong," they hear one of them say. The man speaks with the accent of one from the Empire.

"We don't have time to take care of it now," another one replies with the same accent.

As the riders pass by where they're hiding, one of them glances over at the window they're looking out. Ducking to the sides of the window, James and Jiron quickly move out of view. The man must not have seen them for he turns back and continues riding through town. Twenty riders in all pass by on their way through the town.

They wait for several minutes, allowing the riders to move further down the road before they exit the building. James peeks out and sees the riders have already ridden out of sight.

Seeing no one else on the road in either direction, he asks Delia, "Can we leave now?"

"I'm sorry for putting us in jeopardy," she says a little guilty, "but I couldn't leave without knowing."

"We understand," Jiron says, "but think before you act next time, our lives may depend on it. Okay?"

"Alright," Delia says.

Once the horses have been brought back outside, they remount. Then with James in the lead, they head south out of town, making their way into the grasslands.

Several times during the afternoon, they have to make detours when riders appear in the distance. Each time they were sure they would be discovered, yet each time the riders continued on until they were again out of sight.

When the sun begins to dip toward the horizon, they are still out in the middle of the grasslands. They decide to make camp, forgoing a fire in favor of not alerting the countryside to their presence.

They quickly eat before the sun sets completely and picket the horses close by their camp, leaving the saddles on in case they need to leave quickly. Not good for the horses, but necessary.

"Do you think we're catching them?" Cassie asks while they're eating.

"Who?" James responds. "The slavers?"

Cassie nods her head and says, "Yes."

"I would think so," he answers, nodding his head. "They have lots of people walking while we're riding, even though we are taking a more roundabout way we have to be gaining on them."

They sit there in silence for the rest of their meal. When they're done, they all settle down and get ready for sleep. James lies there and stares up at the sky as it continues to darken into full night.

"James?" he hears Delia say.

"Yeah?" he replies.

"Where're you from?" she asks.

"A long ways from here and probably won't be back for quite a while," he replies. "Why?"

"Just curious is all," she answers.

"Is everyone there mages?" Cassie asks.

"No, there are actually none there," he says. "I may be the first."

"You're the first one I've ever met," she says.

"Do I live up to your expectations?" he asks, amused.

"No," she said, "you're nice."

James laughs then sobers up and asks, "Are all the mages here mean?"

Tinok says, "Most people believe them to be. All you ever hear about is how mages ruin things and hurt people. Seeing what you've already done, it's not hard to understand why that is."

"It's all perspective," James says, "plus most tales of how mages help won't be believed and only the interesting ones are told again and again. Those tend to be the ones where they are not very nice."

"Suppose you're right," he concludes.

"Maybe we should all be thinking about going to sleep," Jiron's voice cuts through the night. "We have lots of ground to cover and people to find."

"You're right," James agrees. Turning over, he tries to find a comfortable spot on the ground. *I hate sleeping on the ground!* Eventually, he's able to drift off to sleep.

The morning dawns beautifully and James wakes up stiff and aching due to another night spent on the hard ground. After getting up, he rummages through his backpack and comes up with some food for breakfast. While he eats he begins walking around the camp, trying to work the kinks out of his muscles.

It doesn't take long before they're all up, eaten, and ready to ride. Once everyone is mounted, they continue south, hoping to find where the slavers are heading. At one point during the morning, James takes out his compass and locates the general direction of where the slavers are. The needle points off to the southeast, more east than south. *We're gaining on them,* he thinks to himself. Putting his compass away, he continues on, beginning to feel much better about the possibility of a rescue. *Just hang on Miko.*

They don't travel much further before a running man appears from the east. Behind him, two fast moving riders are in hot pursuit, racing to intercept the man.

"We must help him," Delia cries.

Jiron and Tinok glance at one another and with a cry, they kick their horses to a gallop as they ride to aid the fleeing man. James and the girls follow behind at a safer pace, keeping an eye to the east for any other pursuers.

One of the riders aims a crossbow at the fleeing man, and James sees the man's pace falter as he's struck by the crossbow bolt. Stumbling, he loses his balance and hits the ground.

The riders, so intent on the man they are chasing, they fail to notice Jiron and Tinok until they are practically upon them.

Riding straight for them, Jiron and Tinok jump from their horses and each grabs one of the men, dragging them to the ground. When they hit the ground, they roll and come to their feet quickly, knife blades flashing in the sun.

The two riders get to their feet quickly and draw their swords as the two teens advance upon them. James sees Jiron divert a thrust of the man's sword and then strike with his other knife, dropping him to the ground. Tinok's man is wielding a sword in one hand and a knife in the other and is pressing Tinok backward.

Tinok sees out of the corner of his eye that Jiron's man is down and quickly begins a series of fast attacks. The pattern makes the man defend and through precisely timed and aimed attacks, causes him to leave a spot open where Tinok strikes, puncturing a lung.

The man stumbles backward and begins coughing up blood. Falling to his knees, he chokes on the blood filling his lungs. Unable to breathe, he soon falls to the ground, dead.

"Took you long enough," Jiron says to Tinok as he wipes his blades on the dead man's clothes.

Tinok just looks at him and they both start laughing.

Cassie by this time has made it to the man whom they were chasing, lying in a puddle of his own blood. The crossbow bolt must've struck an artery in his leg, for the blood is flowing from the wound quickly.

James comes over, and sees the amount of blood on the ground and when Cassie looks at him, just shakes his head, indicating there is nothing that they are going to be able to do for him.

"Thank you," the man says when he sees them approach.

Cassie comes to him and asks kindly, "For what?"

"For letting me die a free man," he tells her. He's dressed in just a loincloth, the garb of a slave.

"Were you part of the people who were captured when the City of Light fell?" James asks. "We're seeking friends who were taken by the Empire's forces."

"It fell?" the man asks incredulously. "Bad news indeed." The man begins to get a glazed look in his eyes and his voice gets weaker. "They'll probably be taken to Korazan, to the slave markets. That's where I heard the slaver say we were being taken, before I escaped."

"Korazan?" Jiron asks intently, "where is it?"

"Don't know," the man says, weakly, "somewhere to the south...I...think." The man takes one last light breath and then death takes him.

"Poor man," Delia says sadly.

"At least he didn't die a slave," Jiron says. "We should bury him before we go."

"I agree," Cassie says. She gets up and looks around until she finds a rock. Then she begins to scrape out a grave for the man. The others find rocks and sticks and before too long have a fair sized grave dug. Jiron and Tinok carry the man over to it and lay him respectfully within. They cover him with the excess dirt and when they are done, mount up and ride on.

"Korazan," James says after they get going, "anyone heard of it?"

"No", Delia replies, the other just shake their heads no.

"It must be within the Empire," he guesses, "at least we have a destination now."

"How do you know if they're actually being taken there?" Cassie asks.

"Don't," James replies, "but it's all we have to go on."

The rest nod in agreement.

They continue on, eating in the saddle to save time. A couple more times before nightfall, they see riders off to the east. Angling more to the west each time to avoid being seen, they find themselves gradually being pushed more and more westward. By the time night begins to approach, they begin to be able to see the Silver Mountains off in the distance to the west.

"Didn't realize we had been going so far westward," James says when they stop for the evening.

"What do you mean?" Jiron asks.

He points over to the mountains in the west and says, "That's the Silver Mountains, they run the length of the border between Cardri and Madoc."

"Are we going away from Korazan?" Cassie asks him.

"Can't say," he explains, "since we have no idea where it is."

"Oh, right," she says a little embarrassed.

"But I would think that the further we are to the west, the less of the Empire's soldiers we will encounter," he reasons. "Of course, that assumes that the Empire and Cardri haven't gone to war yet."

"Think they have?" she asks.

"Doubt it," he assures her. "The Empire probably has all it can handle with Madoc right now."

"I hope so," she says as they get settled in for the night.

Chapter   Four

The morning dawns cloudy, a relief from the sun that had been beating down on them throughout the day before. It takes them little time to be ready to go and soon are off, heading south to find Korazan.

Throughout the morning hours, they are able to hold a fairly southern course, only once having to travel westward to avoid roving patrols. About midday they begin to see a large river flowing from the northwest to the southeast. It spans several hundred feet and runs deep.

As they approach the banks of the river, James looks both upriver and downriver but is unable to see any bridge that they may use to cross. There is also no place along the course of the river shallow enough to allow them to ford. He turns to the others and says, "It appears we have a problem."

"Can't we go down one way or the other until we find a way to cross?" Cassie asks.

"That's what we're going to end up having to do," he replies. "The question is, should we go that way," he says as he points upstream to the northwest, and then points downstream, "or that way?"

"If we go downstream, that will take us closer to Korazan," Tinok says.

"And closer to the Empire's forces," Jiron concludes.

"It's probably safe to say that any bridge to the east of us will be used by the Empire," warns James, "possibly even guarded."

"Then we go west?" Delia guesses.

"But how far will we have to go and will it take us too long to get back?" Jiron questions. "If we spend too much time going west and then have to backtrack, we may be too late to save Tersa."

"Let's go west for a day, and if we don't find anything suitable, then we'll turn around and go east," offers Tinok.

"A day!" Jiron exclaims. "I'll not waste two whole days when Tersa is being marched to the slave markets!" He looks around at everyone defiantly and says, "I go east! You can all do what you want!" He then turns his horse eastward and gallops away, not looking back to see if they are following.

Tinok looks to James and says, "I guess we go east."

"It would appear that way," he replies. They all turn their horses and gallop after Jiron.

They follow the river for several miles before a town begins to come into view along the river ahead of them. It sits on the north bank of the river and at the southern edge of town, a bridge spans the river. They see several figures moving in and around the town, plus several upon the bridge itself. They pause only a moment before turning back toward the west and ride until the town is once again out of sight behind them.

"That bridge would be perfect to get across," James says. "But it looks as if there's guards posted on it. I think we should wait for night and see if we can't find a way to sneak across."

Indicating Jiron and himself, Tinok says, "We can take out the guards before they even know we're there."

"But that would tell everyone that there are hostiles in the area," James counters, "then they would be searching for us. If we can sneak across somehow," pausing for effect, he looks at Tinok and says with emphasis, "without killing anyone, then we may be able to get further south before they even know we've been through here."

"Can we sneak across?" Cassie asks.

"Won't know until tonight," James replies. "Let's find a spot away from the river where we can have a bite to eat unobserved while we wait for dark."

"Why do we have to move away from the river?" Cassie asks.

Sighing, James explains, "In the event that someone is traveling down the river, we don't want them to alert those in the town as to our presence."

"Oh," she says.

They move about a half mile away from the river and find a spot near a hill that provides them some cover. They keep watch for anyone coming and remain undisturbed until night has fallen and they're ready to make the attempt to cross the river.

Once night has deepened enough that the only light is that of the stars, they mount up and ride back toward the river. They follow it until the town's lights appear and then come to a stop. Jiron says, "I'll go and scout the town, then we can decide what to do."

"Alright," James agrees, "but be careful."

He gives James a look that says, 'Of course', and then disappears in the night as he heads for town. Twenty minutes go by before they hear his return.

"Well?" James asks when he rejoins the group.

"Looks to be about twenty soldiers garrisoned there," he explains, "with four on duty at the bridge and two walking patrol within the town itself. Most of the others are gathered in a tavern located near the center of town."

"Is there a way to create a diversion that would draw off the guards at the bridge?" Tinok asks.

"Maybe setting fire to a building or two," he says, "that may do it. Unless the guards at the bridge have an extraordinary sense of duty and remain there."

"Most likely they are bored and would leave just to see what's going on," James suggests.

"Probably," Jiron says. Looking to Tinok, he says, "Wanna come start some fires with me?"

"Every boy's dream," Tinok replies with a smile.

"Now make sure it looks like it could've been an accident, or the search may be on," James cautions.

"Do the best we can," Jiron says. "When we're done, we'll meet you back here."

"Good luck," Delia says.

"Be careful," Cassie says with concern.

"We will," Jiron assures her, and then he and Tinok run off toward town.

James mounts his horse after some time passes and advises the girls to do the same, "We may need to be ready to move fast should they return with soldiers in pursuit."

They sit on their horses and wait. "Where are they?" Cassie asks after an hour has gone by, concern in her voice.

"Don't worry," Delia assures her, "they're just taking their time to make sure they are not caught."

"I hope so," Cassie says.

Me too, Delia says to herself as she watches the town for their return.

Suddenly, two shadows approach. "Get ready," they hear Jiron say as he mounts his horse. Tinok mounts his as well.

They all sit and wait, but nothing happens.

"What did you do?" James asks.

"We found a stable where they had most of their horses," Jiron explains. "A guard was there sleeping in a pile of hay, with a bottle of wine lying next to him."

"Yeah," Tinok says, chuckling a little. "We took one of the lanterns down, lit it and laid it beside him on the hay. The hay was just beginning to smolder as we left."

"But he might burn to death!" Cassie gasps.

"Fortunes of war," Jiron says, with little feeling.

"Besides, it'll look like an accident," Tinok explains. "It'll look like he got drunk and was careless."

"And with their horses in danger," Jiron says, "they'll want everyone to help with putting the fire out, which should draw the men off the bridge."

"Let's hope so," James says.

Suddenly, from the north side of town, a reddish glow blossoms as the stable catches fire. Even from this distance they can hear the horses neighing in terror. From within the town, they hear the cry as the soldiers move to combat the fire and save their horses.

The men on the bridge turn and see the flames reaching high in the sky as the fire roars to life. As one, they race away from the bridge and head for the inferno at the stables.

"Now's our chance," James says, once the guards have left the bridge. Getting their horses moving quickly, they make their way toward the bridge and race across it to the other side without anyone raising the alarm.

A road crosses over the bridge heading south. They follow it for some distance before James slows them down to prevent a horse from accidentally putting a hoof in a hole and breaking its leg. They continue to follow the road for another mile or so before deciding to pull off a ways and make camp within a small copse of trees. A quick meal of cold rations and then they turn in. Jiron, Tinok and James all taking their turn at watch.

Next morning, they're on the road again before the sun has risen very far above the horizon. James uses his compass and with relief finds that Miko is now a little to the north of east now, instead of south of east. *We're ahead of them,* he thinks to himself with satisfaction. To avoid encountering Empire soldiers, they move off the road to the west and run parallel to it.

The Silver Mountains are also getting closer on their right as they proceed south. It's not long before they are close enough to be able to make out the individual trees covering the mountain's slope

Over the course of the next couple hours, they see several columns of troops going north on the road to the east of them, before James quickly moves them further west to avoid detection. An hour before midday, they begin to see another road running along the base of the mountains as it meanders through the foothills. Currently no one is traveling upon it, and since the one to the east had troops moving upon it, they decide to use it. If they move any further west they will be riding along the slope of the mountain.

"Should we even be on this road?" Cassie asks, nervously.

"There's no one on it," James explains, "at least not right now. If we were to go further east, then we run the risk of meeting troops going north. If someone comes, then there's always the mountain."

She looks over to the mountain but doesn't look too happy at the prospect of going there.

Early afternoon, they pull off the road to have some lunch and to rest the horses. They find an area to the west, behind some of the rolling hills, which will keep them out of the view of anyone who may be traveling upon the road.

"How are we going to get to Korazan?" Delia asks.

"What do you mean?" Jiron asks.

"I mean, how will we get there without being seen?" she clarifies. "Once we cross the border, we're going to stand out as northerners, we don't even know the customs."

Jiron and James look at each other and James says, "Well, I hadn't actually thought that far yet."

"Did you think we would just ride in, find them, and then be allowed to ride away free and clear?" she asks incredulously.

"I'm sure we'll figure a way," Jiron assures her.

She looks at them and says, "You're both going to get us all killed if you don't do a little planning ahead."

"How?" asks James. "It's true we don't know the customs, but there's no way to learn before we get there anyway. We may stand out now, but once there, we can acquire clothing that will enable us to blend in."

"Besides," Jiron adds, "are they really going to be expecting a group, such as ourselves, to be up to mischief? I'm sure we can wing a plausible reason should one be needed."

"Then you better think fast," she tells him.

"Why?" Jiron asks.

She points behind him to the six riders wearing Empire uniforms who are approaching their camp from the foothills, three have crossbows loaded and aimed at them. One who looks to be the officer in charge of the group comes toward them, flanked by the remaining two.

They all stand as he approaches. "Well, what do we have here?" he asks with a smile, coming to a stop a few feet away.

Cassie clings to Delia while James steps forward to speak, "Just some friends out having some fun is all."

"I see," he says, a small smile playing across his lips. "And what kind of 'fun' would bring you to this area?"

"We we're camping up in the mountains and had come down to get some more supplies," he explains. "We ran out."

"Ah, yes," the leader says. "And what town were you heading to for the supplies?"

"We don't actually know where any are," he admits. "You see we're from Lornigan over in Cardri…"

"But," Jiron jumps in, "we figured if we were to follow this road, it would eventually lead us to one."

The officer nods his head and signals the crossbowmen to lower their weapons. "Then you're in luck," he says, "we were just on our way to a town just south of here. You're more than welcome to accompany us and purchase your supplies there."

"That would be great," James says. "Just give us a moment and we'll be ready."

The officer nods his head and takes his men a short distance away, where he speaks to one of them in a language that none of their group understands. After a few short words, the man turns his horse and races off to the south.

The officer sees James looking at the departing rider and says, "He's just gone ahead to keep a lookout for rogues." Giving James a disarming, charming smile he continues, "You can't be too careful."

James comes over to his horse and gets ready to mount, when Jiron places his hand on his arm and whispers, "Are you crazy?"

James gives him a look of desperation and replies in a hushed whisper, "We've got no choice. We'd never be able to stop the crossbowmen before they fire, someone could get killed. Let's just bide our time, and see what opportunities develop." He mounts his horse and continues, "We can't risk having the girls hurt."

Not happy about it, Jiron mounts his horse as the officer and his men approach again. "Ready, are we?" he asks.

"Yes, we are," James replies. "We appreciate the escort, though it's not really necessary."

Smiling a charming smile, he says, "Not a problem, really. As I said, we were already heading in that direction."

The remaining man without a crossbow heads out first, leading the way. The officer rides next to James while his three crossbowmen take up position at the rear behind the girls.

James is very uncomfortable with the 'helpfulness' of the soldiers. Having three crossbowmen behind the girls doesn't leave much opportunity to get out of the situation. Trying to appear nonchalant, he asks the officer, who's riding next to him, "So what are you doing out in these parts?"

"Just on a routine patrol," he replies, "making sure no one makes mischief, that sort of thing."

"What town are we going to?" James asks.

"The locals call it Mountainside," he explains. "Not a very original name if you ask me."

"No," comments James, "I suppose not."

They ride for a short time before the town comes into view. "Ah," he says to James, indicating the town up ahead, "there it is."

Sitting at the base of the mountain is a rather small town, even though it's at a junction of roads. A little over two dozen buildings are apparently all there is to it. As they approach, James begins to realize there are no people out amidst the buildings, just more of the Empire's soldiers. As they pass a few houses, he can see faces peering out from windows. Faces full of fear and worry.

Suddenly very nervous, James glances back at his companions and can see his fears mirrored in their faces. But with the three crossbowmen behind, he dares do nothing yet.

They are led to a large, two story building on the edge of town, where several soldiers are standing around outside. One says something to the officer, who answers back in the same language. James sees them smile and one even laughs a little.

The officer stops his horse in front of the building and says, "You can get what you need inside, I am sure." He gets down, handing the reins to a soldier who's standing there and starts toward the door, where he pauses. Glancing back at them, he asks, "Coming?"

James gets down and the rest of them follow suit. Then the officer goes in through the front door, leaving it open behind him. They glance to each other, fear in their eyes, but not knowing what else to do. The three crossbowmen are still sitting astride their horses, looking casual but with the crossbows pointed in their general direction. Not exactly threatening with them, but they could definitely aim and fire in very little time.

With James in the lead, they walk up to and then pass through the front door. They enter a large room where the officer is already seated behind a desk across the room. "Do come in," he says to them as they hesitate in the doorway.

"There're no supplies here!" James says accusingly as they enter the room. Tinok, who's bringing up the rear, is nudged in the back with something sharp. Looking behind him, he sees one of the crossbowmen right behind him, the crossbow close to his back. The other two crossbowmen have dismounted and are following them inside.

The officer smiles at them and says, "Of course not, I'm surprised you even believed me." He gestures to four other crossbowmen on the second floor balcony overlooking the room. "Please, don't try anything," he says to James and the others, "it would be, unpleasant."

"What are you going to do?" Jiron asks.

A couple soldiers enter from a side door and begin taking their things from them, including James' backpack. "My orders are simple; detain anyone passing through the area."

They search them and take their weapons, including the knives of Jiron and Tinok.

"What happened to the people who use to live here?" Delia inquires.

"Alas, they objected to us being here so had to be dealt with," he explains.

"Dealt with?" she asks, afraid of the answer.

"Yes my dear, dealt with," he says to her. "Now they stay in their homes and don't bother us any more."

When they're done with removing everything from them but the clothes on their back, they place all of it on the desk. The officer says a few words to one of them in their language and then turns to their prisoners. "Now, just follow this soldier here and he'll take you to your cell."

"Why are we being locked up?" Tinok asks angrily.

"Would you rather we just kill you now?" he asks.

James can hear Cassie gasp and quickly says, "No, that won't be necessary."

"Good," he says, giving them a smile, "then please follow along peacefully and you won't be hurt."

A soldier leads them through a back door into a hallway lined with solid looking wooden doors, each containing a small barred window. The soldier opens the cell doors and has them enter, one per cell. He puts three of them on one side and three on the other. Once they're in and the doors are secured, the soldier takes up position in a chair at the end of the hallway.

James hears Cassie sobbing, but fortunately everyone has the good sense to keep quiet while the guard is there and can overhear everything they say.

"Don't worry Cassie," Tinok's voice can be heard saying. "I'm sure they'll let us go once they realize we're no threat to them."

James can hear someone enter the hallway from the outer room and the footsteps pause before his cell. He can see the officer looking in through the window in his door and then hears him say something to the soldier with him. A key turns in the lock and the door swings open, the officer walking in. Framed in the doorway is a soldier with a crossbow who has it aimed at James to prevent any mischief.

Once he's in the room, the officer holds up the amulet James bought from a merchant a while back, the same one that ol' One Eye had questioned him about earlier in the warehouse back in the City of Light. "Where did you get this?" he asks.

"I bought it at a merchant's stand a couple weeks ago," he replies. "Why?"

"Hmmm…" he says as he considers what James had said. "Be that as it may, this changes things."

"How?" James asks.

The man looks to James but doesn't answer. He leaves the room and James can hear him mumble to himself as he leaves, "Yes, this definitely changes things…"

The soldier with the crossbow closes his cell door and James is left alone to ponder what he just heard. *Why does having that amulet change things? That amulet must mean something special, even ol' One Eye was extra curious about it.* Unable to come up with any idea that makes sense, he just sits on the floor with his back against the wall and thinks of his options.

The hallway door opens and then closes as the officer leaves the cell area. Jiron whispers, "James, the guard left with him. What are we going to do?"

"I don't know," he replies. "It's not too long until dark, we better wait until then. Can you pick the lock?"

"No, they took my lock picks when they searched me. You?" he asks.

"Probably," James responds. "Let me think about it."

"I'm scared!" they hear Cassie cry pitifully from her cell at the end of the hallway.

"We all are," Delia tells her. "Just be patient, I'm sure we'll be able to get out of this."

"I hope so," she says, as she once again starts to cry softly.

"This was a stupid idea!" Tinok's voice rings out. "We should've taken 'em out when we first met them. Now there's a whole lot more to deal with."

"We couldn't risk the girls," Jiron says.

"Think they're any safer now?" he asks angrily.

"Shut up!" Delia whispers sternly. "This isn't doing us any good!"

Everyone quiets down after that. James looks out the little window that overlooks the back alley, but all he can see is the rear of the building across from him.

Just then they hear the hallway door open again and the chair creaks as the guard retakes his position again at the end of the hallway.

They sit there for another hour in silence, each occupied with their own thoughts. James sits by the window and listens to the goings on outside, but aside from the sounds of the occasional horse going by the front of the building, or conversations in the Empire's language, he fails to hear anything useful. He contemplates several means where magic could facilitate their escape and plans several contingencies.

Outside, the sun begins to go down and the light slowly starts to fade. Suddenly, the door at the end of the hallway opens and two soldiers come in and begin talking to the guard. They exchange words for several minutes, then James can hear them chuckling. The two men begin to make their way down to the end of the hallway and stop outside of Cassie's door.

He hears a click and then a squeal of rusty hinges as they open her cell door. He hears them saying something to her in their language, and then suddenly a cry from Cassie.

"What's happening?" Jiron asks.

Tinok, who's in the cell across from her, says, "They're going to rape her!"

"Jiron, Tinok, go help her," James says as he releases the magic. Everyone hears an audible click as their doors unlock.

Without any thought but to help her, Jiron and Tinok burst out of their cells and rush into hers. James comes out and turns to the shocked guard at the end of the hallway. Loosing the power, James slams the man against the wall, knocking him out.

He rushes down to Cassie's cell and finds the two soldiers dead on the ground, with Delia helping Cassie to her feet. Jiron and Tinok are standing over the dead men, with the dead men's knives in their hand, dripping blood.

As James enters, Jiron says, "Time to leave?"

"I would think so," James replies. They come out of her cell just as the doorway at the end of the hallway slams open. The officer strides in to see what the commotion is all about. He comes to a sudden stop when he sees the guard lying before him on the floor unconscious. Looking down the hallway, his eyes widen when he sees their cell doors open and them out of their cells, two with knives that are red with blood. He begins yelling as he quickly turns and exits the hallway, returning back to the front room. Even though James can't understand what he's saying, he has a pretty good idea.

"Jiron," he says, "give Tinok your knife, quick!"

When Tinok has both knives, James says to him as he points down the hallway, "They're going to be coming through that door. You've got to stop them for a minute or two."

Tinok glances at Cassie, then with an evil grin he says, "You got it." He walks close to the end of the hallway and awaits the first soldier to pass through the door.

Grabbing Jiron's arm, James says, "Come with me." He leads him to the rear cell where Tinok had been, whose little window overlooks the same narrow alley that his had. The girls follow them in there.

"What are we doing?" he asks James.

"Just wait," he replies as he begins concentrating.

Jiron hears the clash of metal from the hallway and sticks his head out to see how Tinok's doing. One soldier lies on the floor, bleeding to death, while his knives dance with another. A third soldier has entered the hallway behind the one battling Tinok, but the narrowness of the corridor allows but one to come at him at a time.

He turns back to the cell and watches as James begins tracing the seams of the stones surrounding the barred window. His finger follows the seam all the way around and when he reaches his starting point, he stops and says, "Alright, give me a hand."

Reaching up to the bars, he begins pulling on them. Jiron steps up and lends his strength to the effort.

"Give up," they hear the officer exclaim from down the hallway, "you've got nowhere to go!"

"Bring 'em on!" they hear Tinok's reply. More clashes can be heard as he parries and blocks, giving them time to do what they need to.

"What's the count?" Jiron yells over his shoulder to Tinok.

"Four!" they hear him hollering back.

James and Jiron pull with all their strength on the bars and a section of the wall surrounding them suddenly slides outward half an inch.

"Five!"

Delia joins them and together, they slowly pull the bars and the adjoining stones away from the wall until the whole thing crashes to the floor with a thud.

James looks out the hole and doesn't see anyone around, while Jiron goes back to the dead guards in Cassie's cell and retrieves a sword.

Coming to the hole, he tosses the sword through and then follows it, climbing through the hole.

"Six!"

He takes the sword and comes back to the hole. "Cassie," he says, "come on!" Keeping an eye out for anyone entering the ally, he offers his hand to help her through.

James and Jiron help Cassie make it through the hole, and then Delia. Once they're safely on the other side, James climbs through as well. "Tinok!" Jiron yells, "Time to go!"

"Seven!" they hear just before he runs through the door. Upon seeing the hole in the wall, he yells, "Stand back!" as he races toward it and dives through. He sails through the opening, hits the ground on the other side, and then rolls, coming to rest against the wall of the opposite building.

James sees guards rushing into the room after him. When they see the hole in the wall, one yells something back down the hallway as most of them turn and race back the way they had come.

"Let's get out of here!" James says, as he leads them down the alley. As they reach the end, he looks back the way they had come and sees soldiers entering the alley, hell bent on catching them. They turn and run down the lane, trying to make the edge of town. A guard runs around a corner in front of them, and before he even realizes they're there, Jiron has cut him down with the sword.

"Good with a sword too?" asks James, panting from the exertion.

"Didn't always use the knives," he replies, "I just prefer them."

When they come to the end of the lane, they realize they've made it to the edge of town, rising before them is the mountain. Behind them are dozens of soldiers racing after them and several crossbow bolts fly past, missing by a narrow margin.

They make a break for the mountain and the relative safety of the trees. The ground begins to rise as they reach the treeline.

From behind, they hear the soldiers in pursuit. James glances back and realizes they're gaining on them. As he runs, James searches the ground for rocks, but in the dusk of early evening, it's hard to make any out. Spotting a couple, he pauses only momentarily to pick them up before he races to catch up with the others.

He glances back again and now can make out about a dozen and a half soldiers are in pursuit, it doesn't look as if the officer is among them. "We're either going to have to convince them to not follow us, or take them out," he says to the others. "We'll never outrun them."

Jiron looks back and says, "I agree."

"Ladies," James says, "you continue on up, we'll find you."

Delia grabs Cassie's hand and together they continue on up the mountain as fast as they can.

"Alright gentlemen," he says, "let's do it." He stops and turns to face the soldiers while Jiron and Tinok split off to either side.

He finds the crossbowmen and using the stones he collected, begins taking them out one by one. Jiron and Tinok move forward to engage the oncoming soldiers. Jiron using his sword and Tinok with his knives, they weave a dance of death that begins felling soldiers at a quick pace.

James stays to the rear and continues throwing stones, with the added speed and accuracy only magic can achieve, until all but a couple of the soldiers have been eliminated. Turning tail, the remaining soldiers promptly retreat back to town.

When they come back together to watch the retreating soldiers, James notices Jiron has acquired two knives from the fallen soldiers. "Let's find the girls," he says as they turn and hurry to catch up to them.

Chapter   Five

"Are they dead?" Delia asks when the boys catch up with them.

"Most of them, the rest fled back to town," Jiron replies.

With relief evident in her voice Cassie asks, "Then we're safe?"

"Until morning at least," James assures her. "But you can bet they'll be coming after us at first light."

"And they'll probably bring everyone," adds Tinok.

"Quite likely," agrees James. "We've killed over a dozen soldiers and embarrassed their leader. So yeah, they'll be coming."

"What are we going to do?" Cassie asks, scared.

"Let's get higher in the mountains and at first light, try to find a place to make a stand," James says.

"Good idea," agrees Tinok. Anger still burns in him over the attempted attack on Cassie.

They proceed further up into the mountains, the dark of night making the way difficult at best. When they come across a somewhat level area, they make camp. Tired, hungry and a little scared over what the next day will bring, they lie down and do their best to get some sleep, the boys taking turns at watch.

James takes the first watch and sits there as he hears his companions, one by one, fall asleep. He knows that tomorrow's outcome will depend heavily upon him and what he can do with magic. Going over in his mind different strategies and solutions that he came up with in similar situations back home, during their role playing campaigns, he tries to find one which would work the best giving their situation. Thank god he at least has a couple of good fighters to hold them off while he does his thing. After coming up with several nasty ideas, he finishes his turn at watch and then wakes Tinok for his turn. Lying down, he does his best to fall asleep.

Morning dawns overcast, the sky beginning to lighten even though the sun is still behind the mountains. Jiron returns to camp just after dawn from reconnoitering down the mountain for signs of the enemy to find no sign of James. Worried, he wakes up everyone else and is about to begin searching for him when he sees him walking back toward the camp, a couple of rabbits in hand.

"Here," he says as he hands the rabbits to Cassie, "take these further on up the mountain and cook 'em."

"But a fire will lead them straight to us," objects Jiron.

"Exactly," James says. "We want them to think we're just a bunch of stupid kids who think they've gotten away from them. That we are lulled into a sense of security and are careless enough to light the way for them."

"There's a spot another hundred feet up that would be prefect to set up camp," he tells them.

"What will you be doing?" he asks.

"While the girls are up there alerting them as to which way to come," he explains, "we'll be down here setting up several nasty surprises for them."

"Surprises?" Delia asks.

"Yeah," he replies, "surprises." He points down the way they came last night and says, "We inadvertently followed a game trail up the mountain and I'm betting they'll follow it too. Especially when they see the smoke from the fire."

"What should we do?" Cassie asks.

"You and Delia go up the mountain and begin cooking the rabbits," he says. He then points to Jiron, "You stay with me." To Tinok he says, "You need to stay with the girls in case anyone gets past us."

Tinok nods his head in agreement though he's dismayed about missing the fun.

"Save some for me and James," Jiron says, indicating the rabbits.

"We'll see," Tinok says, a grin playing across his face.

As Tinok and the girls begin to head up the mountain, James and Jiron start setting up the surprises. "Just what do you have in mind?" Jiron asks him.

"Well, you see…" he then explains what he plans to do as they make their way down the trail.

"Here they come," Jiron says from where they hide behind a fallen log. The first man can be seen coming up the trail below them. "They're following the trail just as you figured."

"I wasn't sure they would," admits James. "Though I'm glad I was right."

"Looks like they brought the whole garrison," Jiron observes as more and more men come into view.

"Hope so," James says, "can't afford to miss even one."

"You're a bloodthirsty one, aren't you?" Jiron asks.

James turns to him and says, "I don't like killing, to me it's just a waste. But if I have to, then I want to make it so they'll never trouble me again."

"See your point," he says.

They watch as the men proceed further up the trail. "You ready?" James asks him.

"Yeah," he replies with a grin, "let's do it."

They stand up from behind the log as James throws two stones in quick succession, killing two of the forward soldiers.

Then they yell as if scared, "Run!" and turn to race back up the trail, the soldiers immediately follow in hot pursuit.

They don't run too far before they come to an area where the trees and plants all look like they're wilting, dying. They continue on until they are back into the healthier part of the forest, then abruptly stop and turn to face the oncoming soldiers.

Their pursuers are following the trail for the most part, though some have fanned out into the forest alongside the trail. "We're not going to get all of them," Jiron says.

"Perhaps," James agrees, "but hopefully we've planned well enough for that."

They watch as the soldiers begin to enter the wilted area as they race to reach James and Jiron. When the men in the front nears the end of the wilted area James shouts, "Walls!"

Six foot high walls of force spring up around the men in the wilted area, boxing them in. The men in front run full force into the forward wall of force, coming to an abrupt halt as if they'd run into a brick wall. The men are confused at first and then panic sets in. James can see the officer who locked them up near the back of the men trapped within the invisible walls. He's trying to keep his men under control but the fear of being entrapped by invisible walls overrides whatever discipline he's trying to establish.

Jiron watches the men trapped inside, hitting on the invisible walls with their hands and weapons in an attempt to break free. He can hear their screams of terror.

"Shut!" James shouts and the walls slam together, pulping the men inside, abruptly silencing their cries. He can hear Jiron next to him exclaim, "Good god!"

"We haven't gotten all of them," James says, indicating over a dozen men, standing stunned over the fate of their comrades on the trail.

James takes out another stone and begins to head back down the trail toward the soldiers, Jiron beside him.

When the remaining soldiers see them coming forward, the men lose heart and turn to flee back down the mountain. Letting fly his stone, James takes out another one. Again and again, he lets fly with stones, striking one after another.

When the remaining men reach a certain tree with a cloth that he tied to it earlier, he says, "Fire!"

Fire erupts from the ground in a circle over a hundred feet across. The fleeing men scream as it burns and consumes them. The trees in the area burst into flame as the dry leaves and needles crackle as they catch fire. The wind coming up the mountain begins to blow sparks from tree to tree, spreading the fire rapidly.

"Crap!" James exclaims, as he sees the fire beginning to burn out of control.

"What?" Jiron asks.

"The fire!" he says, pointing to the blaze. "The wind is going to push it this way! We've got to get out of here!"

As they turn to race up the mountain, Jiron asks, "Do you think we got everyone?"

"I think so," James says, "no way to be sure now. At least the fire will hide the evidence of what we did here." Smoke is beginning to thicken as more and more of the forest becomes ablaze.

"Let's get the others and find a way around the fire!" James yells.

They hurry up the mountain and before they reach the camp, they see Tinok and the girls coming down to meet them.

"What's happening?" Tinok says, as he gazes down the now thickening smoke.

"James set the forest afire," Jiron tells him.

"What?" Tinok exclaims. "Why did you do that?"

"Didn't mean to," admits James, "it just sort of happened. Anyway, we have to get out of here before we're cooked alive."

James heads them southeast since the wind is blowing from the east. Running as fast as the forest will allow, they move laterally along the mountainside, trying desperately to gain the far side of the fire before it cuts them off.

Smoke is thick and he can hear the others begin to cough as the smoke in the air thickens. In her haste, Cassie snags an exposed root with her foot and stumbles, falling to the ground. Her screams bring the others to a halt as she rolls down the mountainside, closer to the approaching fire. She comes to a stop amidst a tangle of undergrowth and fallen branches.

"Help me!" she cries out when she realizes she's stuck within the tangled mess and the fire is quickly approaching her.

Tinok bolts down the mountainside after her and quickly reaches her side. "I'm here," he assures her as he begins pulling back the brush which has her trapped. The fire is burning closer and a tree no more than ten feet away suddenly bursts into flame.

"Hurry!" she urges, her eyes on the tree being engulfed by the fire. At last he manages to free her and helps her to her feet. He has her lean on him as they make it back up to where the others are waiting for them. Behind them, more trees burst into flame as the wind spreads the fire rapidly.

Looking at the treetops, James notices how the fire hopping from one tree to the next, reminiscent of a documentary of the Yellowstone fire he saw years earlier. As Tinok and Cassie join them, they once more begin moving as fast as possible away from the quickly approaching inferno.

Suddenly, they break from the confines of the forest and stumble upon a small road running due east. Ruts line the road, showing that wagons have moved through here. Turning onto it, they're able to make better time.

The fire behind them is gaining rapidly, they begin to feel the heat of the raging inferno drawing ever closer. James looks up again and sees that the treetops above them are already beginning to catch. *There's no way we're going to outrun this!*

Continuing on as best they can with the smoke thickening rapidly, their lungs burn from the heated smoke they're breathing. Cassie falls to her knees, coughing, overcome by the smoke and unable to continue. In desperation, Tinok picks her up and carries her onward. James looks in dread as the trees along the road ahead of them begin to catch fire, the wind pushing the blaze ever forward.

"We're not going to make it!" Delia cries out to him over the roar of the fire.

The forest before them suddenly opens up to a wide canyon, five hundred feet across. A rope suspension bridge, barely wide enough to accommodate a wagon, spans it.

Thank goodness! James thinks to himself when it comes into view. Just then, a branch being consumed by flame falls upon the bridge, twenty feet from the edge. James stares in disbelief as the fire which is consuming the branch begins licking the ropes holding the bridge in place.

"Move!" he yells, allowing Jiron and Delia to cross first and then Tinok with Cassie right behind. Once everyone is on and crossing to the other side, he steps upon the bridge and begins to cross.

Delia comes to the point where the burning branch has fallen upon the bridge, but it's burning so hot, she has to pass by as far to the side as she can. The wooden planks she's walking upon are beginning to burn as well as the supporting ropes.

When James gets to the fire on the bridge, he can see that the ropes have already almost completely burned through, only a few strands keep it from snapping in two. "Hurry!" he shouts as they quickly make their way to the other side.

Jiron reaches the other side first, just ahead of Delia. Then Tinok reaches the other side and carries Cassie away from the edge of the canyon before he lays her on the ground. James is almost to the end when one the remaining strands of the support rope snaps, causing the bridge to skew suddenly, throwing him to his knees.

"James!" Delia cries out when she sees the bridge lurch to the side and James almost plummeting to his death on the rocks far below.

Jiron comes to the edge and reaches out to help him the last of the way. Seeing the hand before him, James stretches his arm out, trying to grab hold of it. Before he's able to take Jiron's hand, the remaining rope suddenly snaps, causing the bridge to break in two and each half falling against their side of the canyon.

James loses his grip and falls. Reaching out in panic, he tries to grab hold of one of the wooden planks of the bridge. He finally manages to stop his plummet ten feet further down as he catches hold of one of the planks that's still attached securely to the rope. He holds on tight as the bridge slams into the side of the mountain and prays he doesn't fall. Once the section of bridge he's clinging to settles down, he looks up and sees Jiron looking down at him from the top, twenty feet away.

"Come on!" he yells. "Climb up, you can make it."

James makes the mistake of looking down at the river far below. Panic overcomes him for a few seconds, causing him to hug the board in a death grip. The panic slowly subsides when he realizes he's not going to immediately plummet to his death. After taking a couple deep breaths, he reaches up to grab the board above him and starts climbing up.

One by one, he climbs the boards on his way toward the top. Suddenly he hears one of the girls scream and looks up, but Jiron is no longer there. He continues climbing and when he is less than five feet from the top, a body flies over the edge and falls, narrowly missing him.

What the hell? Climbing as fast as he can, he reaches the top only to find Jiron and Tinok standing shoulder to shoulder as they face three men with swords. Six men already lie dead on the ground. As James climbs over the top, another of the men falls to the ground as he holds his stomach where Jiron had sliced him open. Then in a flurry of motion, Jiron and Tinok each take out one of the remaining two.

Coming over to them, he asks, "Everyone okay?"

Jiron has a wound in his side oozing blood, other than that, its just minor scrapes and cuts. Delia comes and helps him to bind it, while James goes over to where Tinok is holding a coughing Cassie and asks, "Is she going to be okay?"

"I think so," he replies. "She just needs to get the smoke out of her lungs."

"What happened?" he asks, referring to the dead men.

"They came out of the trees just after the bridge broke," he explains. "I think they were robbers, probably in the area and coming to see about the fire. When they saw us, they attacked without warning."

At mention of the fire, they all look across the chasm at the roaring inferno consuming the road they just left. Some embers are being carried across the canyon, but are failing to start any fires.

"Let's search them and see if they have anything we can use," James says.

He and Jiron go about the task of searching the bodies, but only come up with a pouch for each of them and a belt knife. They also find some coins, though not nearly replacing the amount that is still within his backpack back in town.

By this time Cassie is doing better, just coughing a little bit. "Ready to go?" James asks as he comes over to her.

She nods her head yes and then gets up with Delia's help. James and Jiron again take the lead as they continue to follow the narrow road through the forest. Behind them across the canyon, the fire still blazes with violent intensity. Even from this distance, they can feel the heat.

They follow the road as it twists and turns among the trees, continuing its way through the forest, leaving the canyon and the heat from the fire behind. They don't travel very far before the road opens up to a clearing. Within the clearing they find two wagons as well as two men sitting on the ground next to a fire. Twelve horses are secured in a picket near them.

At their approach, one of the men turns toward their way and begins to say, "Herec, what did you...?" He stops abruptly when he sees them entering the clearing. Grabbing a crossbow sitting on the ground next to him, he hollers to his friend who grabs one as well. Without even a word of warning, he lets loose a bolt, taking James through the right shoulder, knocking him backward to the ground.

Knives flash as Jiron and Tinok advance upon the men. Cassie and Delia come to render what aid they can for James.

The second man, seeing Jiron and Tinok coming toward him, lets fly with his bolt but it goes wide, missing Tinok by scant inches. Drawing their swords, the men prepare to defend themselves.

Tinok closes with the first man, while Jiron goes after the second. Knives dance as they parry the sword thrusts, but the men are no match for them and are soon lying on the ground, dead.

They come over to James where he's lying on the ground, blood welling out from where the bolt had struck him. Jiron rolls him over slightly to look at his back and sees that it hasn't gone all the way through. He looks in James' eyes and says, "It's got to come out."

James just nods his head in understanding and braces himself.

"Hold him tight, Tinok," Jiron says. Tinok comes and holds James firmly as Jiron grabs hold of the bolt. "Alright, on three, okay?" he asks James.

James nods his head again and braces for it.

"One...two..." and then he yanks it out, causing James to cry out in pain before passing out. Turning to Delia he says, "Look through the wagons and see if there is anything we can use for bandages."

She rushes over to the wagons and then comes back with a couple of shirts that she quickly tears into strips. Jiron takes them from her and uses them to bind James' wound.

"We camp here for the night," he says. "Tinok, find some wood to keep the fire going until dawn. Cassie, search the wagons for any food and drink." Turning to Delia he says, "You stay here with James, I'm going to scout a little further down the trail to see what's there. I'll be back shortly."

Getting up he hollers over to Tinok who's gathering wood, "I'll be back shortly."

"Be careful," he hollers back.

Turning toward the east, he breaks into a quick jog which soon has him disappearing down the road.

When he returns, he finds James awake and having a meal of trail rations that Cassie had found in one of the wagons. "How do you feel?" he asks.

"Shoulder hurts bad," he says. "I can barely move my right arm."

"At least you're alive," Jiron says.

"There is that," he agrees.

"There's nothing down the road for a while but more trees," Jiron says as he sits on the ground next to him. Seeing a pile of papers on the ground near James he asks, "What's that?"

"Had Tinok search the wagons and he found bills of sales and contracts," he explains. "Seems we ran across some smugglers, at least I think they were. No honorable trader would've attacked us like that." He holds one up and says, "This one here is for a shipment of..., I'm not exactly sure what it is, to a man in Korazan."

"Korazan?" Jiron asks excitedly.

"Yeah," James replies, "seems we caught a break on that one." He holds up another paper and says, "This one is in a language that I can't read, but it has what looks to be an official seal here at the bottom. I'm hoping it's a letter allowing us to travel through the Empire, though we won't know until we put it to the test."

"If you're wrong, it could be bad," he says.

"Probably," he agrees, "but we don't have much choice."

"So we're going to pretend to be those guys there?" he asks, pointing to the two stiffs lying off in the woods.

"That's the plan," he replies. "Oh, we found a chest filled with gold and some gems. So things are looking better."

"We probably should stay here until tomorrow," James tells him, "give me a chance to heal and everyone could use the rest. Then we'll push on down the road and see just where it leads."

While they take their ease, Tinok comes over to him and asks, "You didn't get all weak and tired like you did the last time you did magic. Why not?"

"Last time I had used the power within me," he explains. "This time I had time to plan ahead for the battle, so was able to harness other sources of power."

"Other sources?" he asks. "What do you mean?"

"I set up spells that would slowly absorb power from the trees and other living things around them, storing it up until needed. Over the course of several hours, they had absorbed all the power they required for their spells. So when they went off, no power was drained from me. That's why a lot of the vegetation around them had begun to look wilted."

"Impressive," Tinok says.

"Thanks," he replies.

The rest of the day, they just sort of relax and take it easy, recovering from the ordeal of the last two days. Near sunset, some of them walk back toward the canyon to see how the fire's doing.

Smoke still fills the air and across the canyon the trees are all blackened where the fire had raged. Pockets of fire are still visible here and there, but for the most part, it has consumed the readily available fuel and moved on. They can see it as it continues to burn further up the mountain, the flames arcing up from the tops of the trees where it's still burning furiously.

They make it back to the camp just as the sun dips below the horizon and the light begins to fade. The rest allow James to sleep as they take turns standing watch.

Chapter Six

When they wake in the morning and are ready to begin hooking the horses to the wagons, they come to the realization that no one knows how. Each wagon takes two horses, which ones were easy to figure out, as they were bigger and more muscular than the others. But the problem comes when they attempt to hook the traces to the horses.

The first time they thought they had it figured, the horses had walked right out of their harness when Tinok flicked the reins to get them moving. The girls laughed so hard at the expression on his face when the horses began racing down the road and the traces fell to the ground. He was almost pulled from the wagon but had let go of the reins in time.

"Nice," Delia says, her brown eyes dancing in amusement.

Trying to ignore the reaction of the girls, Jiron runs after the horses and quickly brings them back. Taking their time and lots of trial and error, Jiron and Tinok eventually figure it out, finally enlisting James' aid. Once they're sure the horses aren't going to leave their traces behind again, they board the wagons.

On one wagon rides Delia and James, with Delia attempting to drive the wagon but is finding it much more difficult than she had thought. Tinok is driving the second wagon behind them with Cassie sitting beside him. Jiron is on a horse in the lead, the rest are strung in a line tied behind Tinok's wagon.

Once the wagons start rolling, they begin to learn the finer points of controlling a team of horses. Delia at first has her wagon weaving from one side of the road to the other and once they abruptly stopped for no apparent reason. By the end of the day, however, both she and Tinok have begun to be able to control them with some skill.

The road they're following is barely wide enough to accommodate the wagons. At one point, Delia was afraid one of her wheels would slide off the narrow road and cause the wagon to slide down the mountainside. Near the end of the day they locate a good spot to make camp, an area little more than a widening of the road amidst the trees. From the campfire ring they find there, it would seem the smugglers have used this spot on more than one occasion.

James' shoulder hurts worse than the day before. When they're done with removing the horses from their traces and tethering them to a nearby tree, he has Delia take off the bandage and inspect it. The area around the wound is turning red and is warm to the touch.

"I think it's getting infected," she says to him, concern in her eyes.

"Great," he moans. "Is there any alcohol in the wagons?" he asks her.

"Why?" she replies.

"It may help to purify the wound," he explains. "Maybe even kill the infection."

"I'll see," she says as she goes over and begins rummaging around in the wagons. She returns shortly with a bottle. "This is all I could find," she explains, holding it out to him. "Not sure what's in it though."

"Just put it back," he tells her. "I'd rather not take the chance."

She returns the bottle to the wagon and then goes over to confer with Cassie, far enough away where he can't hear them. They talk briefly for a few minutes and then Cassie walks over and enters the forest. Tinok sees her leaving and runs after her.

Delia comes back over to him and says, "Cassie has had some training with herbs, she may be able to find something that will help."

James just nods as he lies there, beginning to feel worse. His face is starting to feel flushed and his body aches all over, a sure sign of a fever.

Cassie and Tinok come back after a few minutes with various leaves and petals. She takes a bowl from a wagon and proceeds to mash them all together within it. Once it has been combined, she tears a new set of bandages from a cloak found within one of the wagons and applies the mixture to it before bringing it over to James.

Taking off his old bandage, she tosses it into the fire before she applies the new one. When the mixture touches his skin, it brings a cool, soothing sensation. The pain noticeably diminishes and he is able to lie there more at ease.

"Thanks," he says appreciatively to her.

"You're welcome," she replies with a smile, happy to have eased his pain.

He then closes his eyes and shortly falls asleep.

Cassie says, "I don't like the look of his wound. The poultice I applied will ease the pain, but will do nothing to stop whatever is causing the redness and fever."

"What can we do?" Jiron asks.

"Wait," she says. "All we can do is wait."

"Can you find more of those herbs?" he asks her. "He may need them again later."

"I'll pick more," she says. She then walks over to the wagon and removes a basket she found inside before returning to the forest.

"I'll go with you," Tinok says as he gets up to accompany her. Seeing the look on Jiron's face he adds, "There may be wild animals out there, you never know." Then he hurries to catch her.

Jiron turns to Delia and says, "There may be something developing between those two."

She watches them go into the forest together and replies, "You may be right, but I doubt if they even realize it yet."

Cassie and Tinok return some time later with the basket full of herbs and roots. She places them in the wagon and then comes over to inspect James. He's hot with fever and is beginning to perspire. "This is bad," she says, concern in her voice.

"Bad?" asks Jiron.

"How bad?" asks Tinok at the same time.

"If he gets too hot then he'll die," she explains. "I've seen people who have died because their fevers became too high."

"What can we do?" Jiron asks, worried.

"As I said before, wait. Either it will go away on its own or it will kill him, only the gods know for sure." She takes a moist cloth and dabs his forehead with it as she tries to keep him cool, wiping away the sweat that is beginning to form.

They sit there and wait, afraid of what may happen.

The night explodes with light, startling them out of their sleep. They find James standing up and staring off into the woods. He raises his hands and cries out with words none can understand. Trees on the side of the road simply explode, shattering into millions of pieces.

"We're under attack!" Tinok yells as he comes to his feet, knives at the ready. A rain of wood splinters falls all around them from the blasted trees, the larger ones causing pain when they strike exposed skin.

"Where are they?" Jiron yells to James. He comes to stand with him, knives in hand and stares off into the dark forest in the direction he's facing.

Not paying them any attention, James sends a wave of energy into the forest, beyond the jagged stumps of the trees which had already been shattered. Dozens of trees bow and break, many snapping in two as they crash to the ground from the force of the power James is unleashing.

"I don't see anyone!" Tinok yells to Jiron.

"Protect the girls!" Jiron yells to Tinok as he runs closer to the devastated area, seeking their attackers.

James cries out again and the wind begins to blow with increased ferocity. The trees begin swaying first one way and then the other, limbs can be heard breaking off and falling to the ground.

Cassie yells to Tinok over the roar of the wind as he approaches, "There is no one!"

"What?" he yells back.

"There is no one," she cries and then she points to James. "Look at his eyes, he's not really seeing. It's the fever! He's having a hallucination!" She pulls her long yellow hair out of her face from where the wind continues whipping it.

As understanding dawns upon him, he sheaths his knives and then runs over to Jiron. Before he gets there, James cries out again and lightning flashes from the sky, striking trees near where Jiron stands, the force of which knocks him backward. He lands on his back, dazed, just as Tinok reaches him.

Tinok kneels down next to him and then looks up when James screams incoherently. As he begins running into the forest, Jiron tries to get back to his feet to follow. Tinok places a hand on him and says, "He's fighting dreams!"

"What?" Jiron asks in confusion, not sure if he heard correctly.

"James!" Tinok yells, pointing to where he ran into the forest. "It's the fever making him do this. We're not under attack!"

Once he realizes what Tinok is trying to tell him, he says, "We've got to help him!" He gets to his feet and looks toward the forest where James entered just as another explosion of immense proportion erupts to the sky.

"We can't!" yells Tinok over the wind. "He'll kill us without even realizing it."

"But..." Jiron says, wanting to help him, but recognizing the truth in Tinok's words. Then he looks around the camp, wood everywhere, a section of the forest near their camp is simply gone. Trees are toppled over, most of the horses have run off, frightened. They gather together and he asks Cassie, "What should we do?"

"Nothing to do," she explains. "He doesn't realize what he's doing. It will run its course if it doesn't kill him first."

"How long?" he asks.

Shrugging, she says, "Who knows? I guess we'll find out when the noise stops."

They look off into the forest as more lights are seen and explosions heard. A light rain begins to fall a few minutes later and after it has fallen for awhile, the sound of explosions from the forest lessens until it is once again quiet, bringing an eerie calm to the night.

"Should we find him?" Delia asks as the rain continues to fall, plastering her short, dark brown hair to her head.

Shaking his head, Jiron says, "Not in the dark, we might get lost. Besides, there is no guarantee that he's done." So they settle down to wait for dawn. None are able to get any rest, what with the rain soaking them and their concern for their friend. Sometime before morning comes, the rain stops.

When dawn at last arrives, they are able to see the extent of the damage wrought by James during his fever induced rampage of the night before. Around them, trees are either blown apart at the base or toppled over, one upon another. Pieces of wood are simply everywhere, the wagons themselves have a layer of broken branches and wood chips covering them.

Most of the horses have found their way back, three of the draft animals and four of the mounts. A quick look around the surrounding area turns up one more mount and the other draft animal.

"Should we go look for him now?" Jiron asks Cassie.

"Since we haven't heard anything for a couple hours, it's fairly safe to say that he is no longer a danger," she says. "We need to find him to see if he's okay."

Indicating the path of destruction, Tinok says, "I don't think it is going to be too hard to follow his trail."

"No," agrees Jiron, "it won't." Leading the group, he follows the trail of broken trees through the forest. They come across area after area that shows signs of rampant destruction. "I wonder what he thought he was fighting last night?" he says.

"Yeah," Tinok replies. "What could warrant such power?"

"In his state of mind," Cassie explains, "he could have been imagining almost anything."

They come to a section of the forest where the trees look odd. Delia taps one out of curiosity and gasps, "It's stone!"

The others come over and feel it, mystified at how James could have done something like that. "Incredible," exclaims Tinok.

Continuing on, they finally reach a point where the destruction ends, but James is no where to be seen. "James!" Jiron calls out, looking through the trees as far as he can.

When there's no answer, Delia says, "We better split up."

Jiron nods, saying, "That might be wise, but let's not get too separated." He looks at each in turn and says, "If in five minutes you haven't found him, turn around and come back here."

They all agree and then head out into the forest, each calling for James.

Weak as a new born lamb and his shoulder aflame with pain, James regains consciousness. His head is fuzzy and it's hard to formulate thoughts. He realizes that he's covered in leaves and tree limbs, and that everything is damp. Unable to even lift his arms to remove the foliage from him, he lies there, wondering just how he came to be here.

"James!"

Suddenly alert, he hears his name being called from far away. *They'll never find me here!* Afraid they might pass him by, he starts to panic. He tries calling out but only a weak rasp comes out, "Help!" *Why am I so weak?*

He tries again, "Help!" this time managing a little volume.

"I think I heard something!" he hears someone shout.

"Where?" another voice asks.

"Not sure," the first voice replies. "James! Where are you?"

He can hear several people moving through the forest, near and around him. Giving it one last try, he shouts, "Over here!" Again, it only comes out barely audible.

"There!" he hears someone shout. "It came from that way."

Suddenly, Delia comes into view as she walks right by where he's laying. He moves his hand slightly, but it catches her eye.

"Here he is!" she cries out excitedly. "Are you alright?" she asks him as she places her hand on his forehead.

Shaking his head no, he just lies there.

When everyone approaches, she says, "His fever's gone, but he says he isn't good."

"Let's get him out," Jiron says when he sees him lying there, all but his head and one arm is hidden beneath the broken branches.

They all help to get the limbs and leaves off of him and then help him to stand. But in his weakened condition his legs are unable to support his weight and they just give out under him. So Jiron and Tinok move to help him, Jiron on the left and Tinok on the right.

When Tinok tries placing James' right arm over his shoulder for support, he cries out in pain from the stress that's being put on the wound from the crossbow bolt. Realizing they're not going to be able to do it that way, Jiron tries lifting him in his arms, but James is too heavy for him to attempt to carry all the way back to the campsite.

"I got an idea," Cassie says. Grabbing Tinok she says to the others, "Just make him comfortable and we'll be right back."

They run back the way they came, back toward the wagons.

Jiron sets James down on a fallen log and stays beside him, keeping him upright. "What's she going to do?" he asks Delia.

"Not sure," she replies.

"What happened to you last night?" Jiron asks James.

"Hmmm? What do you mean?" he asks in a voice barely above a whisper.

"Don't you remember anything from last night?" Jiron asks him.

"Last thing I remember is lying on the ground back at camp," he explains. "Then nothing until I woke up here, hearing you calling my name. Why?"

"You woke up in the middle of the night and all hell broke loose," he tells him. "You were fighting something, Cassie thinks you were just being delusional because of the fever. You were throwing magic around, creating havoc as if you were under attack."

James just stares in disbelief as Jiron recounts what happened and the destruction they saw as they came to search for him.

"At first we thought we were under attack," he continues, "but then realized it was the fever doing it to you. Then you suddenly ran off into the forest and for a while we heard you blowing things up. It lasted well over an hour before you finally stopped. Couldn't come for you until morning, didn't want to risk getting lost and separated."

"Sorry," James says apologetically.

"No one got hurt," Delia says, "and it seems that it was good for you, the fever's gone."

They sit there and wait for the return of Cassie and Tinok. Just when Jiron is about ready to leave to find them, they show up carrying a stretcher they made with two long tree limbs and a couple of blankets.

They set it down near James and then Tinok and Jiron help him onto it. With Jiron in the front and Tinok taking the rear, they begin to carry him through the forest and back to camp. As they enter the areas of destruction, James is reminded of a similar instance back near Trendle. He just shakes his head in regret at all the uselessly destroyed trees.

When they pass by the petrified tree, Tinok asks, "How did you do that?"

"What?" he asks, lifting his head a little to see what he's talking about.

"That tree there," he replies, indicating it with a nod of his head.

"What's wrong with it?" he asks again, confused.

"It's as hard as stone," he explains.

"Let me see," he says and they carry him close enough so he's able to touch it. When he feels the tree, he tells them, "Petrified, I would guess."

"Petrified?" Cassie asks.

"Petrification is when minerals in the ground are absorbed by a living organism and over time turns as hard as rock," he explains.

"How did you do that?" Tinok asks.

"I don't know," he admits. "But I plan on thinking about it, now that I know it can be done."

They resume carrying him until they get back to the camp, where they lay him down and start a fire to warm him. Cassie replaces his bandage with a fresh one containing more of her poultice.

Once they have the fire going and James has eaten his fill, he says, "We better get going, we've still got to get to Korazan before the slavers do."

"Are you well enough?" Jiron asks.

"No, but we have little choice," he replies. "I can rest well enough in the wagon."

"Alright," Jiron says, "let's get ready to go." He and Tinok begin the process of securing the traces on the draft horses. When they're set, they help James up onto the wagon, again next to Delia. Tinok and Cassie take up the second wagon and Jiron rides point. The five remaining horses are tied in line in the rear.

"Let's go," Jiron says, as he begins to ride down the road with the wagons following behind.

This time, Delia and Tinok are much more able to properly control the wagons, and are able to make better time. They follow the road for the rest of the day, at times having to stop while everyone except James, gets down and helps push one when it gets stuck in the mud.

Just a brief stop for lunch and then they resume their journey. James drifts in and out of sleep throughout the day and by the time they make camp that night, he's regained enough of his strength to be able to come down from the wagon by himself.

They get the horses unhitched and picketed before making camp. Tinok gets a roaring fire going to help keep them warm through the night and then they eat the last of the rations that were in the wagons. "Hope we get somewhere soon," comments Tinok.

"Afraid of going hungry?" Delia asks with a smile.

"No," he replies defensively, "just tired of being in the mountains."

"I find it relaxing," James interjects. Everyone turns and looks at him as he continues, "They've always brought me peace."

"There is something tranquil about them," Cassie adds. She then rests her head on Tinok's shoulder who places his arm around her, keeping her warm. Jiron and Delia glance at each other and smile.

They sit there by the fire, the pop and crackle of the wood lending a peacefulness to the night. It isn't long before James has fallen asleep. The rest soon follow.

The next morning, the overcast sky of the day before has made way for a beautiful sunny morning, once the remaining cloud cover has burned off. Everyone's mood is much improved and are soon on the road. As he rides along in the wagon, James realizes that the sun is rising on their left. *Heading south,* he figures.

About midday, the road begins to descend gradually and everyone is glad that they will soon be out of the mountains. Everyone that is, but Tinok who says, "I don't know why you're all so happy."

"What do you mean?" Delia asks. "I thought you wanted to be out of the mountains."

"I do, but once we're out of the mountains, we're going to be in Empire territory again. Doesn't that make you the least bit nervous?" he asks.

"A little," she replies, "but I like to hope for the best."

"Besides," adds James, "we now have a reason for being there. I think we've even got a letter that will allow us to pass through."

"I hope so," Tinok replies. He quiets down, keeping his brooding thoughts to himself.

The trees begin to thin and they can see off in the distance where they will be coming out of the mountains. A road appears further down, running along the base of the mountains going east to west.

An hour later, they finally reach where the road they've been following will be leaving the protection of the trees as it makes its way out to the main road. They pause only momentarily as they check for any travelers who might observe them leaving the mountains. Not seeing anyone upon the road, they quickly make their way out upon it.

"Which way?" Jiron asks James.

"Let's try east and see if a road hooks up with this one that's heading south," he suggests. "If we find that this road turns to the north further along, we'll double back and see what's to the west of us."

Jiron turns his horse eastward and leads them down the road.

Chapter Seven

They travel half a day after leaving the mountains when they see a town coming up ahead. It appears rather small, just several buildings at a juncture of converging roads. As they near, they realize this town shows no sign of the Empire's occupation. The citizens go about their daily business and children can be seen running around, playing in the streets.

"Wonder why this town remains untouched by the Empire?" James wonders.

"Maybe it's in the Empire?" suggests Delia.

"Could be," he agrees. "I guess we'll find out soon enough."

Jiron leads them toward the town and as they draw near, the people become aware of their approach. Most only pausing a moment to glance in their direction before continuing about their business.

One of the buildings has a sign of three barrels hanging above the door. Figuring it to be a shop where they can purchase supplies, they pull up and stop in front. James and Jiron go inside while the others wait with the wagons.

Within the shop, they find a man in the process of straightening up his inventory. When he sees them coming through the door, he turns toward them and smiles. "Welcome, welcome," he says as he goes over to greet them. "How may I help you today?"

"We just need some supplies before heading on," James tells him.

"We have a wide selection of goods for the traveler," the shopkeeper says. "What might you be interested in?"

"Just some travel rations and water bottles," he replies.

"You don't seem very busy," Jiron comments when he notices they're the only ones in there.

"Business has been a little slow of late," he says. "With the war going on and all." He places several packages of rations on the counter, and then asks James, "How many water bottles do you require?"

"Five," he replies.

The man reaches up to a shelf and removes five water bottles, placing them on the counter next to the rations.

"The Empire didn't come this way?" Jiron asks.

"We're sort of on the border," he explains. "We're not really apart of anyone, yet they all think we are apart of them. Sometimes it's confusing, but everyone tends to leave us alone her in Bindles."

"How far is it to Korazan?" Jiron asks.

"About three to four days," the man says. "Are you going there?"

"We have some goods to deliver there, yes," James replies.

"If you would deliver a couple packages for me," he offers, "I could let you have this for free." He indicates their goods on the counter. "Plus, when you delivered them, you would receive a bonus as well."

James thinks for a second and then says, "Sure, we could do that for you."

"Excellent," the merchant exclaims. "I've been waiting for some time for a trader to pass through who would be willing to take it. Just wait here a moment and I'll bring it out."

While he's in the back, Jiron comes closer to James and whispers, "Why are we doing this?"

"Gives us more credibility if questioned," James replies.

Jiron suddenly understands and gives James a nod with a slight smile.

The man returns from the back with three packages and a bill of lading. "Take these three packages to Zi-Aldan in Korazan. Not sure exactly where he is located, but if you inquire at the local merchant's guild, they should be able to direct you to him."

"Very well," James says as Jiron collects their goods. The merchant hands him the bill of lading and then picks up his packages to carry them out to their wagons. James holds the door open for him as they leave his shop. Tinok gives them an odd expression as the merchant walks over and deposits the packages in the back of his wagon.

Extending his hand, the merchant says, "I appreciate you doing this for me."

James shakes his hand and replies, "Glad we could be of assistance." He climbs up onto the wagon and sits next to Delia. Then he gives the merchant a slight bow as he says, "May you have prosperous dealings."

The wagons begin rolling away as the merchant says, "You too sir, you too."

They continue through town and when they come to where the roads converge, Jiron automatically turns to follow the road going south. As the town begins to fall away and finally disappears behind them, the terrain gradually becomes more arid. Trees and bushes make way for scrub brush, as well as the occasional tumbleweed. *Kind of looks like the area around Bakersfield,* James thinks to himself.

The air becomes drier the further south they progress and the temperature starts to rise. They had warm, even hot days before, but nothing like this. James is literally baking under the sun, sure that he's going to end up with a dilly of a sunburn.

The road meanders along this desert-like territory for many miles before they begin to approach another small town. The citizens here all wear long flowing robes, kind of like the middle easterners wore back on Earth.

There's a company of the Empire's soldiers garrisoned here and when they enter the outskirts of town, an officious looking man steps out of a building just ahead of them. James' pulse begins to beat faster when he realizes the man means to intercept them. As he approaches he raises his hand, signaling for them to stop.

"Greetings," he says to them as they roll to a stop.

"Good day to you as well," James replies, giving him a small bow.

"What brings you through Arakan, good merchant?" the official inquires.

"Traveling through to deliver some goods in Korazan," James replies nonchalantly.

"Do you have a letter of travel?" the official questions. "Anyone not of the Empire requires one to be allowed to pass through our territory."

James reaches into his shirt and brings out the official looking letter and hands it over to him. His heart racing, he glances to Jiron and sees his right hand on a knife as he stares intently at the man as he reads the letter. He knows if it's not what James had been hoping it was, they'll have a fight on their hands.

The man reads the letter and then hands it back to James, saying, "Very good, all seems to be in order. Hope you enjoy your stay here in Arakan."

Everyone visibly relaxes as James takes the letter back. "Do you have a carpenter here in town?" he asks.

"We do have a blacksmith who doubles as our carpenter in emergencies," the official says. "You'll find him further down the road and a little off to the right. You can't miss him."

Signaling Delia to get the wagon moving again, he says, "Thank you, sir."

"You're most welcome," he replies as he turns to walk back to the building he came out of.

"A carpenter? What for?" Jiron asks.

"I want some shade to keep the sun off me," he explains. Already the back of his neck, not to mention his nose, cheeks and arms are all beginning to turn red. He can feel the heat burning into them.

They go down the road and soon hear the sound of metal being hammered. Turning off the road toward the sound, they come to the blacksmith's shop. They find him working under an awning, hammering some hot metal as he turns it into a horseshoe.

When he sees them approaching, he hammers the metal a few more times, inspects his work and then lays the horseshoe atop the anvil. He places the pincers he was using to hold the horseshoe on a nearby table and then comes over to greet them.

"What can I do for you today?" he asks.

"Was wondering if you might have some long boards and nails I could purchase?" James asks. "And maybe the use of a hammer for a few minutes?"

The man nods, and says, "Got what you need out back," he replies. "But if there's any hammering to be done, I'll do it. Follow me." He leads them around the side of the awning covered area to where he has piles of rough cut boards along with a pile of scraps. "What will you be needing it for?" he asks.

James gets down and walks over to him, "We're not use to the intensity of the sun down here, so would like to create a framework above the wagons which we could secure some blankets to, in order to have some shade."

He looks at the wagons and says, "I got the stuff for that, it'll cost a gold and seven silvers."

"Alright," James says as he opens his pouch and takes out the money, handing it over. "How soon can you have it done?" he asks.

"About an hour," he replies. "I have to finish the shoe I'm working on before I start."

"Is there a place where we can eat while we wait?" he asks.

The blacksmith points back the way they came and indicates a two story building. He says, "You can find something over there at the Cracked Pot."

"Thank you," James says as he returns to the others. "It's going to be about an hour," he tells them, "so we may as well get something to eat while we wait."

They get down from the wagons, Jiron and Tinok secure the horses to a hitching post near the blacksmith's shop. They then walk over to the building the blacksmith had indicated and find an old pot with a sizeable crack running down the side hanging out front. Opening the door, they enter the common room and sit at a table near an open window through which a slight breeze is blowing.

Once seated, a girl comes over and starts to talk to them in the Empire's language. James holds up his hand and says, "I'm sorry, but we don't speak your language."

"Sorry," she says with an accent as she switches to their speech, "but we don't get many who don't speak our language."

"That's alright," replies James. "What's available?"

"We have roasted goat or sliced goat placed between chunks of bread," she says. "The goat is a silver each, and the other is four coppers."

"Sliced goat?" James asks to everyone. They all nod their heads and he says, "Okay, five of those please, and ale all around." He digs out two silvers and hands them to her, "Will this cover it?"

"Yes sir," she says, placing the money within a pocket. "I'll have it out in just a few minutes." She then turns and heads to the kitchen to prepare their meals.

"Sure is hot here," Jiron comments to no one in particular.

"You said it," Tinok responds. "I've never seen it like this before. I mean, sure, back home it got hot, but this is insane."

"Just make sure to drink lots of water so you don't get dehydrated," James tells everyone.

The girl returns from the kitchen with a tray laden with a large heap of sliced meat and three loaves of bread balanced on one hand, while in the other she has a pitcher and five mugs. Jiron gets up to help her as it looks like she's about to lose it.

"Thank you," she says gratefully, smiling at him as he takes the tray from her and places it on the table.

He gives her a slight bow and says, "Anything for a pretty lady."

The girl blushes, then places the pitcher and the mugs on the table. "If there's anything else you require, just let me know." She then returns to the kitchen.

"Stop bothering people," Delia says to Jiron sternly.

"What?" Jiron exclaims. "Can't a guy give a girl a compliment?"

She just glares at him.

James takes his knife and cuts off two slices of bread and then takes a slice of meat, placing it between them. Taking a big bite, he's reminded of a hamburger from back home, though the flavor is a little stronger than what he's used to.

Everyone begins taking the bread and making 'goat burgers'. The break from the trail is nice, what with being in the shade and a nice breeze coming in through the window. They finish eating before the hour is up and relax around the table until it's time to return to the blacksmith's. Tinok takes the last of the bread and stuffs the remaining goat inside it as he leaves the table, eating it on the way over.

They're surprised at what awaits them back at the blacksmith's. Not only did he construct a frame for each wagon, but has also installed an off-white cloth covering for each as well.

Seeing them enter, he comes over to them and asks, "How do you like it?"

"Very nice," James replies admiringly. Not only will anyone sitting on the driver's bench be out of the sun, but it covers the entire wagon as well, shading the holding area.

"You're mounts looked thirsty," he tells them, "so I took them over to the well and gave them water." He indicates a well off to the side with a two foot trough sitting on the ground next to it.

"Thank you," James says.

"You're welcome," the blacksmith says as he leaves them to go back and work on more horseshoes.

They get back on the wagons, Jiron on his horse, and resume their journey to Korazan. The shade provided by the covering helps immensely to alleviate the worst of the sun's heat. Though it's still incredibly hot, at least they're no longer at risk of severe sunburn. Jiron though, doesn't seem to be bothered by being out in the sun on his horse.

After riding for a ways, Delia asks, "What would you have done if that paper turned out to not to have been a pass?"

James shrugs, "I don't know, that would have depended on what he did."

"Think we'll be able to play this off in Korazan?" she asks.

"Hope so," he replies. "Not sure what else to do if it doesn't."

They continue on in silence, every once in a while passing a caravan or other travelers going in the opposite direction. After one of the caravans passes, Jiron slows down until the wagon James is riding upon comes abreast of him and then asks, "Did you see those men in the caravan, the ones wearing only a brown loincloth?"

"Yeah," James said, "I noticed them."

"I think they were slaves," he tells him. "The people who were captured when the City fell were dressed similarly when they were being marched south."

"Thanks," James replies, "I didn't know that."

Jiron gives him a quick nod then resumes his place at the front of the caravan.

As time goes by more and more travelers pass, some having slaves accompanying them, others not. Whenever he sees them his anger blossoms, even though he is impotent to do anything about it. He would free them all if he could, but doing that would bring down the wrath of the powers that be. Miko must be his first and foremost concern right now.

Not having reached the next town by the time the sun begins to near the horizon, they decide to pull over and make camp off the road a ways. The wagons are pulled in close to one another and the horses are picketed in a group nearby. They set about making camp when Tinok comes over to James with his water bottle and asks, "Have you got any extra water? Mine's all gone."

"A little," he replies. "I was trying to make it last."

"Can I have some?" he asks.

"Sure," he says, handing him his bottle.

As Tinok drinks the last of his water, he begins to realize they may be in trouble. Out in this heat, they're not going to last long without water. Then he glances over to the horses and realizes they've not had any water since the blacksmith's earlier in the day. *They must be really thirsty by now.*

He looks around the horizon for a source of water, but only scrub brush can be seen. *This could be bad,* he realizes. Calling them all together, he asks, "Who has water left?"

Cassie and Jiron raise their hands, while Tinok and Delia shake their heads.

"Seems we've gotten ourselves in a situation," he says. "We're going to die out here if we don't find some water soon, not to mention the horses."

"What are we to do?" Jiron asks. "We're miles away from anywhere and," he glances around the horizon, "it doesn't look like there's any water to be found."

"There's always water," he tells them, "it's just a matter of getting to it."

"I don't see any water around here," Tinok says as he looks around the horizon.

"It's beneath us," he explains, pointing to the ground. "Under the surface."

"How are we going to get it?" Tinok asks.

"Magic?" Delia guesses, looking questioningly toward James.

He nods his head, "Magic. Now what I plan to do is to search with magic beneath the ground and when I've found it, get it to come up to the surface."

"Neat," Cassie exclaims.

"Just stay here and watch for anyone coming," he says to them. He then turns and walks away from their camp, looking for a depression or hole where the water would be able to pool once he managed to bring it up. It wouldn't do to spend all that time and energy to bring it up only to have the water run off and be absorbed back into the ground.

He eventually comes across a place not thirty feet from camp that will suffice, and then sits down next to it. He begins concentrating and the magic flows out of him, down below the surface as he searches for water.

Surprisingly, he finds water not very far below the surface, only about twenty feet or so. He sends his senses further down and discovers that there's a sizeable reservoir there. Coming back to himself, he gets up and walks back over to the group, informing them of what he's found. His head is dizzy from the heat and the effort it took to find the water.

Incredibly hot and thirsty after the ordeal, he asks "Cassie, could I have the rest of your water?"

She nods and then hands him her water bottle which he drains completely. "Thanks," he says as he hands it back to her.

"Now what?" Jiron asks.

"Give me just a few minutes to rest and I'll attempt to bring it up." He goes over and sits down on a wagon, taking advantage of the shade the newly acquired covering gives. Even though the sun is about to go down, it's still fairly hot.

Once he's rested and no longer feels dizzy, he gets down from the wagon and walks back to the area where he will attempt to bring up the water. Standing next to the depression he begins to summon the magic, sending it below the surface to where the water lies.

He takes his time, finding fissures and cracks, weak spots that can be loosened and widened, making a way for the water to reach the surface. Little by little, as he widens a crack here and breaks through stone there, he begins to sense the water being forced to the surface by the pressure below.

Once he's created a fissure halfway to the surface the ground begins to shake, breaking his concentration and ending the spell. He stumbles as the shaking increases, cries of confusion come from the others who are watching him from over near the wagons.

Suddenly, the ground cracks open and water geysers out of the ground, shooting twenty feet in the air before falling back down into the depression. The area rapidly fills with water as it continues surging out of the ground.

Jiron reaches James' side and claps him on the shoulder as he says, "You did it!"

The others come to his side, congratulating him. They watch as the water fills the depression to capacity and begins creating a small pond, thirty feet in diameter. Then the water starts spilling over the side and is quickly absorbed by the ground.

Tinok kneels down by the water and cups his hands, tasting it. He looks over to the others and shouts, "It's good, and cool!"

They all come over and drink their fill from the pool of cool water. The horses smell the water and begin straining against their tethers in an attempt to reach it.

Jiron runs over and releases them, allowing them to come and drink their fill. Everyone fills their water bottles before returning to the wagons.

"We were lucky there was no one around," James says as he lies there near the campfire, relaxing.

"Why?" Cassie asks.

"Don't want anyone to know I can do magic," he explains. "They may still be on the lookout for the rogue mage that caused the destruction back at the City. I really don't want them to begin putting two and two together."

"What does two and two have to do with anything?" asks Tinok.

"Sorry, that's just an expression from where I come from," he replies. "It just means they might connect me with the things I did at the City. If they knew I was a mage, that is."

"Oh," he says.

"Maybe the next town we come to, we should buy several water barrels to carry with us," Jiron suggests.

"That may be a good idea," agrees James. "We should have plenty of money left in the chest."

"What is the next town?" Cassie asks.

"Haven't a clue." James admits. "I've never been here before."

"How do you know that we're even going in the right direction, then?" Jiron asks.

"I figure Korazan should be further south," he replies. "A major slave market would hardly be on the edge of the Empire. They would want it accessible to a large number of their people, so it stands to reason that it would be further into the Empire. Thus, south."

As they relax around the campfire, James absentmindedly reaches for his backpack, but then remembers that they left it back in Mountainside when they broke out of jail. Thinking of the things that are now lost to him, he gets sad and then mad. *This place is just going from bad to worse,* he thinks to himself. *Now I've gone and lost my backpack.*

"Oh my god!" he suddenly exclaims, sitting up abruptly.

"What?" Jiron asks.

"My backpack!" he replies.

"What about it?" Tinok inquires as he joins the conversation.

"It's back at the jail," he explains.

"So?" says Tinok. "We all lost some things when we left there. We were in a little bit of a hurry."

"You don't understand," exclaims James "I had some papers in there, notes I had been keeping about magic and other important stuff."

When he sees that he's not getting through to them, he says, "My notes will make them realize that a mage was there. If they assume I'm the same mage as was at the City of Light, then they will know we're heading south."

"And the only reason we would be heading south," continues Delia, "would be to rescue someone from the slavers that had been taken when the City fell."

"That's one reason," James agrees. "And if they come to that conclusion, they'll be waiting for us there."

"What do we do?" Cassie asks.

James looks to Jiron and says, "Someone needs to go and retrieve it. Or at least destroy it and the papers it carries."

He flashes James a dark look, "You mean go all the way back there, on the chance that no one has yet looked inside and seen them?" He shakes his head, "I don't know."

"You're the only one who can do it," James urges.

He sits and thinks for a few minutes, everyone else remains quiet, waiting for his response. "Alright, I'll do it," he finally says. Getting up, he goes over to his horse and begins putting the saddle and tack back on.

"Shouldn't you wait till morning," Cassie asks.

Shaking his head, he says, "No, I better get started now. The sooner I get there, the less likely someone will have read the papers."

James comes over and gives him some coins. He looks at them and James tells him, "For traveling expenses."

He takes the coins, putting them in a pocket. Once he has the horse ready for travel, he mounts and says, "Where shall I meet up with you?"

"Well continue down the road and stop at the next main town," James explains. "We'll stay there for a day, and if you don't show up we'll continue on to Korazan."

"Alright," he says. "I'll meet you there."

"Be careful," Delia and Cassie say at the same time.

"I will," he assures them. "See you in a couple days." He then heads his horse back down the road to the north and kicks it into a gallop as he races for Mountainside.

"Hope he'll make it back," Cassie says, worry in her voice.

"He will," Tinok says with confidence. He looks into the night where Jiron had disappeared and says again, "He will!"

Chapter   Eight

Jiron leaves them quickly behind as he races through the cool of the night. As frustrated as he is at James for having to go back and retrieve his stupid backpack, he finds it refreshing to ride in the cool of the night, on his own.

Making very good time, it's not long before the lights of Arakan appear in the road ahead of him. Remembering the soldiers stationed there, he swings wide to avoid being spotted. As he rounds the town, he spies one of the townsfolk standing outside one of the outermost buildings, his form silhouetted by the light coming through an open doorway. The man must've heard the sound of his horse, for he turns in his direction and peers intently, but is unable to see him in the darkness. Sensing no threat, the man returns to what he was doing. Jiron finishes bypassing the town and then returns to the road, soon leaving Arakan far behind.

Continuing to race north, another hour finds him at the quiet village of Bindles. Only a few lights can be seen amongst the buildings, the rest are dark as the inhabitants are asleep in their beds for the night.

He swings wide around the town and reaches the juncture of roads on the far side, where he follows the road eastward. The mountains now loom large on his left as he races down the road. He begins to detect the faint odor of burnt wood, testament to the forest fire they escaped from some time earlier.

Once he's several miles east of Bindles, he gets down from his horse and walks for a while, giving his horse a break. Ten minutes later, he's back in the saddle and riding hard.

As he continues north, the odor of smoke becomes stronger and stronger. After another two hours, he begins to see a glow coming from far ahead, where the fire is still raging upon the mountain. As he rides, the glow becomes more and more pronounced, until he's finally able to see the flames themselves as they arc into the sky.

Off to the east, the sky begins to lighten with the coming of dawn, enabling him to see an incredibly large cloud of smoke extending for miles in every direction.

Down the road ahead, a town comes into view amidst the smoke. The fire is within a mile of the outskirts and at first looks to be deserted. As he comes closer to the town, he sees that it isn't as deserted as it had first appeared. A few people are seen passing from building to building and they all have cloths tied about their faces to protect them from the smoke.

Realizing an opportunity when he sees it, Jiron pulls up to one of the houses at the outskirts of town. He ties his horse to a tree out back before going up to the backdoor. Finding it locked, he moves to a window and looks inside, the place looks deserted. Going back to the door, he looks around quickly to make sure no one is near and then kicks it open. Entering quickly, he shuts the door behind him.

The house is quiet, the people most likely having fled the approaching fire long ago. He quickly finds a cloth and ties it around his face, effectively disguising himself. Coming back out to where his horse is tied, he remounts and tries to find where the jail had been.

He passes several people moving along the streets as he makes his way through town, but no one gives him a second thought. Up near the fire, he sees dozens of people trying to halt the advancing flames with axes and shovels, doing their best to save their homes but it doesn't look as if they're being too successful. Just as a group has a space cleared in the hopes of preventing it from spreading, a tree engulfed with flame falls across the cleared area, starting new fires past the fire break. People rush to beat them out before they have a chance to spread but are having limited success.

None of the firefighters on the mountain look to be soldiers, though from this distance and with all the smoke it's hard to be sure. As he continues toward the jail, he doesn't come across any soldiers here in town either. *Guess we got them all up on the mountain.*

Out of the smoke ahead of him, the jail suddenly comes into view. Cautiously, he slows down as he takes a good survey of the surrounding area for any soldiers. Not finding any, he makes his way toward the jail all the while continuously scanning for anyone approaching. But with all the smoke in the area, they would have to be really close before they would even know he was there.

Upon reaching the jail, he secures his horse to the rail outside and goes up to a window to look in. A quick look reveals the jail to be empty, a lucky break. Off to one side of the main room a table had been overturned, most likely during their jail break. Spilled on the floor beside it is James' backpack along with their knives and other belongings.

Surprised and pleased to see all their stuff still there and apparently untouched, he glances around to make sure he's unobserved and then enters the jail. Hurrying over to where his knives lie on the floor, he picks them up first and belts them on, feeling good now that he has them again. Stuffing Tinok's knives into the backpack, he then slings the backpack over a shoulder and proceeds back to the front door. The sound of approaching horses stops him before he opens the door.

Moving to a window, he looks out and discovers twenty enemy soldiers approaching on horseback. He watches them for a few seconds, and when he realizes they're on their way to the jail, he runs to the cells in the back and slips through the hole in the wall James had made during their escape. By the time he's reached the alley behind the jail, the sound of them talking can be heard from where they've stopped out front. What they are saying is unknown as Jiron doesn't speak the Empire's language.

He slips around the back to the side alley and moves to the end where he can peer around to observe the riders out front. The majority of the soldiers are still upon their horses, one lone horse stands without a rider. Jiron's horse sits in the middle of the group and it doesn't appear as if anyone is paying it any attention. Shortly, a soldier's voice can be heard calling out to the others from within the jail.

The one whose attire marks him to be an officer barks out orders and half of the remaining men dismount, as does he. The others remaining on their horses turn and proceed to move quickly in different directions through the town, as if they're looking for something. Then he hears another soldier's voice from inside shout excitedly as he finds the hole in the cell.

Jiron looks longingly at his horse sitting there amidst the others for a moment and then begins to hurry back to the alley running behind jail. When he reaches it, he turns to follow it away from the jail. Just as he reaches the end of the alley, he pauses a moment and glances back toward the jail. A soldier sticks his head out of the hole in the wall, looking first one way then the other.

He quickly slips around the corner to avoid being seen by the soldier. Not hearing any outcry from him, he breathes a sigh of relief at not having been spotted. He continues down the side alley until he comes to a door. Finding it unlocked, he slips inside and closes it behind him.

This one looks to be another residence, the room he finds himself in has two tables, four chairs and a one long couch. It was probably where the lady of the house would greet guests and have tea. He moves to a window and keeps a lookout on what the soldiers are doing.

They appear to be searching for something, maybe he and the others. The riders seem to be combing the streets while the officer stays within the jail with several of the others. He hopes they'll just up and leave so he can retrieve his horse. He'll never make it back to the others without it.

The entrance to the jail is barely discernable through the thick smoke that envelopes the town, but he's able to see the officer come out, obviously upset and angry. He barks out more orders and several of the men on foot climb back into their saddles, racing off to the south. The officer stands there a moment as he looks at the fire and the people trying to halt its course.

Jiron continues to watch as two of his men appear out of the smoke with a man held between them. They bring him over to the leader and when they're five feet from him, force the man to his knees.

The officer asks the kneeling man in the northern tongue, "Where are the men that were stationed here?"

The man on his knees just shakes his head.

The officer signals and one of the men twists one of the man's arms, making him cry out. "I said, where are my men?"

"I don't know!" the man cries out.

"Something happened here," the officer says and then comes forward. Grabbing the man's hair, he yanks his head back and stares into his eyes. "What!" he demands.

Gasping through the pain in his arm, the man exclaims, "I don't know! They brought some people in and had them imprisoned in the jail."

"Who were they?" the officer snaps.

"We never found out!" the man cries, tears rolling down his face from the pain he's experiencing.

The officer lets go of the man's hair and then nods his head to his man who releases his grip on the man's arm. "Then what?" he asks.

Holding his arm tight across his chest, the man keeps his head down while he answers. Jiron has to really strain to hear what was being said. "Then that night, all hell broke loose. We heard shouting and fighting and when it was calm again, there was a hole in the wall of the jail and several of the soldiers were dead."

"How could people in cells have caused all that?" he looks intently at the man. When the officer pauses for an answer, the man looks up but just shakes his head. The officer continues, "Did the townsfolk help them?"

"Oh, no!" the man cries. "We did not! We didn't even realize they had anyone there until after it was over." He looks to the officer, hoping to be believed.

"Then what?" he asks.

"You're men gave chase as the prisoners fled up into the mountains," the man replies, bowing his head once more. "Some time later the soldiers returned, several of them having been killed I heard. The next morning, the officer in charge took his whole garrison up after them, but none came back. Shortly after that, the fire swept down the mountainside, almost like magic, engulfing tree after tree."

"Magic, you say?" the officer asks intently.

The man looks up at the officer's eyes boring into his, "It seemed like it, as fast as the fire spread."

"Hmmm," the officer mumbles as he thinks to himself. "Let him go," he says to his men who then release the man. To the man he says, "If you and your folk had a hand in the killing of my men, I will cut the throat of every man, woman and child here and raze this town to the ground!"

Fear in his eyes, the man exclaims, "We didn't!"

"We'll see," and then waves his hand, dismissing him. The man turns and flees down the street as fast as his legs will carry him, never once looking back.

The officer and his men confer for a few minutes and then return inside the jail.

"Damn!" Jiron quietly exclaims. *Why did he have to say 'magic'! Hopefully they won't put, as James says, two and two together.* He continues watching but everything remains quiet. His horse remains tied to the post outside the jail, along with the others.

Figuring on a wait before he'll be able to reclaim his horse, he looks through the house and discovers some bread and fruit in the kitchen. He pulls a chair close to the window so he can keep an eye on what's going on outside as he eats.

Nothing of interest happens while he's eating, soldiers continue to come and go from the jail, and the occasional townsman runs past carrying a shovel or some other item used to combat the fire. After he's finished, he tries to think of a way to retrieve his horse while he sits there looking out the window. The last twenty four hours begin to catch up with him and he finds himself yawning and rubbing his eyes.

Deciding on a short nap since he has to wait anyway, he climbs the stairs to the second floor and finds a bedroom with a suitably large bed. He places the backpack beside him on the bed as he lies down and then takes out one of his knives, keeping it in his hand in case of trouble.

Closing his eyes, he quickly falls asleep.

Voices from below waken him. He sits up abruptly and then makes his way to the bedroom door to listen. He can hear two, maybe three people downstairs talking in the Empire's tongue, soldiers most likely. Returning to the bed, he grabs the backpack and then silently makes his way to the top of the stairs.

Looking down, he can see one of the soldiers with a partially filled sack in his hand, opening drawers and looking through them. Occasionally, he would take something out and put it in his sack. *Looting*, Jiron thinks. The soldier says something to the others and then makes his way to the stairs, looking as if he means to go up to the second floor.

Thinking fast, Jiron hurries into the bedroom again, flips a coin on the bed and then swings the door all the way into the room as he hides in the space between it and the wall. Shielded behind the door, he listens to the footsteps of the soldier as he comes up the stairs.

His heart beating fast, Jiron hears the soldier coming down the hallway toward him. When the footsteps come to the open door, he hears the soldier pause and then gasp as he sees the silver coin sitting on the bed. Jiron then hears him enter the room, hurrying over to pick up the coin to put in his sack.

As the soldier reaches the bed, Jiron silently comes out from behind the door with both knives drawn. Catching the soldier by surprise, he's able to quickly take him out with minimal noise. Easing the dead body of the soldier onto the bed, he takes back his coin and then returns to the hallway, shutting the door behind him.

Returning to the top of the stairs, he listens as the other two are still rummaging around downstairs. One of them raises his voice and then pauses. He speaks louder this time and again pauses. The two down below begin whispering among themselves and then Jiron hears them both hurrying to the foot of the stairs.

Jiron returns quickly back toward the room with the dead soldier and enters a closet sitting across the hallway from the room. He closes the door just enough to leave a thin opening through which he can see out. Looking out through the crack, he observes the other two coming down the hallway, going from room to room as they holler for their companion.

When they come to the room where the dead body lies, they both rush in. He hears them say something and then a moment later one of them exclaims and they begin to hurry out of the room.

When the first one exits and is close enough, Jiron kicks the door to the closet open, catching him in the shoulder, causing him to stumble and fall to the floor. With both knives drawn, he advances on the other soldier as the man exits the room.

Having seen his friend being knocked down by the swinging door, the last soldier draws his sword and thrusts at Jiron's midsection.

Easily deflecting the blade with the knife in his right hand, Jiron slashes with his other, scoring along the man's forearm. Keeping an eye on his companion, he presses the man with a series of attacks which soon has him bleeding from several different wounds.

The soldier on the floor gets back up and advances on Jiron with sword drawn, coming to his partner's aid. He thrusts at Jiron but fails to connect when Jiron twists to avoid the incoming blade.

As the blade goes past, Jiron strikes out and stabs the man in his exposed armpit, puncturing a lung. The man goes down coughing and blood begins welling out of his mouth as his lungs fill with blood.

Seeing his partner fall, the remaining soldier goes back into the room where the dead soldier lies, and then grabs a chair and throws it through the window. As the window shatters, he runs over to it and begins hollering to someone outside. He then turns and looks at Jiron with an evil smile and says something to him in his language.

Realizing he's about to be inundated with soldiers, Jiron turns and races for the stairs, hoping to escape the house before they make it inside. When he reaches the top, hears the door downstairs slamming open as many soldiers rush into the house. He turns and sees the remaining soldier coming out of the room, sword drawn and ready.

Looking around, he sees a trap door in the ceiling down the hallway, past the soldier. He throws the backpack at him, causing him to move to avoid being hit. Jiron advances upon him fast with a flurry of attacks that soon has him lying dead on the floor. Picking up the backpack again, he races to the trapdoor and pulls on the rope attached to it. He can hear soldiers running up the stairs.

The trapdoor comes down and a step ladder unfolds, allowing access to the attic. As he begins to climb the stairs, he hears someone shout behind him. He turns and sees enemy soldiers running down the hallway toward him.

When he reaches the top, he tries to pull the ladder up but one of the soldiers has already gotten a hold of it, preventing him from retracting it.

Next to the trapdoor he sees a chest. Taking hold of it, he pulls it over to the trapdoor and drops it on the soldiers below. He hears it crash down the stairs and into the soldiers, followed shortly by curses and one cry of pain.

Having only seconds, Jiron quickly glances around and the only exit visible is a small window on the far side of the attic. He quickly picks up several other things of moderate weight and throws them down in quick succession at the soldiers below before running over to the window.

The window is hinged and he's able to swing it open. Sticking his head out the window, he looks down and sees a straight drop to the street below. Looking up, he sees the edge of the roof a mere two feet above the window. Pulling himself to a sitting position on the sill, he reaches up and grabs the edge of the roof, quickly pulling himself up. A crossbow bolt hits the eave next to where he's climbing up onto the roof. Glancing down, he sees a dozen soldiers there watching him, two armed with crossbows. Another thud, and he feels a crossbow bolt embed itself in the backpack.

Finally gaining the roof, he rolls away from the edge and the deadly barrage coming from the streets below. The roof is shrouded by thick smoke coming from the fire not to far away. He pulls out the cloth again and wraps it once more around his face, trying to keep the smoke out of his lungs. In a low crouch, he gains the center of the roof and quickly surveys his options.

A narrow alleyway separates this building from the one behind it, the buildings on the other sides are too far away to attempt to jump across. Keeping low, he runs and leaps across the gap to the other building, landing easily. Looking back, he sees a soldier gaining the roof by way of the window in the attic. He sees Jiron and pauses as he points to him, shouting to the soldiers in the streets below. Then he starts running toward him as another begins to climb up from the attic.

Glancing across the roof to the other side, he sees that the buildings continue along close together for a while. Having no other choice, he runs and begins jumping from rooftop to rooftop as he tries to find a way out of this situation. After jumping to the third building, he begins to feel the heat of the fire and realizes that it has reached the edge of town and is consuming the building at the end of the row he's been jumping across.

Looking behind him, he sees several soldiers running and jumping from building to building behind him. With no other choice, he races toward the end of the line of buildings and the fire until he reaches the last building that's yet to catch fire. He slings the backpack over his shoulder and turns to face the oncoming soldiers. The heat from the fire consuming the building behind him is almost intolerable as he awaits their arrival.

When the soldiers get to the building before his, they stop and begin shouting to him. Unable to understand what is being said, he just stands there with his knives ready, planning to sell his life dearly.

A popping noise behind him causes him to turn his head and look. The building he's standing on has now caught fire and the fire is creeping closer to where he is standing. He tries to take a step away from the flames, but the roof under his foot cracks and then caves in.

He falls through the roof to the floor below, smoke and fire are everywhere. He hits the floor hard and then comes up quickly as he looks around for a way out, the thick smoke stinging his eyes. Spying a doorway, he makes his way toward it through the smoke. He begins coughing, the smoke is so thick here, it's even getting through the cloth tied to his face.

Passing through the doorway, he finds the hallway to his left is aflame, the heat from the flames searing his skin. A sudden thought crosses his mind, something James had said before he left, '*Someone needs to go and retrieve it. Or at least destroy it and the papers it carries.*' **The backpack!** He takes it, throws it into the flames and watches for a brief moment as they begin to consume it and the letters inside.

Turning, he runs down the hallway away from the flames to the stairs, where the smoke is billowing up them like a chimney. With no other choice, he races down through the dense, hot smoke, barely able to see and coughing as his lungs try to expel the smoke.

At the bottom of the stairs, the flames wreathe one end of the hallway, the heat causing his hair to begin to curl and smoke. Unable to even see any longer through the smoke, he turns and moves in the opposite direction, away from the flames. Putting the heat behind him, he keeps one hand in contact with a wall as he moves blindly down the smoke filled hall. Suddenly, he feels cool air hit his face and is able to breathe a little better. Running, he makes it through the front door where he collapses on the ground, coughing and gasping, trying to get the relatively clean air into his lungs.

He hears a footstep beside him and looks up to see the officer standing there with two men holding crossbows aimed at him. The officer says something in their language and two of his men grab him and bring him to his feet as they carry him toward the jail.

Chapter Nine

The following morning when James wakes up, his first thought is on Jiron and how he's making out. *Hope he makes it back soon,* he thinks to himself. Getting up, he walks over and looks at the small pond that has developed over night. A small stream has begun to run the excess water off into the desert. It doesn't get far before being reabsorbed back into the ground.

Waking everyone up, he then gets grain for the horses while the others have a quick meal before getting on the road.

"Wonder how Jiron's doing?" Cassie asks.

"I'm sure he'll be alright," Tinok assures her. Looking over to the pond, he says, "Pretty impressive!"

"Yeah," agrees James with satisfaction and pride. He's created a new oasis here in this desolate land. Once the horses are fed, he takes some rations for himself and eats them quickly.

After everyone is finished eating he begins to get the horses harnessed to the wagons with help from Delia, while Tinok fills all the water bottles from the newly formed pond. By the time the sun has completely topped the horizon, all is ready and they begin to roll down the road. This time Tinok rides point, while James drives the lead wagon, with Delia and Cassie bringing up the rear with the other.

They travel for about two hours before they begin to make out a green oasis with several palm-type trees and bushes surrounding it ahead of them. A small town has grown in the vicinity, from the apparent age of some of the buildings, the town must have been here for a very long time. As they draw closer, they see a large gathering of people at the edge of the oasis.

It soon becomes apparent that all is not well here, people are heard crying and wailing. The group by the oasis has their attention focused on a man in robes speaking animatedly to them. As they pull closer to the town, James asks someone what's going on but no one understands him, they speak the Empire's language.

"Something's obviously got them upset," Delia comments as she pulls her wagon closer to James'.

"Wonder what?" he replies as he watches those gathered over by the oasis.

Tinok pulls up close to them and says, "That guy they're listening to seems to be some kind of priest or leader or something."

"I think you're right," agrees James.

As they enter the town, a man comes out of a store and stops when he sees them. Gesturing animatedly, he tries to tell them something but no one understands him.

"We don't understand what you're saying," James explains to the man.

The man pauses a moment and then continues in their tongue, "You must leave this place!"

"Why?" James asks.

"We are cursed," the man says tragically. "We have lost the favor of the gods and bad things are happening."

"What do you mean?" Delia interjects.

"At first, we thought nothing about it," the man explains. "One of Azrahn's ewes went dry and several people took sick, but we just thought they were normal occurrences, these things happen from time to time you see. Then last night, our oasis, the oasis that has sustained our people here for a hundred generations, went dry."

James feels a shiver go up his spine as he remembers tapping the underground water the day before.

"Zalim, one of our town leaders has sought the counsel of our clerics but they all say the gods are not doing this, that we have not displeased them." He stands there, wringing his hands as he continues, "But most of our people feel an atonement of some sort will bring back the water, I fear what they may do in their fear."

"James..." Tinok starts to say when James shushes him quickly, shaking his head indicating he should say nothing.

"I must go," the man says. "Please leave before anything should befall you!" With that, he turns and hurries over to where all the people have gathered by the oasis.

When they are once more left alone in the street, Tinok asks James, "Did you do this?"

Nodding his head miserably, he replies, "Most likely." Feeling ashamed for the pride he felt earlier at his accomplishment, he looks to the people whose lives he's ruined.

"Can we do anything to help these people?" Delia asks from her wagon.

"I wouldn't even know how to fix this," admits James. "This is what happens when you use magic on the natural order, people suffer. Trying to quench our thirst, I have inadvertently destroyed this village and hundreds of lives. We weren't even that bad off. Had we simply continued down the road another few hours, we would've come to this town and had enough water. No one would've been hurt."

"Don't blame yourself," Delia says, trying to console him. "You didn't know this would happen."

"That's right," adds Cassie. "You were trying to do what you believed was right."

"They may find the other water down the road and move their town there," suggests Tinok.

"Maybe," says James, not feeling any better about the situation.

From near the oasis, James suddenly hears a woman begin to wail, while at the same time, several others begin shouting. Jumping down from the wagon, he runs over to see what is happening.

"James!" Delia shouts to him. "Come back!"

But he pays her no heed, as he continues on toward the oasis.

Everyone gets down, except Cassie who stays with the wagons, and follows behind him.

As he draws near the gathered crowd, he can see the same man is still addressing the people. In front of the speaker, kneeling on the ground, is a man whose hands are tied behind his back. A woman at the front of the crowd looks to be crying and pleading as she attempts to go to his side. Two men hold her arms tightly to prevent her from reaching the bound man.

Seeing the man he talked to earlier, James works his way through the crowd to his side. "What's going on?" he asks him.

Glancing at who is addressing him, the man says, "Roland there," indicating the man being held, "is going to be sacrificed to the gods come sunset."

"Why?" James cries incredulously.

"To appease them," the man explains. "He's an outsider that came to live with us a year ago. He took a wife," he says as he indicates the wailing woman, "and now has a son, very sad."

"Why are they sacrificing him?" he asks. Looking over his shoulder, he sees Tinok and Delia are moving through the crowd toward him.

"Because he is odd," the man says. "Always has strange notions and makes the weirdest things you ever saw. When the oasis went dry, people began talking and have come to the conclusion that a lot of unusual things have happened since his coming. So they believe his presence among us has angered one of the gods and that his sacrifice will bring back the water."

"What do your clerics say?" James asks.

"They say it will make little difference, that the gods aren't angry," he explains. "But the people are scared, they must do something." The speaker continues talking and James watches the crowd around him as they hang on every word that he is saying. "Hassin there," the man says, pointing to the speaker, "has been the one convincing everyone to sacrifice Roland." He leans closer to James and quietly says, "There's been little love lost between those two."

"I see," says James, understanding coming to him.

"The people here," he says, gesturing to those around him, "are really a quiet, peaceful lot. But they're scared and need an outlet for their fear, and I'm afraid Roland will be that outlet." James can see a tear begin to roll down his cheek.

James stands there a moment and looks at Roland, then at his wife who's beside herself with grief. He then comes to a decision and says, "Thank you for explaining things to me."

"You're welcome," the man replies.

Turning, James heads back toward the wagons just as Tinok and Delia reach his side. Moving to follow him, they ask what's going on but he tells them to wait until they're back at the wagons.

Upon reaching the wagons, he gathers them all together and explains to them what the man told him. "They're going to sacrifice that man for something I did. I can't allow that to happen," he says with determination.

"What are you going to do?" Delia asks.

"At sunset, they're going to kill him. I mean to stop it," he explains. "I can't let his death be on my hands."

"How?" asks Tinok, as he once again mounts his horse.

"Let's go down the road a ways," James says as he takes his seat on the wagon, taking the reins. "Then I'll tell you." With a flick of the reins, he gets the wagon rolling and soon they're past the town and heading south down the road again.

Once they're a mile out of town, James calls a halt and everyone gathers around him once again. "I plan for us to travel until a couple hours before sunset. Then I'll return on horseback in an attempt to rescue him while the rest of you make camp for the night."

"I'm coming too," Tinok says.

"You need to stay with the girls," James tells him, "in case there are bandits or something."

"I'm sure we're going to be alright," Delia says. "Besides, we need you to make it back. We should be okay for a few hours."

"Alright," James agrees, "I definitely could use the help in this venture."

Grinning, Tinok says, "Better than just riding guard on a bunch of wagons."

"We'll see," he says as he flicks the reins to get the horses moving once more. For the next several hours they roll on down the road until the sun begins to descend to the horizon and it's time for them to head back. They pull off the road and while the girls set about making camp, James saddles one of the spare horses. With a quick goodbye, he and Tinok are off as they race back toward the oasis.

They get to the town just as the sun nears the horizon. The town is eerily quiet as they pass the first couple of buildings. At the oasis, they find the entire town assembled to watch Roland's sacrifice.

They tie their horses to a post at the edge of town and walk the remainder of the way to the oasis. They see Hassin in front of the crowd and his voice can be heard loudly and clearly as he speaks to the people. Though they're unable to understand what is being said, the meaning is unmistakable as they lead Roland over to stand before Hassin.

The crowd becomes even quieter as they make him kneel before Hassin. James looks for the woman who had been making the scene earlier but she's nowhere to be found. They must've removed her so she wouldn't spoil the proceedings.

James whispers to Tinok, "Make your way as close to the front as you can. I'll create a distraction and you get him out of there." As Tinok nods and begins to make his way closer to where Roland is kneeling, James grabs him by the arm and says, "Don't kill anyone."

Tinok winks at him as he pulls away and enters the crowd.

James skirts the edge of the crowd until he comes near the now dry oasis. Looking over to Hassin, he sees him draw a long knife and approach closer to Roland. Holding the knife high, he begins speaking loudly to the gathered people. James begins to concentrate…

"…now, with the spilling of the cursed one's blood, our gods will be appeased and life will flow back into our oasis!" Hassin, exuberant and ecstatic, raises the knife high as every eye in the crowd is upon him.

Suddenly, the mood of the crowd alters and they begin to murmur. He looks to them and their eyes are no longer on him but are looking at something behind him. Irritated at being interrupted in his moment of retribution on the man who had wronged him, he turns his head to see what they're all looking at and his eyes grow wide at what he sees.

Lights, many lights are glowing above the oasis. Pulsating, they begin moving in an intricate pattern over the oasis, as if they're dancing to the beat of unheard music.

Tinok is amazed by the dancing lights, and then he looks over and sees James' eyes closed as he concentrates on maintaining the spell. Knowing this is his friend's work, he begins to edge closer to Roland.

The murmuring begins to grow as the crowd continues watching the beautiful pattern of lights. As the lights continue to swirl, their pattern begins to tighten as their dance brings them closer and closer together. The lights begin to change from their brilliant colors, turning a darker, foreboding color. Suddenly there's a brilliant flash as all the lights come together, and where many lights once stood, now only one remains, a dark sphere that pulsates a red, purplish glow.

Tinok hears the crowd's murmur of wonder begin to change to one of fear and uncertainty. He shoves his way to the front of the crowd, now only feet from where Roland kneels. He sees Hassin has turned toward the sphere, intent on what it's doing. The two men who are guarding Roland have also turned to watch it, Roland momentarily forgotten. Glancing over, he sees James staring at him and then he sees his head nod before closing his eyes once more.

This is it! he thinks to himself. Suddenly the sphere begins to bulge and change shape, the people in the crowd gasping at the sight. He runs the few feet to Roland and quickly severs his bonds with his knife.

Roland looks at him, fear in his eyes. "Come with me if you want to survive," Tinok whispers to him. With sudden understanding that he may not die, he nods and quickly gets to his feet.

Over at the oasis, the sphere has begun to form into the shape of a humanoid creature, with glowing red eyes and two foot long horns sprouting from its forehead. The crowd has begun shouting in fear as panic erupts. All thought of Roland's sacrifice is abandoned as the people begin to flee the area.

Hassin turns at just that moment and sees Tinok there helping Roland to his feet. He shouts out, but is unable to be heard over the cries from the crowd. He advances on Roland with the long knife, intent on killing him.

Tinok sees him advancing and is able to easily deflect the long knife with one of his own. Remembering what James told him, he strikes out with the blunt end of his other knife and connects with Hassin's temple, dropping him to the ground. The two men there with him are oblivious to what is happening to him as they continue to watch the creature take shape.

"Let's go!" he hollers to Roland as he directs him over toward James. He looks over his shoulder at the now fully formed vision of Hell that is walking out of the oasis toward the panic stricken people who're fleeing for their lives. *You're good, James.*

Reaching James, they turn and race through the town together, toward where the horses had been left. They help James, as he is still trying to maintain the hellish vision. Throughout the town, cries can be heard as some people race back to their homes, slamming and barring their doors. Others just race out into the desert as fast as their legs can carry them.

When they reach their horses, Roland says, "I don't know how to thank you!"

James opens his eyes just as a flash of fire comes from the creature and then it slowly disappears. "We've got to get you out of here!" he says to Roland.

"I can't leave!" cries Roland. "Not without my wife and child!"

"But they'll try to sacrifice you again if you remain," Tinok exclaims. Then he looks in Roland's eyes and sees the determination there.

"Do you have a horse?" James asks him.

"Yes, I do," he replies.

Turning to Tinok, he says, "Go with him and get his family, then meet me back here."

He gives James a nod then turns to Roland and says, "Lead the way."

Roland hurries down the street, followed closely by Tinok. They soon leave James behind as they turn down another street, making quick speed through the darkened town. He goes past several more houses and then turns down one more side street, stopping in front of the third house. The light from a single candle comes through an open window and voices can be heard coming from within.

They look through the window and see his wife sitting in a chair surrounded by three men, one of whom is Hassin. He's yelling at her, gesticulating wildly with his hands, obviously demanding to know where Roland is.

She just sits there crying, not saying anything as she glances through the doorway to where the baby lies. Tinok can hear the baby's wail.

Smack!

He backhands her across the face when she fails to answer his questions. Not waiting to see more, Roland runs over and slams open the door with his shoulder, bursting into the room and tackling Hassin.

Seeing him come crashing through the door, his wife cries out, "Roland!"

Tinok is right behind him, knives flashing from the light of the candle. He immediately engages the other two men, the same two who had been guarding Roland during the ceremony.

They quickly draw their swords, but the speed of Tinok drops one of the men to the floor with a stab through the chest before he even gets his sword all the way out of its scabbard.

The other guard tries to slash at Tinok but he parries the sword with the blade of one knife while striking with the other one. The guard steps back, blood now oozing from a fresh wound in his left shoulder.

Roland is on the floor, struggling with Hassin for control of the long knife. Curses from the two men fill the house as they roll back and forth.

The guard grabs a small chair from the floor and uses it as a shield as he strikes out with his sword.

Tinok easily blocks the thrust, but is unable to adequately close with the man as the chair is keeping him at a distance. He continues exchanging blows with the man when suddenly Roland's wife comes up behind the guard and strikes him across the back of the head with the long handle of a broom.

The man is dazed by the blow and Tinok easily gets within his guard dropping him to the floor.

Tinok comes over to the struggling pair on the floor, neither one has been able to gain the advantage over the other. Laying his knife across Hassin's throat, he looks into his eyes and can see him contemplating different courses of action and their consequences. Suddenly, he makes his decision and releases his grip on the knife. His eyes flick murderous hate between them both as Roland gets to his feet, holding the knife.

Roland looks and sees his wife standing there with their baby clutched in her arms, eyes filled with uncertainty and fear, her face turning red from where Hassin had slapped her. She says something to him and he goes over to her, replying in the same language. Giving her a hug for reassurance, he speaks to her again and she nods a reply as she goes and gets a satchel which she begins to fill with clothes and other things.

Turning back to Tinok, who still has his knife to Hassin's throat and his knee on his chest, he asks, "What are we going to do with him?"

"You know him better than I do," replies Tinok, never taking his eyes off his captive. "Should we kill him or not?"

At that, Hassin's eyes widen slightly but gives no other response to what is being said.

"I hate to kill someone who's helpless to resist," Roland replies. "Even one who tried to kill me."

"I have no such qualms about this piece of trash," Tinok says seriously. "Take your family outside and wait for me." He looks intently at Roland then turns his attention back to Hassin.

Roland takes the satchel from his wife and then ushers her out the front door, closing it behind them.

Once the door is shut, Tinok turns his attention back to Hassin and says, "Since your people destroyed my city, I have been waiting for my revenge and the time has come for a part of it." Looking into eyes now filled with fear where contempt and hate had been, he continues, "This is for my little brother."

With a quick motion of his hand, he slits Hassin's throat and stares into his eyes as the life slowly leaves them. Choking and gasping from the blood filling his lungs and spreading across the floor, Hassin tries to stop the bleeding with his hands, but is unsuccessful. Tinok gets up and stands back as he jerks in his death throes until finally becoming still.

Wiping his blade on the dead man's shirt, he says to the now lifeless body, "Thus begins my revenge for the destruction your people has brought unto mine." Turning his back to the room filled with death, he goes to the door and leaves, joining Roland and his family outside.

Roland leads them around back where there's a stable with two horses inside. Roland saddles them while Tinok keeps an eye out for anyone coming. When he's done, he helps his wife up onto the horse and then hands their baby up to her. Swinging up onto the other horse, he takes her horse's reins and leads them out to where Tinok is waiting at the front of the house.

Moving as quickly as they can, they make it back to where James is waiting.

"Any trouble?" he asks Tinok.

"None worth mentioning," he replies as he mounts his horse.

Roland just glances over to Tinok but says nothing.

The baby starts crying and his mother bares a breast and begins to feed it as they ride through the town. Riding as quickly as they can, they clear the edge of town, which by now is completely deserted. Everyone has either fled or is in their homes with the door barred.

Moving quickly along the road for a couple hours, they come to where Delia and Cassie wait with the wagons. James is relieved when he sees the wagons and girls are fine and undisturbed, he had been worried about them. The girls have a fire going, and Cassie is awake as they approach. When she sees who it is, she wakes up Delia, saying excitedly, "They're back!"

Delia wakes up, happy at seeing them back unharmed, but surprised at the appearance of his wife and son.

"We couldn't leave his wife and child there," Tinok explains, "so we brought them with us."

Cassie comes over to help his wife down from her horse and coos when she sees the baby. "Can I hold him?" she asks.

His wife, understanding her request, nods her head and hands the baby over to her. Cassie takes the baby and holds it close going "Gootchi, gootchi, goo!" and other inane child noises. The baby laughs, obviously they'll be getting along.

Once they have all the horses settled for the night, they gather around the fire and Roland asks, "I appreciate you rescuing me and all, but why did you do it?"

They look at each other and leave it to James to answer. "We did it because we didn't feel it justified for you to be sacrificed in vain."

"How do you know it would've been in vain?" he asks.

James looks at the others and says, "Well, you never know for sure of course, but we just felt that it was wrong this time. After all, even your own clerics were talking against it."

"True," Roland admits.

"Now what do you plan to do?" Delia asks. "Is there elsewhere you can go? Family?"

Shaking his head, he says, "I have no family, at least not around here and Ezra, my wife here, all her family is back there." He points back to the town they just rescued him from. At the sound of her name, she smiles at him.

"Does she understand what we're saying?" Cassie asks.

"A little," he replies. "She's been picking it up from me over the last year, ever since we got married. She doesn't speak it too well, but is able to understand most of the words being said." He looks over to her and she just smiles and nods her head in agreement.

Sighing, he says, "I really don't know what we're going to do, I just know we can't go back home, not with the dead bodies there." He puts his arm around Ezra and continues, "Hassin has many powerful friends and they would cause no end of trouble for us, maybe even kill us."

"Well, you're welcome to come along with us," James offers. All the others nod their agreement for the idea.

"We don't want to be a burden," he says, "but we don't have any other choice. Thank you."

A small laugh erupts from the baby where Cassie has him in her lap, playing with him. Ezra smiles fondly at the sight.

"Just where are you heading?" Roland asks. "Are you traders?" He glances over to James, not really believing that they are, what with the display back at the oasis.

"Not exactly," James replies. Then he smiles and says, "Now just where are my manners. My name is James and Tinok here you've already met." Tinok nods his head, Roland returns the gesture. "Here is Delia," who gives him a smile, "and the one who's taken over your son is Cassie." Cassie gives him a big smile and says, "Hi."

"My name is Roland," he says to the group. "I am originally from Cardri but for one reason or another wound up here where I met Ezra, the light of my life." He gives her a kiss which causes her to blush slightly. "That little wiggle worm that your Cassie is holding is Arkhan, Arkie for short."

"Arkie," coos Cassie to the little baby, "what a cute name."

"We're currently heading south," James tells him, "going by way of Korazan. We have some packages to drop off there, and then we'll see."

"Then I think we'll come along," he says to them. He goes over to Ezra and begins talking to her in their language as they get Arkie settled down for the night.

Everyone is pretty tired and begins to get ready for sleep. Delia draws James away from everyone else and asks, "With what we're heading to, do you think it's wise to have them along?"

"Probably not," he replies. "But they're better off than they were. Besides, we'll have more of a chance of not standing out if we have others with us."

"Maybe," she says. "I've also been going over the items we're carrying as well as the delivery orders and it turns out we're carrying some very high priced items." She looks at him and continues, "The person who actually owns this may come looking for it."

"If so," James says, after contemplating what she just said, "he'll have to find us first."

"Maybe we should hire some guards?" she suggests.

"We'll look into that when we get to the next big town," he replies.

"That may be wise," she agrees as they make their way back to the group. Ezra and little Arkie have already lain down near the fire and the rest have bedded down as well. James and Delia join them, the last thought going though his mind before sleep takes him is what's going on with Jiron.

Chapter Ten

Before they head out in the morning, they transfer as much cargo as possible from one wagon to the other, clearing a spot for Ezra and Arkie. Roland and Tinok ride point on horses while James drives the now fully loaded wagon. Delia takes the reins of the other while Ezra and Cassie ride in the back with Arkie.

Everyone is becoming quite thirsty since they gave the bulk of their water to the horses, enabling them to continue pulling the wagons. Pushing on, they continue under the glare of the desert sun, slowly eating away the miles. Roland tells them of an oasis along the road ahead where they'll be able to get water.

A little past midday they arrive at the small oasis and note several other travelers who are already there, filling their water bottles and taking a break from the road. A man sees them coming and waves a friendly greeting, Roland answers and then turns to James, saying, "He's just a merchant, nothing to worry about."

In dire need of the water at the oasis, they pull in and Tinok takes the horses over one by one to drink their fill. Delia and Cassie gather everyone's water bottles and take them over to the pool to fill them.

James sees Ezra near the palm-like trees growing around the oasis, picking some of the fruit hanging from the branches. "What's she picking?" he asks Roland.

"She's taking some dates off the trees," he replies. "It's the custom to take a few, leaving the rest for other travelers."

James nods his head in understanding and walks over to the closest tree, picking one. It's an odd looking fruit, purplish in color with red lines going through it. Placing it to his mouth, he takes a bite and discovers it has a slightly bitter taste, though not altogether unpleasant.

When Roland sees that he's finished the fruit, with only the pit left, he says, "You're suppose to throw it near the edge of the oasis."

"What?" James asks.

Indicating the pit in James' hand, he says, "Throw it on the ground, away from the other trees. It's a tradition, so that other trees may grow thereby filling the desert with fruit."

Finding a likely spot, he tosses the fruit over near the edge where it lands amidst some bushes. Looking back to Roland, he sees him nodding his approval.

The other merchant, who had been sharing the oasis with them, begins to leave and waves a cheery goodbye as his wagons pull back onto the road, heading north.

They make their stop brief, just long enough for all the horses to drink their fill and have a quick meal. Cassie stays in the wagon with Ezra, having her meal with a playful Arkie who continually tries to grab her food. Tinok casts glances over to her every time he hears her laughing.

James notices that he's longing to go over to her so he says, "Why don't you go help Cassie watch Arkie and have your meal. I can finish this alone."

"You sure?" Tinok asks, hopefully.

"Wouldn't have offered if I wasn't," he replies.

"Thanks," he says and then hurries over to the wagon, climbing in beside Cassie. She sees him coming to join her and smiles.

"That was nice," Delia says to James as she comes up behind him.

Looking back over his shoulder, he replies, "Oh, it wasn't much. Besides, we were almost finished anyway."

"They sure do like each other," she observes as they both watch them sitting and talking together, Arkie going from first one then the other.

"Yes," he agrees, "they sure do."

James finishes the watering and feeding of the horses then takes his meal and walks over to sit under one of the trees by the water. Peaceful, just the way he likes it. As he eats, he can't help but worry over the delay of Jiron's return. *He should have been back by now,* he reasons. Thinking nothing but the worst, he continues eating.

Before he's done, he hears several riders coming down the road from the north. Getting up, he hurries back to the wagons and reaches them just as the riders turn off the road into the oasis. *Soldiers!*

Seven enemy soldiers and a civilian enter the oasis and dismount by the pool of water, letting their horses drink. They glance occasionally over at James' group, but otherwise pay them no heed.

Roland notices how everyone has tensed up with the appearance of the soldiers. He comes over to James and whispers, "What's wrong?"

"Nothing," James replies, not wanting to get Roland involved.

"Right," he replies in a tone saying he doesn't believe that.

James just looks back at him, not giving him anymore of an explanation.

The soldiers have all dismounted and are filling their water bottles from the pool. The civilian, oddly enough is remaining on his horse. James glances over to him and realizes that he's staring right at him.

A shock of recognition runs through him. *Jiron!* His eyes widen in recognition and then he nods his head, letting Jiron know that he recognizes him. Not wishing to alert the soldiers to the fact they know each other, James leisurely makes his way over to where Tinok is in the back of the wagon with Cassie.

As he approaches, Tinok hops out of the wagon and comes up to him. Excited, he starts to say, "James! Do you…"

Putting his finger in front of his lips for silence, James nods and whispers, "I know."

"What are we going to do?" he asks quietly, casting glances over to where Jiron sits.

"Let's take the wagons down the road a ways and wait for them to come," he replies. "We could ambush them."

"We should do it now!" insists Tinok, a little too loud. A soldier looks over in their direction at the outburst, but otherwise continues about his business.

"What about the girls?" counters James.

"If they leave here," Tinok argues, "we may lose the chance to get him back!"

Roland comes over and joins them, "What's going on?"

"They have our companion over there," James tells him, nodding toward where Jiron sits, secured to the horse.

Roland looks over and sees him there, "Are you thinking what I think you're thinking?" Looking into their eyes is answer enough. "Are you crazy? Do you know who that is over there?" He indicates the officer in charge.

James shakes his head and says, "No."

"His insignia shows him to be a Commander of Ten," continues Roland.

"So?" Tinok replies, obviously not impressed.

"A Commander of Ten only becomes one by being the best with the sword and usually totally ruthless," he explains. "Any ordinary man taking him on, dies!"

"Still, we must rescue our friend," insists James.

Nodding, Tinok agrees.

"You're both crazy!" Roland exclaims.

Tinok grins and says, "Probably."

James tells him, "Go back and have the girls start moving the wagons out of here."

Roland gives him a look of utter disbelief at what they intend to do, but he turns and starts walking back toward the wagons.

Tinok looks at him in surprise and James says, "You're right, we need to do this here, now, before they have a chance to get back on their horses."

They watch as Roland reaches the wagons and begins speaking to Delia and Cassie. Delia looks at them and slowly nods her head, Cassie starts to cry out to Tinok, but Delia puts her hand over her mouth and quietly whispers in her ear. With a pained look to Tinok, Cassie gets on the second wagon and is soon following Delia, who's leading the first wagon back to the road.

Looking to Tinok, James says, "Are you ready?"

"Yeah," he replies, "Let's do it!"

James gathers several stones and Tinok readies his knives. About this time, the Commander of Ten has noticed that the wagons are rolling away, yet two have stayed behind. He says something to one of his men and the soldier starts walking over toward them.

As the soldier approaches, he says something to them in his language. Getting no response, he puts his hand on his sword as he continues to advance. By this time, all of the Commander's men are aware of what's transpiring. They start to flank out, and begin encircling them.

Not waiting any longer, James lets loose with a stone, propels it with the force of his spell and strikes the approaching soldier square in the chest, blasting out the back.

As his man falls to the ground, the Commander shouts out a command and his men, as one, draw their swords. The whisking of them all coming out at the same time makes an eerie sound.

James throws a second stone and takes out another of the advancing men. The four remaining soldiers fan out quickly, coming at them from different directions. Suddenly, he feels the prickling sensation that tells him magic is being worked just before he hears a shout from the

Commander. Turning in his direction, he sees a green blob arcing through the air toward him.

Thinking fast, he creates a shield surrounding himself just before the green blob hits. It begins to spread, covering the shield in a green, sticky substance. Through the green goo, he sees Tinok being hard pressed by the man he's fighting, with the others coming fast. His opponent is very skilled with the blade and there's three more coming to join him.

James changes the nature of the shield and it bursts into flame, searing off the green goo, leaving him covered in a film of fine ash. Quickly, he tosses his last stone at one of the men advancing upon Tinok and catches him in the thigh, literally blasting off his leg at the hip. The man falls to the ground with a cry of pain.

Out of the corner of his eye, he sees that Roland has snuck around the oasis and is coming toward where Jiron sits tied to the horse. But then his attention is again turned to the Commander who's drawing his sword and advancing upon him.

James readies another spell and a bolt of energy flies from his extended hand, striking the Commander full on the chest where it explodes in a shower of sparks. When the sparks clear, James sees him still standing there, untouched.

Grinning evilly, the Commander continues his advance upon him.

Another spell and the ground erupts under him. Still, he marches on.

James quickly glances over to where Jiron had been, but now only sees the horse with an empty saddle. Turning his attention back to the advancing Commander, he considers the situation. *He must be protected in some way!* James begins backing up, prolonging the inevitable contact, trying to come up with some sort of solution to the problem.

Catching a flash of movement out of the corner of his eye, he sees Jiron coming to Tinok's aid as he joins the fight.

If I can't use magic on him directly...

Concentrating once more, he brings his hands together and then as he lets loose the power, he spreads them apart.

With a crack, the ground under the Commander opens wide. Losing his balance, he falls into the gaping hole. Once he's fallen below the top of the hole, James again unleashes the power and with a clap, brings his hands back together again. The sides of the hole containing the Commander smash together, closing with finality.

He looks around quickly and sees Roland, Tinok and Jiron coming over to him, the remaining soldiers lying dead on the ground.

Jiron is covered in bruises and his clothes are stained with blood, but otherwise in high spirits. "Thanks," he says when he approaches James.

"You're welcome," he replies. "Glad to see you're alive."

"So am I," Jiron replies. "I didn't ever expect to see you two again."

"We were beginning to get worried about you," Tinok chides him. "What happened?"

"I'll tell you when we catch up with the others," he says. They each grab one of the soldier's horses and mount. Riding quickly, they catch up with the girls in no time at all.

The girls stop the wagons when they see them coming. Once her wagon has come to a stop, Delia gets down and rushes over to Jiron, giving him a big hug when he dismounts from his horse.

Returning the hug, he asks her, "Miss me?"

With tears of relief running down her face, Delia replies, "A little." And then she smiles.

Cassie runs and gives Tinok a warm hug and kiss as well. He kisses her repeatedly until Jiron finally has to break them up. A little red faced, they realize what they were doing.

"Now," Tinok says, "what happened?"

"Well…" he begins as he relates to them all that had happened, up to the point where he ran out of the burning house and was captured. "When they took me back to the jail, the Commander had someone begin interrogating me."

"How?" Cassie asks, wide eyed.

"The usual, I'm sure," he replies. "Anyway, this messenger comes in and gives him a letter. When he's done reading it, he barks out some orders and before I knew it, I was being tied on a horse and we all began riding hard to the south. We eventually stopped here, fortunately for me, and the rest you know."

"What were they asking you?" James inquires.

"Mainly, they wanted to know what happened to the men that were garrisoned at Mountainside," he explains. "Since I was hiding there and had killed a couple soldiers, they felt I obviously knew something."

"Of course you did," interjects Tinok.

"Of course," agrees Jiron. "But they didn't realize that."

"What about the backpack?" James asks.

"I left it in the building that was on fire," he says. "I saw it catch fire myself so there should be no more worries from that."

"Thanks," James says. "I'm sorry you got hurt, though."

Looking at James tiredly, Jiron says, "So am I." He then turns his attention to Roland and says, "Just who are you and why did you untie me? Not that I'm complaining or anything."

They relate the events which led up to Roland and his family joining them. When Tinok explains the devilish monster walking out of the dried up Oasis, he breaks into a laugh, "Wish I could've seen that!"

Leaving Jiron with the girls and the wagons, the other three return to the oasis. There they drag the dead bodies of the soldiers out into the desert and bury them. Once they've hidden and removed all traces of the battle which had raged there, they return to the wagons and resume their trek to Korazan. Jiron sits in the back of the wagon with the girls and Arkie in order to rest, soon falling asleep.

Everyone becomes quiet for awhile as they let him sleep, understanding that he really needs it. For his part, James is relieved at having Jiron back. *Now if we can just get Miko and Jiron's sister!*

They ride on until late in the afternoon when they begin to see the outlines of a fairly sizeable city coming up ahead. With Tinok and Roland out front, they approach the town. Off to the east they see an area where several caravans have made their camp.

"Looks to be a caravansary," Roland says, indicating the groups of wagons.

"Should we stop there for the night?" James asks him.

"It's what it's there for," he explains.

"Alright then," agrees James. "Let's find a spot for the night."

As they near the caravansary, a man comes over to them and says, "Good day to you sirs."

"You speak our language?" James replies, astonished.

"I speak many," the man explains. "I am Ahlim, the Caravansary Master."

"I am James," he replies, "and we are looking for a spot to stay the night."

"To stay here will be a silver a day," he says.

James looks to Roland who shrugs his shoulders. Turning back to the man, he digs out a silver and hands it to him, saying, "Very well."

Ahlim takes the coin and says, "Find any spot around here that suits you." He then turns and hurries off toward town.

They find a suitable spot that's not too close to any of the others and start settling in, when another man comes over. "Greetings, fellow traders."

"Greetings," replies James.

"Ah, I'm not one to cause trouble," he says, "but I saw you talking to Ahlim just a moment ago?"

"Yes?" James replies, nervous.

"Did he say that he was the Caravansary Master? And that you had to pay to stay here?"

"Yes, he did," James replies. "Why?"

The man starts laughing, "You didn't pay him did you?"

"A silver," admits James.

The man starts laughing harder.

"What's so funny?" James asks, getting a little mad.

"He's not any kind of a Caravansary Master," the man explains, wiping tears from his eyes as his laughter calms down. "He's a beggar who does this from time to time with new arrivals."

From behind him, he hears Tinok break into laughter, "That's funny."

"What's so funny about it?" James angrily turns to him, asking.

Tinok just laughs more as he shakes his head and turns to go back to where the others are getting their camp ready.

"Don't be too hard on him," the man says. "Ahlim that is. He's had a bad lot."

"We'll just see how bad it is when I meet up with him again," James insists.

"Well, good day to you," the man says. As he returns back to his caravan, James can hear him chuckling to himself.

When he turns back to the others, he can see them trying to hold back smiles whenever he's looking in their direction. Finally, unable to contain it, they all start to laugh.

"This isn't funny," James says, which only makes them laugh the harder.

Their laughter is infectious and soon he's unable to stop a smile from coming to him. "Okay," he admits, "maybe it is."

He goes over to Roland and asks, "Would you be willing to come with me into town to see about getting another wagon and some barrels for water?"

"Sure," he agrees.

Going back to the others, he announces, "Roland and I are going into town to see about purchasing some barrels for water. Just stay here and watch the wagons, keep everything safe."

"Not a problem," Tinok says with his arm around Cassie's shoulder.

Jiron just nods his head from the back of the wagon where he's been resting all afternoon.

"Be careful," Delia advises.

"We will," James assures her. Turning to Roland, he says, "Ready?"

Roland says a few things to Ezra and then turns to James, nodding his head, "Let's go."

James goes over to the wagon with the money box, and takes a large bag of coins out, placing it inside his shirt. Then with a nod to Roland, they begin to walk toward town.

Delia watches them go and then turns to Tinok, saying, "Could you go over and find out what town this is?"

"Why?" he asks.

"There may be deliveries here we could make to give us more coins," she explains.

"Sure," he replies and then makes his way over to one of the neighboring caravans.

She watches as he approaches some of the men sitting around a campfire. They exchange a few words and then Tinok returns.

"Zereth-Alin," he tells her.

Excited, she exclaims, "There are three small packages that are marked for here." She hurries over to the wagon loaded with the majority of their cargo and begins rummaging through it. She finally comes up with the three packages and looks to Tinok, a gleam in her eye.

"Tinok?" she says with a certain tone to her voice.

"You want me to help you deliver them?" he asks her.

"Yes!" she replies. "Will you?"

He looks over to Cassie sitting there with Ezra, longing to remain with her.

"We could get Cassie a present should we receive any money for these," she suggests, temptingly.

"Alright," he says, giving in. "But I want to be back fast."

"We will," she assures him, "I promise." Letting the others know what they'll be about, they take the three packages and head into Zereth-Alin.

Chapter   Eleven

James and Roland enter the town, and with Roland playing the role of translator, they are directed to a place where they can buy barrels for water, maybe even a wagon to carry them.

On their way, they pass by an inn from which a mouth watering aroma emanates. His stomach growls loudly, insistent on something with more substance than what they've been having over the past several days. He gives Roland a grin before altering his course and making a beeline for the entrance.

"What are you doing?" Roland asks when he catches up with him.

"Getting something to eat," he explains.

"What about the others?" he says.

Waving away the question, James says, "We'll get something for them on the way back." He pushes open the door and enters the building. The aroma is even more mouth watering here than it was outside. Finding an empty table, they wait for a server, who arrives promptly.

The server says something and then Roland answers as he orders for both of them. When he's done, he tells James that it's going to be four coppers and waits while he digs them out of the pouch. James hands the coins over to the server, who then bows slightly and heads back to the kitchen.

"I assume you wanted whatever it is that we've been smelling?" Roland asks him once the server had left.

"Absolutely," James replies.

"Good, that's what I did," he says.

They sit back and relax while they wait for their food to arrive. The people here, aside from their different language and attire, are really the same as those he encountered back in Cardri. Just people. *People are people no matter where you go,* that's what his grandmother had always said.

He sees their server coming toward them with two plates, topped with several skewers containing meat and vegetables along with two mugs. As their server places the plates in front of them, he can still hear sizzle coming from the meats. Once the mugs are on the table, their server says something and Roland gives him a reply before going over to another table with two gentlemen.

Keeping his voice low, Roland says, "You guys don't seem much like merchants to me."

James looks at him with a mouth full of food and doesn't reply.

"What is a," lowering his voice to a whisper, he asks, "*mage,* doing running a caravan?"

"It's rather complicated," James replies and then takes another bite.

"I think I have the right to know what is going on," he asserts quietly. "If for no other reason than I've brought my wife and child along. I mean, you guys take out a Commander of Ten like he was nothing!"

James glances around but no one seems to care about their conversation. Turning back to Roland he says, "We're looking for someone."

"Who?" Roland asks.

"A friend of mine who was taken captive at the fall of the City of Light," he explains in a hushed tone. "As well as Jiron's sister, who was taken at the same time."

"How?" he asks, incredulously.

"We've reason to believe they're being taken to the slave markets at Korazan," he explains. "We mean to go there and find them, buy them if possible, rescue them if not."

Roland sits back in his chair and just stares at James, as if he is unsure if he actually just heard what he did.

"You're welcome to leave at any time if you think it's too dangerous for your family," James tells him.

"I don't know," he replies. He continues to eat, thinking about what James told him.

"A man back where we rescued you said that you made things?" James asks him.

Blushing slightly, Roland says, "Nothing, really."

"What?" he asks again.

"Well, I had this idea that if you filled a bag with hot air, you can make it float," he explains then sets himself as if he expects to be ridiculed.

"You would probably need an air tight bag of little weight," James suggests.

Surprised at someone finally taking him seriously, Roland says, "Exactly! But I haven't been able to find anyone able to make what I would require. All the cloth I've been able to afford has been too heavy."

"That could be a problem," James agrees. "What do you hope to do with it?"

"Do?" Roland asks as if the question had never even occurred to him.

"Yeah, do," he says.

"I've never really thought past getting it done, actually" he admits.

"I'm sure you could come up with something," James says hopefully. *Could think of several applications, mostly military ones in this society,* he muses to himself.

Finishing the last bite of his meal, James sits back in his chair, stomach gurgling most contentedly. Once Roland is done, they leave the inn and head over to where they've been told they can acquire some barrels and possibly a wagon.

They come to a building with an adjacent large open courtyard containing wagons, barrels and several other various items constructed of wood. A sign outside the door shows a wagon with two barrels.

"This must be the place," James says to Roland.

"Looks like it," he agrees as they go up three steps and open the door.

They enter a fair sized room, with dozens of barrels of varying sizes stacked against the walls. A man is busily stacking small buckets upon a table and turns around to greet them when he hears the door open. He says something in the Empire's language and stands there expectantly.

When Roland replies to him, explaining that James cannot speak the language, he immediately switches to the northern tongue. "Welcome to Salli's Barrels," he says to James. Placing his hand on his chest he continues. "And I am Salli, how may I help you fine sirs today?"

"We understand that we may be able to procure some barrels from you?" James explains. "As well as a wagon, perhaps?"

Nodding his head, Salli says as he gestures around his shop, "As you can see, I have many barrels for every need, as well as a couple of wagons available out in the courtyard."

"We would like to purchase a wagon and about six large barrels," James tells him. "We are taking a trip and need sufficient water to sustain us through the journey."

"Ah," says Salli, "I have just what you would need." He goes over to where several large barrels sit against a wall and then says, "These barrels are made for just such a use. See," he says as he holds up a round wooden lid, "I have even made lids, especially for these, so the water will not slosh out during your journey." He shows them how easy it is to seal the barrel and to reopen it again.

"How many do you think we would need for about ten horses and eight people?" James asks.

Thinking for a second, he says, "Probably four would be sufficient, provided you are able to replenish them every three or four days."

"Very well," he agrees, "we'll take four. Now, can we go see what wagons are available?"

"Certainly sir," he says as he leads them out a back door to the adjacent courtyard. Outside are four wagons of varying size and age. One is really old and looks to be falling apart, another is brand new with lots of ornamentation. Seeing James looking at the one with ornamentation, he says, "Sorry sir, that one has been special ordered by another customer. I do have these other three available."

He takes them to one that is neither old nor new and looks to have seen service at some time or another. "This one here, though not new, is sturdy and will last you a long time."

James and Roland inspect it, the wheels don't show signs of cracking and overall, it looks to have been very well cared for. "How much?" James asks Salli.

"For the barrels and the wagon," he replies, placing his hand on his chin in contemplation, "ten golds."

"Ten?" James says in mock shock and then begins what he really hates, haggling. "Surely this wagon has seen better days, I would think six would be more than adequate for such a well *used* wagon."

"Six!" Sallie exclaims. "Why not just steal it from me right now!" With a look of outrage, he says, "Surely you can see that this wagon, though having been used, still has many, many years left in her. I couldn't part with it for less than nine."

"Hmmm..." James murmurs as if he's contemplating the offer. Turning to Roland, he says, "Wasn't there that merchant trying to sell his extra wagon for seven over at the caravansary?"

"I think so, yes," Roland says with a smile as he plays along.

"Eight, good sirs," Sallie counters. "And I'll throw in a couple buckets to help in the watering of your horses."

James thinks about it for a second and looks to Roland, who nods. "Alright, eight it is," he says, holding out his hand to clench the deal.

Beaming again, Salli takes his hand and shakes it firmly. "Thank you good sirs," he says. "When would you like to pick it up?"

"We could just take it right now," James replies as he hands over the eight golds.

"But you brought no horses," Salli says, taking the coins. "Surely you two will be unable to pull it yourselves."

James looks at Roland, "How could we forget about the horses?"

"I hadn't," Roland explains, surprised that James had. "I just thought you wanted to purchase the wagon first."

Turning to Salli, he asks, "Where can I get a couple horses?"

"There's a horse trader on the other side of town, a man by the name of Jiharan," he explains. "Just tell him Salli sent you and he'll treat you fairly."

"Thanks," James replies, "we'll do that."

"I'll have everything loaded and ready upon your return," he assures them.

Leaving Salli's Barrels behind, they head across town to find Jiharan. They continue down the main thoroughfare, asking directions from the locals. At one point, James catches out of the corner of his eye someone who looks like Delia among the crowd. When he turns his head to get a better look, she's gone. Figuring he's just seeing things, he continues on and they soon arrive at the horse trader's establishment.

Jiharan greets them upon entering and when they tell him that Salli sent them, he breaks into a smile and cordially takes them to the back where he has a dozen horses of varying size and shape.

James tells him of their need for horses to pull a wagon and he shows them two that would fit the bill perfectly. After some haggling, James hands over most of their remaining money and they leave with two fine horses. Jiharan, graciously enough, threw in the traces they would require to attach the horses to the wagon. He even went so far as to have one of his apprentices carry the equipment back to Salli's and help them with putting it on.

Back at Salli's, he's pleased to discover that not only are the barrels awaiting them in the back of the wagon, but Salli was nice enough to have them already filled with water. With the apprentice's help, the horses are soon attached to the wagon and they give him a couple coppers for his time before he returns to his master.

Salli waves a friendly goodbye to them as they pull out of his yard, James at the reins. As they make their way through town, he sees a chandler's shop and stops. He buys some much needed supplies like better food than just travel rations, and a couple ladles to use for getting water to drink from the barrels.

Now with an almost empty coin pouch, they resume their way back to the caravansary where the others are waiting. When they get there, James is in for a shock. When they left, there were two wagons, now there are four. Two boys are there with the others as well.

As they ride up, Delia comes out to meet them before they have a chance to get to the camp. Beaming like a cat that had eaten the canary, she says, "Good news!"

"What?" asks James, looking a bit perplexed.

She hands him a pouch, heavy with coin. "While you were gone, Tinok and I delivered a couple packages that were to be dropped off here and was paid for them."

"How much?" he asks.

"Forty gold, ten silver," she replies.

"What about those other two wagons?" he asks as he nods his head in their direction.

"One of the merchants that we delivered a package to needed to get a load to Korazan as quickly as possible," she explains. "When he found out we were headed there, he asked if his lads could tag along. Couldn't see any harm in it, so I agreed." She could see that he was dubious of the whole thing, "Besides, he gave us an extra four golds."

Beginning to see the advantage in having others with them, he nods and says, "Good job."

She beams back at him and walks alongside the wagon as he brings it back to camp.

Once the wagon is in position with the others, he gets down and calls Tinok over to help with watering the horses. He comes over with Cassie holding his hand, they're both smiling and happy.

"What's this?" he asks when he sees a new necklace around Cassie's neck.

"Oh, I bought it for her while I was helping Delia deliver the packages," Tinok replies.

"Isn't it beautiful?" Cassie asks as she holds it up for his inspection. It's a gold, heart shaped medallion with two small diamonds in the middle.

Unable to help himself, he breaks into a smile as he says, "Yes, it's very nice."

Glancing over to Delia, he sees her grinning at him. He nods his head and then he and Tinok proceed to water the horses from the barrels, using the two buckets Salli had given them.

By this time, the sun has finally fallen below the horizon and James takes out some of the food that he bought earlier in town. Everyone is glad to have a break from travel rations and sets to with gusto. While they are eating, James spies Ahlim, the 'caravansary master' walking off in the distance. He watches as he greets another caravan and scores some more coin. He just shakes his head and chuckles to himself, able to see the humor of it when it's not happening to himself.

The two lads who will be driving the other wagons stay off by themselves, apparently having brought their own provisions.

During the meal, Delia asks him, "Weren't we planning on hiring guards?"

Having totally forgotten about it but trying to hide the fact, he says, "We sure are. Roland and I were going to go back into town after dinner and hire some." He looks over to Roland and asks, "Right?"

With a slightly confused look on his face, Roland says, "Uh, right."

"How many do you think we'll need?" Jiron asks.

"Maybe eight or ten," James guesses, "depends on how much they'll be." Finishing his meal, he stands up and says to Roland, "If you're ready, let's go."

Roland gets up, gives Ezra and Arkie a kiss goodbye and then joins James as he walks toward town.

"He forgot didn't he?" Tinok asks Delia after they've moved out of earshot.

"Probably," she agrees as she watches them walking back to town.

On their way, James asks Roland, "Where do you think would be the best place to hire some?"

"There's usually a guildhall or some other place where merchants contract for guards," he explains. "We just have to know where to look, or who to ask."

After they enter town, they walk down the main thoroughfare until Roland sees one of the city's guards on patrol. He goes over to him and after a brief discussion, comes back to James and says, "He says that if we continue down the road, we'll come across the merchant's guild where we'll be able to hire guards."

"Great," he replies as they hurry down the road.

After several blocks, they see a three story building coming up on their right. It stands a floor taller than any other building near it, and its imposing architecture can only mean this is the merchant's guild. Stepping up to the door, they open it and enter a room decorated to impress those who enter. Expensive rugs, statues spaced around the room and finely carved furniture all say, money.

Several people are seated in plush chairs, sharing some kind of drink as they converse. One man, whose attire shows him to be a servant, comes over to them after they enter and says something, at which Roland replies. He says something again and then turns to cross the room, exiting through a side door.

James looks to Roland, who explains, "Apparently, only members are allowed within here and only members are allowed to hire guards from here as well."

"Where did he go?" James asks.

"He went to get his superior," he replies. "Perhaps we could join the guild in order to hire some guards?"

"Maybe," says James, dubious at the prospect.

They wait only a moment before the door opens again and a man emerges, dressed similar to the first one except this one's clothes are of much finer quality. Seeing them standing there, he comes over to them. He addresses Roland again and then they begin a conversation.

Frustrated, James can only stand there and wait for the translation.

The other man pauses while Roland turns to James and says, "It's unlikely that we'll be able to join. You must be either a partner of a current member, be referred by a member, or over time be invited to join based on your successes as a merchant."

"So what do we do?" he asks Roland.

Roland turns back to the man and they exchange several words before he again translates for James. "He says we could try the bars, that there are often mercenaries there who may hire out."

Not at all liking that idea, he shakes his head.

Roland says a few words to the man and then they each bow to the other before the man turns and leaves through the door he came out of.

"Now what?" Roland asks.

"We go back and explain why we're returning with no guards," James says.

As they leave the merchant's guild, a man is waiting for them outside and approaches as they start walking away from the building. "Excuse me," the man says, in words heavy with accent.

They pause as James replies, "Yes?" He looks at the man; he's dressed well, neat and trim with a sword hanging at his hip.

"I was inside and heard that you are looking for some guards for your caravan?" he inquires.

"That's right," James says.

"My fellows and I have just finished a contract that wasn't renewed with a merchant, here in the city," he explains. "And we currently find ourselves looking for other work. If you are still in need of guards, we are available."

"Just a moment," James says to him as he pulls Roland aside. "What do you think?" he asks him in a whisper.

"I don't know, it just doesn't feel right," he replies.

James nods his head in agreement, "I feel the same way." Turning back to the man, he says, "Actually, we really don't need your services right now, but thanks for offering."

"As you will," the man says, "apparently, I was mistaken." Bowing, the man turns and walks away, disappearing into the crowd.

Once the man is gone, they resume making their way back to their camp at the caravansary. When they arrive, Delia asks, "Where are the guards?"

"You have to be a member of the merchant's guild in order to hire any through them," James explains. "So we will do the best we can without any for right now."

Delia hands him a sack. Opening it up, he sees a sling and twenty iron slugs within. "What's this for?" he asks.

"So when you do your thing with the stones, it won't seem so," she explains, pausing momentarily, "magical."

"Thanks," he says graciously.

"You're welcome," she replies, "I'll teach you how to use it when we are out on the road."

"Alright," agrees James. Going over near the campfire, he upends the sack and pours the sling and the slugs on the ground and begins inspecting them.

Cassie and Tinok are sitting close together, heads leaned against one another as they sit there, Tinok with his arm around her. Both are looking quite content.

Jiron comes over to where James is looking over his new toy and sits down. "Do you think they're at Korazan yet?" he asks him.

"Maybe, though I can't be sure," he replies, stuffing the slugs and sling back in the pouch. He secures the pouch on his belt to keep it handy.

"Can't you do that compass thing?" he suggests.

James nods over to the two lads and says, "Don't want to alert them about my abilities until it becomes absolutely necessary. Don't know how they'll react, or even who they would tell." Pausing a moment, he turns his head to look at Jiron in the eye and says, "It doesn't matter if they are or not, we can't get there faster."

"True," Jiron says, crestfallen. "I just wanted to know."

"So do I, I'm worried about them. But they should be alright until they get sold and hopefully we'll be there before then."

Jiron just sits there, his mood dark as thoughts of his sister and what may be happening to her run through his mind.

Not too long after, they break up and turn in. The two lads sleep under their wagons while the rest of the group stays together around the campfire.

Chapter Twelve

They're up and ready to roll by the time the sun crests the horizon. Now a much larger caravan, they decide to have Roland drive the wagon in which Ezra and Arkie ride. Jiron again rides point now that he's mostly recovered from his ordeal, while Tinok and Cassie drive the water wagon. James and Delia take the front wagon with the two lads eating dust at the rear. They still have the string of five horses they acquired earlier, as well as Roland's two, just in case.

The road south of Zereth-Alin slowly begins to turn hilly the further they ride. The hills are sparsely covered with scrub brush, the occasional snake or lizard makes an appearance. There's not too much traffic on the road, the heat of summer must keep all non essential travel to a minimum.

During a stop to water the horses, Delia approaches James and asks, "Ready?"

"For what?" he replies.

"To learn how to use your sling," she replies.

Getting down from his wagon and the cool of the shade he says, "Sure." He then rummages in the pouch at his waist and pulls out the sling as well as five of the slugs.

She leads him away from the others and then takes the sling from him. She also takes one of the slugs and puts it into the sling's pouch. "What you want to do is hold it by the two loops on the ends like this," she says as she demonstrates the proper technique. "Then you slowly wind it up and release one end of the sling when it reaches the proper position that will enable the slug to fly where you want it. Watch."

She quickly winds up the sling and then lets go of one end while still holding onto the other. The sling opens up and the slug flies through the air, hitting a small tree ten yards away. Turning back to him, she says, "Easy."

Giving him the sling, she watches as he gets ready to place a slug in it. She adjusts the way he's holding it and then gestures for him to insert a slug. "Now, wind it up and when it feels right, let only one end loose so the slug will fly free, got it?" she asks.

"I think so," he says. Winding up, he gets the sling whirling fast and then lets go. He hears a chuckle coming from behind him as the sling leaves his hands and goes flying out into the desert, the slug still remaining within its pouch. Turning around, he sees Tinok standing there, shaking his head and grinning.

"Don't mind him," she tells James. "Just retrieve your sling and let's try it again."

Once he's returned with it, he stands the way Delia instructs him to maintain his balance and remain centered, then gets it whirling quickly. This time when he lets go, he manages to retain one end of the sling, but he hears more laughter as the slug hits one of the wagons behind him.

"Watch it!" Jiron says from where the slug almost nailed him.

"Sorry!" James hollers over to him.

"Better," says Delia.

"How is that better?" he exclaims. "I almost killed Jiron."

"You didn't lose the sling this time," she explains. "Now, do it again and concentrate less on retaining the sling and more on the target."

Placing another slug within the sling, he gives her a look and receives one of encouragement back. Behind him, he hears Tinok loudly say in amusement, "Be alert, he's trying again."

Trying to concentrate on the small tree that she hit earlier, he begins to twirl and then releases. To his satisfaction, the slug goes in somewhat the desired direction, though still hitting the ground ten feet away from the tree.

"Not bad," she says encouragingly. "A little more practice and you'll have it down. Just don't expect to be perfect too soon, it takes time to learn."

Taking another slug and placing it within the sling, he whirls it and lets it loose while at the same time adding a touch of magic to it. The slug flies unerringly to the tree where it strikes it dead center, punching a hole right through.

Delia looks at him and says, "That's cheating."

James shrugs and gives her a grin, and then he puts it away as they prepare to get underway.

At one point they come across where an old building had once stood, its wooden frame now lying broken and vacant. At a suggestion from Tinok, they stop and jury-rig a canopy for the water wagon from the building's wooden remains. They find four boards that they manage to secure to the wagons frame and then tie a blanket atop it. Not exactly stylish but it helps. The two lads just smile and shake their heads at it all, they're just fine riding in the sun on their wagons.

The rest of the day passes fairly uneventfully, just endless miles of dry hills with only the occasional traveler coming from the south. By the end of the day, they've already emptied one of the barrels of water and have begun to drain a second. They have had to stop every other hour to give each horse some to drink.

With the sun settling close to the horizon, they pull off the road to make camp. Once the horses are taken care of, they settle down around the campfire and have dinner while they swap tales and songs. Before the end of it, the two lads come over and join the fun. One of them, Hakim, even sang a song while his bother, Hakir, told a story that only Roland could understand. He did his best to translate and everyone enjoyed it.

As the fire begin to burn low, everyone starts turning in. James can't seem to fall asleep, worry about Miko keeping him awake. So he just lies back and stares at the stars, still amazed at just how much clearer they are here than back home. *Must be 'cause there's no smog here,* he figures. Whatever the reason, they seem to work like counting sheep for before he even realizes it, he's asleep.

He wakes in the middle of the night, noise from where the horses are picketed having disturbed him. The fire has long since burned out and the only light is that from the stars above. He sits up and looks around but doesn't see anything out of the ordinary, everyone else is still asleep. Even Hakim and Hakir are snoring peacefully under their wagons.

Then one of the horses snorts again and he can hear several others begin to pace around. Suspecting trouble, he quietly crawls over to Jiron and wakes him with a gentle shake. "Trouble," he whispers to him as he comes fully awake.

He sees him nod his head in the starlight as he sits up, looking around. "The horses are skittish for some reason," James whispers to him. "Go check it out and I'll wake Tinok."

Again, Jiron nods his head as he gets up, silent as a cat and begins making his way over to the horses.

Just as James reaches Tinok's side, he sits up, a knife in his hand as he strikes out. Stopping the blade just inches from James' nose, he asks, "What the hell are you doing?"

"Quiet!" James whispers intently. "Something's going on."

Suddenly very alert, Tinok looks around.

"The horses," James whispers to him, "something's got them…"

Suddenly, a cry splits the night, coming from where Jiron had gone to check on the horses. Without even thinking, James casts a spell and his glowing orb appears over the camp, brightly illuminating the area. There they can see Jiron in battle with two men, armed with swords and others approaching out of the desert.

Everyone else comes awake, Cassie screams and James says to the rest, "Stay together!" as he and Tinok race over to where Jiron is being hard pressed by the bandits.

As he runs, James takes out one of his iron slugs and casts it at an oncoming bandit, taking him through the stomach. As the slug exits through his back, gore flies as he falls over dead.

As they reach Jiron, Tinok kicks out and knocks one of his opponents down and then begins to battle another, knives flashing in a blinding arc of speed.

Having Tinok distracting one of his attackers, Jiron is able to be more on the offense with deadly results as another of the attackers falls to the ground.

Two men appear out of the night, coming straight for James. One of them is the man who had offered them his services outside the merchant's guild. "It appears you did need our services after all," he says with a grin full of malice.

"Not necessarily," James says as the power surges out of him. A wave of force throws them backward and he takes one out quickly with a slug. The other man, the one who approached them outside the merchant's guild, gains his feet quickly and comes at James with sword in hand.

Just before the man closes with James, Jiron comes running and imposes himself between the man and James. The man strikes out with his sword and Jiron deflects it with one knife while following through with the other. Dancing backward, the man pauses a moment as he takes in the situation. He's the only one left standing.

Turning, he begins to race away when a slug flies from the other side of camp and strikes him between the shoulder blades. A snap can be heard as the man's spine is shattered. He falls to the ground and lies still, whimpering with pain, paralyzed.

"Good shot!" Tinok says to Delia who is putting away her sling.

Jiron moves to the man lying on the ground and can see the pain in his eyes. Bending over, he takes his knife and ends the man's misery. Turning to James he asks, "Who were these guys?"

Pointing to the dead man at Jiron's feet he says, "That one offered me the service of his band for guard duty, but I turned him down. Guess he figured we were easy prey."

"Guess he thought wrong," Tinok says, chuckling. Cassie runs over to Tinok, burying her head in his shoulder, crying.

Jiron and James check the horses and find them fine then return to the camp. A fire has already been started from the embers of their earlier one. "Everyone alright?" James asks as they return.

"We're fine," Delia replies. The two lads had come out as well, knives at the ready, but have sheathed them again now that the fight was over.

James can hear Tinok trying to calm Cassie by saying, "It's okay, it's over."

Jiron begins the task of dragging the bodies out into the desert away from camp, while everyone else takes stock of the situation.

As James sits down by the fire, the two lads stare at him with eyes wide. "What?" he says to them.

They reply in their own language.

"I would appreciate it if you would never mention this to anyone?" he asks, an edge to his voice. He's surprised when they both nod their heads in quick agreement. *Maybe they can't speak it, just understand it.*

When Jiron returns, he says to James, "You're getting better, less tired."

"Been getting a lot of practice lately," he says. "Too much if you ask me."

"I'll say," Tinok agrees from where he stands nearby with Cassie, though he doesn't seem too disappointed at being able to 'practice' with his knives.

After a while, when everyone has calmed down, they all try to go back to sleep, only this time taking turns at watch.

The next day they see scavengers over at the dead bodies, having a little morning breakfast. As quickly as possible, they hook up the horses and get on the road, none wish to remain a second longer near the dead bandits.

For the rest of the day, they make very good time, having only to stop to water and feed the horses. A little before sunset they come to a small cluster of buildings, hardly large enough to even call it a village.

"Looks to be just a way stop for travelers," guesses James.

"Could be," agrees Jiron. "Look," he says as he points to a group of wagons already camped a short ways from the buildings, "you may be right."

James says, "Looks like as good a place as any to stop for the night."

"I agree," replies Jiron.

Turning off the road, Jiron leads them a hundred yards from the nearest building, to a place where pits for campfires are available. Once the wagons and horses are set for the night, Delia, James, Jiron and Roland go over to the buildings to investigate. Cassie, Ezra and the two boys remain behind with the wagons.

There are only four buildings, one has a sign of a cracked egg and another one with crossed shovels. Deciding to try the one with the cracked egg, they go over and enter through the front door.

Inside, they find a large room with a central hearth containing many tables. A man comes over as they enter and says, "Welcome. How may I serve you today?" Heavy with accent, but understandable.

"We just arrived and were looking around, seeing what is available here," James explains.

"Ah, first time here?" the man asks.

"Yes," Delia pipes up.

"Here at the Broken Egg, you can get a meal and a room if you desire," he tells them. "The other shop across the street has many goods that a traveler may require." He pauses for a response and when none is forthcoming, asks, "Would you care for a room, or perhaps a bite to eat?"

Shaking his head, James says, "Not right now, we may come back later though, thank you."

"You're welcome sirs," and then with a slight nod to Delia he adds, "ma'am."

They turn to leave and once outside Jiron says, "Nice place."

"Maybe we could take turns and come here for dinner this evening," suggests James.

"That would be an excellent idea," agrees Roland. Jiron and Delia nod in agreement.

Crossing over to the store, they enter and find a small man, almost a midget, asleep behind the counter. They all look at each other wondering what they should do and then Jiron closes the door loudly, startling the man awake.

He sits up and looks around, rubbing his eyes. Seeing them standing there and recognizing them for northerners, he greets them in their tongue.

"Hello," he says from his chair, not bothering getting down. "How may I help you today?"

"We just arrived and are looking around to see what's available," Delia says.

"Of course," the man says sleepily as a yawn escapes him. He settles back down in his chair and watches them as they browse through his merchandise.

It looks to be just an ordinary, traveler supply store. Just the same old things as are in every other one. James does see a kit with a small mirror, a comb and a pair of scissors. Thinking of his unruly hair and how it's been too long since it's been properly taken care of, he picks it up and asks the man, "How much for this?"

The man looks over, squinting as if he can't see it very well and replies, "Two silvers."

James takes a single silver out and says as he holds it up, "Give you one for it."

"Alright," the man says as he holds out his hand for the coin.

Taking the coin over to the lazy man, James drops it into his hand. He immediately takes the mirror and looks at himself in it. What's looking back is almost unrecognizable. His hair is an unruly mess, obviously running his fingers through it has been ineffective. Stubble, actually a scraggly beard that's not completely growing in everywhere, now covers his face, his dirty face. "GAH!" he exclaims as he looks at himself, rubbing his free hand over his patchy beard. *I knew it was coming in, but my goodness!*

"What?" Delia asks.

Putting the mirror away, he says, "Nothing." Looking around he tries to find a shaving kit, but such a thing doesn't appear to have been developed in this world yet, or at least there isn't one here.

Seeing a small knife, he buys it for three coppers, thinking that later he might try to put a spell on it that will enable him to shave without scraping all his skin off in the process.

"Anyone else getting anything?" he asks.

Roland looks around and picks up a small piece of cloth, saying, "Ezra would like this." He haggles briefly with the man and then hands over the coins.

Delia and Jiron just shake their heads, not interested.

They look around for a few more minutes and then turn to leave. James glances over to the man to say goodbye but he's already fallen back asleep.

Once they've returned to the caravan, they tell everyone about their plan to have dinner at the Broken Egg. James stays at the caravan with the two lads as everyone else goes over for dinner. "I'll send one of the boys over if there is a problem."

"There shouldn't be," Jiron replies.

"You never know," he says.

After everyone has left for the Broken Egg, he takes a bucket and fills it with a little water from one of the water barrels and then sits down by the fire. Taking out the little knife, he holds it up in front of him and contemplates a spell that will enable it to shave the hair off his face while at the same time, leaving his skin intact.

After about five minutes of working it out, he turns his concentration on the knife and lets the magic flow. After completing the spell he feels the edge of the knife with his thumb, it doesn't seem to have changed at all. It's barely sharp and it would take a whole lot of pressure to cut anything with it. But then, that wasn't what the spell was supposed to accomplish.

Taking out the mirror, he holds it up so he can see his scraggly looking face in it. Then taking the knife, he very carefully runs it down along his cheek. He can feel a slight drawing of magic from him by the knife, must be taking the magic it needs to work from him. To his delight and amazement, the hair is scrapped off like frosting from a cake. Excited, he continues until all the stubble has been completely removed and then splashes his face with the water from the bucket to get all the residual hair and dirt off. Holding up the mirror, he's pleased to see the familiar face that had been hidden by that horrible, scraggly beard.

Next he takes the comb and begins to run it through his tangled hair as he attempts to restore it to its proper look. Painful as it is, he gets the job done and then realizes his hair is getting a little bit long, especially over the eyes. Taking the 'hair' knife as he calls it now, he begins to very carefully cut off the ends, making them as even as possible. *What barber wouldn't pay a lot for this?* he thinks to himself as the hair comes off so easily.

Looking in the mirror when he's done, he once again resembles the man he was oh so long ago. Quite pleased with the results, he starts whistling as he cleans up and then puts away his shaving kit. That's when he notices the two lads watching him, whispering to one another.

When they realize he's noticed them watching him, they smile at him and then resume the game they've been playing, a game with sticks and dice.

A half hour later, the others return and when Delia sees James, she says, "My, don't we look nice."

Cassie takes a closer look and ads, "You do look good." At which Tinok gives her a look of annoyance.

"Couldn't stand it any longer," he tells them. "How was the food?"

"Pretty good," answers Roland. "But don't have the goat, it's a bit tough."

As James prepares to head over there, he says, "Thanks, I'll keep that in mind."

Leaving them behind, he walks over and enters the Broken Egg. The place isn't that crowded, probably since only one other caravan is here. Having his pick of seats, he takes one by a window overlooking the road outside.

A girl comes over and asks what he would like.

"What is there?" he asks her.

"There's roast goat or our specialty which is eggs and ham with a spicy sauce," she explains.

"I'll try your specialty and some ale if you have any," he tells her, remembering what Roland had said about the goat.

Nodding her head, she says, "It'll be just a few minutes for the special, but I'll bring your ale right over. That'll be a silver three."

Once he's handed the silver and three coppers over to her, she returns to the kitchen, returning momentarily with his mug of ale.

While he's waiting for his dinner, he sits and looks out the window. He's surprised when Delia, along with Tinok who's carrying a box, comes into view. Curious, he watches as they go into the store across from the inn. *Wonder what that woman is up to?*

His meal arrives shortly after that and while he eats, he keeps an eye on the store. Finally, he sees them leave and Tinok is no longer carrying the box. *Curious.*

Before he's done with his meal, which is surprisingly good if a bit spicy, a group of enemy soldiers ride up to the Broken Egg and tie their horses to the rail outside.

Upon entering, the soldiers cross the room and sit at a table not too far from where James is. The serving girl comes over to them and begins taking their order.

Nervous, James finishes his meal quickly and then gets up to go. As he crosses the room, one of the soldiers addresses him in their language. Frozen with fear, James pretends that he doesn't realize he's being addressed and continues to the door.

One of the soldiers gets up and comes over to him, stopping him by grabbing his arm.

James looks at him and says, "Sorry, were you talking to me? I didn't understand what you're saying."

The soldier looks back to his officer, who asks him, "What is your business in these parts?"

"Just part of a caravan coming through," he replies. Taking out the letter, he walks over and gives it to the officer.

Taking it, the officer scans through it and when he gets to the signature at the bottom, returns it to him saying, "Very well." He nods to the soldier who has a hold of his arm, who then releases him. "Sorry to have bothered you, but you can never tell."

"I understand," James assures him and then proceeds to the door, exiting the Broken Egg. Legs shaking, he makes his way back to the camp. *What does that letter say?* he can't help but wonder.

Returning to camp, Tinok comes and greets him before he even reaches the wagons. "Can I ask you a question?" he asks him.

"Sure," James replies.

"Can you show me how you got the hair off your face?" he asks, somewhat embarrassed.

"Doing it for Cassie?" James asks, trying to keep the smile off his face.

Nodding his head, he says, "She just keeps going on about how nice you look. So, I thought if I did it too, she would be happy."

"No problem," James replies. "Just wait here and I'll get my stuff."

"Thanks," he says, relief evident in his voice.

Going back to the wagon, he grabs his kit and then returns to where Tinok is waiting. Showing him what to do, he holds the mirror while Tinok runs the knife over his face, removing what little hair he has. When he's done, he runs his hand over his now smooth face and says, "Thanks a lot."

"Glad to help," James assures him.

He watches as Tinok goes back over and sits next to Cassie trying to get her to see his newly shaven face, without letting on that he wants her to. She, unfortunately, has no clue about what he just did and he's crestfallen when she doesn't immediately recognize his efforts.

James just smiles and shakes his head at Tinok's attempts to get her to notice. Replacing his kit back in the wagon, he goes over and joins them. The rest of the evening, Tinok continues trying to gain Cassie's attention until finally taking her hand and rubbing it along his jaw line.

Her eyes open wide as she finally realizes what he's done and he at last gets the praise and attention that he's been wanting.

Before they fall asleep that night, James hears the hoof beats of the soldier's horses as they leave, heading to the north.

The following morning before they head out, they fill their barrels at the inn's well, which only costs them a couple coppers. They also find out that Korazan is about two more days to the south. Eager to get there, they set a quick pace all that day, until having to stop for the night along the road.

Shortly after starting the following morning, they pass through a village with not much more than huts and goat herds. The people there don't seem too friendly, they just hurry out of their way, glaring at them as they pass. Having no reason to stop, they continue on through and soon the village disappears behind them.

For the rest of the day, they're all fairly quiet as they ponder the likelihood of rescuing their friends from the hands of the slavers. Jiron pushes them onward, impatient whenever they must stop in order to water and feed the horses.

James is anxious too, hoping Miko has survived the trip down.

When the sun is high in the sky, they begin to see a large lake in the distance. "Tears of the Empress," Roland says.

"What?" asks James.

"The water there," he replies, "they call it 'The Tears of the Empress'. Don't know why."

"Interesting," James says.

"Korazan is situated next to it, probably on the other side," he says.

"Good," Jiron exclaims.

As they follow the road around the lake, they can see numerous fishing boats out upon it. From the smell in the air, James figures it to be fresh water. The road follows the shoreline, curving around until they begin to see a large city appearing on the shore ahead of them. Korazan.

Chapter Thirteen

The snap of the lash across his back wakes Miko from another restless, dream-filled night. He quickly gets to his feet before the lash strikes again and looks around at the others in the slave line being kicked or lashed awake. There are a number of empty spots along the lines where those who were unable to keep up are no longer with them. He tries not to think about them, lying dead in shallow graves along the road.

He remembers with anguish one old timer who collapsed in line and was lashed to get moving before they realized he was already dead. They had a couple of the other captives in line dig a hole in the ground to put him in. Thankfully, he was spared that duty.

The first night they stopped was the worst. His body ached from the long march and his mind was dizzy from the heat, as well as the lack of food and drink. But that wasn't what had made it so horrible. After they stopped and everyone had been fed and given water, the slaver returned to the girl who had insisted that she wasn't a slave and removed her from the line. She screamed the entire way as they took her to one of the tents they erected. The memory of her screams and cries as they echoed through the night still continue to haunt him. No one got any sleep that night, even after her screams had finally stopped, several hours later.

The next morning when he was awakened by the lash, he saw the girl had already been returned to her place in line. One eye was blackened and multiple bruises showed on every part of her body that wasn't covered up. There was a vacant look in her eye and when given food she wouldn't eat. Given water, she wouldn't drink.

When the line made ready to move, she still remained sitting on the ground. Two slavers came over to her and proceeded to whip her until she came back to her senses and stood up. Once she was on her feet, crying with tears streaming down her face, one of the slavers steps in front of her and says loudly enough so everyone can hear him, "Are you a slave?"

A barely audible, "Yes," escapes her lips.

The lash strikes her across the shoulders and he just glares at her. "Yes, master!" she cries out loudly.

Nodding, the slaver returns back to the front of the line by the wagon. Everyone in the slave line is quiet, unable to even look at the ravished, punished girl.

Miko shudders at the memory as he gets his bowl of food and cup of water to drink. He hungrily consumes it all, wanting more, but knowing better to ask. After all the bowls and cups are collected, they get moving.

He can't remember how long he's been walking in the line, the days are a blur of pain and exhaustion. The only thing keeping him moving is the certainty that James will come. *He will!* he insists to himself.

It's early in the afternoon when a commotion draws his attention to the front of the line. Looking up, he sees them pointing to a large body of water coming into view ahead. A large city sits on its shore.

"Korazan," announces one of the slavers. "There you will be placed at auction and sold to your new masters."

A hushed silence falls upon all of them as they continue marching toward Korazan, dreading what fate may befall them there.

Every last person in line is quiet when they pass through the gates of Korazan. Miko looks around at the people in the streets and notices that they don't even look at them there in the slave lines. It's almost as if they aren't even people to them.

They're taken through to a large complex at the edge of town, holding pens for those awaiting the auction block. There, Miko is removed from his line and the slavers begin separating the captives by age and sex. He's herded into a holding pen with other boys and young men.

Several fights break out by those being separated from wives and children, but in the end they go where they're told, usually with blood running down their backs from the numerous lashings required to subdue them.

Once they've been in their pen for awhile, one of the lads a few years older than Miko comes over to him and says in a whisper, "We gotta get out of here!"

Miko just looks at him and asks, "How?"

"Rush the guard, or something," he says.

"I don't think it would do any good," Miko tells him.

Obviously not getting any support for his idea from Miko, the lad goes over to another group of boys where he can hear them whispering amongst themselves. *I hope they don't do anything stupid to get me killed,* he thinks as he glances over to the older boys, huddled with their heads together.

He gazes over to the other pens in the area and sees many such as his, holding young boys and men. The women and girls must have been taken elsewhere for he doesn't see any sign of them.

Another young man in the pen with him comes over and says, "Wonder what's going to happen now?"

Shrugging, Miko says, "Don't know."

"Name's Viktor," he says holding out his hand.

Taking the hand, he replies, "Miko."

Viktor glances over to the group of boys who are conversing together quietly. "Think they're right?" he asks.

"What? Those guys?" Miko asks, indicating the group planning escape.

When Viktor nods his head, he says, "I doubt it. I would think the slavers are going to anticipate something like that, they've been doing this for a long time."

"But what choice do we have?" Viktor asks, his voice trembling slightly.

"Right now, none," he replies.

Viktor starts sobbing, "I want to go home!"

"So do we all," Miko says, uncomfortable at the show of emotion Viktor is displaying.

Viktor goes back over to a corner and sits down by himself, with his knees up and lays his head in his arms, silently crying.

Doing his best to hold back his own emotions, Miko sits and stares out of the pen.

An hour passes before several slavers come and bring them food and water, as well as a bucket for use as a slop bucket. When they get close to the door of his pen, the boys from the group move closer to the door and Miko gets set for trouble. Two of the slavers have crossbows, armed and casually aimed at the boys while another says, "Back up!"

When the boys don't move, he signals the crossbowmen who take direct aim on them and then he says again, "Back up."

With two crossbows staring down at them, the boys back up several feet, allowing him to open the door and place a platter of bread and old meat on the floor. Stepping back, he closes the door and then proceeds down to the next pen.

When the door shuts, Miko dives for the food and grabs himself two big handfuls of meat and bread before the other boys have a chance to take it. The meat is a little ripe but the bread is only slightly stale. Not caring, he wolfs it down quickly before someone gets it into his head to take it away from him.

Two of the boys are left with nothing to eat, one of them is Viktor. He just sits and stares at the empty plate, as if not believing that there's nothing for him. Miko sees him start to say something to one of the slavers, but then he remembers the girl that had complained on the road and shuts his mouth. Rolling onto his side, he gets into a fetal position and starts sobbing all over again.

The other boys look on him with disdain, and one of them says, "You better be faster next time." The others just laugh. Miko feels bad for the boy but is unwilling to share his meager food with him. Even though he got as much as his hands could grab, it still wasn't enough to quiet the grumbling of his belly.

Miko goes over to a small window that overlooks a large inner courtyard. Looking out, he sees a large platform on the other side that looks like it could be used for auctions, though it's empty now.

Smelling something foul, he turns around and sees one of the boys using the slop bucket and he thinks it could get pretty ripe in here after a while. Leaving the window, he finds a spot as far from the bucket as possible and settles down to rest. The light outside is beginning to fade as night falls.

During the night, he hears many of the boys crying and sobbing all around him, some crying out for their mothers. He eventually breaks down too, as silent tears roll down his cheek. One boy in a nearby pen loses it and starts screaming and trying to break through the bars.

Suddenly, the door at the end of the pens opens up and two slavers come in with torches and long sticks. They move to the pen where the boy is screaming uncontrollably and opens the door. As soon as the door opens, the boy tries to leave and that's when they start beating him with sticks until he quiets down. Either he stopped on his own accord, or they beat him into unconsciousness, Miko couldn't tell but he was glad when the screaming ended.

Once the guards left and it was again dark and quiet, he begins to hear whispers coming from others in his pen.

"...there were only two of them..."

"...no crossbows..."

"...might be our only chance..."

He hears some of the boys begin to move toward the door and then lie down near it. All of a sudden, one of them begins to act just like that other boy, screaming and banging on the door trying to get out.

Just as before, the two guards enter the pen area and open the door to their pen. When the door opens, the slavers rush in and begin beating the one who's crying out. With the landing of the first blow, all the boys who had stationed themselves by the door spring up and attack the two slavers. In short order, the slavers lie on the ground unconscious at the boys' feet.

The boys, now with the torches and sticks, and filled with hope of escape race out of the pen. Miko stays where he is and watches as they race down the hallway toward the open door the slavers had entered through. Suddenly, he sees one fall backward as a crossbow bolt strikes him in the chest. Another boy twists about then falls with a cry when another bolt strikes him in the shoulder.

Soon the hallway is filled with slavers and the ill fated escape attempt is soon squashed. The boys caught outside of the pen are taken away and a couple slavers come back to where Miko and a few of the others had remained. They remove the unconscious slavers the boys had attacked and then begin to leave. One slaver pauses a moment as he looks at those remaining in the pen and then says something before closing the door to Miko's pen. He turns to follow his fellow slavers across the room and through the door, closing it behind him. When the door closes, the pens are once more plunged into darkness.

Miko can hear Viktor giggling over in the corner. He tries to shut out the noise and attempts to fall asleep.

Early the next morning, shortly after sunup, they begin to hear a commotion coming from the courtyard outside of the small window. Miko rushes over to it, as do others in the pens along the same wall. Outside, they see the boys who had been captured in the escape attempt the night before being marched over to where a pole stands near one side of the courtyard. A hushed whisper can be heard as some of those in the adjoining pens relay what's going on to those on the other side of the holding area.

When the boys reach the pole, one slaver stands there as he begins to address the slaves still in the holding pen. "Last night, a few of you decided to try to escape," he says loudly, so all can hear him. "These eight here are those that survived. Should any of you be contemplating similar attempts, let this be a lesson in what happens to those slaves who try to flee."

He says something to the other slavers with him and then the first boy is taken over to the pole where his arms are tied to ropes. A slaver behind the pole pulls on the ropes, pulling the boy's arms high above his head, stretching him until only the tips of his toes are touching the ground. Then a man with a multi tongued whip comes forward and begins to lash him.

As the lash strikes him for the first time, a hushed silence falls upon those in the pens. The boy cries out as the lash strikes him the second time. Each time the lash strikes, it leaves long, red welts which after the fist couple of strikes, begin to well blood.

After ten lashes, the boy is screaming incoherently and blood is flowing freely down his back. At twelve, he loses consciousness and they remove him from the whipping pole, taking him away.

Once he's been removed they bring up the next boy, who by now is gibbering with fear. "I won't try to escape! I won't!" he screams, pleading with the slavers. As they string him up, he continues to cry and plead, to no avail. When he's struck for the first time, his bowels let go and he soils himself.

Boy after boy take their turn at the whipping post until they've all either been given fifteen lashes or they've slipped into unconsciousness. As the last boy is taken away, the man in charge looks around at the faces peering in horror out of the windows, then turns without a word and walks back into the building. The ground at the base of the pole is stained red with the blood that the whip had drawn out of the boys' backs.

Not long after that, they begin to bring in food and water again. This time, when the plate is placed within the pen, there is enough for everyone. The screams of the boys as they were being whipped continue to echo through Miko's mind, causing him to shudder.

A couple hours later, the courtyard begins to fill up with all sorts of people and a string of girls are brought out onto the platform. One by one, the girls are brought to the front, have their clothes stripped off and then the people begin bidding for them.

Miko watches through the window as girl after girl are auctioned off, knowing that soon it will be his turn. He turns his attention back inside when he hears a commotion brewing at the entrance to the slave pens.

A man of obvious importance is entering with a slaver walking beside him that Miko has seen here in the pens before, obviously distraught. The slaver appears to be pleading with the other man, but whatever he's saying is having little effect.

Several guards are following them and as the man walks through, he points to pens and the guards begin taking out the boys within and tying them to a line. When he gets to Miko's pen he points to it and soon Miko and the others are tied to the end of the line. The guards come to Viktor who is lying on the floor, gibbering to himself. They look back over to the man and one of them says something. The man looks to Viktor and then shakes his head. His men leave him there as they move on to the next pen.

After half the pens have been emptied, he says something to the slaver who looks to be about ready to argue with him. With a stern look, he stops any complaints the slaver might have had about him taking the slaves. With resignation, the slaver follows him back outside, the boys he's selected following along behind.

They're marched through several adjoining pens until they come to the outside where several wagons are waiting. The guards untie the boys from the line and then direct them to climb up onto the wagons. The official gives a letter to another man who then climbs up onto the lead wagon and then they begin to roll out.

Miko isn't sure just what is happening, but at the moment he's just happy to be out of there. They roll through town and are soon exiting through the southern gate. Unbeknownst to Miko, on the far side of town, James is entering Korazan from the north.

Chapter   Fourteen

As they approach Korazan from the north, a large complex of buildings comes into view over on the eastern edge of town with many pens full of slaves. "That must be where we'll find them," observes James.

"Let's go," Jiron urges.

"We need to get the caravan settled in first," insists James. "Then we can go scout around for Tersa and Miko." Seeing that Jiron is going to be stubborn, he continues, "If we don't behave like an actual caravan, we might gain attention that could prove awkward."

Seeing conflicting emotions running across Jiron's face, he waits. After only a moment's deliberation, he nods and says, "Okay, but let's do it fast."

"Agreed."

During their approach, they notice a large caravansary off to the north of town, closer to the lake. When they turn to leave the road and head for it, Hakir and Hakim take their leave, continuing on toward town to deliver their goods.

At the caravansary, they find a suitable location and quickly settle in. After the horses and wagons have been taken care of, Jiron looks to James and urges, "Let's go!"

James turns to Tinok and says, "Stay here and take care of things, okay?"

Tinok's face begins to fall as he realizes he's being left behind. Just before he starts to protest, Cassie calls over and asks, "Tinok, can you help me please?" Torn between conflicting desires, he finally says to James, "Alright," as he heads over to see what Cassie needs.

By this time, Jiron has changed into native garb, having chosen one that partially covers his face. If there are people from the City of Light in the pens who would be able to recognize him, they won't inadvertently give him away.

Taking Roland with them to act as translator, they make their way to the main gate leading into Korazan. Here, as nowhere else, the ratio of slaves to citizens is staggering. Wherever he looks, James can see slaves engaged in almost every facet of work. Hardly anyone is walking down the street without at least one slave of one kind or another trailing along behind. Many are carrying packages and other items, most though are simply following behind their owners.

James is totally disgusted by the whole thing and almost intervenes when they come across a man beating a young female slave for some slight infraction. Jiron takes hold of his arm which causes him to stop. "Not now," Jiron cautions when James turns to look at him, "we have people, our people, depending on us."

Coming to his senses, James realizes he was about to jeopardize the whole mission and says, "Sorry."

"We understand," Roland assures him. "But it's too ingrained, too well established to do anything about."

As they resume walking, James tries to shut out the crying, begging of the girl as she pleads with her master to stop, that 'she will do better'. Similar scenes are played out over and over again as they continue toward the slave markets. All he can think of is to get Miko out of this as quickly as possible.

When they finally reach the fence surrounding the slave pens, the guard posted at the entrance holds up his hand and says something. Roland makes a reply as he slips him a couple copper pieces. The guard takes the coins and then nods as he waves them on through.

"What did you tell him?" Jiron asks once they're past the guard.

"I simply told him that we wished to view the slaves before the next auction," he explains. "It's really quite common for a prospective buyer to do that. Usually you give some coins to the guard for the privilege"

"You seem to know a lot about slave market customs," Jiron accuses.

"I took a trip down here a while back with an associate who was interested in purchasing some laborers," he replies.

Once through the gates, they find themselves in a large courtyard with two large platforms on either side that most likely would be used during auctions. Off to one side, James notices several posts sticking up from the ground stained a dark red, it looks like its blood. One appears to have been recently used. *Whipping posts*, he assumes, shuddering.

Another slaver greets them as they walk across the courtyard and he exchanges words with Roland. Turning to the others, Roland says, "I told him we wish to see the girls. That we are from a northern brothel and wish to purchase some at the next auction."

"When will that be?" Jiron asks.

Roland asks the man and then says, "Tomorrow."

Jiron nods his head in understanding, "Thanks."

The slaver leads them to a set of pens holding females and they walk slowly through them as if they were actually who they claimed to be. As Jiron searches the pens for his sister, James looks closely at the faces of those in the pens. The hopelessness, the fear and the degradation he sees there is almost more than he can bear. He feels a strong desire to let the magic destroy this entire complex and free everyone here.

Jiron looks anxiously at all the girls within the pens and then turns to Roland and James, shaking his head. Roland turns to the slaver and exchanges a few words before saying, "There is another pen which is full of recent arrivals. He says that you would not be interested in them as they haven't yet learned their place and would be difficult at best to handle."

Excited, Jiron says, "That's where she would most likely be."

Roland turns to the man and explains that they wish to see those girls as well, that many of their customers like to 'break them in'.

The slaver nods in understanding and then leads them out of this holding area to another. The noise level in this one is much greater than the last as the majority of the girls are either crying or talking amongst themselves. When they enter, all the girls turn their attention on them and it suddenly gets very quiet.

James can tell the difference between these girls and the previous ones. Some of these still have a defiant look about them that the previous ones had lacked. Some even look with content upon them as they pass by, others are fearful and sobbing.

Suddenly, he hears a barely audible gasp escaping Jiron. Glancing at him, he sees him nod his head, indicating that he's found her. "Roland, that's her," he says quietly, indicating a young woman with long auburn hair.

"You sure?" Roland asks as he locates the girl he's talking about.

Jiron just stares at him like he's stupid or something.

"Okay, okay," he replies. Then he turns to the slaver and points her out saying they want a better look at her.

The slaver motions for two guards to come over and they enter the pen. When the girls realize they're going to enter their pen, many squeal and they all press as far away from the door as possible.

When Tersa realizes that they're coming for her, she tries to escape to the back of the pen but the guards grab her. Scared and terrified, she tries to get free of them but to no avail, they drag her out of the pen and bring her to stand before them. The slaver asks Roland if this is the one they're interested in. With a nod from Jiron, Roland says that she is.

As Roland makes as if he's inspecting her, Jiron stares intently into her eyes. Suddenly, her breath catches as she realizes just who is standing there.

He barely shakes his head, telling her to say nothing and then gives her a wink.

With a barely perceptible nod, she tells him that she understands.

Jiron indicates to Roland that he's ready to go and Roland tells the slaver that they've seen enough. Once Tersa is put back in the pen, Roland asks if this batch will be auctioned at tomorrow's auction.

Shaking his head, the slaver says that these won't be ready for auction for at least a week.

When Roland relays that to the others, Jiron exclaims, "A week! We can't wait a week."

James digs out a gold piece and offers it to the slaver as he tells Roland, "Ask him if there is any way he can expedite it for us."

When Roland asks the slaver, the slaver takes the coin and nods. He tells Roland that the earliest is in two days and when Roland starts to protest, he says no matter how much they gave him, there is no way it can be done any quicker.

"He says two days and that is the best he can do," Roland explains to them.

Jiron looks back to his sister and says, "Two days then."

The slaver then leads them back out to the courtyard as Tersa is returned to the pen. Jiron glances back to her just before they leave and sees her there, staring at him, her hands gripping the bars. Jiron hates leaving his sister in there but doesn't have any choice.

"Can we see the young men now?" James asks, intent upon finding Miko.

Roland asks the slaver who nods and then alters his course as he takes them over to the other side of the courtyard. He leads them through a door and down a hallway which runs between several pens of young men and boys.

Two slaves are busy scrubbing blood stains off the floor and James asks, "What happened here?"

Roland asks the slaver and then translates the reply, "He says last night several of the new arrivals had tried to escape and two of them were killed."

James and Jiron glance at each other, suddenly worried about his friend. Hoping to find him still within one of the pens, he walks down the hallway. His nervousness rises when he fails see him within any of the pens. Chills run though him as he fears the worst.

While waiting on James, Jiron looks at the faces of the men and boys in the pens. His eyes widen in surprise when he recognizes a couple of the fighters from the fight clubs that he had fought with and against. One, a slim individual who is exceptionally deadly with sword and shield is leaning against the bars near the hallway. He walks down the hallway slowly toward him, acting as if he's inspecting them. Roland and the slaver remain back near the door.

When he comes close to the one by the bars, he whispers so only he may hear, "Don't move, say nothing."

The young man's eyes flick to who's speaking to him and widen when they recognize Jiron. He starts to say something when Jiron barely shakes his head and whispers, "Quiet, man." Sudden understanding comes over him and he settles down.

"How many are here?" Jiron asks in a voice barely audible.

"Five left that I know of," he replies softly. "There were more but a bunch made a break for it last night and two died, the others got their backs flayed off them this morning as an example to the rest of us." Then in an urgent whisper, he says, "Jiron, get us out of here!"

"I'll see what I can do," he says. "But don't tell anyone and I mean anyone that I am here, understand?"

With a slight nod, the young man agrees. Jiron turns and walks back toward where the others are and has Roland ask when these are scheduled to be auctioned off.

The slaver replies and Roland says, "Three days."

James is getting frantic at not finding Miko here and Jiron worries he may do something rash. Roland asks if there are any more fresh arrivals and the slaver replies, no.

Roland thanks the slaver and tells him they're ready to go. Grabbing James' arm, he gets him moving as they follow their guide out of the slaver's compound.

Once outside the compound and back on the streets of Korazan, they head back toward their caravan. James is quiet the entire way as he deals internally with not finding Miko. Roland says to him, "You don't know he was one of the ones killed last night."

"That's right," agrees Jiron. "There are many other reasons that could explain why he wasn't in the pens with the others."

"Like what?" James asks.

At a loss, Jiron just says, "I don't know, but you can't assume the worst until you know for sure."

"I should raze the whole place to the ground," he threatens. "Do the world a favor."

"But you won't," Jiron says, "you just aren't that way."

"I can think it though," growls James.

When they arrive back at the caravan, Jiron explains what's happening to the others. Delia says, "Can't you do some magic thing to see if he's still alive?"

As if the thought hadn't even occurred to him, James sits up as an idea forms in his mind. Excitedly, he says, "There may just be." He hurries over to the wagon and pulls out his shaving kit, removing the mirror.

Sitting down, he looks into the mirror and concentrates on seeing Miko's face, his face as it is right now. Everyone gathers around him and he can hear them gasp as the image in the mirror begins to blur and then refocus on a boy riding in the back of a wagon. "That's him!" James exclaims excitedly. "He's alive!" In his excitement he loses concentration and the reflection returns to normal.

Behind him he hears Delia say, "Now all we have to do is find out who has him and where they are going."

"Maybe tomorrow we could ask around and find out?" suggests Tinok.

"Alright," James agrees, "just be careful and don't draw attention to yourself."

"That's right," says Jiron, "we still have Tersa to save." He pauses for a moment and then adds, "We may be in luck as well."

"How do you mean?" asks James.

"Well, it seems there are several guys back there," he points back toward the slaver compound, "who were participants in the fight clubs back in the City. If we were to buy them, we would have ready made, loyal guards."

"Who?" Tinok asks excitedly.

"I talked briefly with Yorn," he explains. "And I saw Scar and Potbelly over in a different pen. Yorn said there were another three in there somewhere, but I didn't see them."

"Can they be trusted?" James asks.

"After what they've been through," Tinok exclaims, "you can be sure of it!"

"I agree," adds Jiron.

"So," James begins, "we have Tersa's auction in two days and I believe they said that the guys were to be auctioned off in, three?" He looks to Roland for confirmation who nods in agreement.

"Since it's beginning to get late, we may as well stay here through the night and then see about discovering where Miko is heading first thing in the morning." James looks around and everyone seems to be in agreement.

"It will also give me time to drop off the packages that I have for Korazan," Delia announces. When James looks to protest, she says, "It will give us more coins for the auctions and supplies."

"Alright, but don't go alone," James advises.

"I won't, I promise," she assures him.

The next morning, Delia takes Tinok and Roland with her as well as a wagon to deliver her packages. After they leave, James takes his mirror out and finds Miko still riding in the wagon. "He's heading south," he announces.

"How do you know?" Cassie asks as she sits next to him in order to look in the mirror.

Pointing to Miko and the wagon, he explains. "See how the shadows fall? They're falling to the right of the wagon, so that means the sun is to the left of them. Which in turn can only mean he's heading south."

"Oh," she says.

Replacing the mirror back in his shaving kit, he then takes out his shaving knife and proceeds to remove what little stubble has appeared since the last time. While he's shaving, Cassie remains sitting next to him and he asks, "You like Tinok, don't you?"

Blushing slightly, she says, "Is it that noticeable?"

"Well, you two are hardly seen apart," he explains.

"He is so nice and brave," she says. "I didn't care for him at first, but now that I've come to know him, I do."

"I think you two are very good together," he tells her.

Smiling, she says, "So do I."

At just that moment, Arkie begins crying so she gets up and hurries over to help Ezra. James smiles at her retreating back as she walks over to where they're sitting in the shade of the wagons.

Finished with getting the stubble off, he replaces his knife and mirror back in the kit. He notices Jiron pacing impatiently about the camp as he waits for the upcoming auction. When his pacing brings him near, James says, "Relax."

"Can't," he replies as he pauses a moment.

"Tomorrow won't get here any faster," he tells him.

"I know," admits Jiron, "but I can't just sit and do nothing all the while knowing she's stuck in there." He then resumes his pacing.

Several hours later, Delia and crew come back with a wagon much emptier than had left. "How did you do?" James asks as they roll up.

"You're not going to believe it!" she exclaims. "We received two hundred golds for one package alone! Altogether, we collected seven hundred and fifty six golds." Beaming, she pats a small chest resting on the floor of the wagon by her feet.

"Impressive," he says as he helps her down from the wagon.

"Thanks," she replies.

Tinok says, "We were unable to find out anything about your friend. We didn't push too hard for answers since we wanted to avoid drawing attention."

"I understand," responds James. He goes over to Roland and asks, "Would you mind going into town with me? There's something I'd like to get."

"Sure, what?" he asks.

"I want to find someone who can make a belt for me to hold my slugs," he explains.

"Right now?" he asks.

"If you don't mind," says James.

"Alright." He says a few words to Ezra and then with Jiron tagging along, they head back into town.

After inquiring with several locals, they at last make their way to a clothier who specializes in leather. Walking into the store, they see many different types of goods made almost entirely of leather; belts, coats, hats, etc. Bent over a table is a man currently working on stitching a belt together. When they enter, he looks up and says, "One moment, please," and then finishes up with a few more stitches.

Thankful that the man speaks his language, James says, "Not a problem."

When he's done, the man sets the belt aside and then asks, "How can I help you?"

Stepping up to the table James says, "I am interested in a belt, one that will hold the slugs for my sling so I can have ready access to them."

"Like what?" the man asks.

"I want firm pockets attached to the outside of the belt, just large enough to hold each slug firmly so it won't fall out as I move," James explains. "There should also be a slit up the middle where I can grab it with my finger to pull it out."

The man takes out a piece of parchment and begins drawing what James is describing. After a couple corrections, James is satisfied the man understands what he's asking of him. "I could get something like this done for you," the man says, "for about five silvers."

"I'll give you six if you can finish it by sundown tomorrow?" James offers.

Shaking his head, the man says, "I have another order that I must do first, but I can have it ready by day after tomorrow, for six."

"Alright," James says as he hands over three silvers. "I'll give you the rest when I pick it up."

Taking the coins, the man says, "Very well, day after tomorrow."

James shakes his hand and then they leave his shop.

They make it back to their camp and spend a restless evening as they wait for the morning, and Tersa's auction.

The sun no more crests the horizon before Jiron is itching to get going to the slave market for his sister.

"Relax," Roland says, "the auction doesn't start until two hours after sunup."

"Still," Jiron says as he resumes his pacing.

Once they've had breakfast, Jiron, Roland and James leave for the auction. Jiron sets a fast pace and the coins in James' shirt that he had brought for the auction can be heard jingling with every step.

At the gates to the slaver's compound, they find a line of people has already begun to form to enter. They wait their turn and finally pass through into the courtyard beyond.

They see that one of the platforms on the edge of the courtyard has been set up for the auction. Pressing through the crowd they maneuver to get as close to the front as possible. Jiron looks around at all the people waiting for the opportunity to purchase a living being and it just makes him angry.

Several slavers are already in position there on the platform, watching the crowd as the courtyard fills up. Each has a whip hanging at their waists. Jiron stands there impatiently for over ten minutes before a door finally opens in the side of the courtyard and a line of girls comes out. Jiron looks over at them anxiously but doesn't see Tersa among them.

The auctioneer steps to the front of the platform and calls for the first girl to be brought forward. When she approaches the front of the stage, one of the auctioneer's assistants removes the girls clothing. Standing there naked, she starts crying as they turn her around, showing her off to the crowd.

Once the auctioneer has spoken to the crowd, the bidding begins and James sees those in the crowd raising their hands. When the bidding is done and the girl is being led to the man who bought her, Roland says, "She went for seventy five gold."

"Is that a lot?" James asks.

Shrugging, Roland replies, "I don't know, I've never been here for this kind of auction."

One by one they watch as the girls are brought forward, displayed and then sold. Once sold, each has a tether attached around their neck before being led off the platform to be received by their new owner. One girl collapses in a faint and has to be carried away. The onlookers laugh while some call out to the new owner as he goes to take his property.

The next line of girls are brought out and at the head of the line is Tersa, not looking nearly as nervous as the rest of them. James can see her searching the faces of the crowd, trying to find her brother, but isn't able to.

When she is brought to stand next to the auctioneer and stripped, James thought Jiron was going to run up there, killing everyone. But to his surprise, he took it stoically and endured this so he may have her back. The bidding commences and Roland raises his hand to make a bid. It had been decided he should be the one to bid on her since he understands the language.

During the bidding, James watches Tersa as her eyes move from one bidder to the next in a hopeful attempt to locate her brother. He can see a slight uplifting at the corners of her mouth when her eyes stop their roving and settle on her brother standing next to one of the bidders. A slight smile escapes her as she stands there on the platform, knowing her brother is out there.

Roland continues bidding until all but a few are still with him. Then, from the back of the crowd, a loud voice says something and the crowd becomes positively silent. Looking back over the crowd, James sees a large man, easily a head taller than anyone else in the courtyard. Bald head and extensively tattooed, with two swords strapped to his back, he strides to the front as the crowd quickly parts for him like the sea for Moses.

All the other bidders are silent as the man strides forward, confident that she is his. When Roland doesn't say anything, Jiron says, "Bid!"

"But…" he stammers.

Jiron, having picked up a little of the language after having listened to the bidding, shouts out a bid in their language.

The crowd collectively catches their breath and the auctioneer pales. The giant of a man suddenly stops and turns to see Jiron staring fiercely back at him. He cries something out and again the crowd gasps.

"What's going on?" James asks.

"That's a Parvati," he says, "terrible fighters."

"And?" Jiron asks.

"They have a custom that is supported by the Empire," Roland explains. "They may call for a blood duel if anyone crosses them."

James looks shocked by that, "Why in god's name would they support a custom like that?"

"They serve the Empire loyally and fiercely," he explains. "That's why no one crosses them, those that do, die." He looks at Jiron and says somewhat nervously, "He has called one on you for challenging his right to this slave."

Jiron looks over at the Parvati and sees him staring back at him. The crowd begins to widen into a circle, a wide circle.

"So now…" begins James.

"Jiron must fight him, right here, right now," he finishes. Looking to Jiron, Roland says, "You have no choice in the matter and it's to the death."

Jiron looks toward Tersa, who is standing there on the platform, uncertain now that things are not going exactly as she had anticipated. He removes his excess native attire and with a glance to the waiting Parvati, he pulls his knives and advances.

"Good luck," says James.

"Thanks," Jiron says nonchalantly, "just like back in the pits."

As he advances, the Parvati draws both swords, one slightly shorter than the other. Not nearly as confident as he's making out, Jiron sizes up his opponent as he would in the pits.

When he's within about six feet of the Parvati he stops and waits for the attack. Knives are no good against an opponent who's prepared and waiting for your attack, you've got to get them moving so an opening will present itself that you can take advantage of. Those in the pits who failed to learn that didn't last too long.

With a roar, the Parvati slashes with his longsword while keeping his shorter one close for defense.

Jiron dances back and lets the sword pass by in front of him, mere inches away, never once taking his eyes from the Parvati's.

The Parvati studies Jiron and then begins a series of attacks using both the long and short sword.

Jiron easily deflects each blow, trying not to absorb too much of the impact. *He's good, but not the best I've seen*, Jiron thinks as his knives move to counter each attack.

The Parvati stops his attacks and steps back as he stares in disbelief at the little man with the two knifes. The expression on his face says he doesn't understand why Jiron is still standing.

Again the Parvati closes to attack Jiron and launches complicated pattern, using attacks and feints to try to get within Jiron's defense. Unable to breach it, the Parvati begins growing frustrated at not being able to kill this upstart. Suddenly, pain erupts from his left outer thigh and he's shocked to see blood beginning to well from a shallow cut that Jiron had managed to land.

The crowd gasps, utterly surprised that this man with knives against swords had managed to draw first blood, especially against a Parvati.

James nudges Roland who turns to see him there with a smile on his face, "He's good."

"I see that," Roland says, amazed.

His pride wounded at not drawing first blood, the Parvati screams and presses the attack, trying to connect less by skill than by brute strength.

This new series of attacks begins to leave Jiron's arms fatigued from having to take more of the force of the blow on his knives rather than deflecting it away. Deciding to change tactics, Jiron goes on the offensive, startling the Parvati who's not used to such a maneuver from an opponent.

With amazing agility, Jiron manages to get within his guard and scores another slash across his chest. Not deep, but it's a staggering blow to the Parvati's ego. Jiron takes a few steps back to catch his breath as he watches to see what the Parvati will do next.

The Parvati stands there staring at the blood coming from his chest and then looks over to Jiron. His eyes begin to turn red and flecks of foam can be seen at the edges of his mouth. *Berserker!* Jiron recognizes the signs from others he had faced in the pits. Berserkers are incredibly dangerous, but often leave themselves open for counter attacks, providing their opponent lives that long.

With a cry unlike any he had uttered thus far, the Parvati races toward Jiron, swords flying with incredible speed. Jiron's knives deflect blow after blow, his arms deadening from the impact of a berserker's strength.

Then the moment comes that he was waiting for, a series of attacks that will bring the longsword into just the right position. He catches the longsword between his knives and twists while at the same time jerking the longsword. To the amazement of the onlookers, the Parvati's longsword flies out of his hand and sails over the crowd. Onlookers dive out of the way as the sword strikes the ground, its point sinking a foot into the ground. Everyone looks in awe at the weapon standing upright a dozen feet from the combatants.

The loss of his sword snaps the Parvati out of the berserker's rage which greatly diminishes his strength. All berserkers use up most of their stamina while in the rage. He staggers backward, staring at his empty hand, not understanding what had just happened.

Taking the offensive, Jiron advances upon him, knives whirling in a pattern that a single sword is unable to defend against.

Doing his best, the Parvati, who had been so sure of victory, now was trying to merely survive. Cut after cut springs open upon his body; arms, legs, and chest all begin to well blood. Greatly weakened by the berserker rage, he's increasingly becoming unable to block Jiron's blows. Until at last, Jiron gets within his defense and slices him across the wrist, severing the tendons. Unable to hold the sword any longer, he watches as it falls from his now useless hand to the ground.

Without even pausing, Jiron moves in and finishes him off with a stab through the chest, puncturing his heart. To the shocked awe of the crowd, the Parvati falls to the ground, dead.

Coming over to him, James asks, "You okay?"

Nodding, Jiron says, "Just tired." He then reaches down and cleans his knives on his opponent's shirt. Once his knives are sheathed, he takes the Parvati's purse and walks up to the auctioneer. Roland joins him before he reaches the platform.

The auctioneer says something and Roland says, "She's yours, Jiron, free and clear."

Jiron turns to Tersa as she comes down the steps off the platform. They give him a slave shift for her and he puts it on her. Giving her an apologetic look, he takes the tether that had been placed around her neck and then leads her out of the courtyard while the onlookers move aside, clearing a path for them.

She tries to give him a hug once they're outside the slaver compound, but he stops her saying, "Not here, not now." Understanding, she continues to play the part of a slave until they reach the caravan.

Chapter   Fifteen

When they leave the city and are seen approaching the caravan, Delia and Tinok leave the others and race toward them. Delia gives Tersa a big hug while Tinok pats Jiron on the back.

Jiron takes hold of the tether around his sister's neck and uses one of his knives to cut it off of her. The world seems to stop for a moment as they finally look at each other, reunited after so many hardships. Allowing herself to finally express her emotions, Tersa hugs her brother as tears begin to fall.

The others remove themselves closer to the wagons to give them a moment alone and James relates the events back at the slaver compound. When he gets to the part where Jiron is fighting the Parvati, Jiron and Tersa join the group. After he's finished, Tinok says, "Wish I could have been there."

Delia goes over to one of the wagons and brings back a small, rectangular box and hands it Tersa. Opening it, she finds a beautiful new dress inside. She looks to Delia, almost ready to break down into tears again. "Thank you!" she exclaims as she removes the dress from the box.

Smiling, Delia says, "I just thought you would want something other than slave rags to wear."

Jiron gets up and hugs Delia, saying, "I never even thought about clothes for her, thank you."

Returning his hug, she pats him on the shoulder as she says, "You're a man. I figured you wouldn't."

Tersa turns to her brother and asks, "Are we going back home?"

"I don't think there's any home to go back to," he says, hating the words even though he knows they're the truth.

"But," she says, apprehensively, "what are we to do?"

"First thing is to get you out of those rags," Delia says as she leads her over to a wagon where she has a couple blankets already set up for privacy while Tersa changes.

"Just what are we to do now?" asks Tinok while Tersa is changing.

"Miko is still heading south," James replies and then he explains how he figured that out. "I plan to continue south and find him." He looks around at everyone else before adding, "You needn't feel obligated to accompany me, now that your sister is back with you."

Jiron gives him a look and says, "We're not about ready to turn our back on you, James."

"That's right," Tinok joins in. "Besides, where would we go?"

"Right now, we're together and being together gives us security," Roland adds. "No point breaking it up just yet. I figure as long as we act the part of traders, we will be left alone." Looking around at the group he says, "We don't exactly look the part of spies or invaders."

"True," agrees James. "I'm not sure how far my quest for him will lead us, though."

"Doesn't matter," Jiron replies. "We're standing by you till you see it through."

"Thank you," James replies, "I was hoping you would."

Just then, Delia returns with a much changed Tersa. She had brushed out her hair and cleaned her up. The guys catch their breath at the vision of feminine beauty walking toward them.

"Tersa," Jiron exclaims, "I can't believe that's you."

"Do I look alright?" she asks.

"Alright?" Tinok says with a smile. "You're gorgeous." Cassie gives him an annoyed look. "But not as gorgeous as you," he tells her which softens her expression.

James can only nod his head, words escape him.

"Thanks," she says, blushing slightly.

"But I think we need to get her other more practical, traveling clothes," Delia says. "This dress will hardly be suitable for the road."

"Good idea," James says, "we all could use a change of clothes. We're not leaving until after tomorrow anyway."

"Then it's settled," Delia announces, "Roland, Ezra and I will go in and purchase more clothes." Turning to Tersa she says, "It would probably be best for you to stay here."

Tersa nods her head in agreement, "I would prefer that."

"When we get back," she says to the others, "then you guys can go and get some extras for yourselves as well."

"Maybe we should get equipment for the guys we're going to buy tomorrow?" Tinok asks.

"Might not be a bad idea," agrees James. "Do you know what we're going to need for them? And the sizes?"

"I think so," says Jiron. "I know who three of them are, so we can at least get those three set up and then just see about the rest once they're here."

"We have six additional horses," James says. "Will they be able to ride?"

Jiron and Tinok look at each other and laugh.

"What's so funny?" James asks.

"I don't think they've ever been on a horse before," Jiron says.

"Yeah, they're going to be sore!" Tinok exclaims and then commences laughing once again.

Delia and her group head out toward town to do their shopping while the rest just hang around the wagons, waiting. Jiron and Tersa swap stories of what's happened to them since the last time they were together. When he mentions James and his ability to do magic, she looks over to him with wide eyes, a little fearful.

"You've nothing to worry about," her brother assures her. "He's nothing like the stories of mages that we grew up on, he's okay. Besides, without him I wouldn't be here."

Seeing him noticing her looking at him, she flashes him a quick, slightly embarrassed smile and then resumes her conversation with her brother.

Several hours later, they finally see Delia and her group returning. Trailing along behind are a couple boys carrying armloads of packages.

"Think you got enough?" Jiron asks, a slight smile on his face.

"Hope so," she says, oblivious to his sarcasm. "Just a few necessities that will be needed."

Ezra has a new sling for Arkie slung across her chest, his wide, curious eyes peering out from within.

"Just put them in that wagon there," she tells the porters. When they've placed them in the desired location, she gives them each two coppers and they return back to the city.

"Shall we?" Jiron asks James.

"Yeah, lets," he agrees. So this time, James, Jiron, Tinok and Roland go into town to get the equipment they'll need tomorrow for their new 'guards', as well as some extra clothes for themselves.

Their first stop is a clothier where they each purchase a second set of clothes, as well a set for the guys they'll be purchasing tomorrow. James arranges to have them delivered back to the caravan.

Outside the clothier's, Roland asks, "Now where to?"

"Need to get some weapons for them as well," Jiron says. "If they're going to be guards, they won't do much good without them."

"True," agrees James. Asking a passerby, Roland learns of a blacksmith across town that usually has a surplus supply of weapons for sale. They proceed over there to see what he has available.

On the way they see a group of Parvatis coming down the street toward them, five of them, their distinctive tattoos giving them a menacing appearance. Unsure as to how they are likely to react over the outcome of the fight earlier, James leads them down a side alley. Hiding in the shadows against one of the walls, they wait until they see the group pass by the mouth of the alley. Then Jiron returns to the end and peers around the corner to see if the coast is clear. When he sees the Parvatis have moved down the street, he gives the others an all-clear signal and they return to the street.

"That was close," Roland says.

"Don't know if we could have fought off that many," James says. "Not and avoid unwanted attention."

Keeping a lookout for more roving bands of Parvatis, they continue toward the blacksmith's.

Having to ask for directions two more times, they finally arrive outside of an open courtyard where metal being hammered can be heard coming from within a building off to the side. Entering the courtyard, they see where the side of the building opens up and in the shade given by an overhang, a burly man is busily hammering a piece of metal upon an anvil. To James' relief, the man appears to have originated from the north.

At their approach, he puts the hot metal into a bucket of water, a steaming hiss and a cloud of steam appears when the hot metal hits the water. He holds it there but a moment before quickly removing it. After a quick inspection, he places the piece of metal upon a nearby table and turns to greet them. "Good day to you sirs," he says.

"Good day to you as well," replies James. "We were told that you may have some weapons available for sale?"

"That I do," the blacksmith tells him. "If you'll follow me, I'll show you what I have."

"Thank you," says James.

Following the blacksmith, they enter the building through a side door where they find many racks holding various types of weapons. There are swords, knives, maces and several others that James has never seen before, all looking very deadly.

"What exactly are you interested in?" he asks.

James turns to Jiron and looks at him questioningly.

"Yorn usually used a longsword and shield," he says.

"Potbelly likes two swords and Scar uses a shortsword and knife," Tinok adds.

"If you gentlemen would like, feel free to look around and examine the weapons," the blacksmith suggests.

"Thank you, we will," replies James.

They inspect the various weapons while the blacksmith looks on. James is totally at a loss as far as telling if a weapon is good or bad, so he stands back and lets Jiron and Tinok decide.

After inspecting all the swords and knives, feeling for balance and sharpness, they settle on the ones that are the best of the lot. Unfortunately, the blacksmith doesn't have any shields, they'll have to find an armorer for that. James lets Jiron do the haggling and then hands over the coins.

When James asks if they can be delivered to their caravan, the blacksmith says, "My apprentice is currently out for his midday meal, but when he returns I can have him take them out first thing."

"Thank you," says James, "we would appreciate that."

Leaving the blacksmith's shop, they go in search of an armorer for a shield for Yorn, there's no way they'll be able to afford any armor. They find a shop boasting a sign bearing a shield upon it not very far from the blacksmith's shop. Inside they find many different shields available in different sizes, thickness and strength. Jiron finds one that he says is similar to the one Yorn had used back in the pits.

Handing over the coins, James realizes that they've all but exhausted the money that he brought with him. They take the shield with them, since it would be no burden to carry back.

After leaving the armorer's shop, they head on back to the caravan. On the way, they again run across the group of Parvatis, only this time the Parvatis see them first and alter course to intercept.

Seeing them approaching, James fears the worse and readies one of his slugs. The Parvatis come close before stopping in front of them, the leader of the group takes a further step forward and says something.

Roland replies to him and then he says something else. Turning to the others, Roland says, "He's asking if you're the man who fought the blood duel with the Parvati earlier in the slaver compound." Looking worried, he asks, "What should I tell him?"

"Tell him the truth," Jiron replies and turns his gaze to fixate on the leader.

Turning back to the Parvati, Roland tells him that Jiron is in fact the one, pointing him out.

The leader turns to Jiron and reaches into his tunic, bringing out a necklace with three spherical stones. He says something to Roland as he hands it to Jiron.

Taking the necklace, Jiron looks questioningly to Roland.

"He says that to defeat a Parvati in a blood duel is an amazing thing," he explains. "He also says that it shows great skill and this necklace will show any Parvati that you are to be treated with respect. It kind of makes you one of them."

Jiron gives the Parvati a slight bow and says, "Tell him I am greatly honored to be accounted as one of the Parvatis."

Roland translates for the Parvati, who breaks into a smile and says something else. Then he turns and the group walks away.

"What did he say?" James asks.

"He said 'May your knives drink deeply'," Roland tells him.

Jiron places the necklace around his neck as he watches the departing Parvatis.

"Thought we were in trouble for a moment there," admits James.

"Me too," adds Roland.

"Let's get back to the caravan," Jiron says as he begins walking.

It doesn't take them very long to find their way back and they're surprised to find that the packages containing their clothes have already been delivered.

"If we keep buying stuff," James observes when he sees the water wagon is beginning to be filled with their things, "we'll need to get another wagon just for belongings."

"Probably," Delia admits.

Shortly after the sun crests the horizon the following morning, James, Jiron and Roland are again heading back into town for the auction. Before leaving, James fills his money pouch once more from the chest and realizes that they've spent almost all of it. He mentions the fact they're running out of money to Delia and she says, "I'll see what I can do."

"Alright," James replies.

As they leave, Delia hollers out, "Don't get into any fights this time!"

When they arrive at the slaver's compound, people recognize Jiron from the day before. Many come up and congratulate him on his victory over the Parvati. Due to his notoriety, they are allowed to proceed to the front of the crowd for the auction.

After a wait of about fifteen minutes, they begin to see slavers coming onto the platform and shortly afterward, the first line of slaves is brought out. These are men this time and they look as if they are all from the fall of the City of Light. Their ages range anywhere from fifteen to fifty, some look to have had an exceptionally hard time if the number of bruises covering their bodies is any indication.

"Recognize any of them?" James asks.

"A couple," Jiron replies, "though none of the ones we're interested in."

The auctioneer begins and they quickly go from one to the next until the entire line has been sold. "They're going for a lot less than the girls had," Roland tells them.

"Wouldn't be surprised," James comments.

When they bring the next batch out, Jiron says to Roland, "I see Yorn. He's the third in line."

Roland nods and waits until the first two have been sold and then joins in the bidding for Yorn. Whether it's because he's with Jiron or because no one wants him, the auction lasts only a few rounds. Having outbid everyone else, Roland moves forward and pays for him. Leading Yorn by his tether, Roland brings him over to the waiting group. Upon seeing Jiron there, he smiles briefly before resuming the stoic look of a slave.

Jiron gives him a nod and then turns his attention back to the auction. The rest of the line is auctioned off quickly and then another batch of slaves is brought out. "There are Scar and Potbelly," he tells Roland.

"Which ones?" he asks.

"Scar's the first in line and Potbelly is the fifth," he points them out. "Did you tell them about me?" he whispers to Yorn.

He shakes his head and whispers back, "You asked me not to. But they saw you fighting here yesterday, so when they mentioned it to me, I let them in on it."

Jiron nods his head as he turns back to the auction. When Roland goes up to get him, Scar gives him a look that says he's dead and gets a lash across the shoulders for it. When he's led back to the group, he begins to smile when he sees Jiron and Yorn standing there, then remembers himself and again dons the look of a dejected slave. They wait for Potbelly's turn and in just a few minutes, he's standing there amongst them too.

When the next line is brought out, James hears Jiron gasp. "What?"

"See that little guy there," he says, "second in line?"

"Yeah," James replies.

"He's another of the knife fighters, not as good as Tinok and me, but good," he explains. "He used to show me how he could hit an apple thrown in the air with his throwing knives, though of course he was never allowed to use them in the pits." Turning to Roland, he says, "We want him and number five."

Roland nods and commences to bid for them when their turn comes.

"Number five's name is Stig, he's good with mace and shield," he explains.

Soon, they're standing with the group as well. Jiron has to silence them on more than one occasion when they begin to talk amongst themselves.

The next line doesn't contain anyone that they're interested in, although Jiron gets a satisfied look on his face when they're brought out. James notices his expression and asks him about it.

"The third guy in line," he says, pointing him out. "He once tried to accost Tersa and had to spend two weeks recovering when I was through with him. Glad he's up there."

He gets bought by a farmer whom they hear needs help on his farm. "Back breaking labor," Jiron says. "Good!" He watches with great satisfaction as the man is taken by the farmer and led out of the compound.

The next line finally yields the last one they're here for, a young man of average build, who Jiron says is very deadly with the quarterstaff. Once he's bought, they lead their newly acquired slaves out of the courtyard and back to the caravan.

After they arrive at the caravan, Jiron removes their tethers and says, "You guys are expensive."

They all laugh at that, "Thanks, man," Yorn says to Jiron.

"Don't thank me," he says, "thank James, he's the one who paid for you."

They all express their thanks to him. Delia begins to hand out the clothes that they bought for the ones they knew about and they quickly remove their slave clothes and don the others.

While they're changing, Jiron explains what's going on and that they're still searching for James' friend, Miko. How they're going to act as a caravan and that they'll be playing the part of the guards.

"You know," Scar says after he hears about Miko, "an official came through and took a whole bunch of them the morning after the escape attempt."

"Yeah," says the little guy whose name, accurately enough, is Shorty. "The slaver in charge seemed really unhappy about him coming and taking them all away."

"It seemed like he had no choice in the matter," adds Potbelly. "Your friend is most likely in that group."

"Think we could find out where they're headed?" James asks. "I do know they are at least headed south."

"Maybe," Jiron says.

"We still need some weapons, too," Shorty pipes up.

"We got enough left for that?" Jiron asks James.

"Might have," he says.

"Let's go back in and get the rest of it then," he says.

"May as well," James replies as he grabs Roland and with Jiron, head back into town. The newly acquired 'guards' are more than happy to stay behind and catch up on what's going on with Tinok and the others.

Their first stop is to the clothier to pick up James' belt for his iron slugs. He's managed to have the belt ready and James tries it on, a perfect fit. Taking a slug out of a pocket, he tries sliding it in. It's a firm fit and is unlikely to fall out on its own. Using his finger, he presses against the slug through the slit in the side of the pouch and is able to slide it out with little difficulty.

"Perfect," he tells the man as he hands over the remaining three silvers he owes.

"I'm glad," the clothier says as he takes the coins. "I've never seen anything like that before."

"Common where I come from," he says, thinking of gun belts. "Thank you," he says as he makes ready to leave.

"You're very welcome," the clothier says. "Do come again."

After leaving the clothier's shop, they complete the rest of their shopping quickly, this time carrying their belongings with them since there isn't quite as much as before.

When they return to the caravan and distribute the clothes and weapons, Shorty is absolutely ecstatic about the set of throwing knives they bought him. Taking one out, he throws it at nearby tree where it strikes point first and embeds itself three inches into the trunk. He runs over and removes it, replacing it back in the belt with the others.

James takes in the newly dressed men and is satisfied that they should now be less likely to stand out, as well as better protected.

"James," Delia says to him as she approaches.

"Yeah?" he asks.

"Do you think it would be possible to find out where your friend Miko is heading?" she asks.

"Why?" he asks her.

"I've found out there are two main roads to the south and if I knew which one we'll be taking, I may be able to arrange for cargo to help replenish our depleted supply of coins."

"Maybe," he says as he gets up to retrieve the mirror from his shaving kit. Settling on the ground with the mirror cupped within his hands, he concentrates on Miko.

Delia sits down next to him and watches as Miko appears, still riding in the wagon. "Can you expand the image? Try to see more of the surrounding area," she asks. "One of the roads follows the river that flows out of the lake."

Nodding, he concentrates and they watch as the view expands and sure enough, the road is following the river. "Does that help?" he asks her.

"Yes, it does," she says. Getting up, she signals Roland and Tinok and they follow her as she heads back to town.

He relaxes the rest of the afternoon, watching as the men get familiar with their new weapons, sparring with one another. James is amazed at the speed with which they move their weapons, also surprising is that no one is even nicked by a blade during it all.

The lad with the quarterstaff works primarily by himself, whirling and twirling the staff until it begins to whine. He sees James watching him and gives him a nod, smiling, before resuming the practice.

Several hours later, when the sun begins to dip toward the horizon, Delia returns. Tinok is carrying a large sack full of food, "I thought everyone could use one last good meal before we hit the road tomorrow," she explains.

"Good idea," he says.

"I did manage to acquire a couple consignments, nothing major, that are to be delivered at a few towns along the road," she tells him. "They'll be bringing them out to us in a little while."

When the smell of the roasted meat contained within the sack hits the guys practicing, all practicing halts as they hurry over to get some.

Ravenous for some real food, they pretty much consume it all, but not before everyone else was able to get some for themselves.

Over the next hour, three different wagons come and deliver the goods for transport, transferring them to their wagons.

Delia comes over to James and sits down, saying, "I neglected to mention to you that the road your friend is traveling on leads to the capitol of the Empire."

"Oh?" he replies.

"Doesn't that make you nervous?" she asks.

"A little," he admits, "but there's not much I can do about it, is there?"

"No, I suppose not," she replies.

When they all settle down for the night, there is one thing that James realizes that he forgot to get for the new arrivals, bedrolls. But they don't seem to mind, sleeping free is good no matter what.

Chapter Sixteen

The next morning they begin rolling with the rising of the sun, everyone is anxious to leave Korazan and the slave market behind.

With Jiron riding lead, the rest of the guards space themselves along the caravan with Potbelly at the rear. Getting them into the saddle that morning brought back the time when he first started riding back in Trendle. Smiling at the memory, he watches as Jiron and Tinok attempt to show them the proper way to mount a horse.

After several attempts, which remind James of an old Three Stooges' episode, they manage to get everyone one into the saddle. The first couple of miles are the worse as the novice riders begin to get the hang of commanding their horses, as well as staying upon them. By the end of the first day, they're all sore and stiff; oh the complaining that was heard around the campfire that night. You would've thought they had just fought a hard and long campaign and suffered grievous wounds.

"You poor little babies," Tinok says mockingly as they sit and moan about their sore posteriors. "Do you want me to rub your bum bums for you?"

"Shut up!" Scar says to him.

"Yeah, or we'll beat your head in," adds Potbelly as he gingerly sits down near the campfire.

Tinok just laughs and says, "By this time tomorrow, you should be really stiff and sore."

They just give him an ugly look and say nothing.

"It takes a few days for you to get use to sitting on a horse," Jiron assures them. "It does get better, once your muscles become accustomed to it."

"I hope so," says Qynn, the quarterstaffer.

Delia sees James sitting a little ways off by himself and goes over to him. "You okay?" she asks him.

"Just worried about Miko is all," he tells her.

"Did you check the mirror again?" she asks when she sees it lying next to him.

"Yeah, it just shows him still traveling," he replies. "I think they're making better time than we are."

"Not too surprising since they don't have wagons slowing them down," she reasons.

"It just seems like we're getting further and further behind," he says despondently. "Sometimes I feel like I'll never be able to catch up with him."

"They've got to stop some time," she assures him.

Sighing, he says, "I know, it just gets to me once in a while."

"Come on over to the camp and join the rest of us," she suggests. "It'll take your mind off your worries for a time."

Nodding his head, he gets up and comes back over to the campfire, where Scar and Potbelly are regaling everyone with their exploits at the fall of the City of Light.

"...and then when the last one fell," Scar is saying, "we ran, trying to find a way out of the City."

"Yeah," Potbelly joins in, "by that time there was only four of us left. We didn't get far before Hinck and Olin bought it."

"A squad of soldiers had come upon us and the fighting was fierce. Me and Potbelly stood back to back, Hinck and Olin did the same. After the last of the soldiers we were facing fell was when we saw them lying dead," Scar says. "From the stack of bodies surrounding them, they must've taken out over a dozen before being overpowered."

"Those of the pits are hard fighters," Jiron says.

Tinok nods his head and adds, "The best."

"Then what happened?" Cassie asks from where she's sitting next to Tinok, eyes wide at their account.

"They took us the only way you can take a pit fighter," Scar explains. "We rounded a corner and came face to face with half a dozen crossbowmen and that was that."

"Yeah," Potbelly adds. "They bound us and before we knew it, we're tied in the slave lines outside the City with the rest of them that were took."

Jiron holds up his water bottle and says, "Not much to toast with, but here's to the pit fighters who didn't make it through the last battle."

The others hold up theirs, pausing in a silent toast, and then take a drink.

Suddenly Arkie begins to cry and Roland and Ezra make their goodnights as they take Arkie to the wagon where they bed down for the night.

Shortly after they've left, the rest begin to turn in, until the only one still up is Stig who managed to draw first watch. He begins walking a perimeter in the dark around their camp. The sound of the crackling of the fire and his footsteps as he walks around the camp are the only sounds James hears as he tries to fall asleep. Worry about Miko's fate, as well as those traveling with him, weigh heavily upon him. Eventually though, sleep wins out.

The next morning, Tinok takes great pleasure in watching as his friends get up and begin to work the stiffness and aches out of their legs.

"You all look like a bunch of old ladies the way you're hobbling around like that," he informs them, smiling at their misery.

"Leave 'em alone, Tinok" Jiron tells him.

"Alright," he agrees when he sees how serious Jiron is, "I'll leave 'em alone."

They're able to get back in their saddles, but not without groans of pain. "You wouldn't think they had spent years in the pits to hear them carry on so," Jiron whispers to James.

"This is different," he replies. "Besides it may not be just the pain, but an outlet for the fear and humiliation they've endured while they were slaves."

Jiron nods his head and says, "Perhaps."

After leaving the caravansary, they pull back onto the road. At the gates of Korazan, they come to where the road splits. They can either continue on through the gates and into Korazan, or turn left to follow the road around the walls rather than trying to forge their way through the crowded streets.

Jiron leads them to the left and around the walls. On the far side of the city, they rejoin the main road and follow it as it follows the shoreline of the lake. Before they reach the southern shore of the lake, the road splits. One branch continues following alongside the lake while the other takes a more southeasterly direction.

James hollers to Jiron to continue following the road by the lake. He glances back and nods as he turns his horse to follow it. Not too long after that, they come to the southern shore of the lake and begin to follow the river flowing out of it to the south.

The road is quite busy with many people, both walking and riding, passing them on their way to Korazan. At one point, a long caravan passes them going north, James counts twenty five wagons and almost thirty guards.

A couple of hours past midday they come across a man on the side of the road who's standing by a wagon with a broken wheel. When Jiron comes abreast of him, the man says something but he's unable to understand what.

"Can't understand you," he says to the man.

Looking frustrated, the man starts speaking to Jiron again, and this time talking real slow. He takes extra care to pronounce his words more carefully and clearly, as if that would enable Jiron to understand better.

By this time, Roland rolls up in his wagon and begins conversing with the man. With a look of relief, the man begins talking rapidly and when he pauses, Roland says to everyone gathered around, "He's asking if we can take him and his cargo on to the next town, a place called Inziala. Apparently, there's some kind of celebration going on there and he's been contracted to supply wine."

James looks at the poor man for a second before Roland says, "He's willing to pay us five golds just to transport him a few miles down the road."

"Sure," James agrees, "we've got the room." Turning to Stig and Scar he says, "Could you please help this gentleman transfer his barrels into the water wagon? There should be enough room for them."

They get down from their horses and proceed transferring the barrels from his wagon to theirs. The man starts speaking again and Roland tells them he's thanking them for their help. He then removes his horses from their traces and ties them to the rear of Roland's wagon. Once his horses are secured, he climbs up and sits on the seat next to Roland as he waits for his cargo to be transferred.

James can hear Stig mumbling, "Lazy merchant…"

"Yeah, he could've at least helped…" Scar says to Stig.

When all the barrels have been transferred, they get back into the saddle and their caravan continues on down the road. Roland talks with the merchant and then says to James in the next wagon, "It seems the celebration is a yearly festival where people come from far and wide to just have fun."

"Kind of like a county fair," states James.

"What's that?" Roland asks.

"It's a festival where I come from that happens every year," he replies.

"Oh," he says.

"Maybe we could stop for the night there?" Delia asks him. When he looks at her, she says, "It wouldn't take much time away from traveling, especially since we will need to stop for the night anyway. Also, I have a couple deliveries to drop off there as well."

"You guys can go have fun," he tells her, "but I don't think I'll be in much of a mood."

Three hours later they come to Inziala, a large city sitting at a crossroads. To the north of the city along the river is a large area with hundreds of tents spread out. A crowd of people are moving in and around the tents. *That must be the festival.*

To the east of town is an area where the caravans have all gathered while they're enjoying the fun. Finding a good spot near the other caravans, they set up camp while Delia takes the merchant with his wine over to the festival. She takes Scar and Potbelly along for protection.

After they're settled in, Tinok, Cassie, Jiron and Tersa along with Roland, Ezra and Arkie deicide to go and enjoy the festival. "Do you want to come along?" Cassie asks James.

Shaking his head, he says, "No thank you. Someone needs to stay here and look after things. Besides, I'm not really in the mood for fun."

"Miko?" she asks.

He just nods his head yes.

"I'm sorry," she says and then giggles as Tinok takes her by the hand as they head over to the festival. Over her shoulder she says, "Goodbye!"

"Have fun!" James hollers after them.

The four guards remaining see them walk over toward the festival and say, "When do we get to go?"

"I'll need four of you here at any one time to discourage any thieves," he replies. "When Scar and Potbelly get back with Delia, you can draw lots and then two at a time can go."

"Alright," Yorn says.

An hour later, they see Delia trundling her way back to their camp with Scar and Potbelly riding along beside.

"Everything okay?' he asks as she pulls up.

"Everything's fine," she assures him. "Got the five golds and another thirty for the packages I delivered."

"Great," he says.

Looking around, she says, "Just where is everyone?"

James indicates the festival and replies, "They left shortly after you did."

From the group of guards, he hears several curses and a cry for joy as they draw lots to see who gets to go. Stig and Shorty walk over to James with happy expressions on their faces, "So you guys get to go first?"

"That's right," Shorty says.

"Could we perhaps have a few coins to spend?" Stig asks.

"Sure," James says as he gets up and goes over to the money box. He takes out four silvers for each of the guards and hands them over.

"Can I come with you two?" Delia asks when she learns they are going over to the festival.

"Sure, milady," Stig says as he offers her his arm. His shield is slung across his back and his mace hangs at his hip.

Taking his arm, she says to James, "I'll be back later."

"Just send your escorts back in a couple of hours so the others can have their turn," he tells her.

"Okay," she replies. Then she turns to her escorts and says "You heard that, right?"

"Yes, ma'am," Shorty affirms.

They quickly make their way over to the festival. She feels bad about leaving James back at the wagons, but understands how he feels.

Many minstrels roam the grounds providing music and atmosphere to the festival. There are tents and booths set up throughout the area where festival goers can purchase a multitude of various items. She pauses in front of one that is selling small, wooden carvings of horses and admires the intricate workmanship that went into them. When the merchant asks if she would want to purchase one, he's disappointed when she shakes her head no and moves on.

They make their way further into the sea of tents and come across Roland and his family. Arkie is holding one of the wooden horses from the display she examined earlier, happily sucking on its head.

"Where are Tinok and Cassie?" she asks him.

"Don't know," he replies. "They went off with Jiron and Tersa shortly after we arrived."

"If you should run into them, tell 'em I'm here," she says.

"Sure, no problem," he replies. "James didn't come?"

Shaking her head, she says, "He didn't feel like it, still worried about his friend Miko."

Roland nods his head in understanding. "Want to stay with us?" he asks.

"Thanks, but I want to find Tinok and Cassie," she says as she glances around at the crowd of people, "somehow."

"Good luck," he says as they move further on, stopping at another booth selling colored bottles.

Delia and her escorts wind their way through the people, occasionally stopping at booths to browse the items on display.

They come to an open area where a man is trying to entice passersby to test their skill. He has a target set up over a hundred feet away and in front of him are several throwing knives. It looks like you throw one of the knives and try to hit the bull's eye in the center of the target.

Intrigued, Shorty comes up and takes one of the knives testing it for balanced. The man starts speaking to him but no one understands him. "Do you understand the common tongue?" Shorty asks him as he continues examining the knives before him.

"Yes sir," the man replies. "For just two coppers, you may try your skill and if you hit the bull's eye, you get one of these." He indicates a selection of jewelry and bracers.

"Alright," he says as he hands over one of the silvers James had given him. The man takes it and gives him his change. By this time a few onlookers have stopped to see how he'll do.

He selects the first knife he examined and then stands with his feet a foot apart so he's well balanced. Taking careful aim at the target, he takes a couple deep breaths and then throws the knife. It sails through the air and to the amazement of the crowd, strikes the target dead center. The onlookers cheer and the man says, "We have a winner, see how easy it is." To Shorty he says, "Please take your choice."

Selecting a necklace, he turns and offers it to Delia, saying, "I would be honored if you would accept this from me."

When she hesitates, he says, "You needn't feel it's a commitment, I would just like you to have it."

Taking the necklace, she puts it around her neck saying, "Thank you Shorty."

He smiles and blushes slightly.

As they move on, another person tries their luck but the knife flies wide, missing the target.

"Only one of the knives is balanced properly," he tells them. "If you were to use the others, you'd be in danger of hitting yourself," he continues, laughing.

They move along and eventually find the others sitting at a table enjoying a meal as they listen to a group of musicians. There's an open area in front of where the musicians play where people can go and dance if they like, a few couples are already out there.

As Delia approaches them, she catches Tinok's eye and asks, "Why aren't you out there dancing?"

Blushing slightly, he says, "I don't know any of the dances they're doing."

Taking a seat next to Cassie, she asks, "Need any help getting him out there?"

"Yes I do!" she says, acting as if she's put out. A smile on her lips tells her that she's not really.

The musicians finish their song to a smattering of applause and then begin another one, this time a fast paced song.

"Okay," Delia says to Tinok, "now's your chance, get moving."

Cassie gets up and practically drags him over to the dancing area.

"I never thought she would get him out there," Jiron says as he watches Tinok doing his best.

"For someone who's graceful in battle, he's sure clumsy out there," Tersa adds.

When Tinok looks over to them, with an expression bordering on fear, they all give him encouragement. After a few minutes he begins to get the hang of it and begins to flow with the music.

"Your turn dear brother," Tersa says as she drags him out there as well.

Delia sits and watches as Jiron and Tinok both fumble and misstep as they dance. Shaking her head and silently amused, she just sits back and enjoys herself.

Long after the sun has gone down, James finally sees them returning. "Have a good time?" he asks them.

Cassie comes straight to him and says, "Tinok and I are to be married!"

"What?" he exclaims, looking over to Tinok who's looking both happy and scared out of his mind.

"He proposed to me while we were dancing," she tells him.

"Congratulations," he says to them both, shaking Tinok's hand. "When will you be getting married?"

"We want to wait until we're back home or maybe in Cardri," Tinok says with his arm around her waist.

"That's right," adds Cassie. "We didn't want to be married in the Empire."

"I'm happy for both of you," he asserts warmly.

Cassie gives Tinok a big hug as they settle down around the fire and then leans her head on his shoulder. Tinok just sits there with a happy and contented look on his face as he holds her tight. Putting their heads together, they talk together quietly.

James awakens the next morning to find Tinok and Cassie sleeping together, wrapped up in each others arms. He begins to get the horses in their traces as everyone wakes up. Shortly, they're on the road again, making the best time they can.

He pushes them the entire day, anxious to get to Miko before something happens to him, only allowing a few short breaks before pressing on again. The miles quickly pass and by nightfall they've made it to a town called Jihara.

A small town, barely more than a village really but it has an inn where they can find some decent food. James offers to spring for a room for the two love birds but Cassie turns him down, saying it wouldn't be right for them to have one when no one else does. Much to the disappointment of her betrothed.

So they spend another night together wrapped up in a blanket on the ground. Everyone can see that the two of them are deeply in love and belong together.

The following morning, they get an early start. Before the sun has risen much above the horizon, they're already a mile down the road. A little before noon they begin to enter rolling hills, which James can see stretches a long way ahead of them. The road continues to follow the river as it winds its way through the hills.

Ever since Jihara, the other traffic on the road has dropped off to almost nothing, only the occasional rider or caravan is encountered. At sunset when they set up camp, they find an area adjacent to the river where they can have ready access to water. James even wades out into the river and does his fisherman routine and bags several large reddish orange fish.

"Neat trick," Roland says when James brings back his third fish.

"It comes in handy," he replies.

Everyone enjoys the fish and after dinner, they take turns telling stories or singing songs. Most of them seem to be love songs or stories about those in love. Stig begins recalling his first amorous encounter but Cassie begins to blush a deep red, causing him to cut it short. Tinok gives him a stern look before someone else breaks in and begins another song, this one a fast paced silly song for Arkie.

"Better get to sleep," James announces when the song is finally over. "I'd like to get an early start tomorrow." Some grumble about having to turn in, but most take it in stride. The only ones who don't seem to mind are Cassie and Tinok, who readily lay down together. Cassie lays her head on his chest and quickly falls asleep.

James looks over and sees Tinok's head up and he's looking around.

"What's the matter?" James asks him.

He gestures to Cassie sleeping on his chest and then whispers, "I gotta go pee!"

James tries to hide his amusement but fails as he just shrugs his shoulders at Tinok's predicament.

He starts to get up and Cassie wakes up. "I'll be right back," he assures her.

She lays her head down on the ground and says, "Hurry up."

In no time at all, he's back and she lays her head down on his chest again.

James lies down and continues to chuckle as he begins to fall asleep.

Ahhhh!

A cry in the night startles James awake just in time to see Qynn fall into the fire with an arrow piercing his chest. Without thought, he causes a great burst of light to explode over the camp and in that brief instance, sees a dozen or more attackers approaching from all directions.

Everyone comes awake when the light bursts overhead.

"We're under attack!" he yells as he gets up, trying to find the bowman.

Everyone bursts into action, the girls hiding under a wagon while the guys all grab their weapons and move to engage the enemy. With light to see by, the surprise the attackers held in the dark is now gone. The pit fighters rush to engage the attackers, wreaking havoc with skills honed by years in the pits.

James locates two bowmen who each get an arrow off before James has a chance to take them out. An attacker is rushing him and is almost upon him when a knife flies out from the camp, imbedding itself through the man's left eye. He turns and sees Shorty standing atop a wagon as he lets fly another knife at an approaching attacker.

Scar and Potbelly are standing back to back as they hold off three attackers while Jiron and Tinok are busy slicing and dicing ones of their own. He looks to see Stig engaged with a large attacker wielding a longsword. Stig deflects the thrust of the man's sword with his shield and then follows through with his mace, pulping the man's face. Seeing Scar and Potbelly engaged with three, he runs over to render aid.

Scar, with both swords weaving a pattern of death, takes out one of the ones pressing him and Potbelly. Turning to engage the other, he watches as a hole opens up in the man's chest, blood and gore spraying out his back. He looks behind him and sees James there with another slug as he prepares to take out another attacker. Between Potbelly and himself, they quickly take out the last of the attackers near them before Stig has a chance to join them.

Scar quickly looks around for another to engage but all he sees are dead bandits lying everywhere. Shorty jumps off the wagon and races over to where Qynn is burning in the fire and pulls him out. The smell of burnt flesh and hair permeates the entire area.

"Tinok!" he hears Delia's anguished cry. He looks over and sees her cradling Cassie's head in her lap, blood from where an arrow sticks out of her stomach rapidly spreading across her dress.

"Cassie!" Tinok's cry echoes across the battlefield as he races over to her.

He drops to his knees, tears falling from his eyes as he looks to Delia. She just shakes her head.

"Tinok," Cassie says weakly when she sees him there.

"Yes, my dearest," he says, trying to hold back the sobs.

"I can't wait to be your wife," she says, distantly.

"You will be soon," he says as he takes her into his arms, brushing strands of her golden hair out of her face.

"Don't leave me!" he cries as he starts to sob.

"Silly boy," she says as she looks into his eyes. "I'll never leave you. I love you."

"I love you too," he says to her. A tear falls from his face onto hers.

"Maybe tomorrow," she says as her voice begins to grow faint, "we can dance again." And then she smiles as he kisses her on the forehead. She closes her eyes as her body relaxes in death.

"Cassie!" Tinok cries as he gently shakes her as if she was just sleeping, "Oh my god, Cassie!" He then holds her tight to his chest as sobs rack his body. He just sits there holding her as he rocks back and forth.

His head snaps up as he looks to James with red, tear filled eyes, "You can save her, can't you?"

Shaking his head as his own tears fall, he says sadly, "Some things I'm unable to do."

"But..." and then he starts sobbing all over again.

Everyone leaves Tinok alone in his time of grief. Each in their own way cared for Cassie and her passing has touched each of them deeply. While Tinok mourns the loss of his beloved, the others go through the grisly process of removing the dead from the camp. James and Jiron go through all the dead bodies and collect what money they can.

"I think they were just bandits, out looking to rob us," Jiron says.

"It looks that way," agrees James. Then he gestures over to Tinok, "Think he'll be okay?"

"I don't know," Jiron says, "he really cared for her."

By this time, Yorn and the others have wrapped Qynn in a blanket. As they pick him up, he says to Jiron, "We're going to go bury him out in the desert."

Nodding, he replies, "Just a second and I'll come with you."

He was about to go over to Tinok when he all of a sudden stands up, holding Cassie in his arms. Without a word, he begins to carry her out to the desert. When he sees Jiron coming toward him, he just shakes his head and then is soon lost in the dark as he takes his beloved out into the desert to bury her.

"Alright," he says to Yorn as he joins them, "let's go."

James watches as they carry Qynn out to be buried, taking a different direction than Tinok so as not to intrude upon him.

James and the rest remain in the camp and wait for the others to return. No one feels like talking, each is lost in their own reflections.

In a little bit, Jiron and the others return from burying Qynn. He looks around and asks, "Tinok hasn't returned yet?"

"No," Delia replies.

He turns and looks out toward where he disappeared into the night with Cassie, worried for his friend. An hour later, Tinok comes back to camp. Eyes red and swollen from crying, and covered in dirt from where he dug her grave, he looks a pitiful sight. The necklace he had recently given her hangs around his neck. His knives are caked with dirt, obviously what he used to dig her grave. That above everything else gives Jiron cause to worry for his friend. Nothing has ever before meant more to him than his knives and for him to not have cleaned them cannot bode well.

He sits near the fire and stares vacantly into the flames. They try to engage him in conversation, telling him of their sorrow for his loss, but he doesn't respond. Eventually he just goes over to his bedroll and falls asleep.

The others stay up for a little longer, discussing their worries for Tinok and the loss of their friends. But soon they all grow tired once again and one by one, drift off to sleep.

In the morning, Tinok is gone.

Chapter   Seventeen

"What do you mean he's gone?" Jiron exclaims after James gives him the news of Tinok's disappearance.

"He's gone," James tells him again. "Sometime last night, he must've saddled a horse and taken off."

"And no one heard him?" he asks, looking around at everyone.

They all shake their heads indicating they hadn't.

"We must go after him!" he says.

"No, we shouldn't," Delia tells him. She grabs him by the arm and stares him straight in the eye as she continues. "With the wagons we will never be able to catch up with him. And if we abandon them, we lose the reason we're in the Empire."

He looks at her in anguish and she says softly, "Let him go, you have more immediate concerns."

"Like what?" he cries.

Pointing to his sister she says, "Like her."

Defeated, he nods his head acknowledging she's right. "Let's get the horses hitched up and get out of here," he says miserably. He climbs to the top of one of the nearby hills and turns toward the desert, standing there as he looks out across the rolling, desolate hills. "Tinok!" he yells as his eyes scan the horizon. "Tinok!"

Nothing, dejected at the loss of his friend, he climbs back down and helps the others with getting the caravan ready for the road.

"He'll be okay," offers Yorn as he comes up behind him, laying a hand on his shoulder.

"Yeah," adds Scar, "he's a tough one, he is."

He turns and looks into the faces of his friends and says, "Thanks." Then he turns back and finishes saddling his horse.

It's a somber group that heads down the road this morning. Each remembers the fallen in their own way.

"Remember when Qynn was going up against that sailor who thought he was hot stuff?" Potbelly suddenly says, breaking up the silence.

"Yeah," Stig replies, chuckling, "the guy thought that Qynn was going to be easy pickings." Laughing, he continues, "He sure made him respect the quarterstaff that day."

"I remember," adds Scar, nodding. Then breaking into a smile, he says, "Remember that tune he would always hum as he was whacking someone to its beat?"

Laughing, Potbelly exclaims, "And how he started doing that stupid dance, making the poor guy even more humiliated!"

Everyone from the pits starts laughing at that, James looks over and can see the beginnings of a grin appear on Jiron's face.

After several more stories of Qynn's antics in the pits, the mood is lifted somewhat. Apparently, he had been quite the clown at times.

A little past noon they leave the foothills and are once again in flat desert. The river curves to the south, as does the road and after another two hours they begin approaching another sizeable city. From a fellow traveler on the road they learn its name is Morac.

Even though it's not getting dark yet, they decide to stop for the night here. Pulling to the northeast of town, they find a suitable spot for a camp and proceed to arrange the wagons and picket the horses for the night.

Delia says to James, "I'm going to take Scar and Potbelly with me to deliver a couple packages. Roland too."

"Alright," he says, "just be careful."

"I will," she assures him.

Once the others are aboard the wagon, she turns it and begins rolling on into town. In the course of her deliveries, she comes across a temple to Coryntia, The Hooded Lady. If you light a candle in one of her temples after a loved one's passing, it's said that she will help them to find their way to the afterlife and not be stranded or lost along the way.

She pulls up to it and tells them, "I'll just be a moment." Getting down from the wagon, she goes inside the temple and approaches a table with many candles. Sitting in the middle of the candles is a single silver bowl. Placing a coin into the bowl, she takes a candle and carries it over to where a statue of a veiled woman stands. A couple candles are already lit there at her feet and she lights hers from one of the ones already burning, before placing it alongside them. Kneeling down, she says a prayer for Cassie, that she will find her way.

After several moments, she gets up and turns as she walks back toward the exit. Once outside, she climbs back aboard the wagon and then continues on with her deliveries.

Jiron has been moping around the camp ever since Delia left, hurt that Tinok ran out on him. Tersa comes over to James and asks, "What should we do?"

"About what?" he asks.

"About Jiron," she says as she gestures toward him. "I don't like seeing him like this."

"Not much we can do other than just be here for him," he replies. "He'll work it out on his own, all we can do is to simply allow him the time to do it."

"I suppose," she says, not entirely happy. "But I feel so helpless."

"I know," he assures her.

Yorn comes over and joins the conversation, "When the others return, we're going to take him to get drunk."

"Why?" she asks.

"To help him forget about things for awhile," he replies. To James he asks, "You want to come?"

"No, I'm not into that sort of thing," he tells him.

"Your loss," he says as he wanders back to the others.

From the wagon where Ezra and Arkie are, they can hear poor little Arkie crying. "He misses her," Tersa says. "She always played with him after we stopped."

"We all do," he admits, "she was special."

A little while later, when Yorn sees Delia approaching, he grabs Jiron and the pit fighters all head into town. They pause momentarily at the wagon and soon Scar and Potbelly join the group as it continues on its way.

When Delia gets to the camp, she asks James, "Where are they going?"

"To get drunk," he explains, "at least that's what Yorn said."

"Hope they don't get into any trouble," she states as she watches them go.

The first place they find is an old tavern with questionable clientele. Walking in, they see the mangiest group of derelicts this side of the gutter. "Perfect!" announces Scar as they sit at a large table off to one side.

A woman with a small beard and a patch over one eye comes up to them and says something that none can understand. Despite the language barrier, they finally make her understand that they want drinks. She brings them over several bottles of a foul smelling concoction that makes their eyes bug out and slightly burns as it goes down.

"Like mother's milk," Potbelly squeaks out after downing a large swallow.

"I hope they're not trying to poison us," Scar says as the liquid burns its way down to his stomach.

They sit there and drink for awhile, trading tales both true and improbable when a group of tough looking men walk into the tavern. They see them sitting at the table and walk over toward them. When they reach the table, one of them says something belligerently to them, which of course no one understands. Their failure to respond only makes him all the madder.

"What do you suppose is wrong?" Shorty asks.

A man sitting at a table next to theirs says, "You're sitting at their table and they want you out."

Jiron looks at the spokesman for the group and he says, "No, you find your own table. This one's ours."

Even though he couldn't understand the words, he understood the meaning behind them. The man suddenly reaches out and grabs Jiron by the shirt as he starts hauling him out of his chair.

Jiron stands up while at the same time swinging his fist with all his strength and connects with the man's jaw, sending him stumbling backward several feet into his fellows.

Then pandemonium erupts as one of the man's friends takes a swing at Jiron and both sides join the fray.

"For Tinok!" Scar yells as he trades blows with a large individual, finally sending him to the floor with two quick blows to the stomach and then one to the face, breaking his nose. Turning, he sees Shorty being tossed through the air where he hits the wall with a thud.

The other tavern's patrons quickly make for the sides of the room or out the door to avoid becoming embroiled in the fighting. Some join in, those who always enjoy a good fight no matter the reason.

The fighting remains fairly even until the town watch shows up. When Potbelly sees them enter he yells, "The town watch!" They all turn to see a dozen uniformed men entering wielding clubs, which they use to start felling brawlers.

Trading a few more blows, they turn and race to the other side of the tavern where they dive through the windows or run out the door into a side alley, to avoid being taken in. A quick survey shows them all there and then they race down the alley.

"Man that was a good fight!" exclaims Yorn, wiping blood away from his nose.

"Just what I needed," Jiron adds, smiling.

Stig says, "I think one of my teeth are loose," as he wiggles one.

Walking down a little further, they find another tavern where they're able to resume their drinking once more. An hour passes and they're beginning to get fairly drunk, having a grand time. A girl comes over to them and asks, "So, are you boys new in town?"

"Yeah," Stig replies as she makes herself comfortable on his lap, "just passing through." He places his arms around her as she leans against his chest.

"I've got some friends who would like some company tonight," she says sultrily and she runs her fingers through Stig's hairy chest. "If you feel up to it of course."

"How many friends do you have?" Potbelly asks.

"Oh, more than enough to satisfy you, I'm sure," she assures him.

"Well, what are we waiting for?" Scar says, grabbing the bottle and then getting up from the table.

She gets up off Stig's lap and leads them out of the tavern.

James is pacing by the fire, *Where are they!* Everyone else has already fallen asleep and it's well past midnight. *Probably passed out in the street somewhere.* Having to know, he takes the mirror out of his shaving kit and concentrates on Jiron as he gazes into it.

Slowly, Jiron's image begins to appear and at first it looks like he has in fact passed out somewhere. Broadening the image, he realizes they're not passed out, but tied up and lying on a dirt floor. He can see the others lying next to him, some are struggling trying to loosen their bonds.

Damn! What did they get themselves into now? Unable to see much more, he puts the mirror away and goes over to wake up Roland.

He gently places a hand on Roland's arm and gently shakes him.

"What?" Roland says groggily as he wakes up.

"We got trouble," James whispers to him, trying not to awaken Ezra who's lying next to him.

Sitting up abruptly, he looks around the camp but doesn't see anything. "What trouble?" he asks.

"Not here, in town," he explains. "The guys are in trouble and we need to go get them."

Roland gets up, gently disengaging himself from Ezra and then goes over to the remnants of the fire with James.

"What happened to them?" he asks.

"I'm not sure," he says and then explains to Roland what he saw in the mirror. "But we better do something."

"I agree," Roland says once he understands their predicament.

James goes over and wakes up Delia, explaining the situation to her so she won't worry if she were to wake and find them gone. Then he and Roland head into town to try and locate them. James makes sure that he has the belt with his slugs around his waist just in case.

"How are we going to find them?" Roland asks as they enter the town.

He moves over to a side alley and then glances around to make sure no one is watching. "Watch," he tells him as he lets the magic flow and a shimmering, transparent bubble forms in the air before them. In the dark of the alley it's almost impossible to see unless you know what to look for. "I've been working on this the last couple of days," he says. "Thought it might come in handy in finding Miko when we finally catch up with him."

"Amazing," Roland says as he reaches out his hand to touch it.

"Don't," says James as he lays his hand on Roland's arm. "It would most likely disappear if you do."

Taking his hand back, he says, "Sorry."

The bubble begins to float away as it leads them in Jiron's direction. Several times it floats past people on the streets, but in the dark, they fail to notice it. Whenever James loses sight of it, he has it flash a very dim light until he once again spots it and is able to follow.

It takes them through the city, all the way to the other side, where it comes to rest near the door to an old house with a single light emanating from an upstairs window. The bubble starts to dimly flash in the dark.

"They're in there," he tells Roland as he cancels the spell.

"Now what?" he asks.

As James approaches the door, he says, "We knock and ask for them back."

"What if they don't admit they're here?" he asks nervously.

"Then I'm afraid I'll have to insist," he says as he knocks loudly upon the door. When there's no answer, he pounds a little harder.

From the other side they hear footsteps approach and the door opens a crack. A little old lady sticks her head out, "Yes?"

"Good evening ma'am," James says, somewhat surprised to see such a harmless woman here. "I'm sorry to disturb you in the middle of the night, but I have reason to believe that some friends of mine are here."

"There's no one here but me," she says.

From a window upstairs, Roland sees a shadow move across it. "Someone's upstairs," he whispers to James.

"I'm afraid I'll have to ask you if I can come in to see for myself," he tells her.

"I'm not letting you into my home!" she says sternly as she starts to close the door.

James kicks out with his foot, causing the door to swing open and accidentally knocks the little old lady to the floor where she begins calling for help.

Coming in quickly, they shut the door and James says, "Gag her and tie her up so she'll be quiet."

Roland stuffs her mouth with a rag lying on a nearby table and then proceeds to tie her hands behind her back. "Sorry ma'am," he tells her, feeling bad about doing this to an old woman.

Hearing a creak, James turns to see a younger woman standing on the stairs to the second floor. She has a crossbow armed and aimed directly at him. "Release my mother," she commands.

James concentrates on the crossbow and the wire snaps, rendering it useless. "Come here," he says to her, motioning for her to come down into the room.

"How did you do that?" she asks, fear in her eyes.

"A little trick I picked up," he tells her. "Now, come here!" he says sternly.

When she hesitates, he says, "We have your mother, don't make this difficult. I only want my friends back."

As she comes into the room, fear in her eyes, she asks, "What are you going to do with us?"

"That depends on how helpful you are," he tells her. Seeing that Roland has the mother secured, he indicates the daughter and says, "Sit her down by her mother."

Nodding his head, Roland comes over to where she's standing and takes hold of her arm and brings her over, sitting her down on the floor near her mother.

"Now, where are my friends?" James asks her.

Defeated, she says, "Downstairs in the basement." She indicates a door under the stairs she had been standing on earlier.

He crosses the room and opens the door. He's greeted by the smell of alcohol coming from below. Glancing over to Roland he says, "Keep an eye on them." When he sees Roland's nod, his glowing orb appears in his hand and he descends the stairs.

Upon reaching the bottom, he finds them lying there in the middle of the basement floor, tied up and helpless. "Well, well, what have we here?" he asks as he makes his way over to them.

"Glad to see you," Jiron says.

Scar asks, "Man, how did you find us?"

James takes out his knife and cuts through the rope as he frees Jiron. "Take care of the others, I'll be upstairs," he tells him and moves to return up the stairs.

Over on a side table are their weapons, Jiron goes over and retrieves his knives before beginning to cut through Scar's bonds.

When he leaves the stairwell and rejoins Roland with the ladies he asks, "Now, just what were you going to do with them?"

"Sell their weapons and them to slavers," she admits.

"Done this before?" he asks.

"Couple of times," she admits, ashamed. "You don't know what it's like to be a woman alone here, without a man," she cries. "If we didn't, my mother and I would lose everything and have to live on the streets."

"No excuse," he says to her. He turns as he hears footsteps coming up from the basement. Still inebriated, the guys are quite a sight as they stagger along. He smiles and shakes his head.

"What to do with you two," he muses as he turns back to the women.

"Are you going to kill us?" the younger woman asks, fear in her voice.

"Should I?" he asks. "Or can we leave without anyone but us knowing what transpired here?"

"We won't tell anyone!" she cries out. "We swear!" Her mother nods her head in agreement.

"Alright," he tells her. "But if we hear about this from anyone else, I'll be back. Understood?"

"Yes!" she cries, relief evident upon her face.

Turning to Roland, he says, "Let's go." He unties the younger woman and then helps the stumbling drunks out of the house. Being the last to leave, he gives the daughter one final, meaningful look and then closes the door.

With Roland's help, he gets them moving in the right direction as they work their way through town. They finally meander their way back to camp where the drunks collapse and pass out.

192 Fires of Prophecy

"Everything go okay?" Delia asks when they arrive.

"We're here aren't we?" he asks her.

"What happened?" she asks.

Too tired to want to talk, he just says, "Tell you in the morning." Lying down, he's soon fast asleep.

The boozehounds all have incredible hangovers from the night before and not too surprisingly, most don't remember being tied up in the basement. Jiron and Scar remember it somewhat, but mainly it's all just a blur.

Smelling far worse than normal, James has them all go to the river, clothes and all and at least make an attempt to get the stink out.

While they're gone to the river, he and the others work to get the caravan ready for travel before they return.

"You going to tell them what happened last night?" Roland asks James as they secure a team of horses in their traces.

Grinning, he says, "If I do, I'll probably make up a bunch of stuff."

Roland breaks out laughing and then they finish securing the horses to the wagon. Everything is set to go by the time they see them coming back toward the wagons, drenched and cold. With the heat of the day already beginning to rise, it won't take long before it dries them out.

Sitting atop his horse, James watches and waits while they return and mount their horses. This day, Jiron is to drive the wagon while James gets to ride point. James is wearing his floppy hat that he bought back at Korazan to keep the sun off.

When everyone is ready, he takes the lead and soon they're back on the road following the river south. After riding for several hours, an odd fog bank appears off to the east, several miles away. "Do you see that?" he asks Jiron when he pauses to allow the wagon to catch up with him.

Shielding his eyes against the glare, he replies, "Yeah, so?"

"I've never heard of there being fog in the middle of the desert, in the middle of the day," he says. "Certainly not during summer, the heat should've burnt it off long ago."

When Roland catches up to them, James asks him about it.

"I think it's called the 'Mists of Sorrow'," he explains.

"Why do they call it that?" Jiron asks.

"Don't know," he replies. "I just heard someone passing through mention it once."

By this time the whole caravan has stopped to see what's going on. They all stare at the fog in the distance.

"What is it?" asks Shorty.

"We're not sure," Roland explains. "It might be the 'Mists of Sorrow'."

"Oh," he says.

"We're not getting anywhere by standing here gawking," James says to everyone who's gathered around him. They get back on their horses and wagons as he resumes riding to the south.

Throughout the rest of the day, the fog bank remains a permanent fixture on the horizon, they all can't help but keep glancing at it from time to time. James notices how the traffic is all but nonexistent on this road. The few travelers they do encounter tend to be nonsocial, giving only short responses to greetings if they give any at all.

When the sun rides low in the sky, they stop for the night next to the river. Before the sun goes down, James looks to the east and can still see the fog bank sitting there, miles away.

The next morning, he's shocked to discover the wall of fog had moved during the night. Now it's no more than a half mile from the road. It easily extends fifty feet high and is so dense, you can't see anything within it.

"Wow," says Delia when she wakes up and joins him where he's gazing at it. "Creepy."

"You said it," he agrees.

"Should we go check it out?" she asks.

Shaking his head, he says, "No, it makes me feel uneasy. Might be a good idea if we stayed away from it."

Then suddenly, they see a shadow pass through it along the fringe, the density of the fog keeping them from getting a clear view of it. It was half the size of a horse and was running like a dog.

They look at each other and she asks, "What was that?"

"I don't know," he replies, "but I think we need to be moving."

Waking everyone quickly, they set a new record in getting the caravan ready and moving down the road. With uneasy eyes on the fogbank, they make haste down the road. For the first couple miles the fog stays fairly close but then begins to recede again until it is once again several miles off in the distance. By the end of the day, they're unable to see it any more, much to the relief of everyone.

Next morning, James looks to the east and is happy to still see no trace of the fog at all. After rolling down the road for two hours, they come to another town. A large congregation of people can be seen out in front of a two story building set a little ways into town.

As they come closer, they notice that the people are upset about something and are talking agitatedly among themselves. "Go see what's going on," James says to Roland.

Roland gives him a nod, climbs down off the wagon, and then walks over to the crowd of people. The others wait for him on the road.

James sees him moving through the crowd, talking to several different people until he finally begins to make his way back. "Well?" he asks as Roland returns.

"You're not going to believe this," he says. "Last night the garrison Sub-Commander was murdered."

"So?" Jiron asks.

"He was murdered by a northerner," he says, "and there were witnesses. Also, drawn in blood on his forehead, was a heart with two dots." He turns to Jiron and says, "Sound familiar?"

"Cassie's necklace?" Jiron replies. "It was a heart with two stones."

"You mean Tinok did this?" Delia asks, not really believing it.

He turns to her, "It would appear so, but we have no real evidence, though the description of the murderer matches him fairly good."

"What is he doing?" Jiron wonders, angry. "That fool's going to get himself killed." He turns to James, "He's close, maybe we could find him and help him?"

"Let's get a ways out of town and then I'll look and see what I can discover," he tells him.

Jiron nods his head and they follow the road as it passes through town. Once the town has disappeared behind them, they pull off the road and James takes out his mirror to attempt to locate him.

Settling down on the ground, he gazes into the mirror, concentrating on Tinok and then lets the magic flow. Tinok begins to appear in the mirror, he's riding his horse fast across the desert.

"Where is he?" Jiron asks.

"I don't know," James says, "somewhere to the east, I think. The sun is too high for me to be able to tell for sure by the shadows."

"How far away is he?" demands Jiron.

"I can't tell that," explains James.

"Damn him!" Jiron curses in frustration. He turns and stares out into the desert to the east, hoping beyond hope to be able to see him. "So close!"

Delia comes to him and says, "But he doesn't want us to find him."

"Why do you say that?" he shouts at her in anger. "Why wouldn't he want to be with his friends?"

"I don't know," she replies, gently. "But if he did, he would be here."

"He knows where we're going," Yorn tells him. "He can find us if he wants to."

Potbelly comes over and says, "Sometimes, a man's just got to work things out on his own. And a hurt like he's had could take a long time, if ever."

Jiron continues gazing out to the desert and then his head droops as he turns to walk back to his horse. "Let's go," he says to them despondently.

Chapter   Eighteen

That evening when they stop for the night, James takes the watch in the middle of the night. He likes that one cause it's quiet and peaceful, giving him time to think about things. When he's on watch, he usually goes over the magic he's done and tries to figure out how to make it better, such as the bubble seeker spell he used in locating Jiron the other night.

This evening, he's trying to come up with spells that will be effective against another mage. His last two trials hadn't gone all that well, the first one at the City of Light almost killed him and ended up devastating a wide area. He needs to devise spells that will be effective against a mage, yet not destroy everything in the surrounding area. He might be in a town with innocent people the next time.

Maybe a series of spells, small spells that build on each other to breach the mage's defenses. Two things that all mages need to do magic are concentration and power. You disturb either one of those and his ability to do magic disappears.

A good mage's concentration will not be disrupted easily, something profound or totally unexpected would be needed. James considers different methods that might work as he walks around the campsite, trying to stay awake until Stig's turn at watch.

On his fourth trip around the camp, from off in the distance he begins to see two white lights coming toward him. As they get closer, a roar begins to be heard as well. He's about to wake everyone when he comes to the shocked realization of just what is approaching him.

He stands there with mouth slightly ajar in shock, as a beat up Ford pickup comes rolling into camp and pulls up with the passenger side next to him. James stands there expectantly, but at first nothing happens. Then he sees the driver lean over to his side and opens the door. Looking in, he sees the little creature with the felt hat sitting behind the steering wheel.

"Get in," he says, motioning for James to enter the cab.

He looks around at his sleeping friends and says, "I can't just leave them, I'm on watch."

"They'll be fine," he tells James.

"Are you sure?" he asks.

Giving James a look of annoyance, he says again, "Get in."

James climbs into the cab and shuts the door. With a roar, the little creature hits the gas and they drive away into the dark. He sits there as the truck rolls on, the creature turns the radio on and a George Strait song comes on. "Where are we going?" he asks.

"Going for pizza," the creature tells him.

"Pizza?" he asks. "There's pizza here?"

"Just have to know where to look," the creature smiles as he continues down the road.

Road? James looks and suddenly realizes that they're on a blacktop highway. Up ahead he sees the lights of civilization approaching. There're not many buildings, the one closest to them has a sign out front that says 'Mama's Pizza'.

The creature pulls the truck into a parking spot outside Mama's Pizza and parks it. Shutting the engine off, he gets out. Before he closes the door, he looks back at James who's remained in the cab and asks, "Coming?"

"Yeah," James says, as he gets out of the truck. Theirs is the only vehicle in the parking lot out front of Mama's. The place looks a little rundown, similar to what his grandfather would've called a greasy spoon. He joins the little creature where he's waiting at the door and they enter together.

The little creature opens the door and allows James to enter first. Once inside, he points over to a fat, dark haired woman behind the counter and says, "That's Mama."

She looks over to them as they enter and gives them a big smile, "It'll be ready in a few minutes," she says. He gives her a nod and then leads James over to a table where they sit down.

An old tv is mounted to the wall over by mama who's watching it with rapt attention. James is surprised to see she's watching an old episode of Star Trek.

"She's a Trekkie," he tells him. "You should see her collection in the back room."

James turns back to him and asks, "So why are we here?"

"For pizza, like I said," the little guy replies. "I wanted some and I hate eating alone. It's better with someone who is able to enjoy it with you, wouldn't you say?"

"I suppose," he says.

James watches as the little creature takes the salt shaker and pours a little salt on the table. Using great care he positions the salt shaker on its edge within the salt pile and then slowly removes his hands, leaving the salt shaker cocked to one side. He looks across the table to James with a satisfied smile on his face and asks, "Not bad, eh?"

"You sure don't act like a god," James tells him.

"Never said I was, just work for one," replies the creature, as he continues to admire his accomplishment.

Mama goes into the back and comes out shortly with an extra large pepperoni pizza. She carries it over and places it on the table between them, then fetches a pitcher of soda with two glasses. "Enjoy," she says before returning to watch her show.

Taking a big slice, the creature says, "Go ahead and help yourself."

James watches as he takes an enormous bite, sauce trickling down the side of his mouth. Grabbing a slice for himself, he takes a bite and admits to himself that this is pretty good pizza.

"This is the one where they have to recharge the dilitium crystals," she says from the counter. "I love this one."

The little creature just smiles at him as he continues to eat. James sits there quietly while he eats and ponders why the creature had brought him here. Maybe it's for company as he said, though James considers that highly unlikely.

"You're more talkative this time," he observes.

"That a problem?" the little guy asks through a mouthful of pizza.

James shakes his head and says, "No, just thought you weren't supposed to answer questions."

"Can't you just relax and enjoy yourself?" the creature says, a little annoyed.

"Okay, okay," James replies. "You never told me your name."

"Its true pronunciation, you'd be unable to manage," he says. "Just call me Igor."

"Igor?" James asks about ready to laugh.

"Yes, Igor," he replies. "As in Dr. Frankenstein's assistant."

"Alright," James says, "Igor."

They sit and continue eating the pizza, James is amazed at the speed with which Igor consumes each slice. He's barely had three before Igor removes the last slice for himself. Giving out with a loud, satisfied belch, Igor sits back in his chair while James finishes the last couple of bites.

When the last bite enters his mouth, Igor stands up and asks, "Shall we?"

James swallows the last bite and asks, "We're leaving?"

"Yes, it's time to take you back," replies Igor.

Getting up, James takes his glass and drains the rest of it before following Igor outside.

"Come back again," Mama says from behind the counter as they leave.

On the way back to the truck, Igor pauses as he looks down at a mud puddle by his feet. James pauses before entering the cab as he notices him there. Bending over, Igor picks up something shiny out of the puddle and holds it up for James to see. "A nickel," he says happily. "You never know what treasure you'll find, even in the dirtiest of places."

"That's true, I suppose," James says as he opens the cab door and gets in the truck.

Igor gets in, starts the motor and backs out onto the road. Heading back the way they had come, he soon has the truck speeding into the night.

They both remain quiet until James asks, "Did Cassie have to die?"

"Everyone dies, James," he says, glancing over to him. "It's just a matter of when."

"But they were so happy together," James replies. "Couldn't they have had some time together?"

"Not for me to say," Igor tells him.

Soon, James sees the fire from their camp up ahead and Igor brings him right into the middle of it by the campfire. Looking out the window, he sees everyone still sleeping, the roar of the truck motor not even causing them to stir. "See you later," Igor says as he stops and lets James out.

James opens the door and gets out of the cab. Before shutting it he pauses, glances back and asks, "When?"

"When it happens," Igor says with a smile. "Good luck," he says just before James closes the door. Then with a roar, the truck gets going and James watches until the tail lights have disappeared into the night.

James continues his watch as he ponders the meaning of these visits. *Why does he keep showing up? Is it just for a visit like he says, or is there more to it? And 'Igor', what kind of name is that for a being like him? The pizza was good though,* he thinks as he belches, bringing forth reminiscence of pepperoni.

He begins to grow tired and realizes his time at watch is about over. Moving through the sleeping bodies to where Stig is sleeping, he wakes him up for his turn at watch.

In the morning when he awakens with the dawn, he goes over to where the truck had been and isn't too surprised when he finds no tire tracks in the dirt. Shaking his head, he joins the others in preparing the caravan to get underway. It's not too long before they are once again on the road, heading southwest along the river.

Throughout the day as they continue down the road, they come across little hamlets and villages with increasing frequency. At one point, they have to pull over to allow a long column of soldiers to pass on their way north.

"Must be heading to Madoc," Yorn says, commenting to Jiron as they watch them pass.

"Probably," states Jiron. "Hope they get cut to pieces," he says, barely above a whisper.

Several heads nod in agreement.

Once the column has passed, they're able to bring their wagons back onto the road and continue on their way. The amount of traffic on the road slowly increases as the day progresses, and soon James can smell the familiar scent of the sea. "We're getting close to the ocean," he tells them.

"Azzac, the Empire's capitol, is on the ocean," Roland says.

"Must be getting close to it then," he figures.

After another mile, the great city of Azzac comes into view before them. Larger than any city they have yet seen, it sprawls along the river for over a mile before it meets the ocean. A large wall surrounds the city as it stretches miles in both directions down the coastline.

Upon the water beyond the city are dozens of ships tied to the long line of docks. More are out upon the sea, some leaving and some preparing to dock. "This place is massive!" he exclaims.

"Unbelievable," he hears someone mutter from behind him.

"Hopefully we can get in and find out where Miko is fast, then be on our way," Jiron says.

"Man that's right," agrees Shorty.

"James," Delia says, "it looks like there's a place for caravans to the north of the city."

Looking to where she's indicating, he sees the caravansary and angles in that direction. At the caravansary, an official looking man flanked by two guards comes forward to greet them. "Welcome to Azzac, strangers," he says. "If you could show me your letter of travel?"

James takes it out and offers it to him and the man takes it. The official looks at it, sees the name and seal at the bottom and then returns it to him. "There's a tax of three coppers per wagon to stay here," he tells him.

Taking the coins out of his pouch, he hands them over to him.

"Thank you," the official says. "Find any place you like to set up camp." He then turns and walks back to a tent set up along the road to the caravansary.

They find a good spot near the river and set up camp. Delia takes Roland with her to deliver several packages that are marked for here. She takes Scar and Potbelly along as well.

"You be careful," James warns her. "If there is anyplace we're most likely to be discovered, it's here."

"Don't fret," she assures him. "I'll be in and out fast."

James watches as she drives the wagon into Azzac, worried about the 'what ifs' and 'maybes' running through his mind.

After they've finished getting everything settled in, James takes out his mirror and tries to locate Miko. Jiron and Tersa come over and sit by him as he makes the attempt. They look at the mirror and watch as Miko's face begins to appear. As he broadens the scope, they discover that he's still riding in a wagon. As he expands the scene even further, they're able to see a large expanse of ocean off to his right.

"So he's still following the coast south?" Tersa reasons.

"It looks like it," agrees James. "At least he's alive and appears to be doing okay."

"As long as he's not dead yet, there's still hope," Jiron adds.

"That's right," he says. "Let's get Delia's deliveries done and get the heck out of here."

Stig comes over and asks, "Do you think we might be able to go in and have a drink?"

James just looks at him and says, "After the last time? I don't think so."

"We'll be careful," Stig says.

"No," James tells him, "not here. Down the road maybe, but not here. Too dangerous."

"James's right," Jiron says.

Disappointed, he goes back to his fellows and breaks the news to them. Jiron and James can hear groans coming from them as he tells them his reply. Here the seat of the enemy's power? He would have to be mad to allow it.

Three hours later when the daylight begins to fade, Delia has yet to return. James has been pacing around the last hour, dread growing with every passing minute. "Something's wrong," he tells Jiron when he comes to a stop next to him.

"Not necessarily," he says. "She's been gone longer than this before."

"If she waits much longer she may run the risk of having the gates close on her," James says.

"Do the gates close here at night?" Jiron asks.

"I don't know, but there's always the chance," he replies.

"What should we do?" he asks.

"Let's go and find her," James suggests.

"Good, I'm tired of just sitting here," he says.

"What about the rest of us?" Tersa asks nervously.

"Just stay here with them," James says indicating Stig and the others, "and we'll be back as soon as we find them." He then goes over and explains to them what he and Jiron are about to do and then they begin walking toward the gates to the city.

"We don't even speak the language," Jiron says.

"Hopefully that won't be a problem," James tells him. "I've seen many northerners here so hopefully we won't stick out too much."

"Where are we going to start looking?" Jiron asks before they reach the gate.

"Not sure," he replies.

At the gate, they're looked at by the guards, but other than that cursory examination, are allowed to pass through into the city.

"Going to do that bubble thing again?" Jiron asks.

"Maybe," he says. "Let's look around first through the merchant's district and see if we can't locate them that way." He feels a tingling sensation and looks around. Sure enough, he sees a mage walking through the crowd on the street. He points him out to Jiron as he pulls him close and whispers, "He's doing magic of some sort. I can feel it."

Considering that fact for a second, he whispers back to James, "Will they be able to sense you if you do magic?"

James nods, "I would think so."

"Then maybe we shouldn't do the bubble thing," he says.

"Only if we have to," James replies.

They walk through the streets, looking for any sign of Delia and the others. They pass many merchant's establishments but fail to find any clue as to their whereabouts. By this time it's becoming fairly dark and they see two people with long poles, each with a flame at the end, begin walking the streets. They go from streetlamp to streetlamp, lighting the lamps hanging there to give the people on the street light to see by.

"This is hopeless!" Jiron exclaims, "They could be anywhere."

"I agree, we'll never find them this way. The city is just too large," he says.

James leads Jiron into an empty side alley where he takes out his mirror that he brought along and begins concentrating on Delia. They both gaze into the mirror as her features begin to form. James hears Jiron gasp when they see her sitting on the floor in a small room. The others are there with her and the looks on their faces tells them they're not happy.

"They're in trouble!" says Jiron.

"It would appear so," James replies. "I told her to be careful!"

He expands the view, hoping to see where they are being kept until finally managing to get a bird's eye view of the estate wherein she is being held. He tries to expand it even further when Jiron touches his arm and whispers, "Mage!"

James looks out of the alley to the street where he sees a brown robe walking toward the alley entrance. He stops the spell and immediately the brown robe pauses, turning his head first one way and then the other. It seems almost like he's searching, trying to rediscover the source of the magic. James and Jiron hold their breath and remain pressed against the side of the alley as they watch the mage there in the street, until he finally turns and walks down the street to their right.

"He knew you were doing magic," Jiron whispers.

"Apparently so," James replies as he sticks his head out the alley to watch the brown robe continuing down the street away from them.

"Let's go," he says. "I got a pretty good look at where they're being kept. It's a large estate with plenty of grounds surrounding it."

"Sounds like someone important," Jiron reasons, "or rich."

Stepping out of the alley, they follow the street as it moves closer to the river and the castle. Estates of that size are most likely to be located in that area, hopefully.

They proceed for a few more blocks before coming to the inner wall. A single gate stands open with two guards watching as people pass through.

"Doesn't look as if they're stopping anyone," James says hopefully.

"Maybe it's because they already know them?" Jiron suggests.

Shrugging, James says, "Only one way to know for sure." He steps out, followed closely by Jiron and begins to walk toward the gate, heart beating rapidly in anticipation of a confrontation. The guards see them approach but don't stop or question them as they pass through.

Once through to the other side, James breathes a sigh of relief. They continue down the street, now in a much more affluent section of town. Not too far past the gate, they come to where the street splits. One section continues on toward the keep and the other moves away from the keep. The street moving away from the keep looks to head toward an area with estates.

James glances to Jiron and indicates the area away from the keep. When he sees Jiron nod in agreement, he turns to follow that street.

"Which one is it?" Jiron asks after they've traveled down that street and have begun to enter the estate area.

"I'm not sure," he replies as they continue down the street. Then, on a hill off to their left he sees the estate that was in the mirror. "That's it!" he exclaims as he points it out to Jiron.

"You sure?" he asks.

"Absolutely," James replies.

The estate has a stone wall going all the way around it's perimeter with but a single gate for an entrance. The gate has a well lit guardhouse with a guard keeping watch. The area between the wall and the house is fairly clear except for a small area containing plants and bushes, probably for the lady of the house.

"Let's go around back and see if there's a better spot to try to get in," Jiron advises.

James nods his head as he follows him around the outside of the wall.

"It doesn't seem to be guarded," says Jiron suspiciously.

"We're in the heart of the empire, who would be dumb enough to break into a noble's estate here?" James reasons.

"You may be right," Jiron agrees. He gets close to the wall and jumps up, grabbing the top as he pulls himself up and then quickly scans the area on the other side of the wall for guards.

"See anything?" James asks.

"No, it looks clear," he tells him from the top. Reaching down, he says, "Give me your hand and I'll help you up."

James takes his hand and Jiron pulls him to the top of the wall. They quickly drop down to the other side and squat for a few seconds in the shadows to observe what's going on. The area between the wall and the manor house is dark and they don't see anything moving. With Jiron in the lead, they make their way across the open lawn to the side of the house near a darkened window.

Jiron silently moves to the window and peers inside, but is unable to make out anything in the dark. With great caution, he tests the window and finds it locked. Taking out one of his knives, he slides it in the narrow space between the two sides and lifts the latch. Replacing his knife in his belt, he pulls the window open and then quickly slips inside.

Reaching his hand down, he helps James in through the window and then closes it once again. Jiron begins moving around, trying to find the door when a soft glow begins to fill the room. Looking back, he sees James there with the glowing orb in his hands. The orb is barely giving off any light at all, just enough so they can make out the details of the room and won't be stumbling around.

"Thanks," Jiron whispers.

Grinning, James replies quietly, "No problem."

The light shows that they're in a study of some kind with but a single door leading out. Jiron moves over to it and places his ear against the door, listening for any sound coming from the other side. After a minute, he shakes his head and says, "Nothing."

"Good," James says.

Jiron slowly opens the door and then shuts it again quietly as he turns to James. "They're not going to come looking for magic because of that, are they?" he asks, pointing to the glowing orb in James' hand.

"I wouldn't think so," he replies. "It's hardly using any magic at all."

With a brief nod, Jiron again opens the door and a dim light comes through it. James cancels the orb and it disappears as Jiron opens the door wider. He cautiously looks down the hallway to either side. He turns back to James and in a barely audible whisper, says, "There's a light down to the right, to the left is dark."

"Try the left?" he suggests.

Jiron nods in agreement and then he again checks the hallway. Not seeing anyone, he opens the door wider and silently exits the room to the hallway, making his way down toward the left.

Once he's out of the room, James follows and then closes the door behind them. He can hear muffled voices coming from the room down the hallway to the right where the light is emanating from, but is too far away to be able to make any of it out.

Jiron stays to the left side of the hallway as he quietly makes his way down to the next door on the right. He pauses a moment as he listens at the door. Not hearing anything, he proceeds further down the hallway. They pass two doors facing each other and after a moment's listening at each, Jiron continues past them.

A little ahead of them they see light emanating around the corner where the hallway turns to the right. Jiron turns to James and whispers, "Wait here."

James nods his head and then watches as Jiron silently walks to the edge of the corridor and peers around it. After only a brief look, he brings his head back quickly and then motions James closer. "There's a guard standing in the hallway about ten feet down. There's a torch in the wall near him."

"Should we take him out do you think?" James asks.

"If we do, we may be alerting the whole place that we're here," Jiron replies. "He may not even be guarding Delia and the others."

"Can't think of any other reason to post a guard in a hallway," reasons James. "I say we've got to do it."

"Can you do it?" Jiron asks. "I would need to be closer to take him out before he could raise the alarm."

"Yeah," James replies, not liking the fact of having to kill someone like this, but what choice does he have. He removes a slug from his belt and silently moves to the corner and peers around. Seeing the guard there, he gathers his thoughts before stepping into the hallway. Before the guard even realizes he's there, he releases the magic and throws.

The slug flies straight and true, striking him in the head. The guard sags to the floor unconscious. "Come on!" James says to Jiron as he hurries to where the guard lies on the floor.

"He's not dead!" Jiron exclaims when he realizes the guard lying there is only unconscious. A sizeable goose egg of a bump shows where the slug had hit him in the temple.

"I held back a little," admits James. "I didn't want to kill him that way."

The guard, as it turns out, had been standing in front of stairs leading down.

"Let's put him in one of the rooms we passed," Jiron suggests.

"Alright," agrees James. They lift him up and carry him back to the corner where they pause a moment as Jiron peers down the hallway. Seeing the coast is clear, they go to the first door on the right and open it slowly as they look inside. It's a bedroom, but empty and doesn't looks as if it's been used for some time. They deposit the guard on the bed and then bind and gag him. Once the guard is secured, Jiron returns to the door and opens it a crack as he makes sure the hallway still remains empty. Finding that it is, they leave the room, closing the door behind them.

They quickly make it back to the stairs where Jiron takes the lead as they begin to descend to the lower level. At the bottom of the stairs, they find a door that's slightly ajar. Jiron cautiously opens it further and peers around to the other side where he sees an empty corridor leading away from the door. He opens it further and motions for James to follow him through.

Following the corridor with James right behind, they pass two other closed doors on their way, pausing momentarily to listen at each. Not hearing anything, he continues down to the door at the end, where light can be seen coming through the cracks from the other side.

As they draw near to the door, they're able to hear voices speaking from the other side. "...tell me!" one voice yells and then they hear the sound of someone being slapped hard.

"Again," the voice says and then a female can be heard crying out in pain.

"Delia!" Jiron cries as he races for the door. James readies a slug as Jiron hits the door with his shoulder, causing it to open and swing into the room, slamming hard against the wall. With both knives ready, he quickly surveys the room.

It takes but a moment to realize what's been happening, Roland, Scar and Potbelly are sitting along one wall, hands chained to the wall. Delia lies stretched spread-eagled upon a table, her hands and feet secured with ropes to the corners.

A well dressed man stands next to the table with another whom James can only believe is a dealer in pain. They've been torturing Delia! Two guards spring into action and immediately draw their swords as they move to engage Jiron.

"Jiron!" Potbelly cries out from where he sits against the wall when the door bursts open and sees him enter.

The two guards close with Jiron, one falling when a slug strikes him in the face blasting out the back of his head. Jiron parries a thrust from the other with one knife and then strikes out with the other, catching the guard in the neck, severing the jugular. Grabbing his neck, the guard tries to stop the blood spewing forth as he stumbles and falls to the floor. Jiron kicks out his foot on his way down and can hear a snap when the man's neck breaks.

The well dressed man has his sword out and has the edge lying across Delia's throat. "Enough!" he cries. "Or she's dead."

Jiron stands there, seething with impotent anger. Unable to do aught else, he stops.

James sees a ring of keys on one of the guards and reaches down to pick them up when the well dressed man says, "Don't, or she dies."

"It seems we're in a pickle here," James tells him as he straightens back up. "We're not about to leave without them," he says as he gestures to Delia and the others, "and if you cut her throat you're a dead man."

He just stands there with his sword at her throat, considering the situations. The torturer next to him says with authority, "You dare not hurt the High Lord Cytok. He's the right hand to the Emperor himself!"

"Shut up you fool!" Lord Cytok yells to the man. Turning back to James and Jiron, he says, "You two, get over there next to the others." He nods his head indicating they should go over to where Scar, Potbelly and Roland are sitting along the wall. He menaces Delia with his sword until they begin to move over there.

Delia watches them with her eyes, fear of the sword at her throat preventing her from doing or saying anything.

"James," Jiron says quietly as they move closer to where the others sit, "do something."

"I'm working on it," he replies.

"Go get Kirtch and Prul," he says to the torturer who then moves quickly to the door.

James concentrates on Delia's exposed neck and then releases the magic. "Go ahead," he says to Jiron, "he can't hurt her now."

Trusting in James, Jiron is up in a flash and rushes toward Lord Cytok.

The torturer breaks into a run as he races through the door and begins screaming on his way to the stairs.

Lord Cytok runs his sword across Delia's throat but it only slides along an invisible barrier encasing her throat. Shocked at seeing the ineffectiveness of his sword, he turns to Jiron and prepares to defend himself.

"We need him alive," James says. "We'll never make it out without him."

With a slight nod, Jiron closes with Lord Cytok. Deflecting a thrust with one knife, he strikes out with other but Lord Cytok dances backward and the knife misses by inches. The battle is joined.

James gets the keys from the dead guard and goes over to free Scar.

"Thanks, James," Potbelly says. "We were hoping you might show up."

"Yeah man," Scar says when James had freed him.

He gives Scar the keys to remove the other's shackles before going over to Delia. He takes out his knife and cuts through her bonds. He helps her to her feet just as Roland comes over to assist her. Delia stands up, a little bit shaky and James asks, "Are you alright?"

"I'll be fine," she assures him.

Scar and Potbelly have taken the guards' swords and stand to the door to keep a look out. Scar turns back to the others and cries, "We've got company!"

Suddenly, a crash and James looks over to see Lord Cytok's sword lying on the ground and Jiron with his knife to his throat.

"Tell your men out there to drop their weapons and come inside," Jiron orders him.

A man from the hallway hollers something to Lord Cytok.

Jiron begins pressing the point of his dagger into his throat and says, "One of us understands your language, so don't do anything stupid."

He hollers back to his men.

Jiron looks to Roland and asks, "Did he tell them to drop their weapons?"

Roland shakes his head and replies, "They asked if he was okay and he told them he's okay, but held at knifepoint."

"Tell them to drop their weapons and come inside, NOW!" Jiron insists as a drop of blood wells from where the point of the knife had punctured the skin.

Lord Cytok hollers to his men and James glances to Roland who nods his head.

Soon they hear weapons falling to the ground and then his men, four of them, step into the room. The torturer isn't among them.

"Where's the other guy!" Jiron demands when he realizes he's not among them.

Roland asks and when one of the men replies, Lord Cytok begins laughing.

"What's so funny," Jiron asks.

"He's gone to raise the alarm," he tells him. "Soon this whole area will be swarming with soldiers." With a satisfied smirk on his face, he stares at James.

"We'll never make it out!" Potbelly exclaims.

"Maybe," says James, "if we're fast enough."

"Secure them to the wall," James tells Scar and Potbelly who start taking Lord Cytok's guards and placing them in the chains that had once been theirs. "Gag them too," he advises them.

"Right," Scar says as he picks up the most dirty, disgusting rags available, taking great pleasure in stuffing them in their mouths.

"Now, milord," James says to Lord Cytok. "I hate to ask but please lie down on the table here."

"Never!" he says adamantly.

Once Scar and Potbelly have the guards secured, they come over and force Lord Cytok onto the table, securing his arms and legs to the restraints. "Use a cleaner rag for his gag," James tells them, "after all, he is a Lord."

When he's secured and gagged, James says, "You guys go on up and see what's going on while Roland and I help Delia up the stairs."

"I can walk," she says as the others run down the hallway and up the stairs. Roland puts one of her arms across his shoulders to help support her. For despite her assertion that she can walk, her legs are a little unsteady. With James in the lead, they make their way to the stairs.

When they reach the top, they see Jiron racing back toward them. "Nothing yet," he tells them.

"Good," says James as they continue down the hallway, going back the way they had come. Moving past the room where they saw the light earlier, James notices it's empty now. Most likely whoever had been in there is now back in the room with Lord Cytok, chained to the wall.

A little further past the room, the hallway opens up onto the foyer where they see Scar and Potbelly looking out the front door. Scar turns at their approach and says "It looks clear out there."

"Then let's move," Jiron urges as they leave the house and run toward the gate. The guard that had been there earlier is absent, most likely sitting in the basement with his fellows. Potbelly reaches the gate first and opens it. He moves through to the other side and looks for anyone in the vicinity. Not finding anyone, he motions for the others to pass through to the street.

They begin running, making their way down the road a short ways before they see a large group of armed men running toward Lord Cytok's estate.

They duck down a side alley and remain motionless as they wait for them to race past. Several brown robes could be seen among the running soldiers.

"Mages," James says once they're past. "How are we going to get out of here now?"

"I don't know," Scar replies. "But we better hurry before it's too late.

Jiron looks out on the street and sees the way the soldiers had come is clear for the moment. They step out of the alley and race down the street away from Lord Cytok's estate, hoping to escape the city before it's too late.

Chapter   Nineteen

The streets begin to fill as more soldiers and guards race toward Lord Cytok's estate. Having had to duck into another alley to avoid detection, they wait for the squad of men to pass. Then James spreads his hands wide as ten small floating spheres appear before him. With a wave of his hand, they begin floating away in different directions.

"What're those going to do?" Jiron asks. "Aren't they going to attract any mages in the area?"

"That's the idea," replies James. "Hopefully they'll be so intent on tracking down what they think are rogue mages, that we'll be able to slip though, unnoticed."

"Let's hope so," Jiron says. Once the spheres have left the alley, he takes one more look up and down. Not seeing anyone in the vicinity, he reenters the street with the others right behind. He keeps them to one side of the street as they quickly make their way to the gate leading out of the inner walled area.

As they approach the gate to the outer area, they see a squad of soldiers with a mage stationed there. The mage is looking down the street they are approaching on but has yet to detect them.

"Damn!" James exclaims when he sees them. They duck down an alley where they stop to determine what they're going to do.

"Now what?" Delia asks.

"I'm thinking," he replies as they pause for a moment.

"Think faster," Scar says as he points to several squads of soldiers entering through the gates. The mage there gives them directions as they move past and the squads split up as each moves in a different direction.

A squad turns to head in their direction and looks to be heading for the alley they're hiding in. "Move!" Jiron urges as he leads them further into the alley, away from the approaching soldiers.

"The whole army is on the move to find us," Potbelly says from the rear.

"We invaded the home and humiliated a very powerful and important leader," Roland explains. "They'll not let us just walk away."

The alley ends at another cross street. To their right, the street approaches the wall before intersecting with another street running perpendicular to it. A three story building has been built right up against the wall. James takes a closer look and realizes the top of it is only several feet from the top of the wall.

Jiron glances up to where James is looking and grins, "That'll work." Making sure the street is currently clear of soldiers, they leave the alley and run down the street to the building. It looks to be someone's residence. He goes to the door and tries to open it, but discovers it's locked. No time for niceties, he kicks it in and the door swings wide, slamming into the wall.

Rushing inside, they quickly close the door behind them. Potbelly moves to a window and looks out. "I don't think anyone saw us," he tells the others.

Jiron finds the stairs going up and begins to climb them when a man appears at the top with a drawn sword. The man holds his sword menacingly as he descends three steps before saying something that could only be 'Get out of my home!'

"I don't have time for this," Jiron says as he draws his knives and moves to the top of the stairs. In a quick exchange, the man's sword lies on the stairs and Jiron has a knife threatening him. Turning the man around, he propels him back to the top of the stairs.

A woman is standing further down the hallway with three children held tightly to her. Her eyes widen in fear when she sees her husband emerging from the stairs with a knife held against him. She says something to him and he replies, motioning for them to stay back.

"Tell them to get in that room," Jiron says to Roland, indicating one that's near the woman.

Roland tells them and the woman slowly backs her way into it, taking the children with her. One of the young girls begins to cry and she does her best to quiet her. "Tell them to be quiet and we won't kill them," Jiron says as he pushes the man into the room with his family.

Grabbing his children, the man turns to Roland and listens to what he's being told and then nods his head and replies.

Roland says, "They'll be silent."

Jiron nods his head as he shuts the door on the family. They find another set of stairs leading up and they race to the third floor. "Split up and find the access to the roof," Jiron tells everyone as he continues down the hallway from the stairs. Doors begin to open as they all search the rooms for a way to the roof, they know that time is against them.

"It's in here!" they hear Scar yell from the far end of the building. Set in the roof of a small room is a trapdoor with a rope hanging down from it. Pulling on it, the trapdoor swings open and a ladder extends down allowing access to the roof. With Scar in the lead, they climb the ladder and once everyone is on the roof, James severs the rope for the trap door before pulling it closed behind them.

The inner town wall is just five feet above the roof of the building. Jiron runs over to it and jumps, grabbing hold of the top, and then pulls himself up onto the wall. He reaches down a hand and helps Scar up just as a guard patrolling the wall sees them and begins crying the alarm. Drawing his sword, the guard rushes toward them.

Once Scar has reached the top, he draws his sword and moves to engage the approaching guard while Jiron helps the others up. In trepidation, he observes three more are on their way behind the first guard. "Hurry up man, we've got company!" he hollers to Jiron just before he parries a thrust by the guard.

Jiron helps Potbelly up who rushes to Scar's aid. Delia next, Roland and then James gain the top of the wall.

Scar and Potbelly have disposed of the first guard and are moving to intercept the three oncoming guards. Jiron runs to help them as James tries to figure out where they need to be going. On the other side of the wall, all the houses are at least fifteen feet away. *Makes sense*, he reasons, *they let people on the inside build close because they're not worried about people getting out so much as they are about them getting in.* It's a thirty foot drop to the ground so they won't be jumping down that way. The wall they're on extends all the way to the outer wall.

James looks over to where Jiron and the others are fighting just as the last guard falls. He cries out, "Toward the outer wall, hurry!"

Two more soldiers are running to intercept them from the direction of the outer wall, and the fighters move to engage. Roland and Delia move quickly to follow Jiron and the others, with James right behind. Jiron takes the first one as Potbelly blocks a downward thrust from the second and then follows through with a thrust, taking him through the stomach, just below the breastbone. He kicks the guard off his sword with his foot as Jiron pushes the guard he was fighting over the wall, the man's scream can be heard all the way down until he hits the ground below.

Behind them, eight guards are running down the wall to catch them. One has a crossbow and lets a bolt fly but it goes wide, narrowly missing Scar.

James turns and takes out a slug which he throws, hitting the crossbowman square in the chest, causing him to stagger and then fall off the wall.

"Here!" Roland hollers to them. They turn and see him there with a bucket that's tied to a long rope. "We can climb down," he explains.

James glances down the outward side of the wall and doesn't see anyone there, guess they figured on them not being able to get down here. "Looks clear," he tells them. He and Roland hold the rope as Jiron shinnies down.

Scar and Potbelly have positioned themselves to hold off the oncoming guards, giving the others a chance to get down. As Jiron makes it to the ground, the guards reach Scar and Potbelly, and the crash of swords can be heard as they engage.

Turning to Delia, James says, "You're next." He and Roland hold the rope secure while she makes her way down. Glancing over to the fighting, James sees one of the guards has already fallen but that Scar and Potbelly have to give ground as they're being pushed backward by the remaining seven.

Roland tells James, "Go on!"

Shaking his head, he says, "You first."

Not wanting to take the time to argue, Roland takes the rope and swings over the side as James holds onto it. He glances back to Scar and Potbelly and it doesn't look good. Even though another guard has hit the ground, there's still too many, it's only a matter of time before one or the other falls.

The tension on the rope disappears and he looks down, seeing that Roland has made it to the ground. "Come on!" he hollers up to him.

Securing the end of the rope around a merlon he hollers over to the fighters, "Let's go!"

Scar replies, "We'll never make it!" He parries with one sword and then takes the guard through the stomach with his other. "You go," he tells him, "we'll hold them off!"

Potbelly is holding his own, but there's just too many for them to last. As he watches them fighting, anger and frustration build within him until it's like a white hot sun.

"Scar, Potbelly! Get down, NOW!" his voice thunders behind them.

Almost reflexively, they drop to the ground as an invisible wave passes over them and they watch as the guards are lifted and thrown backward, some screaming as they fall to their deaths to the ground below. Once it's past, they get up and hurry over to James where he's staggering a little. Scar asks, "You okay?" as they steady him.

Nodding his head, James just says, "Let's get off this damn wall." He sees a couple of the guards are getting back up from where they had been thrown backward along the top of the wall.

They let James go first and then Scar with Potbelly coming last. When James reaches the ground, he says to Jiron, "What I did up there is going to be like a beacon for every mage in the city. They're going to know where we are."

"Then let's get the hell out of here!" Jiron says as they start to race toward the main gates to the city. A squad of five men turns into the street ahead of them, coming in their direction. When they see James' group running toward them, they let out a cry and draw their swords as they rush to attack.

A slug strikes one, felling him before they even get close. Jiron takes the next one, knives flashing as they parry and strike.

Potbelly and Scar face the remaining three; Scar's two swords quickly take out one while Potbelly holds his own with the second but is unable to gain an opening to finish him. Scar engages the remaining one and soon has him on the ground as well. "You got him?" he asks, looking over to Potbelly as he continues exchanging blows with the guard.

"Yeah!" he replies as he blocks and holds his opponent's sword with his knife, while following through with his sword, taking him through the chest. His sword gets caught in between his opponent's ribs and is unable to pull it free. Leaving the sword there, he grabs the dead guard's sword just as Jiron's opponent falls to the ground. Then they're off again for the gate.

This area is relatively clear as most of the guards and soldiers have gone to the inner section of the city to hunt for them. They're able to run quickly through the streets without fear of being attacked and it isn't long before the gates appear ahead of them. "There they are!" Jiron shouts to them as they race for freedom.

They come to a quick stop when they see at least thirty soldiers in formation before the gate, as well as a mage. "You cannot escape!" the mage hollers to them where they've stopped in the middle of the street. "You are greatly outnumbered."

James takes a slug and throws it at the mage who erects a barrier, causing it to ricochet off harmlessly.

The mage just smiles, as he makes ready to cast a spell. James counters with a spell he's been devising for just such a time and is able to release it before the other can cast his. The mage knows James has done something but can't detect anything. He releases a bolt of power and the shield he erected around himself to ward off the slug suddenly turns orange as the bolt of power bounces off the shield, turning back onto the mage.

With a scream of pain, the bolt blasts through the mage before hitting the shield again and then bounces back. The bolt then proceeds to fly from one side of the shield to another until finally running its course. James releases his spell on the shield and the mage, now a charred corpse, falls to the ground.

In stunned silence, the guards at the gate stare for a second at the smoking remnants of their mage lying there in the street and then a cry erupts from then as they charge forward.

Crumph!

James releases the power again and the ground under the approaching men explodes upward, tossing bodies and debris in every direction. A few men were forward of the area that erupted and are thrown forward by the blast. Jiron and the other pit fighters quickly take them out before they have a chance to recover.

Behind them, they can hear running feet as hundreds of guards and soldiers, who had been in the inner area of the city, race to catch them. "To the gate!" James cries as he begins running through the devastated area littered with dead bodies before them.

"But it's closed!" Delia cries as she hurries behind him.

"Leave that to me," James tells her as they race toward the gate.

From atop the wall, crossbowmen begin raining down bolts at them. But by luck's good grace, they all fail to hit their mark.

At the gate, they turn to see the courtyard beginning to fill with soldiers, hell bent on engaging them. "There're too many!" shouts Scar.

"James hurry!" Jiron yells as he and the other pit fighters turn to face the oncoming men. Being so close to the gates, the crossbowmen on the wall are no longer able to fire upon them. He glances back and sees James standing next to the gates with his hands resting upon them.

Then with an ear deafening crash, the gates fly open and James sags to the ground. On the other side, two guards stand in stunned amazement at the opening of the gates. Scar and Potbelly quickly turn and move through the gate, taking them out in short order. Jiron helps James up and half carries him as they hurry through the gate.

Behind them, a swarm of men armed with swords fill the streets as they race for the broken gates, hot on their trail. Crossbow bolts fly at them from the walls again once they've passed beyond their protecting cover, but none find their mark.

Suddenly, they hear horses approaching from the southwest, hooves thundering toward them across the bridge that spans the river. Getting set to sell their lives dearly, they're stunned to see Shorty and Yorn racing toward them. Behind them are Ezra and Stig, as well as extra horses for each of them.

"Come on!" Shorty yells as they race toward them. He gets down and helps assist Jiron in getting James in the saddle as everyone mounts. Once done, they quickly get in the saddle and then begin racing back toward the bridge. Potbelly cries out from his saddle as a bolt strikes him in the side.

"Potbelly!" Scar yells as he slows to come to his friend's aid.

"I'll make it!" he yells back to his friend as he holds his side, bursts of pain exploding from where the bolt is sticking out with every stride his horse takes.

As they cross the bridge, James slows his horse and then comes to a stop. He begins to dismount when Jiron hollers to him, "What the hell are you doing?"

"Delaying them," he replies. "I may not be good for much after this, so be prepared for that. I need a few minutes."

Looking back at the mass of soldiers running toward them, he says, "You ain't got a few a minutes!"

James ignores him as he concentrates. Jiron watches as the center of the bridge begins to glow and then becomes dark again. James suddenly sags to the bridge, unconscious.

"Damn!" Jiron says as he dismounts. Coming to his side, he puts James back onto his horse and secures him to the saddle with rope. He gets back on his horse, grabs the reins to James' horse and then leads him quickly over the bridge to where the others are waiting for them.

"What did you stop for?" Scar asks as they approach.

"I'm not sure," he replies. "Let's get going!"

As they gallop away, the first of the pursuing men gain the bridge. *Crumph!*

The concussion wave washes over them and they turn to see the bridge exploding into the air. A twenty foot gap now separates the two sides of the river.

"Damn!" Scar says.

"Let's move," Jiron says. "We don't know how long we'll have before they manage to get around that."

Potbelly groans and then begins to topple off his horse. Scar jumps down and hurries over to his friend's side, catching him before he hits the ground.

Potbelly looks up to Scar as he lays him on the ground, "I guess this is my last fight."

Scar sees Delia there and she bends down to examine the wound. "It's hit nothing vital," she tells him. "If we can get the blood to stop, he should be alright."

Jiron looks back to the river and can see that they've already started moving some boats toward the broken bridge to begin ferrying men across. "We don't have much time," he tells her.

"Won't need much," she says as she tears a strip of cloth off her shirt.

Jiron looks again and sees ten men disembarking from the boats. They begin running to close with them. Two knives fly in quick succession as Shorty takes out two of the attackers.

"Hurry please!" Jiron says as he and the others move to engage with the oncoming men. Side by side, the pit fighters stand, giving Delia the time to administer to Potbelly. Scar is a terrible foe as his anger for what happened to his friend finds an outlet, his two swords weaving a pattern of death no soldier willingly enters.

As she starts to bind the wound, leaving the bolt in his side, Roland asks, "Aren't you going to take it out?"

"No," she replies. "If I do, it'll leave a hole allowing more blood to escape. He's already lost too much as it is."

The attackers fall like stalks of grain before the scythe as they engage the waiting fighters. Keeping her mind on Potbelly and doing her best to ignore the fighting going on fifteen feet away, she finally finishes up with binding his wound. With Roland's help, they manage to get him on a horse, securing him in the same manner as James. When he's secured, she turns and yells, "Let's go!"

She quickly mounts her horse as the pit fighters take out the few remaining soldiers and then run to where their horses are waiting. Glancing back to the river, she sees two more boats disembarking another twenty soldiers. "Hurry!" she yells to Scar and the others as they reach the horses and begin mounting. Crossbow bolts fly at them from the river, but from that distance they're not much to worry about.

Back into the saddle, they turn and race down the road, leaving the enemy far behind. After putting several miles between them, they slow the horses, saving them in case of the need for speed.

"Where did the other horses come from?" Jiron asks Shorty.

"After you guys left, we figured that we might need to leave in a hurry so we traded all the wagons and the goods for the horses," he says.

"What about the money chest?" Delia asks.

"It's divided among the saddlebags," he tells her. "Each horse is carrying roughly the same amount."

Jiron nods his head, "Smart thinking."

Shorty smiles back to him and replies, "We knew you guys wouldn't be able to leave without disturbing a few people."

"Yeah," Yorn interjects. "So we positioned ourselves near the wall and just listened for where the commotion was the loudest and figured that would be where you were."

"You figured right," Scar says as he rides next to his friend Potbelly. "We are going to need to find somewhere to hole up for a while, so Potbelly can recover."

"Any ideas?" Jiron asks.

"We could cut cross country, try to find someplace away from civilization," Roland suggests.

"But that would be the first place I would look if I was them," Jiron replies. "Of course, any place near here will be searched in no time, as well. No, I think we better put as much distance between us and them that we can, stay on the road as long as possible."

Scar understands the logic, but is worried for his friend who doesn't look very good. "Hang in there Pot ol' boy," he says to him.

A little after midnight, James regains consciousness, though is still extremely weak and tired. "What's going on?" he asks, looking around groggily.

"We've been riding all night, ever since you blew up the bridge," Jiron tells him. "Right now we're looking for a good place to stop and rest."

"Can't take the chance that their forces will get ahead of us," he says. "We've got to keep moving."

"Potbelly is in a bad way and the horses are tired," Jiron explains. "We can't keep going very much longer."

"I'll leave it to your judgment then," he says, before passing out again.

Roland comes up next to him and asks, "Why not go off the road here and see if we can find a spot? We've traveled a long ways and hopefully their patrols won't reach this far so fast."

"You're probably right," he agrees. "Anyway, James and Potbelly need to rest." He leads them off the road and they travel cross country for another hour before coming to an old abandoned farmhouse. They bring James and Potbelly inside before they picket the horses nearby.

Delia has them lay Potbelly on the floor in the front room. Scar stays with her while the others see to the horses. She begins to unbind his bandages around the bolt. She looks to Scar and says, "It's time for it to come out." Removing the rest of the bandages, they can see where the skin around the shaft of the bolt is beginning to turn red. Drops of blood continue to well out from around it.

He nods as he watches her take out a needle and remove a thread from her shirt.

When she has the thread through the eye of the needle and tied securely, she says, "Alright, you gently pull out the bolt and I'll sew it close."

He grabs the portion of the bolt sticking out of Potbelly's side and looks to Delia who nods. Then with a gentle, even pull, he removes the bolt as blood begins streaming out.

"Quickly!" she says to him, "pinch the wound closed so I can sew it together."

As he holds the wound together to inhibit the flow of blood, he looks to the unconscious Potbelly and murmurs, "Glad you're not awake for this." He continues holding the wound together until Delia has completely sewn it closed. Tying it off, she has him remove his hands and the stitches hold securely, only a few drops of blood continue seeping through between the stitches.

Taking some water, she washes away the blood from Potbelly's side and then dries it with an extra shirt. Using strips of cloth she tore from a spare shirt, she once more binds the wound. When she's done, she says to Scar, "Hopefully we can rest here at least a day to let this heal. Keep a watch on him and don't allow him to move around very much, we don't want him to tear open the stitches."

"I will," he assures her as he settles down next to his friend.

When the others have returned from picketing the horses, Jiron sets up a watch schedule and takes the first shift. He finds a place outside where he can see anyone approaching and settles in until its Scar's turn.

Shortly after he begins his watch, Delia comes out and sits with him. "You need to get some rest," he tells her.

"In a moment," she replies. "Just needed to get out of there for a bit."

"Potbelly's snores bothering you?" he asks her with a smile.

"No, not really," she replies back. "I just can't get being questioned by Lord Cytok off my mind."

"It'll get better over time," he assures her. "Some things, especially intense situations like that, have a way of hanging around longer with you than others."

"I suppose," she says. She gives him a quick glance and continues, "Did anyone tell you why he captured us?"

He shakes his head and replies, "No, not yet."

"Well, the last package on the list was for his estate," she tells him. "When we went to deliver the goods, the man at the gate called the guards and had us taken. It seems that the smugglers had worked for Lord Cytok, in fact his is the name on that letter James has been showing everyone."

Nodding his head, he says, "That makes sense."

"Yeah," she says. "They held us until he showed up and then began questioning us as to how the letter and the cargo came to be in our possession. He hadn't been at it very long before you guys showed up." She lays her head on his shoulder and he puts his arm around her as sobs begin to wrack her body.

Holding her close, he sits there silently as she lets out all the emotions she's kept bottled up since the ordeal.

When she's done, she wipes her eyes and says, "Thanks."

"That's what friends are for," he assures her. He gives her one more hug and then says, "Now, you go and get some sleep, you look like you could use it."

Nodding her head, she begins to turn toward the house. Then she comes back over to him and gives him one last hug before leaving him there alone.

He watches her go until she's inside the house. Brushing away the tears that had fallen from his eyes in the dark, he turns his attention back to keeping watch.

Late in the night as Stig is taking his turn at watch, he hears horses passing off in the distance. He quickly moves to try to better see where they're going. In the moonlight he's able to see a company of twenty empirical horsemen ride past, going to the east.

He continues watching them until they disappear into the night. When he wakes Yorn for his turn, he tells him of the riders before turning in.

Yorn keeps a watchful eye and ear out for any other visitors, but his watch passes quietly.

"This is not the afterlife," Scar assures Potbelly when he wakes up, thinking he's dead.

"It's not?" he asks confused. "But I died last night." He sits up, even though the pain in his side is throbbing greatly.

"Don't you tear out those stitches!" Scar admonishes him severely. He lays a hand on his friend and says, "You need to rest and let you're body heal."

Potbelly gives his friend an annoying look as he knocks his hand off his shoulder. "Don't need no nursemaid!" he exclaims. "Been hurt worse than this many times in the pits."

"Stubborn," Potbelly tells him, "that's what you are."

Tersa walks over to see how he's doing and he asks, "Are you sure this isn't the afterlife? For there surely must stand an angel."

She smiles at him and asks, "How are you doing?"

"Better," he replies, "seeing as how I'm not dead."

"That's good," she tells him. "Jiron was saying that we might stay here till tomorrow if nobody shows up."

"What for?" Potbelly asks.

"So we can rest and you can heal," she replies.

"Heal? Me?" he asks as if the thought had never even occurred to him. "Now don't be thinking that I need any rest." He starts to get up and says through teeth clinched in pain, "I hardly even notice it."

"Be that as it may," she tells him, "we're here for a while so you may as well take advantage of it and heal the best you can." She gives him a playful, stern gaze.

"Yes ma'am," he replies as he settles back down to the floor.

"Keep an eye on him," she says to Scar, giving him a wink and a smile.

"You can count on it," he assures her as he turns his gaze to Potbelly. "You rest!"

Potbelly gives them both a small smile as he lies back down and soon drifts off to sleep once more.

Over to the other side of the room, James has awakened and is talking with Jiron. "Did everyone make it?" he asks.

"Yeah," he replies, "we're all here. Potbelly took a bolt in the side, but he'll survive."

"That's good," James says. "We should probably get going soon."

"You need rest," Jiron tells him, "and Potbelly could use a day for his wound to heal."

"We may not have that much time," warns James. "They're going to want us bad. Lord Cytok will most likely want revenge for what we did to him." He looks to Jiron and says, "He'll mobilize everything he can to search for us."

"What should we do?" he asks.

"I'm still going after Miko, but the rest of you should try to get out of the Empire," he says.

"You helped me get Tersa back, I'm not going to leave you before you rescue your friend," he tells him.

James looks at him a moment and then replies, "Alright. We're near the coast, or at least we were. Maybe we can sneak into a port town and get passage for the others on a ship, sailing up the coast to Cardri. If the Empire isn't at war with them, then there still should be unrestricted access for Cardri captains."

Jiron nods and adds, "With them out of danger, you and I can go after your friend."

"We just need to figure a way into a port where a Cardri ship is at anchor," he says.

"That's going to be the tricky part," agrees Jiron.

"What's going to be the tricky part?" asks Yorn as he comes over and joins the conversation.

Jiron quickly fills him in on the plan thus far. "You and the others need to get Tersa and Delia to a safe place and hole up while we're rescuing his friend."

"Take her to Trendle, it's a village to the north of Bearn," suggests James. "When you get there, find a Forest Warden by the name of Ceryn and let him know what's going on. He should be able to get you settled in while you wait for us."

"Alright," agrees Yorn.

"Now," James says, "ready or not, we need to get out of here."

Chapter Twenty

"Get away from me!" Potbelly yells at Scar who's trying to assist him in mounting his horse. "I ain't no invalid."

"Alright," Scar replies impatiently as he backs away. "Tear out those stitches then, I hope you bleed to death you pig headed mule!" He stands there and watches as Potbelly grabs the saddle and swings himself up onto his horse with a groan.

"See," he says through teeth gritted in pain, perspiration beginning to form on his face, "don't need your help."

Scar shakes his head at his friend then mounts his own horse. Staying close in case Potbelly needs him, he sits and waits for the others to get ready.

Delia rides over to them, nods to Potbelly as she asks Scar, "How's he doing?"

"I'm fine!" Potbelly answers, irritated at her for talking about him like he isn't even there.

"Stubborn and likely to kill himself because of it," he says with a slight smile, "but I think he'll survive the ride."

"Let's hope so," she says.

Jiron is the last to mount. He turns toward the others and says, "We'll make for the sea and then travel along the coast. First chance we get, we'll acquire some clothes that will allow us to pass ourselves off as Empire citizens."

Yorn asks, "What are we to do if we encounter the enemy?"

"Avoid them if possible," he replies. "Kill them if not."

Yorn gives him a satisfied grin at the thought of a little payback for the sacking of his home.

"Now, let's ride!" Jiron exclaims as he kicks his horse into a trot. Heading to the northwest, he leads them toward the sea.

James rides in the lead with Jiron as they make their way back through the desert to the road. "Think we'll make it?" Jiron asks him.

"We can but try," he replies.

"What do you plan to do once you get your friend?" he asks.

"Make our way back to Cardri," he says. "At least there it's reasonably safe right now. After that, who knows?"

Shorty hollers from the rear, "Jiron! Riders coming from the north! Looks like an advance patrol."

They turn to see ten riders coming directly at them, they have little chance in avoiding contact. "Potbelly! Stay and watch the others," Jiron hollers to him. Turning his horse, he cries to the rest, "We can't let even one escape, or they'll bring more."

Leaving Potbelly to protect Roland and the ladies, the others turn and race to meet the oncoming horsemen. Before they close the distance, two slugs fly from behind each taking out a horse causing the riders to fall to the ground. Drawing their swords and knives, they race forward, closing with the enemy.

Shorty lets fly with a knife and takes out one rider as the knife embeds itself in his chest. He then slows his horse and jumps to the ground, as knives are little use in mounted combat. He dives to the ground to avoid the blows of the mounted riders and regains his feet quickly as he heads for the ones approaching on foot whose horses were knocked out from under them.

Stig closes with a horseman, his shield on the arm holding the reins and his mace striking out. With a clash of metal, the combatants begin beating at one another, each looking for an opening.

James holds back and is looking for a clear shot to take out another rider, but his friends are too close, he dares not try it.

Two swords weaving a pattern of death, Scar engages a horseman and soon has him falling to the ground, blood welling from where his sword took him through the chest. Looking around, he sees Shorty running toward the two men on the ground. Suddenly he notices a horseman riding toward him from behind, sword raised to cut him down.

"Shorty!" he yells, "Behind you!" He watches as Shorty turns to see the horseman almost upon him and dives to the ground, avoiding by inches the sword of the rider. Then Scar's attention is diverted as he's beset by another horseman, having to block an overhand attack with one sword while slicing back with the other.

Yorn is engaged with two and is having a hard time, trading blows with one while turning his horse to avoid the other. Suddenly, the one he had been trying to avoid falls from his horse as one of James' slugs explodes out of his back.

Shorty regains his feet as the two on foot reach him. He circles, trying to keep it so only one is able to attack him at a time. He catches the sword of his attacker on his left knife as he follows through with the other, opening up a long slash along the man's forearm causing him to drop his sword.

Out of the corner of his eye, he sees the rider turn and begin to come back toward him as the remaining man closes in and engages him. Unable to disengage, he tries to quickly finish him off but is distracted by the advancing rider.

Suddenly, just when the rider is almost upon him, another horse runs full tilt into his attacker, knocking the horse off its stride. As Stig's horse crashes into the other, he vaults from his saddle and grabs the rider, dragging him to the ground. Stig lands on top of the rider and gets up first, mace smashing into him as he tries to rise, crushing his shoulder. He follows through with another blow that caves in the side of the man's head. Looking around, he sees Shorty engaged with one of the unhorsed horsemen and hurries over to render aid.

Able now to focus his attention on the remaining man, Shorty circles as he looks for an opening. The enemy strikes out with his sword and he deflects it to the side with the knife in his left hand. He twirls quickly and his elbow connects with the man's face, blood flowing from his broken nose.

The man staggers backward and then comes again at Shorty, who easily deflects another blow. Kicking out, Shorty knocks him backward toward the approaching Stig. As the man regains his balance, he's struck from behind in the head with Stig's mace and falls to the ground, lifeless.

Looking around, Shorty sees the battle is pretty much over, the last horseman is engaged with Yorn. Seeing his fellows dead or dying, the horseman starts to flee as he turns his horse and begins racing across the desert. Shorty is about to holler when the man falls to the ground amidst a gory spray as James' slug exits the man's chest.

"Anyone hurt?" Jiron shouts out over the battlefield.

"Slight cut, but nothing serious," Yorn yells back. Everyone else has sustained only minor injuries as well.

"Are any left alive?" James shouts.

"One!" replies Shorty as he comes to the one he sliced on the forearm. The man is lying there, trying with little luck to stop the blood from flowing out of the wound.

"Roland!" James hollers back over to where he's waiting with Potbelly and the ladies. "We need you!" He continues over to the fallen man as Roland and the others ride up to him.

"How may I help?" he asks when he reaches James.

James indicates the fallen man and says, "Maybe we can find out what their orders were and where they were to patrol."

"I'll see what I can do," he says as he dismounts and comes over to the fallen man. He starts to talk to him, but the man is unresponsive, just stares back at him.

"He's not going to cooperate," Roland tells him.

Looking to James, Stig asks, "Is this important?"

"Could be," James replies.

Stig draws a knife and comes over to the man as he says to Roland, "Ask him again."

Stig holds the knife in front of the man's face, intimidating him as Roland again begins speaking to him.

The man's eyes widen but still he refuses to say anything. "Tell him if he doesn't answer, I'll start removing fingers," he says to Roland as he grabs the man's forefinger, placing the edge of the knife against it.

Still the man doesn't answer, so true to his word, Stig takes a firm hold of the man's finger. He makes ready to slice the finger off and glances meaningfully at the dying man.

The man almost seems to deflate as he cries something out. Stig moves the knife away from the man's finger as he looks to Roland.

"I think he'll talk now," he says, relief obvious in his voice.

James says, "Ask him what they were doing here."

Roland exchanges words with him and then says, "They were looking for a group of assassins who tried to kill Lord Cytok."

"Assassins?" Scar exclaims. "That's not the way I remember it."

"What were their orders?" asks James.

"They were to patrol several miles into the desert and along the road for any sign of us," he says after speaking again with the man. "Apparently, no one really thought that we would be in this area, the main search is farther to the north."

"Good," James replies.

"How do we know we can trust this guy?" Shorty asks. "He may just be telling us this so we won't hurt him."

"I think he's telling the truth," Roland says, "at least as he knows it."

"I agree," James says. "Whether he is or not, it's not going to make any difference on what we're going to do."

"What are we to do with him," Tersa asks.

"We can't let him go or he'll tell them where we are," Stig insists.

"If we leave him here, he'll die," says Delia.

"Then there seems to be only one thing left to do," Stig says as he grabs the man's hair, lifts his head back and slits his throat. Letting go of the dying man's hair, he wipes his knife on the man's shirt as he gurgles and dies.

"Stig!" Delia cries out.

"What?" he asks back, staring her down and daring her to find fault.

She just turns away and goes back over to her horse.

"If he's telling the truth," James says as they all get back on their mounts, "then there may be a chance that we can find a port and get you all out of here."

Shorty comes over and gives James back the slugs he used to take down the riders.

Taking the slugs, James notices that he also recovered his throwing knives as well. "Thanks," he says to him.

"No problem," Shorty says as he goes over to his horse and mounts.

"What happens when they fail to return?" Scar asks. "Isn't someone going to come looking for them? I mean, as soon as they find them, they'll know we're not to the north."

"Then we better hurry and get to a port as fast as we can," Jiron says. Kicking his horse into a fast trot, he once more begins to lead them northwest.

Another hour of riding and they begin to see the road coming up ahead. The only traffic upon it is a caravan half a mile away moving east to west. Not observing any soldiers, they make for the road, coming onto it far ahead of the approaching caravan, not wanting to be close enough to be identified. They follow the road west as it meanders its way along the seashore which lies several hundred feet off to their right.

"If we continue west, we're bound to find a port of some kind," James says to Jiron as they ride along.

"We don't know that for sure, or even how far it's going to be," he replies.

"True, but our only alternative is to go east, back toward the capitol," he says. "And I don't think we'll be doing that."

"You got that right," agrees Jiron.

Up ahead of them, they begin to see a small fishing village appearing along the coast. Several small boats are out upon the water where men are casting out nets and pulling them back with fish ensnared within.

The village is just a small collection of huts so they continue on, hoping for a larger city. A small boy comes running out from between two of the huts as they pass and Roland hails him. When the boy comes over, he asks him something. After giving him an answer, the boy runs back into the village as he continues playing with his friends.

"What did you ask him?" inquires James.

"I asked him how far it was to the next large town," he replies. "He said a day away is the trading port of Al-Kur."

"Good," James says. "If we hurry, maybe we can reach it by nightfall."

"Hopefully not running into any more patrols along the way," Scar adds. He looks to his friend Potbelly, he seems to be doing okay even though a red stain has begun to appear on his shirt from where blood is continuing to seep through the stitches. All this riding is not allowing him to heal properly.

A couple of miles past the fishing village, they come to another town, this one is larger than the one they just passed through. They send Roland, Ezra and Arkie in to see about buying them all clothes so they can blend in with the natives. The rest continue around the town and await their return a mile or so further down the road. Once the town is no longer in sight behind them, they pull off the road and rest while they have a bite to eat.

James paces around nervously, worried about Roland and his family, until Jiron comes over and says, "Relax, they'll be fine. A man with his wife and kid will be the last one the Empire's men would be looking for."

"I know," he replies. "I just can't help but worry."

From where Scar sits with Potbelly, he can hear Scar say, "See! You done tore out a couple of the stitches." He looks over and sees Delia getting her needle ready to redo the stitches. "I hope this hurts," he tells his friend.

Potbelly just gives him an ugly look as he braces himself for the needle. James sees him flinch when she begins and turns his attention back to the east as he continues searching for the return of Roland and his family.

Shortly after Delia is finished with Potbelly, James begins to see two horses coming down the road. With relief, he sees that it's Roland and family burdened with several bundles of clothes. Roland waves and smiles when he sees James standing there.

He distributes the clothes to everyone once they've reached the others, saying, "There wasn't much selection, I hope they fit well enough."

Actually, the clothes do fit well enough, Shorty's is a bit long, but serviceable.

James looks around at everyone in their new clothes. *Not bad,* he thinks. Now if they could just do something about their weapons and shields, but all they can do is pack them away as unobtrusively as possible in with their other gear. Their disguise will uphold under a brief scrutiny, but anything more direct would easily expose them.

"I guess it's the best we can do," Jiron says to James.

"At least we don't stick out nearly as bad anymore," he adds.

"To Al-Kur, then," Jiron says as everyone mounts up and gets underway. Potbelly allows Scar to help him into the saddle this time, due primarily to the scolding he received from Delia when she had to redo his stitches. Possibly from the pain of the restitching as well, but he isn't likely to admit that to anyone.

Setting a quick pace, they make all speed for Al-Kur. They pass many travelers throughout the day, but none give them more than a quick glance or a brief 'Hello'. Roland rides in the lead with James and Jiron so he can field any and all greetings that they receive.

The sun begins to set and still Al-Kur has not appeared upon the horizon. "Maybe the boy was wrong?" suggests Jiron.

"Perhaps," agrees James. "We did have that stopover to get the clothes, let's travel a few more hours and see if it appears. If not, we can camp off the road till morning."

Nodding his head in agreement, he says, "Very well."

When night has fallen completely and the stars are out in all their glory, the lights of Al-Kur appear on the horizon.

Unable to see much of it in the dark, they discover that this town has no defending wall surrounding it. As they get closer, they run across guards and soldiers, but other than a brief glance, they pay them no attention.

Entering the city they find an inn, Roland and James go inside to inquire about rooms for them all.

With Roland doing all the talking, they get four rooms and enough stall space for all their horses. James hands over the money as the innkeeper tells Roland which rooms are theirs.

Going back outside, they get their horses settled in the stable before returning to the inn. Once inside, they divvy up the rooms; Tersa and Delia get one, Roland and family another, James, Jiron and Shorty take the third, with Yorn, Scar, Stig and Potbelly in the last one.

After taking their saddle bags up to their rooms, they meet down in the common area for dinner. They find a large table that will accommodate them all and by the time they're all seated, a serving girl comes over.

Roland orders for them all and pays her before she returns to the kitchen.

"So, what are we getting?" Shorty asks him once she's left.

"Just the house special, it's a slightly spicy stew with meat and vegetables," he tells everyone. "Comes with bread and I ordered us all ale."

Satisfied, they relax and Jiron says in hushed tones, "Tomorrow, we'll start looking for a ship to take us to Cardri."

"Why not tonight?" asks Stig.

"We're all tired," he replies. "Also, most captains have returned to their ships and none like unexpected visitors coming aboard at night."

"Makes sense," he says.

The rest of the evening they spend enjoying themselves as they eat their dinner. Although there's no entertainment provided here, they still have a good time just talking amongst themselves. James tells them of Trendle and what they can expect when they get there.

Roland and family are the first ones to head up to their rooms, Arkie being quite tired from all the riding and Ezra wants to go to sleep as well. The rest stay down there for a couple more hours until they begin to grow tired and eventually drift on up to their rooms.

The next morning when they all gather downstairs for breakfast, they decide James and Jiron, along with Roland, would go to the docks and try to find a ship to take them to Cardri. The rest would remain in their rooms, being as inconspicuous as possible.

They leave the inn and follow the main street as it makes its way down to the dock area. Before they get close to the docks, they observe several soldiers going through the crowd and asking questions. Turning around, Jiron leads them back down the street for half a block where they duck into a side alley.

"Think they're looking for us?" Roland asks, keeping an eye on the soldiers.

Nodding, James replies, "I think we have to assume so. They seem a little bit more curious than would seem normal."

"I agree," adds Jiron. Turning to James, he says, "What should we do?"

"We could go ahead and take our chances by going to the docks," he says. "Or we could remain here, keeping our eyes open and hope a captain just happens to walk by."

"One just walking by doesn't seem very likely," asserts Jiron. "Maybe we could hunt through the taverns in the area?"

"This time of morning?" asks James. "I doubt if anyone would still be there, they would all be back at their ships."

Suddenly, a group of sailors comes walking up the street from the docks, one of them is dressed finer than the others. From the looks of them, they are not from the Empire, but from the north.

Looking at the others, James says, "Fortune may be smiling upon us."

"I'd say," Jiron replies with a smile.

As the sailors pass by, they can hear the one dressed well say, "Damn customs officer, holding my cargo like that."

"He released it didn't he?" one of the sailors replies.

"Yeah," the well dressed man replies, "after holding it for two days. Two days!" He storms down the street with his men following behind.

Exiting the alley, they follow the sailors as they continue further into town before turning down a side street. They continue past several buildings until finally entering a large warehouse. Jiron and the others peer in through a window by the door where they see the sailors talking with a man inside.

"Let's wait until they come back out and see if we can book passage," suggests James to the agreement of the others.

They watch through the window until they see the man shake hands with the well dressed sailor who then turns back toward the door they entered through.

Seeing that they're coming back out, James has them move away from the building for a ways and wait until they leave.

Once all the sailors are completely out of the warehouse, James steps up to the well dressed one and says, "Excuse me."

Stopping, the sailors turn to see them standing there. A couple of them put their hands on the swords hanging at their waists.

"Yes?" the well dressed man asks, looking at James and the others.

"Are you a captain of a vessel?" James asks.

"Yes, I am," the captain replies.

"My friends and I were wondering if you might be heading to Cardri soon?" inquires James.

"Why?" the captain asks him back, suspicious.

"We were interested in booking passage if you were," he explains.

"Hmmm," the captain says and then one of his men whispers into his ear. His eyes widen slightly and then he says to James, "There were some soldiers asking about a group of people, not of the Empire, who might be looking for passage. They requested that we inform them of any that do."

"I'm sure that wouldn't be us," responds James, innocently.

"Don't lie to me boy," orders the captain, "I'm not stupid. I can tell from the way your friend over there got a panic look, that you're the ones they're looking for." He points over to where Roland is standing, beginning to blush.

"What do you plan to do?" Jiron asks, as he unobtrusively takes hold of a knife.

"Do? Nothing," the captain replies. "I hate the Empire and everything it stands for. I'm only here because I was offered enough gold for me to put aside my dislike for this place and come. Plus, some idiot of a customs official decides to hold my cargo for two days because he thought I had slighted him in some way. If you are causing them problems, so much the better."

"Then, will you allow us to sail with you?" Jiron asks. "We can pay you for your troubles."

The captain thinks for a moment and then says, "How many are there?"

"Two women, an infant and six men," James tells him.

"What could you have done with that to warrant such an extensive search?" he wonders.

"We'd rather not say," James tells him.

The captain considers it for a moment and says, "Fifty golds and that's not open to negotiation."

"Very well," agrees James holding out his hand.

The captain takes it, sealing the bargain. "Our ship is the Crashing Wave, it's the second from the end. We sail at first light, if you're late or don't have the money, we sail without you. Understand?"

"Yes, sir," replies James, "we do."

With that, the captain turns and heads back toward the docks, his men following.

"Fifty golds!" Roland cries. "Do we even have that much?"

"I guess we better go and find out," James says as they head back toward the inn.

When they return to the inn and tell everyone what's happening and how much it's going to cost, they pool their money. They discover that they do have enough, though they'll have little left for when they arrive in Cardri.

"Let's sell the horses," suggests Delia. When everyone looks at her, she continues, "We're not going to need them, except two for the two of you who'll be staying behind."

"How much do you think we could get for them?" James asks her.

"Don't know," she replies. "I'll take Roland with me and we'll find out."

"Be careful," warns Jiron, "there're soldiers everywhere looking for us."

"I will," she assures him. "Besides, are they going to be looking for a lone couple out for a stroll?"

Grabbing Roland by the arm, she propels him out the door, but not before he gets a few quick words off to Ezra.

"The rest of us should stay in our rooms until just before dawn," Jiron says. "Then make our way down to the docks."

"Sounds simple enough," adds Stig optimistically.

James hopes his optimism isn't premature.

Delia and Roland leave the inn and make their way to the outskirts of town, which is usually where the horse traders have their businesses. Several times, they cross the paths of soldiers who fail to take any interest in a couple strolling down the street. Coming to the edge of town, they find a large corral containing several horses.

"Looks like the place," comments Delia.

"I would tend to agree," adds Roland as they make their way over to the building adjacent to the corral.

Within the building, they find a man sitting at a table, making notes on parchment. When he sees them enter, he puts his quill in the inkwell and gets up as he comes over to greet them.

Once Roland makes it understood what it is they wish to do, the man becomes all business as he asks about the horses they wish to sell. He tells them that he will be happy to take them off their hands but is unable to name a price until he's actually seen the animals.

Roland explains to him that they'll be back shortly with the horses. Walking out of the horse trader's shop, Roland asks Delia "Aren't we going to draw attention if we're seen leading eight horses through the streets?"

"Hopefully not," she says, "but we need the money for when we reach Cardri."

Back at the inn, she tells them they found a buyer and takes Scar and Stig along to help with the horses. Leading them out to the stables, she has each of them take two horses. They leave the two that James and Jiron will be using to get out of Al-Kur on their way to locate Miko.

As they proceed through the city, the people on the streets only briefly glance in their direction as they make their way toward the horse trader. Apparently the sight of them leading horses through town is not so out of the ordinary to warrant curiosity.

Once at the horse trader's, he has them lead the horses into the corral where he begins an inspection of each one. He looks at hoofs, teeth and overall fitness. When he's done with the last one, he names a price, seventy five golds.

Delia commences to haggle, with Roland as the intermediary and ends up with eighty nine golds. A brief shake of hands to seal the deal and the trader takes them into his office where he pulls out a chest and counts out eighty nine golds. Scar and Stig put the golds into the pouches they're carrying and then they leave, heading back toward the inn.

A man watches them from a doorway across the street as they leave the horse trader's shop. When they're out of sight, he crosses the street and enters through the door they just came out of. The horse trader turns to look at who's entered and his face turns slightly pale when he sees the sign on the medallion the man is showing him.

The man asks, "Those people just sold you several horses?"

"Yes, sir," the trader replies, nervously. "Eight."

"Did they say why they had needed to sell so many at once?" he asks as he looks at the trader closely.

Beginning to sweat as he stands before one of the Eye's of the Empire, a secretive group that seeks out those who would jeopardize or challenge the rule of the Emperor, he replies, "They just said that they needed to leave town and wouldn't be taking the horses with them."

Staring at the trader, the Eye says, "Now, just where would they be going that they wouldn't need horses?"

"I...I don't know," the trader says, beginning to get the shakes. No good ever comes from being questioned by an Eye.

Without so much as a thank you, the Eye turns and walks out of the horse trader's shop. He ponders the question for a moment when his eye catches sight of sails out on the ocean. Nodding his head and smiling he hurries along, there's not much time.

Chapter   Twenty One

That night at the inn was one of the longest James can ever remember. Doing his best to try to sleep, he just ends up tossing and turning all night as he worries about the next day. Sometime during the night, Jiron gets up and heads to the door. "Where are you going?" James asks.

Pausing in the dark, he replies, "Down to the docks. Want to look around before morning."

"Be careful," cautions James, "and be back an hour before sunup."

"I will," he assures him. "Try to get some sleep." He then turns back toward the door and quickly makes his way out of the room, closing it behind him.

James listens to his soft tread in the silence of the night as he walks down the hallway to the stairs as he lays there for awhile. After no longer being able to hear his footsteps he must've managed to fall asleep for the shutting of the door startles him awake when Jiron returns.

"Just me," he hears Jiron say as he walks over to where he's lying on the bed. "We got trouble."

"What?" he asks, coming the rest of the way awake.

"There are twenty or more guards stationed at the docks with more patrols on the streets than there were yesterday," he explains.

"Did you find out why?" James asks.

"No," he replies. "It was all I could do just to avoid being seen."

"How are we going to get the others to the Crashing Wave with all the guards everywhere?" James asks, worried.

"I don't know, but we better think of something fast," he says. "Dawn's about an hour away."

James sits there and contemplates the situation when Jiron says, "Maybe we could draw them off?"

"What do you mean?" he asks.

"I mean, we get the others close to the docks, then you and I go to another part of town and create a diversion," he explains.

Nodding, James says, "That might work. Can we get them close enough to the docks without being seen?"

"I think so," Jiron replies.

"Let's wake up the others and let them know what's going on," he says as he gets out of bed.

Going to the other rooms, they soon have everyone awake and back in James' room for a quick meeting. As soon as everyone's there, they tell them about the guards at the dock and what they plan to do.

"Selling the horses," Delia announces. "That must have tipped them off something was going on."

"Could've been," James agrees, "but we had little choice."

He has them take out the money and makes sure that Roland has the fifty golds for their passage. Then he takes ten golds apiece for Jiron and himself, the rest they divide among everyone else. He turns to Roland and says, "Have Ezra keep Arkie quiet. If he starts crying, it's all over."

Roland nods his head and communicates that to Ezra, who indicates she understands. "Alright," he says, "let's go."

They quietly make their way down to the main floor and leave out the back way near the stables. "We better leave our two horses here and try to get back to them when we're ready to leave town," he suggests to Jiron.

"If we're able," he replies. "We might be a little too busy to make it back here."

Jiron takes the lead and follows a roundabout way through the streets toward the docks. Twice they have to duck into side alleys when they encounter roving patrols. Both times they wait silently until they pass before continuing once more to the docks.

When they're within a couple blocks of the docks, Jiron stops before a door in the side of a darkened warehouse and places his ear against it, listening. Then he turns the handle and opens the door as he motions for everyone to file inside. The warehouse is empty but for a few boxes that look like they have been abandoned here. "You should be able to wait here until you make the run for the ship."

"How will we know when it's time?" Tersa asks.

Jiron looks to James and says, "I think you'll know."

James nods his head.

Tersa gives her brother a hug and says, "You be careful."

He hugs her back and sees the tears in her eyes, "Don't worry, I'll see you in Trendle." Trying to stop his own tears from falling at having to leave her again, he says to James, "We better get going."

"Good luck," Delia says to them before they leave. The others offer their 'goodbyes' and 'see you laters' as well.

With a final look toward the pit fighters, Jiron says, "You keep her safe!"

Scar says, "You can count on us," the others nod their heads in agreement.

With a slight nod of his head, Jiron leaves the warehouse with James right behind and closes the door behind them. Turning to James he says, "Let's go cause some trouble!"

"Right behind you," he says, not nearly as eager as Jiron seems to be.

Jiron leads him through back streets as they avoid the patrols until they've put most of the city between them and where the others wait. Hiding in the shadows of an alley, they watch as a patrol of five guards approach from down the street.

"You ready?" Jiron asks James.

"No," James replies, sighing slightly, "but I never will be. So let's just do it."

They wait for the guards to march pass and then Jiron runs out of the alley and tackles the one in the rear while James causes a light to burst overhead.

His knives strike out, killing the rear guard while James takes out another with a slug. Cries begin sounding in the night and horns start to sound. Jiron quickly gains his feet as the remaining three turn around, momentarily blinded by the light bursting overhead.

Jiron closes with the next one and quickly takes him out. "Let's get out of here!" he hollers to James as they run, leaving the remaining two guards to sound the alarm.

"Think that did it?" James asks as they dash through a side alley to get away from the scene of the attack.

"Probably not enough to draw them from the docks," he says. "We need something a bit more spectacular."

"Alright," James says as they race around a corner.

"Nothing yet," Shorty announces from where he's looking out the window for the signal.

"It's only been a couple minutes," Delia says. "Give them time."

Tersa comes over near Delia and asks, "Do you think they'll be able to draw off the guards at the docks?"

Delia nods her head as she remembers the massive explosion James had produced back at the City of Light, "I'm sure they can manage it."

Suddenly a bright light comes in through the window and everyone runs over to look. A starburst explodes in the sky near the far side of Al-Kur. "Was that them?" asks Tersa.

"Has to be," Delia replies just as horns begin to sound off in the distance.

Shorty runs over to a window that has a good view of the docks and the men stationed there. After a brief look he turns back to them and says, "They're still there."

"What are they doing?" Scar asks as he moves to join him.

"They're looking at the light but otherwise not moving," he says.

"Come on guys," Stig says as he looks out the window toward the starburst that's beginning to fade, "you've got to do better than that."

They can see other guards running toward the commotion off in the distance, but the ones at the docks remain where they are.

"I don't think…" Yorn starts to say when…

Crumph!

A massive explosion rips through the night, fireballs shooting into the air as well as chunks of stone from whatever building had blown up.

"Way to go James!" Scar exclaims jubilantly.

"Some are leaving!" Shorty shouts from where he's watching the docks.

"How many?" asks Stig.

"It looks like all but about ten," Scar replies.

Potbelly says, "That's better than twenty."

"It's unlikely any more will leave if they haven't already," adds Stig.

"I agree," Scar says. "Shorty, can you take out a few before we get there?"

"Three or four," he replies. "I'm running out of knives."

"That will do," he says. "We can take care of the rest." Drawing one of his swords, he opens the door and takes the lead as they begin making their way slowly toward the docks. The rest of the fighters follow him closely with Roland and the girls at the end along with Potbelly, who's doing better but still not up to his best.

When they reach the docks, they pause briefly before passing from the cover afforded by the last of the warehouses. Shorty readies his knives and with a nod from Scar, begins throwing them in rapid succession. The others break into a run toward the guards as the second knife flies by.

They watch as his first knife flies and strikes one of the guards. As the man falls to the ground, the second sinks into the man standing next to him. The rest of the guards become aware of the threat and begin scanning for the source of the flying knives. One of them shouts a warning when he spots them running toward them, weapons out.

A third knife takes out another guard and then Shorty's final knife hits the foremost guard in the shoulder. As he staggers from the blow Scar reaches him and quickly finishes him off with a thrust through the middle.

Potbelly stays behind to guard the women and Roland, his sword and knife ready for any who somehow make it around the others. He keeps an eye out behind them as well for any who may come from within Al-Kur.

Stig faces off with a guard bearing a sword and shield, his mace smashing through the man's shield and breaking the bone of his arm in two. He deflects the guard's sword with his shield while following through with his mace. Connecting with the man's helmet, he caves it in and crushes the skull beneath. As the guard falls lifelessly to the ground, he turns and engages another.

Shorty's fighting knives dance as he joins the fray, blocking the attacks of two guards. Unable to go on the offensive, he's at least able to put up a good defense and keep these two busy while the others deal with the rest.

Suddenly a cry splits the night and Scar turns to see Yorn fall, a guards' sword wedged between his ribs. "Yorn!" he cries, as he strikes out at his opponent severing the man's head from his shoulders. He runs over to where Yorn lies and engages the guard who has his foot on Yorn's chest as he attempts to dislodge his sword. With his sword wedged in between Yorn's ribs, he's unable to defend himself and falls quickly to Scar's swords. Scar looks down to Yorn but knows there's no hope when he sees his lifeless eyes staring out.

Having killed his opponent, Stig moves to help Shorty who's being hard pressed by the two guards he's fighting. Coming up behind one, he cuts deeply into the man's neck, practically severing his head from his shoulder. As the man falls, Shorty is able to utilize both knives in his fight with the remaining man and soon has him on the ground next to his partner.

Swearing at the loss of Yorn, Scar looks around and sees the rest of the guards lying dead on the docks. "Come on!" he yells as he waves to where Potbelly waits with the others.

From across town, another massive explosion rocks the morning. They look and see a large fireball reaching up toward the sky.

The morning is beginning to lighten as the sun peaks over the horizon. Scar looks to the ship, second from the end and sees movement upon the rigging where the sailors are preparing to get under way.

Once Potbelly and the others join them, they begin running toward the Crashing Wave. Reaching the gangplank, Roland hollers up to the ship, "Permission to come aboard?"

The captain comes to the rail and looks down at them. Glancing over to the dead guards lying on the docks he replies, "Permission granted."

"Come on!" Roland says to the others as he starts crossing the gangway.

When they're all on board they stop abruptly as four crossbowmen aim their crossbows at them. From behind the captain, the Eye comes forward and says, "Thank you captain, you've been most helpful."

James is growing quite tired, especially after that last spell which took out the guardhouse. "Do you think that's enough yet?" he asks Jiron.

Grinning back at him, Jiron says, "That should be enough to get their attention in a bad way."

They run down a side alley as they attempt to evade another patrol passing through the area. They've been running and hiding after that last explosion, doing their best to avoid tangling with any large group of guards. James' supply of slugs is beginning to run low, only ten left.

"Maybe it's time to get the horses and leave," he suggests.

Jiron replies as he nods his head, "That would probably be a good idea, they should be on the ship by now."

"I hope so," he says as he thinks of Delia and especially little Arkie.

"Our horses are all the way across town," Jiron informs him. "It's going to take us a while to get there."

"I know," he replies, "lead on."

Looking out of the alley, Jiron checks to make sure the street is clear of guards before exiting. When the coast is clear, they exit the alley and follow the street in the interest of speed. Breaking into a run, they head toward the inn where their horses are stabled.

Street by street they make their way closer to the inn. Many times they've had to duck down alleys or into buildings to avoid being spotted. Back on the street after one such incident, they suddenly see a group of six soldiers turn onto the street ahead of them. Fortunately they're moving the other way down the street so fail to notice them.

"Soldiers now?" James says as they quickly turn off the street into another alley.

Leading them further into the alley, Jiron replies, "Guess we really got their attention."

"That was the plan," James says from behind. "Could be the ones who've been following us the last few days, too," he adds.

"Possibly," agrees Jiron.

Coming to the end of the alley, they pause as they watch a dozen or more soldiers running past on their way further into the city. They're just moving past the alley where James and Jiron are waiting, when from up above them, a woman begins crying out to the soldiers.

James looks up as she continues yelling and pointing to where they're hiding in the alley. Glancing back toward the soldiers, he sees them turning and begin running in their direction.

"Damn!" he hears Jiron curse as they race back down the alley. Before they reach the end of the alley, Jiron grabs James and ducks into a side door of the building opposite the one with the woman.

James slams the door shut and locks it. That's when he realizes Jiron has led them into someone's home. Jiron takes the stairs leading up to the second floor with James following close behind. Before they reach the top of the stairs, banging can be heard coming from the door leading to the alley.

Emerging from the stairs onto the second floor they see before them a long hallway running the length of the home. From the far end a door can be heard slamming shut and what sounds like furniture being piled behind the door to prevent them from gaining access to it.

They do a quick search and locate a narrow stairway leading up to the roof. As Jiron steps upon the ladder to go up to the roof, they hear the door to the alley burst in. Moving quickly up the stairs they reach the roof.

Jiron pauses momentarily as James clears the ladder. "Where now?" James asks him.

He scans the buildings adjacent to them and finds one with a small enough gap between them that they will be able to jump. "Follow me," he tells him as he runs and jumps over the gap between buildings.

James runs as fast as he can and with heart beating wildly, jumps across. Sailing through the air he glances to the alley below and panics. When he lands on the other side, he loses his balance, falls to the roof and rolls a couple of times before coming to a stop.

Jiron is there to help him back to his feet and then they run to the opposite side where they once more jump the gap. James makes it this time without falling.

A noise behind them causes James to turn and he sees soldiers pouring onto the roof of the building they had originally exited. "One more time," he hears Jiron say as he makes once more for the edge of the building where he jumps across to the other side.

Looking over his shoulder before he starts to run for the edge, James sees the soldiers beginning to jump the first gap in pursuit. Bracing himself for another jump, he runs quickly and soars over to the other building where he lands well, maintaining his balance.

Jiron is standing by an open trapdoor that leads down into the building. "Hurry!" he yells over to him as he begins to climb down.

James reaches the trapdoor and starts to climb down when he hears Jiron fighting with someone on the inside. When he clears the top, he sees him there battling with someone in their nightshirt.

The man is no match for Jiron and is soon lying on the ground, blood beginning to soak the front of his nightshirt.

"Did you have to kill him?" James asks as Jiron begins to descend to the ground floor.

With impatience in his voice, Jiron replies, "Didn't have time not to."

Coming to the front door, he pauses a moment and says to James, "I think we're only a couple of streets down from the inn."

"Thank goodness," exclaims James.

He looks out a window near the door and sees many soldiers running past on their way to the building they had originally entered down the street.

Suddenly, they hear the pounding of many feet on the roof as the soldiers chasing them reach the roof from the other building.

Jiron says to James, "There are still a lot of soldiers out there."

"What choice do we have?" he replies grimly.

Jiron throws open the door and quickly engages the closest soldier, taking him by surprise. At the clash of metal, every eye turns toward them. Jiron quickly disposes of the soldier as he turns to face the others.

James pauses momentarily as he gazes at the dozens of soldiers in the street that are now intent upon them.

Crumph!

The ground explodes to their right, throwing soldiers and dirt into the air. Then he releases the power again as the ground to their left explodes upward. Two soldiers are left dazed and standing after the two explosions.

Jiron closes with the first one and in his dazed state, is unable to defend himself. Jiron takes him out in short order. The other soldier gains his senses quickly and draws his sword as he advances.

James looks back to the building they just vacated and sees the soldiers coming down the stairs from the roof, heading for the open door. Almost out of reflex, he unleashes a blast of energy through the door, knocking them backward and slowing them down.

"Come on!" Jiron says to him as the second soldier falls to the ground.

His head bursting with pain and knees wobbly, he hurries as best he can. Jiron sees the condition he's in and takes his arm, helping him toward the inn.

They move along the path left between the two large holes in the road he created with the explosions and move into another alley on the far side. Hurrying as best they can, they come to the rear wall of the inn's courtyard.

The inn's courtyard is crowded with people who begin screaming and running when they see Jiron and James approaching. Jiron is a ghastly site, covered in blood as he is with one knife drawn, glinting in the torchlight. The courtyard is soon cleared of the panicked people. They move to the stable to retrieve their horses that they had left saddled for a quick escape.

Once in the saddle, they ride out of the courtyard and into the street where Jiron plows through a group of soldiers, knocking them to the ground. Riding with all speed, they race for the edge of town, several crossbow blots fly in their direction but all miss their mark.

They gallop with reckless speed through the streets, heedless of anyone in their way as they make for the edge of town. Suddenly, Jiron pulls up and stops. "Why did you stop?" James hollers at him as he slows to a halt beside him.

Jiron points down the street and says, "Look."

Looking to where Jiron is pointing, he gasps when he sees the men stationed along the road ahead of them. There are easily thirty crossbowmen and another fifty foot soldiers barring their way. "Oh my god!" he says. Beyond the waiting men is the edge of town, and escape.

Looking behind them, Jiron sees a swarm of soldiers heading their way. "Looks like we're trapped," he says.

"Jiron," James says.

"Yes?" he replies without taking his eyes off the approaching soldiers.

James removes a rope from behind his saddle and begins tying himself in place. "You may need to lead my horse should I lose consciousness."

Jiron looks over to him and sees what he's doing, "What do you plan?"

"Don't have time to explain," he replies. "Just don't let go of my horse, whatever you do."

Jiron nods his head and takes the reins as James closes his eyes. Behind them, the soldiers are gaining, only five buildings separate them from where he's sitting on his horse. The soldiers barring the edge of town have taken notice of them as well and have begun advancing slowly toward them. *Come on James!* he thinks to himself as he watches the men getting closer.

All of a sudden, two of the buildings behind them blast apart, their stones raining down upon the men running in the street. Cries ring out as the stones crush the men. With great relief, Jiron sees the street behind them is now completely blocked by the rubble.

He looks over to James and sees perspiration beginning to form and course down his face. His breathing is coming in gasps and he's leaning slightly in the saddle.

"James?" he asks but then stops when James shakes his head.

The wind suddenly begins blowing harder as it steadily increases in intensity. Jiron looks to the sky as clouds appear, moving toward them with unnatural speed from all directions. James begins to moan in pain but still he concentrates, directing the magic.

Having just witnessed the power James unleashed on the men now dead under the rubble, the soldiers waiting for them at the edge of town become restless. They become even more so when they see the clouds gathering in the sky above them. Several crossbow bolts fly in their direction, but the force of the wind knocks them awry. A man with a commanding presence, an officer by his bearing, stands there yelling at the nervous soldiers, attempting to bolster their courage.

Jiron looks on in absolute amazement as he watches a section of the clouds begin to descend a little ways down from the dark mass above. And then suddenly, with great speed, it slams into the waiting men below. Nothing can be heard but the roar of the tornado as it rips through the gathered men beneath it. Bodies are ejected from it, flying in all directions to land broken and lifeless. Those not directly under it are sucked into it until they too are eventually thrown out, falling lifeless to the ground.

A very few of the men that were gathered at the edge of town survived the initial plunge of the tornado. Thrown around by the wind, the rest flee for their very lives. Suddenly, a cry comes from James and the tornado splits in two, each half moving away from the center of the street in opposite directions.

Jiron glances back to James who is trying to say something but is having trouble being heard over the roar of the wind. Leaning closer, he's able to make it out, "Now, go between them!" Trusting in James, he gets the horses moving quickly and they approach the towering funnels. The wind whips them mercilessly as he approaches the gap between the two.

The horses balk at going between the two towering tornadoes, but with whips and kicks, Jiron forces them through. "Hurry!" he barely hears James shout as they pass between the swirling masses of destruction. Kicking the horses harder, Jiron at last emerges from the other side, where it takes little encouragement to get the horses into a gallop.

Another cry escapes James before he passes into unconsciousness. Jiron looks back to the tornadoes and sees them melding back together into one large tornado that quickly dissipates. Seeing no imminent pursuit, he turns the horses southeast and races out into the desert.

"Please drop your weapons," the Eye says to them.

Roland glares at the captain, feeling betrayed. The captain just returns his stare, his face devoid of any emotions.

The Eye raises his hand and the crossbowmen take aim as he repeats his command, "Drop your weapons, now!"

With little choice they remove their weapons and drop them to the ship's deck.

"You've given us quite a chase," he says to them. "Fortunately, that is now over." Turning to the captain, the Eye says, "Have your men secure their hands behind them."

The captain glances behind him to his men standing there, "You heard him boys."

"Aye, captain," one of them says as they start to move toward Roland and the rest.

As they pass through where the crossbowmen stand, they suddenly turn and knock the crossbows out of their hands, quickly subduing them. The captain, in a fluid motion, draws his sword and rests the point on the Eye's chest.

"What is this, captain?" the Eye exclaims in anger when he sees the captain's sword threatening him.

"You're not taking them," he informs the Eye.

"I'll have you killed for this, captain!" the Eye warns vehemently. "I'll send your ship to the bottom of the sea!"

"Toss em over, lads," the captain tells his crew, ignoring the threats of the Eye.

One by one, the crossbowmen are thrown overboard until only the Eye remains. "Captain!" one of the men up in the rigging hollers out as he points toward the docks, "we've got company!"

The captain looks over to the docks and sees a score of men running toward his ship. "You'll never get out of this harbor alive," the Eye warns him.

"Cast off," he cries to his men who begin casting off lines and climbing the rigging.

"Your death will be a pleasure," the Eye continues, "watching as you wriggle upon the end of a pole as it slowly pushes its way through your guts from your ass!"

"Would you just shut up!" the captain yells at the Eye. He turns him around, boots him in the butt and watches as he plummets over the rail into the sea below.

"Thank you captain," Tersa says as she comes forward.

"Enough time for that later," he tells her. "You and the others stay out of our way and we may yet live through this."

"Mr. Kerny!" he hollers.

"Yes sir," a sailor yells from the other side of the ship.

"Make for deep water!" he cries.

"Aye, aye captain!" he replies as he begins turning the wheel to steer them out to sea. The wind begins filling their sails as they slowly turn away from the docks and head out of the harbor.

Splash!

A rock hits the water not five feet from the side of the ship. "Look!" Stig cries as another boulder flies through the air toward them. They brace for impact but it flies over the ship, landing with a splash twenty feet away.

"That was close," exclaims Shorty.

"Mr. Kerny!" the captain yells.

"Yes, captain," Mr. Kerny replies.

"Hard to port, evasive actions!" he tells him.

"Aye, aye captain!" and then they feel the ship lurch as Mr. Kerny begins attempting to evade the oncoming boulders.

"Captain, look!" Delia cries as she sees two ships beginning to pull away from the docks.

"I see 'em, lass," the captain tells her, "but if we can beat them to open water, they'll never catch us."

"Ahoy aloft! Full sails!" he shouts to the sailors in the rigging.

Without even a reply, they begin to completely unfurl the sails. Once they're fully extended, the boat lurches as the wind fills the sails.

Delia looks to the ships that are pulled out, but they've already begun to fall behind. She soon realizes that they are not going to be able to catch them.

The captain comes over to where they're crouching by the railing and asks, "So, do you have my fifty gold pieces?"

She nods to Roland who hands over the pouch containing the gold.

The captain opens it and looks through it, satisfied.

"You did all this for fifty golds?" Stig asks incredulously.

"No, son," the captain replies, "I did it because I hate the empire."

"But you've risked your life and your ship for us," Delia says. "How can we ever repay you?"

"Having the pleasure of kicking that son of sea cow overboard was payment enough," he tells her breaking into a big smile.

"Make yourselves comfortable," he tells them. "It's a three day trip to Cardri."

The wind starts to fall off suddenly and there's a cry from up above. The captain looks to the sky and watches in amazement as the clouds begin rushing toward Al-Kur. "What the hell?" he exclaims.

"It's James," Delia whispers to the others.

"You think so?" Tersa asks.

"Yeah, only magic could make the clouds react like that," she explains.

They look back to Al-Kur and watch as the clouds intensify over the town and then suddenly seem to descend to the ground in one spot. After a couple minutes, the clouds begin dissipating and everything returns to normal.

"Hope they're alright," Tersa says, worried for her brother.

"Those two can take care of themselves," Scar assures her.

"I hope so," she says as she watches Al-Kur slowly disappear in the distance. "I hope so."

Chapter   Twenty Two

The days since the fall of the City of Light have blurred together until he no longer knows how long it's been since it all began. His butt has finally stopped aching from sitting on the seat in the wagon and the sore on his leg from the manacle around his ankle is beginning to toughen up and become a callus. His is but one of several wagons loaded with slaves.

Miko stares numbly out at the water of the ocean as the wagon he's in continues its journey. To where, he doesn't know nor care anymore. He was sure that James would've found him by now, but day after day of hope unfulfilled has left him doubting if he would come at all. After all he's only one boy and a street rat at that. Hardly worth risking one's life for. Why did he think James would even bother coming after him?

His arm still throbs from where he got cut by a fellow slave back in the city of Azzac. It was during the night after they arrived at the city and been placed in holding pens with other slaves. During their journey, as they came to different cities, they would stop off at the local magistrate's building and some slaves would be taken off or others added. Often the ones who were added were those who had been sentenced by the courts for some heinous crime and were on their way to wherever their sentence decreed.

It was during one such stop the day before their arrival at Azzac that they acquired an individual who took an immediate disliking to Miko. When the man was put in the wagon, he sat across from Miko. The chain from the manacle on his foot was secured to the same eye ring in the bed of the wagon that Miko's was.

Miko disliked the looks of him from the beginning, he was missing two fingers on his right hand and a scar ran across one eye that was white and obviously blinded. His hair was greasy and dirty, many of his teeth were missing and those that remained were crooked and beginning to turn black. He began to refer to him as Black Tooth, but only in his mind.

Black Tooth kept staring at Miko after the wagon began rolling and then he said something to him. When Miko failed to respond he began to grow agitated. One of the other slaves in the wagon, who had been riding with Miko for a while, said something to him.

Black Tooth turned to Miko and said something else before a crooked smile played across his face, which did anything but put him at ease. The rest of that day, Black Tooth kept staring at him and by the end of the day, Miko was feeling very uncomfortable and worried.

When the slave caravan stopped for the night, they unloaded the slaves and had them all settle in close together for the night, with several slavers armed with crossbows standing watch over them. Their legs were manacled together but their hands were kept free. One by one, they were marched away from camp where they were allowed to answer nature's call and then returned to the others.

Miko was relieved that Black Tooth was nowhere near his place. He did catch him glancing over at him from where he was sitting on the other side of the group. Each time he did, a chill would run through Miko and his nerves would start getting the better of him.

In the morning, when he woke up, many slaves were talking among themselves and pointing off the road to the east. Miko gets up and looks to see a wall of fog off in the distance. No one there speaks his language so he's left to his own imagination as to why they're so excited about it.

Once more led to the edge of camp, Miko takes care of nature's business and then is brought back to the wagon where his manacles are once again secured to the eye ring in the bed of the wagon. Black Tooth is seated on his side of the wagon with two others between them, much to Miko's relief.

All that day they continue riding under the blazing hot sun, Miko is surprised at just how dark he's becoming from the sun. Near nightfall, he sees a large city appearing on the horizon ahead of them. One of the other's in the wagon says 'Azzac' to him as the man points to it.

Miko gazes at the approaching city and wonders if this will be the end of the line for him, where he will truly become a slave. With apprehension, he watches the city grow closer until finally they pass through the gates.

They roll on through the city for awhile until they arrive at a large compound where the wagon stops and they're removed from the wagon.

Feet still manacled, they're led into the building and divided into two holding pens where their manacles are removed.

Miko is the second to enter the pen and he watches with dread as Black Tooth is ushered into his pen behind him. When Black Tooth sees him there, he breaks into the smile that sets Miko's nerves on edge.

Trying to put as much distance between them as possible, Miko moves to a far corner and settles down there. He watches Black Tooth as he goes over to several guys in the corner and begins talking to them. From the way they're acting, it doesn't look to him like the others know him at all.

The only time when Miko leaves his corner is when they're fed and when he has to use the slop bucket. It's not long after they're fed that the light begins to fade with the coming of night. The slaves in the pens begin settling down to get what sleep they can.

Sometime in the middle of the night, Miko is awakened when someone grabs him. Startled, he tries to break free but the man only laughs. *Black Tooth!* Frantic now, Miko struggles harder and strikes out with his elbow, catching Black Tooth in the side.

Black Tooth's grip loosens slightly but it's enough for Miko to wriggle away from him. In his haste to get away, Miko trips over a sleeping slave who cries out in protest.

In the dim light filtering in through the windows, he sees Black Tooth begin approaching him, something held in his hand, glinting in the dim light. Miko starts hollering "Help! Guards!"

Black Tooth says something and then rushes toward him.

Miko keeps hollering as he tries to get away from Black Tooth. The other men in the pen realize what's going on and quickly move to the edge to get out of harm's way. Some begin calling out and before you know it, the whole area is in a roar with words and cheers, none of which Miko understands.

A door opens and light fills the pens from several torches brought in by the guards to see what the commotion is about.

Black Tooth continues chasing him around the pen as the guards enter the holding area, and when Miko gets close to the men at the side, one of them trips him. Falling to the floor, Miko quickly rolls on his back and sees Black Tooth right on top of him.

The knife held in his hand strikes down, opening up a long cut on his left forearm.

Suddenly, the door to the pen is opened and guards rush in and grab Black Tooth before he can strike again. They immobilize his arm and remove the knife from his hand. They holler to others and as they take

Black Tooth out of the pen. Two slavers come in with a wooden block and set it on the floor outside of the pen.

They take Black Tooth to it and lay his right arm, the one that held the knife, across the top of it as one of the guards draws his sword. With a quick motion, he severs Black Tooth's hand from his arm.

Black Tooth cries out in pain as his hand falls to the floor and blood begins to spray out of his stump.

One of the guards takes a torch and places it to the stump, cauterizing the wound and stopping the blood flow, which causes Black Tooth to cry out again as his flesh begins to sizzle in the flames. The smell of burnt flesh and hair fills the pen with a nauseating odor.

When the wound is sealed, they throw Black Tooth back into the pen and one of the guards makes an announcement which Miko is unable to understand. But he gets the gist of it, don't cause trouble or you'll be punished severely.

Then the guards take the block away and once more leave them in darkness as they file out of the holding area. Once Miko's eyes become adjusted again to the gloom, he can make out Black Tooth on the ground, holding his stump as he moans in pain. He can't see, so much as feel the hate for him radiating from Black Tooth.

His own wound seeps blood all night but by morning has stopped and a scab is beginning to form.

That was several days ago, just how many Miko isn't sure. He's lost count as every day is the same. He looks down to where Black Tooth still sits and whenever their eyes meet, naked hatred is all he sees reflected in his eyes. He's sure that given the chance, Black Tooth would kill him. But without his right hand, Miko is confident that he can defend himself against any attack he may try.

A day or so ago, the road turned south as it continues following the coastline. They had rolled into a large city and made their way down to the docks to drop off two slaves while picking up three more. They now number six wagons with sixteen slaves jammed into each.

The ships with their sails gave Miko a moment's pleasure as he imagines sailing upon the seas in them, like many a story he heard from bards and minstrels. To feel the sea air and the spray of the waves as your ship crashes through them, ah, Miko can only dream. But the dream was to be short lived, for they once more returned to the road and continued on their way, leaving the ships behind them.

Miko looks to the sea as they ride and occasionally can see the ships passing by on their way to who knows where. Ever since being in the port, he's had a desire to be upon one.

That night, during the wee hours of the morning, Miko is awakened by shouting as guards begin rushing about. He sees a couple of them with crossbows mounting their horses and heading off into the desert. The slaves begin muttering to themselves until a slaver comes over and tells them to be quiet.

Miko lies back down, wondering just what all that was about. In the morning when he awakens and gets back on the wagon, he sees at the edge of the camp, four dead bodies. Slaves that he later comes to understand had tried to make a break for it last night.

Wish one of them had been Black Tooth, he thinks to himself wistfully.

Another couple of days finds them rolling into another port town and heading toward the dock area. Several ships docked there are in the process of loading or unloading cargo. The wagons pull up next to one and a slaver gets down off the lead wagon and walks up the gangplank onto the ship.

Miko is figuring on them transferring more men either to or from the ship. When the slaver comes back to the top of the gangplank, he hollers to the other slavers and they begin removing all the slaves from the wagons who are then led up to the ship. Excited about being on a ship, but apprehensive as well, Miko looks around as he walks up the gangplank and led over to a hatch where he's led down into the hold.

The hold is a place of stale air and unpleasant odors. They are led over to where eye rings have been secured to the hull and their manacles are secured to them. Left there in the dark, Miko begins to get scared and a little nauseous from the motion of the ship and the smells from the hold.

After what seems like hours, the ship finally begins to move. Even though he's held in the cargo hold as a slave, Miko enjoys the roll of the ship despite being nauseated as it makes its way out to sea.

After twenty minutes into the voyage, one of the slaves further down from Miko starts throwing up when the rocking of the ship gets the better of him, spraying it all over. The odor only adds to the already unbearable stench in the hold. Miko's stomach begins to protest as he continues to smell the other man's vomit.

Before too long, others begin vomiting as well, including Miko whose stomach can no longer stand the combined odor and the rocking of the ship. The voyage that started out as one of excitement for him, now is pure misery as he gets sicker and sicker, vomiting several more times.

At last, the rocking of the ship diminishes and they feel the hull scrape alongside another dock. The ship comes to a stop and they hear footsteps on the deck above them coming over to the hatch. The hatch above them opens, allowing light and fresh air to come in, much to everyone's relief.

A sailor comes and begins removing their manacles from the eye rings in the floor. They're then told to come up and when Miko steps out of that foul hell hole, he sees that the ship is resting next to a small pier on a heavily wooded island, at least he thinks it's an island. At the end of the pier are several buildings as well as a guard tower upon which two guards with crossbows are standing watch.

The men are disembarked from the ship and formed into lines upon the pier. A guard steps forward and takes several papers from the captain of the ship and then turns to the slaves. After making a short speech that Miko is unable to comprehend, they begin marching along the pier toward an area with several large barrels. A slave stands with a bucket near the first barrel.

As the first of the new arrivals reaches the slave with the bucket, he pours the water in the bucket over the slave's head who then commences to rub as much of the filth he acquired in the hold off as he can. When it's Miko's turn, he steps forward and feels the water flow over him gratefully, the stench from the hold of the ship at last being washed away. A faint odor still remains despite his efforts to remove it all, but nothing like what they smelled like before, a hot bath would do the trick a whole lot better. After the last of the slaves has had a bucket's worth of water poured over him, the line begins moving again.

They march for about an hour, the fresh air and exercise is a pleasant change after the length of time on the wagon and then in the bottom of the cargo hold. From out of the forest ahead of them, a wooden palisade suddenly appears and begins running along the side of the road. Guards armed with crossbows can be seen walking along the top of the wall and look their way as they approach.

A gate large enough to accommodate a wagon swings open as they near the middle of the palisade and they're marched through. Once on the other side of the gate, Miko sees a large open pit in front of them, with a winding road that follows the outer edge as it circles down into the depths.

Surrounding the pit are many wooden buildings, with the wall encompassing the entire area. Wagons are rolling along the road as they make their way from out of the depths of the pit. The guards march Miko and the others over toward the road that leads into the pit and then follow the road as it descends into the pit.

Chapter   Twenty Three

James awakens to the sound of waves crashing upon rocks. Though his head hurts like it's about to split open, he sits up and sees Jiron sitting over near the entrance to a cave, staring out at the water. Their two horses are standing over by the opposite side of the cave.

A groan escapes from James as he sits up. Jiron glances back over his shoulder at him and smiles. "Didn't think you were ever going to come back to the land of the living," he says.

Holding his head in his hands to try and ease the pain, James replies with a raspy voice, "Not sure that I have."

Jiron gets up and brings him a water bottle, "Like some water?"

Reaching out his hand, he takes the offered bottle and drains the entire contents. Looking around, he asks, "Just where are we?"

"In a cave near the ocean," Jiron explains.

"How did we get here?" he asks as he hands the bottle back.

"After we left Al-Kur," he begins to explain, "I initially took us out into the desert but ran across a patrol, they saw us and gave chase. I had to back track toward the coast, we didn't lose them until night fell. After that, we rode all night until I saw this cave opening revealed in the moonlight."

"Been here for two days," he tells him. "Wasn't sure if you were going to make it at first, but by the end of the first day you were getting less restless and began to quiet down. I was afraid the noise you were making would alert anyone passing by to our presence here. I did some scouting around and we seem to be in a remote area, I doubt if anyone will think to look for us here."

"Me too," agrees James, his throat still a little raspy. "Do we have any food?" he inquires.

"A little," he replies and then moves over to one of the saddle bags. He takes out a cloth containing some rations and brings it over to James. "I figure we have a day's worth left," he says, "maybe more."

James takes it and when he takes his first bite, his stomach lets out a large growl and he begins eating in earnest.

"Are you going to need more rest?" Jiron asks him.

"I think so," James replies just as a yawn escapes him. "Most likely another day at the most, then I think I'll be okay to travel."

"In that case I better go and find us more food or we'll be out by morning," he tells him. "It looks like you're going to be needing a lot."

"I usually do after major magic like I did back at Al-Kur," he explains.

Jiron looks to him and asks, "Will you be okay by yourself?"

He shrugs and says, "If no one shows up, yes. I doubt if I could do anything to defend myself now if someone should come by."

"I won't be long," he says as he goes over and begins to saddle one of the horses.

James finishes eating and already his body is telling him it's time to rest. Trying to stifle another big yawn he says, "Hurry back."

"I will," he assures him. Leading the horse outside the cave, he mounts and glances back inside to James before he leaves. Already, he's fallen asleep.

Jiron quickly leaves the cave behind as he makes his way through the hills, away from the beach area. The rolling hills give him some cover as he follows the coast south, hoping to come across a town where he can acquire some food.

The light begins to fade as the sun drops below the horizon. The approach of darkness makes Jiron more at ease, in the dark is when he's most effective. Before the sun slips completely beyond the horizon, he comes across a small fishing village. A couple dozen huts and one main building is all there is to it. A small dock extends into the water and several small boats are tied to it.

Satisfied to have found a town so readily, Jiron turns around and leads his horse away from the village. He finds a place back in the hills that will keep his horse hidden while he goes in search of food. Taking the reins, he ties him to a scrub tree in a hollow between two hills. Patting him on the neck before returning to the village, he says, "I'll be back soon, boy."

Working his way back to the village on foot, he stops when he begins to see the light coming from the outlying buildings. He waits there, hidden in amongst some trees and bushes as he observes the inhabitants, thankful that there are no soldiers or guards patrolling the streets. This place is just not big enough to warrant any.

Once darkness has completely set in, he stealthily makes his way to the outskirts of town and over to one of the houses that remains dark. Hoping that since the house is still dark, there would be no one within, he creeps to a window and looks inside.

It's a small home and appears that there isn't anyone currently inside. Going to the door, he slowly opens it and slips inside, closing it behind him. Moving around in the dark, he finds the kitchen area and starts looking through the shelves and cupboards for food. Removing the sack he brought with him, he places a loaf of bread and some vegetables within it.

Moving to another shelf, he finds a few strips of dried fish and other dried meat which he takes as well. Figuring he's taken enough to last them for a few more days, he takes out two silver pieces and lays them on the table.

Stealing from those who have plenty has never bothered him. But taking from those who obviously have nothing, that's something he could never do, so he leaves the coins. Slipping back out the door, he quickly leaves town and heads back to where he left his horse.

As he approaches the area where he's sure he left his horse, he begins to see a light coming from up ahead. Wary of danger, he draws one of his knives and slips closer. Passing between the hills, he sees four teens near his horse. They're bending over where the contents of one of his bags have been emptied upon the ground.

Setting down the sack of food, he approaches them, knife still in his hand. As he enters the light, he says, "Get away from my horse and my things."

All four of the teens stand up and look in his direction. One of them says, "Back off, this is our stuff now." Drawing his knife, the teen threatens him with it as he says, "Go away if you don't want to get hurt." The others stand behind him and draw their knives as well.

Drawing his other knife, he advances upon them saying, "But I do want to get hurt."

The first teen gets an uncertain look in his eye, as if he can't believe Jiron isn't going away.

When Jiron gets to within five feet of the teens he stops and says, "Just put back everything you took and I won't have to kill any of you." Whether it's the look in his eye, or the sure way he's holding himself, the teens all back up a step.

They begin to empty their pockets and coins, as well as a few other things join the rest of the items lying on the ground. He gestures to the pile on the ground with his knife and says, "Now, please put everything back into the bag." He stands there with knives still drawn as one of the other teens complies.

Then he says, "Now everyone back up and away from the horse." He advances on them as they back up until he's next to the bag. Without taking his eyes off the teens, he reaches down and picks it up. After replacing the bag back on the horse behind the saddle, he takes the horse's reins and backs toward where he left the food sack. Reaching down, he picks it up, and then secures it to the horse as well.

He sheaths his knives before mounting. Turning his horse, he gives the boys one last look before heading out into the night. As he leaves, he goes in the opposite direction of where James lies in case the boys decide to tell anyone about meeting him. He doubts they will, though, it would make them look cowardly.

He travels through the hills for a few hundred feet before turning back to the north and to James. Finding the cave in the dark proves difficult but he at last comes across it and is relieved to find James still sleeping and undisturbed.

Securing his horse with the other, he sits back down at the entrance and keeps watch while James sleeps.

When the sun hits James' face, he wakes up and feels much improved over the day before. Lying next to him is a few strips of dried meat and vegetables. "Found some?" he asks Jiron.

"A little bit," he replies from where he's sitting at the cave entrance.

Tearing off a strip of meat with his teeth, he chews it for a bit then takes a bite of one of the veggies.

"Able to ride today?" Jiron asks.

"Yes," he replies through a mouthful of food, "I think so. My head is not hurting as bad as it was yesterday and I don't feel nearly as wobbly."

"Good," he says, "we need to get moving before we're discovered here."

"Let me see if I can find out where he is first," James says as he gets up and goes over to his horse to retrieve the mirror from his shaving kit. Stuffing the rest of the dried meat in his mouth, he pulls the mirror out and takes it over to the cave entrance where he sits next to Jiron. Cupping the mirror between his hands, he concentrates. The image begins to waver and suddenly they see Miko sitting with other people, someplace dark. He expands the picture and after watching it for a few minutes, states, "I think he's on a boat."

"You sure?" Jiron asks.

"Pretty sure," he replies. "He's somewhere dark and if you watch, it seems like the view is slowly rocking back and forth. It reminds me of being on a ship at sea."

"He could be going anywhere then," Jiron says.

"Yeah, I know," agrees James. "It'll be harder to follow him if we're going to need a boat."

"Let's worry about one thing at a time," he tells him. "Where is he?"

James thinks for a moment and then removes a short piece of cloth from his bags. He takes it outside and walks down near the water. Jiron gets up and follows him down to where the waves are crashing upon the beach.

Standing still at the water's edge, he holds the cloth by one end and extends his arm outward as he concentrates on Miko, willing the cloth to point the way. If it worked with a piece of wood, it should also work with the cloth. The cloth in his hand begins to move, not with the breeze coming in off the water, but on its own. Maintaining his concentration, he opens his eyes to see the cloth pointing south along the beach. He turns to Jiron as he terminates the spell and says, "He's to the south and I get the feeling quite a ways away."

"Then we better get going," he says.

James nods his head as they return to the cave to get their horses and leave. Once inside, Jiron asks him to use the mirror to see if the others made it safely on board the ship.

So James takes out his mirror again and concentrates on Delia and her surroundings. The image in the mirror begins to swirl until Delia appears along with several of the others, including Jiron's sister, Tersa. Widening the view, they're relieved to see them on board a boat that's at sea. From the expressions on everyone's face, it would seem they are not in distress.

"Looks like they made it," James tells him.

Sighing with relief, Jiron says, "I'm glad that Tersa is safe, that's been worrying me ever since we left."

"Me too," adds James. Putting his mirror back in his shaving kit, he places the kit in the saddlebag before mounting his horse.

Jiron quickly gets into the saddle as well and then leads them out of the cave. Turning away from the water, they head through the hills, continuing to angle away from the water.

"Why don't we follow the shoreline?" asks James.

"There's a village up ahead along the coast I visited last night," he replies. "They may be looking for someone who took some food. I did leave money, two silvers, but they still may be looking."

James nods his head, leaving it to Jiron's judgment.

As they continue to angle away from the shoreline, they come across the main road running north and south. A quick look reveals no one currently traveling upon the road so they quickly cross and enter the cover of the foothills on the other side. Staying within the hills, they're able to run parallel with the road as they continue their way to the south.

They don't ride very long before they begin to hear the sound of marching feet coming from up ahead of them. Leaving the horses between two hills, they climb to the crest of the next hill and peer over the top.

From their vantage point, they're able to see the road and the army of marching men upon it coming their way. Easily a thousand strong, the army marches north and at their head are two brown robes upon horses, as well as two others who look to be civilians. A wagon train, most likely carrying supplies, stretches behind them for as far as the road is visible. Flanking them out in the hills are several riders, most likely scouts.

"Uh, oh," Jiron says as he indicates the riders in the hills on both sides of the road. "Scouts! We've got to get out of here, fast!"

Glancing back to the brown robes, James says, "Yeah."

Rushing down the hill, they get to their horses and mount quickly. Turning their horses due east, they gallop away, hoping the scouts won't catch sight of them. "Do you think they're looking for us?" Jiron asks.

"It's likely," he replies. "We did sort of upset them back in Al-Kur."

With a short laugh, Jiron adds, "I guess you could say that."

Suddenly a horn sounds behind them and they turn to see a scout upon a horse at the top of a hill. Kicking their horses into even greater speed, they fly through the hills. The scout follows, keeping them in sight and periodically sounding his horn to alert the host behind him as to their position.

"Damn!" James hears Jiron exclaim as they race through the hills.

"At least the majority of the soldiers back there were on foot," James says.

"True, but the mages weren't," states Jiron.

They continue to ride hard and James glances behind them but doesn't see any pursuit developing, other than that annoying scout who continues alerting everyone as to their whereabouts.

"Hold up a minute," James finally says as he brings his horse around and turns toward the scout. He sees the scout holding still, two hills back as he once more sounds his horn. Reaching into his pouch, James brings out one of his remaining slugs.

"Can you hit him from here?" Jiron asks.

"We'll see," he replies as he throws the slug and at the same time, lets the magic flow.

Jiron watches as the slug flies through the air toward the scout on the distant hill. The scout must've seen the slug for he quickly moves down off the hill and out of James' line of sight. The slug alters course slightly and then disappears behind the hill where the scout went. "Did you get him?" he asks.

"Not sure," he tells him. "But let's not wait around to find out."

They turn their horses around and once again race through the hills. After several more minutes of riding, they slow down. "Looks like you did get him," Jiron says when the scout doesn't show himself again.

"Maybe now we can lose them in these hills," James says with relief.

The plan to escape in the hills dies as after a few brief minutes they clear the hills and are once again in the rocky desert with the scrub brush and stunted trees. Turning south, they follow the edge of the hills and only ride a short distance before they again hear the sound of the horn. Turning to glance behind them, Jiron exclaims, "Dear god!"

James turns and sees at least a hundred horsemen charging toward them from the north. Kicking their horses to a gallop they ride fast, hoping to stay ahead of the approaching cavalry. Another horn sounds to their right as they see the soldiers from the road coming into view as they crest the hills. The brown robed mages are at the fore.

Coming to the inevitable conclusion that magic will again become necessary, James takes the rope out of his saddlebag and again ties himself to the saddle. When he notices Jiron looking at him, he just shrugs and pulls the rope tighter.

He begins to feel the tingle that always heralds another mage who is working magic. Glancing back toward the mages on the hill, he sees one has his arms raised. "Fly!" he yells to Jiron as he kicks his own horse into a gallop and rides to the southeast, angling away from the two armies.

The tingles suddenly intensifies and he looks back to see a fireball flying toward them. He counters with a spell and it explodes harmlessly before it even reaches them.

The cavalry has swung to intercept them but aren't gaining very fast. James realizes he's unlikely to destroy both armies without unleashing something cataclysmic. His only hope is to hide, disappear. Suddenly, a memory surfaces of a time he and his family had vacationed in Las Vegas during the summer when a Santa Ana had come through. They had been caught out on the back roads and the flying sand was so bad, his grandfather had to pull off the road and wait it out because he couldn't see the pavement.

He yells to Jiron, "Take a cloth and cover your face!"

"What?" he yells back.

James pulls out a cloth and yells again, "Cover your face!" He then takes the cloth and ties it around his face until only his eyes are showing. He sees Jiron getting the idea and beginning to do the same. James starts concentrating on air pressure and the winds begin to increase.

They've left the armies on foot behind but the cavalry is still gaining ground. Jiron realizes that they're not going to be able to outrun them. He looks over to James and sees him there with his eyes closed. He moves his horse closer to James and grabs his reins so they won't become separated.

As they continue to gallop, the wind begins to pick up. It's almost as if the wind is slamming into the ground and drawing the dirt and sand up into the air. Before too much longer, the air is becoming hazy as more and more of the dirt and sand is being sucked up into the air.

The intensity of the wind hurls the sand into them with sufficient force to sting where it strikes exposed flesh. Jiron looks back but the dust in the air has obscured everything and the cavalrymen are no longer visible through it.

He begins to angle slightly more to the south, hoping to throw off their pursuers. The storm continues growing in intensity and he hollers to James, "That's enough! You're going to get us killed if you don't back off!"

James' eyes fly open and he looks tiredly to Jiron as he nods understanding.

When the storm doesn't subside, he yells to James, "Stop! You're going to kill us!"

Yelling back, James says, "I have! The storm has taken a life of its own. I can't control it any more!"

"Damn!" Jiron curses as they continue galloping to the south.

The winds steadily keep increasing and soon larger stones have been picked up by the winds and begin to pelt them. One stones strikes James on the thigh causing him to cry out. "Stop!" he yells to Jiron.

Coming to a stop, they both dismount. He has Jiron stay close to him as he attempts to create a barrier around them to keep the storm out. Suddenly, all is calm as the dome springs into being, the sand and wind continue pelting the outer side of the dome. The dome extends fifteen feet in diameter and ten feet high.

"How long can you hold it?" Jiron asks, retaining tight hold of the frightened horses' reins.

Considering it, James replies, "It was the initial construction that used the most magic. It's drawing what I call maintenance magic now, just enough to keep it stable. Probably for quite a while."

Jiron says, "Good."

The horses are restless, but appear they'll be okay. Jiron looks out at the swirling mass of sand and stones in awe. "Just what did you do?" he asks as he turns back to James.

"I thought I would make a dust storm to hide us in so we could escape," he explains. "But when I cancelled the spell, it continued. It seems I inadvertently triggered something that was on the verge of happening anyway, though maybe not to this degree." Indicating the storm outside, he says, "It's probably situations like these that make people hate mages, or at least distrust them."

Jiron nods his head and is about to reply when they hear a scream and turn to look as a man, at least they think it is, hits the side of the invisible dome. Most of the skin has been flayed from his bones by the storm. A ghastly appearance, they can see its skeletal mouth opening and closing and then it's picked up again by the wind and disappears.

They look to each other, James feeling very bad about the whole thing. "I guess we're not going to have to worry about pursuit when this is over," Jiron states.

Trying to fight back nausea, James replies, "You're probably right." He looks out to the storm again and then says, "Maybe you should try to get some sleep, I don't know how long this will last."

"What about you?" he asks.

"I dare not fall asleep," he replies. "The barrier might end."

Jiron unconsciously looks out at the storm and nods his head. "Alright," he says as he makes to lie down. "Though how I'm going to sleep in this is beyond me," he states.

James sits there as the storm rages outside the dome. He realizes after a while that Jiron has finally managed to fall asleep and hears soft snores coming from him. As the day progresses, the storm continues in its intensity and as night comes, the light begins to fade.

Casting his glowing orb for light, he keeps it soft so as not to awaken Jiron. The horses finally settle down as they become use to the roar outside the dome. Sitting there with nothing to do as he maintains the domes integrity, he becomes bored and tired. He's beginning to find it hard to stay awake. The events of the last few days and the continual draw of magic to keep the barrier up are starting to take its toll on him.

Getting to his feet, he paces around to keep himself awake and begins to sing songs from home. Some he knows in their entirety and others he gets through the first couple of verses before losing it. All through the night he stays on his feet, refusing to give in to the tiredness that's making his eyes droop and voice start to slur.

Sometime near dawn, the storm finally begins to subside and quiet down. Jiron comes awake and sees James sitting there, head drooped down to his chest, asleep. Startled, he gets up and begins to go over and wake him up when he realizes the dome hadn't collapsed with him falling asleep. It was covered completely with sand, light from the morning sun dimly filtering through.

Calming down, he sits back down and allows James time to sleep, knowing he has to be extremely tired after all he's done the last couple of days. He only has to wait a short time before James awakens. He begins to panic when he realizes that he fell asleep. "Relax," Jiron tells him reassuringly, "you're spell didn't fail."

"Yes, it did," he corrects him. "I no longer feel any drain used to maintain it."

Gesturing to the dome around them, he asks, "Then how?"

Going over to the side of the dome, James examines it and says, "The storm has packed sand and dirt around us so tightly, that it held together when the dome failed."

"You mean we're buried under the sand?" Jiron asks incredulously.

"It would seem that way," replies James.

"Incredible!" Jiron exclaims as he moves over to the dirt packed in around them. He touches the side and a small portion of the dirt comes loose. Then suddenly more begins to cascade down until the integrity of the entire dome fails and collapses down upon them, burying them in a foot of dirt and sand.

The horses panic as the dirt hits them and James cries out but quickly realizes that there's really not that much dirt covering them.

When the dust clears, they see the morning sun just cresting the horizon. Looking around, James doesn't find any sign of the man who had crashed into the side of the dome the night before, nor anyone else for that matter. From horizon to horizon, the land is barren, most of the plants are gone as well as a few of the trees. Of the trees that do remain, most are bent and broken.

Getting the horses out of the dirt and sand, they take stock of the situation. "I doubt if we'll need to worry about encountering anyone for a while," Jiron announces.

"Let's hope not," James agrees. "I'm getting worn out and need to lay off the magic for a day or two if possible."

Jiron pats him on the back and smiles, "If we encounter anyone, we'll ask them if we can fight tomorrow so you can rest, okay?"

"Very funny," replies James as he gives him an annoyed look before breaking into a smile himself.

"We better get going," Jiron says as he climbs into the saddle. "Even though the enemy we encountered yesterday may be scattered to the winds, there still could be others on their way, hunting for us."

Mounting, James says, "I agree."

"Should we go south for awhile?" suggests Jiron.

"Probably," he agrees. "I'll try to find him tomorrow, let's just put some distance behind us for now." With that, he kicks his horse into a gallop and they head off toward the south.

Chapter   Twenty Four

As they follow the road leading down into the pit, they pass several wagons on their way back up. Miko and the others have to press close to the inner wall in order for the wagons to be able to make it by. He looks into the wagons as they pass and sees they're filled with rocks. Once the wagons have passed, they resume their march down into the pit.

When they've descended to the point where they pass the point of direct sunlight, a sound of hammering comes to them from the depths. They continue down and begin passing by the mouths of other passages branching off into the rock from the road. At the third such branching Miko looks down and sees a group of slaves using pickaxes and hammers as they pound away at the rock.

It's a mine!

The slaves then pick up and carry the rocks they remove from the wall over to a wagon standing nearby. *Is this my fate? Am I to spend the rest of my life underground?* Worse fates than this has coursed through his mind at various times since the fall of the City of Light.

They pass by many other branching passages as they continue to make their way down, most have groups of slaves working at removing the rock from the walls as had the earlier one. When they finally reach the bottom, they enter a long, wide tunnel leading off into the distance.

This tunnel looks more a continuation of the road than another offshoot, it's wider than the others have been and has many tunnels branching off like veins from an artery. Spaced periodically along the tunnel are lanterns hanging from pegs in the wall to light the way. Empty wagons are spaced throughout the tunnel waiting to take the place of ones currently being filled. The horses of the empty wagon are removed and then hitched to the full one which is taken out of the pit.

They don't progress far down before a man comes over and they're brought to a halt. He begins talking to them while others divide them up into different groups. To Miko's relief, Black Tooth is taken away by one of the guards and led back up to the top. Five others are grouped with Miko and once the man stops talking, are led deeper into the mine.

"What are they mining?" he asks the guard in charge of them after passing a group of men working on the beginnings of another passage.

The guard replies, "Iron ore, as you soon will be as well."

"You speak my language!" he exclaims.

"Of course," the guard says. "There are many here from the north."

As they continue deeper into the mines, the tunnel they're in begins to narrow. The frequency of other branching tunnels diminishes the further they go. The guard begins talking again, alternating between the empire's language and the north's. "This is where you will spend the rest of your days. We have only three rules here but they are enforced strictly. First of all, if you try to escape, we will kill you."

"Second, you will work hard when and where we tell you. If you fail to, you shall be punished," he says. Pausing momentarily in his speech, he has them move over to the side of the tunnel as several slaves carry others past them. The ones being carried are bloody and a few are even unconscious, maybe even dead. Miko asks, "What happened to them?"

The guard looks at him and says, "Cave-in. It happens sometimes, that's why we need new slaves occasionally."

Once they're past, the guard gets them moving again and they walk in silence until Miko asks, "What's the third rule?"

"Don't hurt or hinder other slaves," he explains.

"That's nice of you," Miko replies.

The guard pauses and turns to look at Miko. "Nice?" he asks with a short laugh. "Hardly. Slaves are expensive and we have a quota of iron ore to mine each day. We'll not have anyone messing with our schedule. Understand?"

Miko nods his head and continues to follow with his group further into the tunnel. It's grown very dark now, with only occasional patches of light from a lone lantern illuminating slaves hard at work to mine the ore from the walls.

They come to a branching tunnel and the guard moves into it. He leads them down the tunnel until they reach a gang of slaves hard at work, chipping the ore from the walls.

One slave, who's carrying a whip, comes over to them. "This is Essin," their guard tells them. "He will be your overseer and you will do as he tells you."

"New bunch, eh?" Essin asks the guard as they near.

"Just arrived today," the guard replies.

"Good," Essin tells him, "we've been falling behind in our quota and old Vorn has been complaining."

"Not your fault though," the guard says, "since that cave-in took out half your group."

Essin nods and says, "I know, but try telling that to him."

The guard laughs as he turns and returns back the way they came.

Turning to the new arrivals, Essin announces, "My name is Essin and welcome to the Mines of Sorna. Whether you live or die will be determined by me, understand?"

Six heads nod agreement.

"Alright," he says as he hands each of them a pickaxe or a hammer, Miko gets a pickaxe. "Here we dig out the iron ore that the empire needs. We have a certain quota that must be achieved each day." He glances around at the new arrivals and says, "We will meet it or you'll wish to whatever gods you worship we had."

One by one he takes the new arrivals and assigns them to work beside a slave who has been there for a while. "Each of you are to work alongside your partner, learn from them and any questions you have be sure to ask them," he explains as he's matching them up.

Miko is partnered with a man of about twenty with sandy hair. "Name's Nate," the man says to Miko as he extends his hand.

Taking the offered hand, he returns with, "Miko."

"Here, let me show you what to do," he says. "You take your pick and swing it at the wall as hard as you can," he says as he demonstrates by striking the wall. "You want to strike near the veins of iron that run through the stone." He shows Miko what the veins look like and watches as he takes a swing at one. "Sometimes it takes several hits before it will come loose. If the first hit doesn't work, then strike in the same place again until some comes away."

Miko raises the pickaxe and swings with all his might. The jolt of the pick hitting the stone causes his hands to sting. "Not bad," Nate tells him. "You don't want to stop though, try to find a rhythm and keep swinging. We have a lot to do before the day is over," he explains as he takes up his own pickaxe and resumes chipping chunks from the wall.

Miko takes up the pickaxe again and strikes the wall, this time a sizeable chunk comes loose and falls to the ground. He looks to Nate who smiles and nods his head in approval. They continue chipping away until they have a sizeable pile at their feet. Then Nate has him pick up the chunks and carry them over to the waiting wagon where he drops them in.

They continue like that for a while, chip away the stone before carrying it over to the wagon. Miko's arms begin to tire and his hands become sore, as blisters start to form.

Nate notices that he's slowing down and says, "Keep up." He nods over to where Essin is watching another pair, "You don't want Essin to think you're slacking."

Doing the best he can, Miko continues to chip away with the pickaxe despite the sores on his hands. After a little while longer, his back and arms begin to ache and hurt.

Essin hollers, "Rest break!"

All the slaves give out a sigh of relief, especially the new arrivals, as they rest their pickaxes on the ground. They go over to where Essin is standing with another slave who is holding a bucket of water and a sack containing stale bread. The slave goes around the group, giving each a piece of bread and drink of water that he draws from the bucket with a ladle.

"We get three such breaks every day," Nate informs him. "They're not doing it to be nice, but so we can have the strength to continue removing the ore all day."

"Oh," says Miko as he takes his piece of bread and drinks from the ladle.

It seems like he just received his bread when Essin announces, "Back to work!"

With a groan, the new slaves return to the wall with their partners and resume the arduous work of removing the iron ore.

Shortly after the break, Miko turns as he hears Essin's whip strike out and hit someone. "Who gave you permission to stop working?" he shouts at one of the new arrivals.

"But my hands are sore and bleeding," the man wails as he holds his hands out, showing Essin.

"I don't care if they fall off!" he shouts, knocking the hands away. "Grab your pickaxe and continue working!"

When the man hesitates, Essin lashes him twice more. The man grabs his pickaxe and starts chipping at the wall again.

"See," Nate tells him, "you don't want to be slacking. He got off easy because he's new. If he's caught again, he'll be put to much worse jobs."

"Worse?" ask Miko after striking the wall again.

"There're always worse jobs," he explains. "Don't ever forget that. Certain sections of the mine cave-in more often than others, the trouble makers and slackers are the ones who get to work those areas. You understand?"

Miko just nods his head as he continues to wield his pickaxe. As bad as this is, he definitely doesn't want to go where it's 'worse'.

After a couple more hours of mining, the sores on his hand begin to rub raw and every strike now causes him pain. His shoulders and back feel like they're on fire, their strength beginning to fail.

Nate sees how he's struggling to continue and says, "I'll do this and you take the rocks over to the wagon, okay?"

Too tired for words, Miko just nods in relief and begins to carry the rocks over to the wagon.

When their group has filled its second wagon since Miko's arrival, Essin announces it's time to head up to the surface. "Take your picks with you," he tells the new arrivals.

Grabbing his, Miko rests it on a shoulder and follows Nate as they begin to leave the mines for the night. "When they first started mining here," Nate tells him, "they used to have the slaves remain within the mines all the time. But many kept getting sick and dying so they started bringing them out every night and the sickness began to go away."

"Quiet back there!" Essin hollers back to them.

Whispering, Nate continues, "Remember worse? The ones at the very furthest end aren't allowed out at night. They stay down here a week at a time as punishment, few make it more than a month."

A shudder runs through Miko when he thinks about having to stay in the mines for days at a time, never seeing the outside or having fresh, clean air to breathe.

They make their way back toward the winding road that leads to the surface. Other slave groups join them as they make their way up and out of the mine. Able to breathe fresh air again, Miko begins to feel a little better and some of his strength returns. Essin leads them over to a large, single story building with many doors spaced along the outside. Coming to one, he opens it up and leads them inside. "This is where you will be spending every night," he tells them as the new arrivals drop to the floors, one even passing out. "No one is permitted outside during the night."

Once they're all in, he says, "In a little bit, someone will bring you food and water." He glances around at the exhausted new arrivals and then to the one who has passed out, "Use this time to rest. I expect you hard at work in the morning."

Just before he leaves, he says, "Share the food evenly, those who don't will go without food for a day." He glares around at everyone before leaving the room and shutting the door.

When the door closes, the new arrivals begin to quietly complain and bemoan their situation. "Shut up!" one of the old timers says.

"You'll get use to it after a while," another adds.

"Yeah," a third says, "the first couple days are the worst, but your hands will toughen up."

Miko looks at his hands in the dim light coming through the cracks in the walls and the one lone window. Open, oozing sores cover his hands, each one adding its voice to the throbbing pain.

When the food arrives, the old timers make it a point to share evenly with the newcomers. In fact, Nate actually gives Miko some of his portion, saying, "You can have some of mine, it looks like you need it." The old timers know that a poorly fed worker only hurts the group, and it's the group that counts down here. Everyone looks out for each other, those who don't, tend not to make it long.

"Thank you," he says gratefully as he takes the offered portion. The bread and meat they're given isn't the freshest he's ever had, but after all the exertion in the mines, it tasted wonderful. Not nearly enough to fill him completely, but enough to quiet the grumbling in his stomach.

After he's done eating, he goes over to a corner where he quickly falls asleep.

It seemed like he no sooner fell asleep before Essin is there waking them up. After a quick meal, they're again marched back down into the mines. His arms and back are stiff and aching, it's all he can do just to carry that heavy pickaxe as he descends into the mines. They arrive back at the same spot they worked the day before and commence to mine the ore.

After the first couple of swings, his arms begin complaining and by the first break, his back and arms are again on fire. His hands are slippery from the oozing sores that the swinging of the pickaxe has reopened from the day before. Nate does his best to help him along, he's thankful that his partner is so nice and helpful. As Nate chips away at the wall, he carries the rocks over to the waiting wagon and deposits them inside.

When Essin calls for the first break, Miko is dazed and exhausted even though his day isn't even half over. When the slave comes over to give him his bread and water, he at first doesn't realize it, but then his eyes focus on who the slave is. Black Tooth!

When he reaches for his bread, Black Tooth gives him a dark look and drops it to the ground before he can take hold of it. When he gives him the ladle, he finds that it's only half full of water.

Black Tooth gives him an evil grin as he takes the ladle back. Nate, standing beside him doesn't fail to notice what is going on. After Black Tooth is gone and the break is over, they return to mining the ore.

"You know him?" he asks, referring to Black Tooth.

"Yeah," Miko replies as he carries the rocks over to the wagon. "He lost his hand because he tried to attack me one night and the guards cut it off, probably because he had a knife."

"That's the general rule," he says. "I take it he doesn't care for you too much, then?"

"You could say that," agrees Miko.

"You'll never survive if he only gives you half rations," Nate tells him.

"What should I do?" Miko asks.

"If he does it again," he explains, "tell Essin. I'll back you up on it."

"Alright," he says, "I'll do that."

The rest of the day passes pretty much as the previous one had. Apparently their quota was four wagon loads a day. "And there better not be just rock in there either!" Essin keeps telling them. At the second to last break of the day, Black Tooth is again the one to bring their bread and water. Miko figures he's given that job because a one handed man is of little use otherwise.

When he comes to Miko, he gives him another of his crooked grins as he fills the ladle again only half full. Instead of taking it, Miko hollers over to where Essin stands, "He's only giving me a half ration of water!"

Black Tooth's smile disappears as he quickly dips the ladle back in before Essin has time to come over to see what he's doing.

"What's going on over here?" he asks, obviously not pleased at having been disturbed.

Indicating Black Tooth, Miko says, "This man here is only giving me half rations of water."

Essin speaks to Black Tooth and gets a reply. "He says you just want seconds," he says to Miko.

Nate steps in and says, "I've seen it. He's been shorting Miko because of an old grudge."

Essin looks from Nate, Miko and then to Black Tooth. Making up his mind he says something to Black Tooth and then walks away.

Black Tooth gives Miko a dark look, dips the ladle and gives him a full measure. Miko takes it and says, "Thank you" to him very pleasantly just to irritate him.

"What did Essin say to him?" Miko asks Nate once they've returned to work.

"He said if he ever shorts one of his workers again, he'll have the other hand cut off," he replies.

"Good," Miko says with malice. He really doesn't care too much for Black Tooth.

Near the end of their shift, there's a rumble from off in the mines and then someone comes running and says something excitedly to Essin.

"Leave your picks boys," he tells them. "There's been a cave-in and we've been told to go help dig 'em out."

He turns and leads them at a quick pace down a side tunnel that has dust belching out of it. They go down it a ways and arrive at a spot where the ceiling has fallen in and has either trapped or killed the men that had been working this area.

They begin to clear the rubble as fast as they can, sometimes several of them have to work together to move a sizeable boulder. Miko works diligently and suddenly sees an arm sticking out of the rubble after removing a stone. "Someone's under here!" he hollers.

Everyone begins to clear that section until the body can be removed. Miko gets sick when he sees the skull has been smashed and the man's brains are oozing through the cracks.

They find three more bodies before they break through to the other side where the rest of the crew had been trapped. One has a broken arm and another a broken leg, the rest of the crew are unscathed.

After they've removed the rubble and the men are being taken to the surface to mend, Essin leads them back to their area. On the way back, Miko sees a group of men coming with timbers and hammers to shore up the fallen area.

Once back and again picking away at the wall, his mind keeps returning to the cave-in and he can't get the picture of the man's skull, crushed by the fallen stone, out of his mind. The tunnel feels smaller than it had before and every noise he hears, scares him as he thinks the tunnel is caving in.

When they at last head back up to their room, Miko is happy to be out of there. All night long, he has dreams of being trapped inside the tunnel as it caves in around him.

Chapter   Twenty Five

The day before, they headed south as directly as they could and had put many miles behind them. Several times they came across dead soldiers and horses, all having been flayed by the storm. Every corpse had a good portion of their skin removed, some even with bones exposed from where the flying debris had shredded the skin and tissue from them.

They remained out of sight of the road to the west while paralleling its course south. Once they detoured further to the east to avoid patrols and each time James had dreaded the thought of possibly having to do magic to escape them. But thankfully, they managed to avoid detection and hadn't needed to use magic.

Close to nightfall, they come across a small spring and made camp. Barely three foot across and two deep, it held enough water to quench their thirst and satisfy the horses. By the time they were done with drinking and filling their water bottles, they had practically drained it dry. By morning, though, it had refilled to its previous level and they were able to top off their water bottles again before setting off.

Prior to leaving, James pulls out his mirror to see if he can determine Miko's whereabouts. When the image begins to appear, he starts to panic because it is so dark. At first he thought he was looking inside a grave but then a light appears and he sees Miko with a pickaxe in hand, swinging it against a rock wall.

"I found him!" he announces excitedly. "It looks like they have him inside some kind of mine."

"A mine?" Jiron asks. "Can you determine where?"

He tries to expand the image but to no avail. Shaking his head he says, "All I see is the inside of the mine, others are there working beside him."

"Must be a big place then," Jiron figures.

"Perhaps," he replies. "I'm sure the locals would know of it, but we don't dare inquire."

Jiron nods in agreement, "Yeah, we would stick out all right, what with us not knowing the language. What do you propose we do?"

Thinking a moment, he takes out a strip of cloth and says, "I'll keep using this to show us the way and eventually we'll find him."

"Even across water?" he asks. "Remember, he was on a ship a few days ago."

"There's no reason to believe he's not on the mainland," James says. "They could've simply used it for quick transport from one city to the next along the coast."

Looking dubious, Jiron shrugs his shoulders and says, "Either way, sitting here isn't going to get us any closer." He tops off his water bottle and then allows his horse a last drink from the spring before mounting. Once mounted, he waits for James to do the same and then they're on their way.

Jiron looks over to James and sees him holding the piece of cloth as it sticks straight out from his hand. It's pointing to the southwest. "Should we head that way now or stay south until he's due west?" he asks.

"May as well head straight there," he says. "We don't know if going south or southwest is the safest way. So we may as well go in as straight a direction as possible." He looks to Jiron and then says, "Until our circumstances change that is."

"Southwest it is then," Jiron says as he turns his horse in that direction. As James turns to follow, Jiron asks him, "What do you plan to do after we find your friend?"

"First thing would be to get him out of wherever he is," he replies. "I still want to try to head back to Cardri. Maybe we could get a ship and sail around the coast."

"Maybe. Then what?" prompts Jiron.

"Oh, maybe rest for a while and perhaps build a house." He glances to Jiron and continues, "There are some things I've been thinking about, things to do with magic that I would like to experiment with. I want to be somewhere safe and away from people where I can work and not be disturbed."

"What about searching for information about this Morcyth? Do you still plan to continue with that?"

"Absolutely," James replies. "There are things I still need to know, but the last few weeks have shown me that I need to be better prepared before

I set out again." He pauses for a few seconds then says, "But I'll worry about that when I get Miko back to Cardri. One thing at a time."

They ride along in silence for a while longer before a road appears in the distance ahead of them. The coastline has begun to curve which has brought the road toward them. Several travelers are upon it, none looking to be military in nature.

Jiron looks to James who shrugs and says, "The road might actually be okay now."

"How do you figure?" he asks.

"Since that large force had just recently come through here," he explains, "it's unlikely they would expect us to be here."

"Possibly," states Jiron.

"Besides, I'm tired of slugging our way through the desert. I want to get to Miko as quickly as possible.

"Alright," agrees Jiron as he leads them toward the road. Upon reaching it, a fellow traveler on his way north says something to them, but they ignore him as they pass.

The man turns and says something, an obvious statement about being rude before he continues on his way.

When they are some distance away from the closest traveler on the road, James says, "It's going to be a problem, not being able to speak their language."

"I know," replies Jiron, "but what can we do about it?"

"Nothing, I suppose," he says.

They follow the road for several more miles and the only traffic they encounter is civilian in nature. James is surprised at the lack of military presence on the roads. Maybe the force he saw before the storm is all they are sending, or are able to send. Hopefully the local garrisons have been depleted to make up that force and are unable to spare any for patrols.

A town begins to appear ahead of them and when Jiron notices it, suggests, "Perhaps we should skirt around it. We could make camp out in the desert and I could sneak in for some supplies after it gets dark."

James nods agreement, "Our supplies are getting a little low."

So they veer to the east and continue until they've reached a spot a good two miles away from the town. They set up camp and wait for the coming of darkness. When the sun reaches the horizon, Jiron mounts his horse and says, "I'll be back in a couple of hours, hopefully not longer."

"Be careful," cautions James.

"I will," he assures him.

As he gets ready to leave, James stops him and says, "How are you going to be able to find me out here in the dark?"

Jiron looks around at the landscape and fixes the landmarks in his mind before he turns to James and says, "Rest assured, I'll find you." Then he turns his horse in the direction of the distant town and rides off into the deepening night.

Upon reaching the edge of town, he skirts along the edge, keeping to the shadows. He comes across several trees growing beyond the edge of town and stops to secure his horse in among them. With any luck he'll still be there when he returns.

Removing a couple sacks from his saddle bags, he folds them up tightly and places them within his belt pouch. He pats his horse on the neck as he says, "Stay quiet," and then melts into the darkness as he makes his way to town.

The wall surrounding the town is not very large, almost seems more for aesthetic value than for defense. A gate stands across the road where it passes through and is being guarded by two men. Jiron pauses for a moment to observe them as he evaluates his chances of making it through.

Deciding not to risk detection, he moves down the wall away from the gate. Reaching a spot where no one can observe him, he jumps up and grabs hold of the top of the wall, then proceeds to pull himself up. He looks over the top to the other side and when he sees it's clear, slips over the wall and drops to the ground.

Keeping to the shadows as best he can, he runs across the distance to where the first building lies. He moves along its side until coming to a window. Glancing in through the window, he discovers it to be some sort of carpentry shop. Not what he's looking for, he continues down to the adjacent building where a light is shining out through a window. Looking in, he finds this one to be a home, most likely that of the carpenter. It doesn't look as if any one is currently within, though it's hard to be sure.

Not wanting to take the chance where someone could be home, he continues on from building to building. Staying in the shadows as best he can, he finally comes across one that is dark, yet seems to be a residence. Hoping for it to have some food, he makes his way around the side to the alley running between it and another building.

Finding the alley vacant, he moves into it and continues down until he comes to a door leading into the building he wants. A moment's listening at the door assures him there's no one on the other side. He takes the handle and tries to open it only to discover it's locked. Taking out one of his knives, he works on the lock until it clicks open.

Pushing open the door slowly, he makes his way into the dark interior of the house, closing the door quietly behind him. Much to his relief, he finds that it is indeed a residence and begins to search the house until he comes across the pantry. Relieved to find it containing food, he takes a loaf of bread and puts it inside one of his sacks as well as some dried fruit. It's not going to be enough to last him and James for very long, but it's a start.

This residence contains many things of value so he doesn't feel obligated to leave any money this time. They won't suffer from the loss of a little bit of food. As he returns to the door leading to the alley, he opens it a crack and looks out to find the alley still remains dark and empty. Leaving the house, he closes the door behind him and starts moving further along the side of the alley until coming to a cross street. He sees hanging outside of the building directly across the street from him, the unmistakable sign of a butcher's shop. *That's what I need!*

Excited at the prospect of raiding a butcher's shop, he looks up and down the street before he crosses. A lone man is walking toward him. Hiding in the shadows of the alley, he waits until the man passes and continues down the street, eventually moving out of sight. A quick scan after the man disappears shows the street to be empty so he dashes across to the shadows of the alley next to the butcher's shop, where he pauses momentarily to glance back along the street. Finding that he's made the dash undetected, Jiron begins searching for another entrance to the shop, other than the one facing the street.

Around back, he finds a door that's locked and no amount of finagling with the lock will open it. Wishing for his lost lock picks, he begins glancing overhead and spies an open window on the second floor.

Searching the alley for something that might help him reach the window, he finds a broken crate lying in the alley several feet away. Going over to it, he checks it quickly to be sure it'll hold his weight, it seems sturdy enough. Picking it up, he brings it over and sets it under the open window. Standing upon the crate, he comes to within inches of the window. Hoping the crate will indeed hold up under his weight, he jumps up and grabs the window sill. He then pulls himself up so he can look through the window.

The room looks to be someone's bedroom, a bed and several dressers are contained within. Snores can be heard coming from the bed, two forms are sleeping under the covers. Not wanting to risk disturbing them, he drops back down to the crate which collapses under his weight with a loud crash. He quickly rolls against the building and holds still.

The noise from the crate crashing and him hitting the ground must've woke up one of the sleepers, for shortly a head sticks out the window and looks around the darkness of the alley.

Lying there perfectly still, Jiron watches as the person continues to look for several seconds before pulling his head back in. He waits for a minute and then lets out a sigh of relief when whoever it was fails to raise the alarm. *He mustn't have seen me here in the dark.*

As he gets up, he sees two shapes coming toward him. They quietly say something to him but he doesn't understand what they're saying. Backing up slowly, he retreats back down the alley, never taking his eyes off the two approaching figures. Suddenly, a noise from behind and a quick glance shows another shadow approaching from behind.

Again, the figures say something. When he fails to reply, he sees them draw knives and can hear the person coming behind him do the same.

Sudden calmness comes over him as he realizes these are just some local thieves out for a score. Drawing his two knives, he quickly advances upon the two approaching him.

They're shocked for a moment as they didn't expect him to launch an attack, and that moment's hesitation is all Jiron needed to drop one to the ground. Quickly engaging the other, he blocks the man's slash with one of his knives while following through with his other.

The man cries out as Jiron's knife penetrates into his side, sinking five inches of steel beneath the skin and puncturing a lung. Falling to the ground, the man begins crying out and choking as his lung fills with blood.

Turning to the last thief, Jiron stands ready and can see the man is about ready to flee. Then suddenly from overhead, the person who had looked out previously now begins shouting, raising the alarm. That's all the other thief needed, he quickly backs up and turns as he flees out of the alleyway.

Jiron quickly follows, deciding that the food he has will have to be enough for now. As he races across the street back the way he had come, another person who had stuck his head out his window to see what the other guy is yelling about sees him and starts to holler as well. Several guards, alerted by the shouting, see him running and give chase.

He dodges between buildings as he tries to throw off pursuit, all the while trying to make his way back to where his horse is tied up. He finally throws his pursuers off by ducking into a building and going out a side window. As they run off in the opposite direction, he makes a beeline for the wall and is soon over to the other side.

His horse is right where he left it. Mounting quickly, he turns toward the desert and kicks his horse into a gallop, putting distance between himself and the city.

Not happy with the small amount of supplies he had acquired, he supposes it'll have to due under the circumstances. He tries to get his bearings in the dark in order to locate the area where he left James.

He rides for several minutes before spotting a light off in the distance. It looks to be a campfire. *Don't tell me James built a fire? That'll alert everyone to our presence here!* Getting mad at a James' stupidity, he rides toward the fire.

As he draws close enough to make out details, he realizes that it's not a fire but several torches. Now much more cautious, he slows down and stops some distance away from the light, then gets down from his horse. Leaving his horse behind, he makes his way closer on foot and sees that the torches are held by soldiers of the Empire. A wagon is there as well and he watches in shock as an unconscious James is being loaded into the bed of the wagon.

A brown robed man is directing those placing James in the wagon and seems to be the one in charge. When James is finally within the bed of the wagon, the brown robed man climbs up onto the wagon seat as he gives orders to the driver. With a flick of the reins the horses get under way and the wagon begins to trundle back to town.

The dozen foot soldiers accompany them on their way back. Jiron is momentarily stunned that James could've been taken with so few soldiers. He's seen him blast away dozens before, the area should've at least looked devastated. But looking around, it looks like they just walked right up and threw him in the wagon.

Whatever happened, he doesn't have time to just stand there and ponder the imponderable. Hurrying back to his horse, he mounts up and follows the wagon at a discreet distance. When they arrive at the town, he's glad they're entering a different area than the one where he stirred things up earlier. Securing his horse to a tree outside the wall, he again jumps up and pulls himself to the other side as the wagon passes through the nearby gate.

He follows them through town, staying within the shadows and alleys. When he comes to avenues that he must cross in order to follow, he just strides right out and blends in with the few people on the street. Looking like you belong has always been the best way for him to remain undetected. If you look like you're about your business, most people fail to even notice you.

The wagon continues rolling through town until it comes to an estate with a wall more formidable than the outer town wall had been. Guards are posted at the gates and the robed man says a few words to them as the wagon passes through. Once the wagon is within the estate, the gate closes. The accompanying foot soldiers turn and march down the street away from the estate.

The wall surrounding the estate has nasty looking spikes along the top to deter anybody from going over. Jiron has scaled those types before, but never made it over unscathed. He's anxious to get in for he doesn't know how much time James will have before they begin the interrogation. Hopefully they'll most likely wait at least until he regains consciousness. But with mages, you never know what they can do to revive someone. He's got to get in there!

He does a quick survey of the wall encompassing the estate, which by the way is fairly large and discovers the spikes run its entire length. Sighing, he comes to the conclusion that he's going to have to risk the spikes.

Going over to a neighboring house, he acquires several shirts which are lying in a heap at the back door. He wraps them around his arms. Though they're not very good protection against the spikes, they're still better than nothing.

Glancing around, he makes sure he'll remain unobserved and then jumps up, grabbing the top of the wall. Using extreme care, he pulls himself up and braces himself as he crosses over the spikes. A sudden pain erupts from his left thigh as a spike pushes through his leggings and punctures his skin.

He pushes his leg off the spike with his left hand and then a pain erupts from his left arm as another spike scores through the layers of shirts. When he finally makes it down to the other side, he has several pinpoint punctures on his arms and legs. Fortunately, none are very deep or serious, just bleeding slightly. He knew people back in the City of Light who had attempted a similar feat and had muscles and tendons tore from the spikes. Removing the shirts from his arms, he leaves them on the ground by the wall.

Looking toward the estate, he watches from the shadows as the wagon stops in front of the main entrance. The brown robed man gets down as several waiting attendants remove James from the wagon. Following behind the mage, they carry him into the house and the door closes behind them.

Continuing to watch the house for a few minutes, he finally sees a light appear in a second story window, most likely where they've put James. Turning his attention back to the grounds surrounding the estate, he takes notice of two guards walking a set path around the estate. After watching them for several circuits around the house, he observes a gap between their paths that he may be able to take advantage of. When the first guard passes in front of the house, the second one is patrolling behind it, leaving a gap of several seconds before he makes his appearance again.

Jiron waits until the first guard has passed over halfway past the front of the house and then leaves his hiding spot in the shadows by the wall. Silently running across the open space to the side of the house, he keeps an eye on the back of the first guard until he turns the corner. Ducking behind a bush, he hides himself from view just as the second guard turns the corner. Holding very still, he watches the guard from behind the bush as he passes by.

Looking up from his position behind the bush, he sees the window that he believes James is in directly above his head on the second floor. The first floor window near him is ajar so he waits for the first guard to pass again before quietly opening it and slipping into the house. Once inside, he closes the window before the second guard turns the corner.

The room he finds himself in looks to be a library, shelves of books line the walls and several comfortable looking chairs are spaced around the room. *James would love this.* A single door leads from the room. Making his way over to it, he places his ear against the door and listens for any sound coming from the other side. Not hearing anything, he opens the door a crack and finds the hallway on the other side to be dark and empty.

Exiting the room, he closes the door behind him and then looks down both directions of the hallway. The hallway to the left is dark, further down to the right is a barely perceptible light. Deciding in favor of the light, he moves silently down the hallway toward it. He passes several closed doors before reaching a flight of stairs leading up to the second floor. The light is coming from the flickering of an unseen candle in the hallway beyond the top of the stairs.

Taking the steps quickly and quietly, he ascends to the top where he pauses to peer around the corner. Several burning candles line the empty hallway, allowing no shadows in which to conceal himself. A door further down to the left stands ajar several inches, voices can be heard emanating from within.

He decides to risk detection and creeps quickly down the hallway to the door, peering inside. Within the room are several people, including the brown robe. James is sprawled out unconscious upon a bed to the side of the room and one of the men is examining his eyes. The man turns to the mage and makes a comment as he lets go of James' eyelids, allowing them to close.

All of James' things are sitting on top of a nearby table, including the medallion that he used to open the secret door back in the City. A few more words are exchanged and then they all turn and move toward the door behind which Jiron is spying on them.

Panicking, he bolts back to the stairs and descends to the bottom as fast as he can to avoid being seen. Once there, he listens from around the corner and hears their footsteps coming down the hallway toward the top of the stairs. About ready to run back down the hallway to the library, he stops when he realizes they're continuing down the second floor hallway past the stairs.

Relieved, he again creeps to the top of the stairs and peers around the corner. Two guards stand at the door to the room holding James. He pauses there at the top of the stairs and ponders the situation. Apparently, they're not going to interrogate James immediately, it didn't look as if he was even conscious. *Gotta get in that room!*

Deciding on a plan that's rather risky in nature, he returns to the room where he initially entered the house and goes back to the window. Watching for the patrolling guards, he soon sees the first one pass. He opens the window and slips outside, shutting it before the second one turns the corner.

The largest gap is after the first one passes, the second one seems to be lagging behind, so he sits and waits until the second one passes. Then, when he sees the first one turn the corner and approach, he makes ready. Once the guard has gone ten feet past his hiding place, Jiron gets to his feet and begins scaling the wall of the estate up to James' room.

He gets ten feet up the wall before the second guard appears around the corner. Holding absolutely motionless there on the wall, he waits for the guard to pass beneath. Sweating, heart pounding fast, he watches as the guard approaches, knowing that if the guard but looks up, he's dead.

Walking toward the spot where Jiron hangs precariously upon the wall, the guard draws ever closer and then passes a scant two feet beneath Jiron as he continues on his way. Stopping the sigh of relief that almost escapes him, he waits until the guard moves further away then he maneuvers to the window and positions himself so he can look inside. He sees James still there on the bed, the door closed and no one else is in the room.

Realizing the first guard is about to turn the corner, he moves away from the light coming through the window and back into the shadows. He holds still as he waits for the guard to turn the corner and pass underneath. Once he's past, Jiron returns to the window and attempts to open it. The window opens easily and he slips inside before the second guard makes his appearance. He shuts the window just as the second guard turns the corner and then moves silently over to the bed upon which James is lying.

He looks like he's sleeping. Jiron shakes his shoulder in an attempt to wake him. *What's wrong with him?* His eyes open a fraction and then he mumbles something incoherently before slipping back into unconsciousness. *Now what?*

Trying to determine the best way to get him out of the house, he realizes going out the door would be a bad idea. The guards standing outside would alert the whole house to his presence. He might be able to hold his own against the guards, but he would stand little chance against the mage. That leaves the window.

He moves back to the window and peers out, trying to avoid casting his silhouette from the candle on the table across the window. Other than the two guards passing at intervals around the house, the only other guard visible is stationed at the gate. A plan begins to form and he waits until the first guard passes by before slipping back out the window. He closes the window once he's securely clinging to the side of the house and manages to maneuver down the side a little before the second guard rounds the corner.

After the second guard passes by below, he drops silently to the ground and immediately ducks behind the bush. The guard pauses a moment as he looks back in his direction. Not seeing Jiron hiding behind the bushes, he turns back and resumes his trek around the house.

He waits for the first guard to pass again before racing across the lawn to the wall and the safety of the shadows there. Pausing a moment to see if he was seen, he then moves silently toward the gate and the guard stationed there. Luckily, the gate is poorly illuminated on this side of the wall so it's easy enough for him to sneak upon the guard and quickly silence him. He pulls the guard's dead body along the wall and stuffs it behind several bushes.

Checking the gate, he finds it locked. Returning to the dead guard, he searches his pockets until he finds a set of keys. Returning to the gate, he uses the keys to unlock it and then places a stone against its base to prevent it from swinging open and announcing to everyone that something's not right.

He goes back to the deeper shadows along the wall as he watches the two guards continuing their patrol. When the first one passes again, he races once more to the side of the house and again hides behind the bush until the second one has passed. Then when the first one rounds the corner and passes by the bush he's hiding behind, he jumps out and grabs the guard from behind. Quickly and quietly he slits the guard's throat with his knife, then drags the body back behind the bush and lays it against the house.

Taking his place behind the bush, he waits for the second guard to round the corner and pass by. He again jumps out and silences him the same way he did the first. When the second guard's body lies next to the first, he begins to scale the wall, this time more interested in speed than in avoiding making noise.

At the window to James' room, he cautiously peers in and with relief, finds him still sleeping and alone. Opening the window, he slips in and closes it behind him. Moving across the room to a chest of drawers, he begins sliding them open until he finds what he's looking for. The third one down from the top holds what he needs, a spare sheet.

He takes it and goes over to James where he begins tying it under his arms. The sound of approaching footsteps coming down the hallway toward the room warns him someone is on their way. Jiron quickly removes the sheet from around James and slides under the bed, scooting as far back against the wall as he can.

The bedroom door opens and two men come in, quietly talking to each other. They walk over to the bed, their feet mere inches away from the spot where Jiron is hiding. It seems as if they're seeing whether James is ready for interrogation or not. After they stand there for a few minutes conferring with one another, both men turn and walk back out the door.

Slipping from under the bed, Jiron again ties the sheet tightly under James' arms. When he has it secured, he goes over to the window and opens it wide. Returning to the bed, he lifts James up and carries him to the widow where he sets him on the window sill.

Taking a firm hold of the sheet, he eases him over the edge and begins to quickly lower him to the ground below. The sheet isn't quite long enough to reach the ground and ends up having to drop him the last three feet to the ground where he lands with a thud. Hoping James hasn't broken anything, Jiron slips out the window and begins to descend the side of the house when he suddenly remembers James' medallion and the other items sitting on the table.

Sighing, he goes back inside and quickly grabs James' empty pouch that's sitting on the floor and scrapes everything off the table into it. Tossing it out the window so it lands near James, he again begins his descent and closes the window.

Once on the ground, he takes the pouch and secures it to his belt, then he removes the sheet from James. Picking him up, he slings him over his shoulder as he heads to the gate.

Running as best he can with James' added weight, he crosses the distance quickly. Upon reaching the gate, he kicks the rock that was set to keep it closed to the side. Pushing the gate open wide, he starts through just as a cry arises from the house. Glancing back, he sees someone at the window to the room where James had been held, hollering and pointing in their direction.

He passes through the gate quickly and closes it behind him, locking it with the key in the hopes of slowing down the pursuit. With James slung over his shoulder, he runs down the deserted street and then enters an alley to cut over to the next street. Running as fast as he can, he quickly reaches the end of the alley and then turns to the right. Racing down another deserted street, he tries to put as much distance between himself and pursuit all the while working to make it to the edge of town.

After running down the street another two blocks, he sees a group of people far ahead of him in the street. Ducking down a nearby alley, he moves into it a short distance before coming to a stop. *It's a dead end!* Turning around, he moves to leave the alley when several figures enter from the street and block his escape.

Chapter   Twenty Six

One of the shadows says something to him as they advance further into the alley.

Still having James slung over his shoulder, he waits to see what they intend before doing anything. They're obviously not part of the pursuit from the estate.

Another shadow says something in an excited and animated fashion while pointing toward him.

Jiron takes in the situation. Without James to worry about, he probably would have little difficulty with these guys. But with him to protect and pursuit on the way, he just isn't sure what to do.

He begins backing into the alley away from them and watches as another ten shadows detach themselves from the dark and join the ones already moving his way. The street behind the approaching shadows begins to lighten up and the sound of running feet can be heard approaching.

One of the shadows from the edge of the alley says something and the one who appears to be the leader of the group barks out a command. Suddenly they all become still as they melt back into the shadows to either side of the alley.

Jiron realizes they're trying to remain unnoticed by those approaching. And then they will finish dealing with him. He decides to take a chance and when those running along the street begin to pass in the front of the alley, he shouts out, "Okay boys, let's take 'em out!"

The men passing by come to a sudden stop and turn to look in the alley. The light from their torches reveals the thieves standing against the walls of the alley, their knives out. One of the men on the street shouts a command and three crossbow bolts fly into the alley. Thieves cry out as they're struck by the bolts and fall to the ground. The men out on the street then rush into the alley with their swords drawn as they move to attack.

The leader of the thieves shouts something to the approaching men, but whatever he says fails to have any effect. Left with little choice, the thieves proceed to defend themselves against the attackers.

Jiron watches in satisfaction as the men and thieves begin to fight. He moves to the rear of the alley, away from the fighting and hunts for a way out. Near the end he finds a closed door. Carrying James over to it he checks it and finds it locked. Drawing his knife, he uses it on the lock and manages to get it open. Passing through the door, he glances one last time at the embattled men and grins as he closes it behind him and resets the lock. The thieves are getting the worst of it.

The sound of fighting follows him as he makes his way further into the dark room, searching for a way out. In total darkness he stumbles about, once almost losing his balance as he trips over a small stool sitting in the middle of the floor. He eventually comes across the door. Opening it a crack, he looks out onto a dark hallway that has a faint light coming in through an open doorway further down.

Moving down the hallway, he reaches the doorway where the light is emanating from. Peering in, he sees an empty living room. The light turns out to be moonlight coming in through a window by the front door. He cautiously makes his way though the living room to the window where he looks out onto the street. First one way, then the other, he checks to make sure no one is out there. Not seeing anyone, he moves to the door and opens it slowly.

Suddenly, banging can be heard coming from the door to the alley, the fighting back in the alley must have come to an end. Floorboards creak overhead as the owner of the house is awakened and begins making his way down to see what all the commotion is about.

Jiron slips out the front door and shuts it behind him. His shoulders begin to ache from James' dead weight as he quickly makes his way along the side of the street, trying his best to keep to the shadows. He passes several buildings until he comes to an inn on the right. Ducking down the alley on this side of the building, he hears his pursuers entering the street from the house he just left. For a brief moment he wonders what happened to the men who had originally accosted him in the alley, but that question will have to remain unanswered.

As silently as possible, he makes his way down the alley to the courtyard behind the inn. The gate is open and he hurries through just as the pursuers pass the mouth of the alley he just vacated, on their way to search for him further down the street.

He glances back down the alley, thankfully discovering none of those hunting for him had thought to come this way. Setting James down against the inner wall of the courtyard, he makes his way over to the stables, in search of a couple of horses.

Once within the stables, he finds a stableboy asleep in a small room at the far end. He wakes him up by placing a knife at his throat and motions for him to remain quiet. The boy nods and remains quiet as Jiron ties him up and places a gag in his mouth to keep him quiet. Then he goes back to the horses and begins saddling two of them.

After he's saddled them, he returns to where he left James. Picking him up, he carries him over to the stable where he puts him on one of the horses. Taking out a length of rope, he ties him securely to the saddle. Once James is secured, he goes over to where the stableboy is tied up and places ten gold pieces on the ground before him. He points to the gold and then to the horses and the stableboy nods his head. Whether he understands the gold is for the horses' owners or not, Jiron isn't sure, but his conscience is clear.

Mounting up, he takes the reins of James' horse and leads him out of the stables to the courtyard. Pausing momentarily at the entrance to the alley, he makes sure it's clear before leaving the courtyard and entering into the alley. He makes his way toward the end of the alley where he again pauses to look in either direction down the street.

For the moment, the street appears deserted, but he can hear commotion on neighboring streets as the search for them continues. He enters the street with James' horse in tow and begins heading toward the part of town that seems to have the least amount of disturbance going on.

Moving as quickly as he can, he continues along toward the edge of town, somehow avoiding the roving patrols. Coming out of an alley he sees the wall ahead of him. Keeping close to the buildings, he rides along in the shadows until reaching a gate. Where before there had been but two guards, now they have been increased to a squad of twenty and the gate is shut and locked. His plan to ride through the guards at the gate is no longer feasible, he'll have to find another way out of the city.

Realizing he's now sitting on useless horses, he makes his way to a side alley and dismounts. James begins mumbling incoherently as Jiron removes him from his horse. "Not now!" he whispers vehemently to him. The last thing he needs is for James' nonsensical ramblings to attract notice.

Once removed from the horse, James continues to mumble, thankfully not very loud. He throws him across his shoulders again as he quickly makes for the wall. Upon reaching it, Jiron pushes him up and rests him across the top before he climbs up next to him. He then carefully lowers him down to the other side and then swings over as he lets go, feet landing on the ground next to where James had settled. It doesn't take him long to realize that he is now on the opposite side of the town from where his horse waits for him.

Shouldering James once more, he begins making his way to the other side of town, detouring occasionally when a search party on horseback comes into view. During one such time while he was hiding among some bushes, waiting for a search party to pass, he notices that James' eyes were open and looking around.

"You awake now?" he asks him.

James nods his head yes, but is still having trouble talking, slurring his speech so bad as to be unintelligible.

"Can you walk?" Jiron asks.

He shakes his head no.

"Damn!" Jiron silently exclaims as he hoists James across his shoulders yet again and hurries along. When he comes to the spot where he had left his horse, he finds that it's no longer there. He quickly looks around the area but finds no trace of it anywhere. Someone must've come along and helped themselves to it.

Without horses, they're not likely going to make it very far. He sits James down and says, "Stay here!" When he gets no response, he asks, "Understand?"

James gives him a wobbly nod.

"I'll be back. I need to get a couple horses," he tells him. Leaving him hidden there among the bushes, Jiron moves through the night until he sees two riders riding leisurely back into town. They're not in any hurry. Perfect!

Angling to intercept them, he races through the dark. The moon above enables him to see the terrain well enough to keep from tripping over the desert shrubs. Just a dark shadow in the night, he maneuvers until he's directly behind them.

The riders talk to each other, occasionally laughing at the witticism of the other, totally oblivious to the impending attack coming up behind them. He paces them for several feet until the space between the two horses closes to just the right distance. Then, running as fast as he can, he races to catch them. As he nears, he jumps and grabs each from behind and pulls them backward off their horses.

As the two men hit the ground, Jiron draws his knives and advances on the one getting to his feet first. He kicks out and connects with the man's middle, knocking him over again and then attacks with his knives before the man has a chance to recover. A quick stab through the chest ends the man's life.

Jiron turns to face his partner who is now ready with sword and shield. The man thrusts with his sword, Jiron able to deflect it easily to the side. He tries to counterstrike with his other knife but it's knocked aside by the man's shield.

They circle each other for a second then the man strikes out with an overhand blow that Jiron has to sidestep to avoid. As the sword swings past him, Jiron strikes out with one of his knives and scores a cut along the man's sword arm.

Angered, the man advances rapidly and begins attacking him with a flurry of blows that Jiron easily avoids or deflects aside. He continues to defend against the man's attack, waiting for his chance. Patience is often a knife fighter's best friend.

Suddenly, the opening presents itself and he strikes out at the man's sword arm. The man cries out as his sword drops to the ground after Jiron's knife severs the tendons in his arm. He pushes Jiron back with his shield as he cradles his arm, trying to stop the blood from pumping out.

Jiron goes on the offensive and after a quick series of blows which the man cannot defend against with just a shield, he sinks to the ground, eyes vacant as death takes him. Jiron wipes his knives on the man's tunic before returning them to their sheaths. Gathering the horses, he mounts one and takes the reins of the other as he rides back to where he left James. It takes a minute to locate the exact spot where he left him, but a hushed call from James leads him there.

He gets down from his horse to help James into the saddle. No sooner is James in the saddle then the hoof beats of a patrol is heard coming their way. Jiron takes a piece of rope and quickly secures him to the saddle, all the while listening to the patrol coming closer and closer. Finished with securing James, he quickly mounts and they wait in silence as the patrol passes by in the dark. He then leads them out into the desert, away from the city. Behind them, the sound of patrol begins to recede in the distance as they move further away. Once the sound of the patrol can no longer be heard, Jiron brings the two horses to a gallop as they begin to cover the miles quickly. After traveling for some time, he hears James holler, "Stop!"

He brings the horses to a halt and then looks back to see James untying himself. Slipping off the horse, James doubles up and begins to retch into the dirt. Once his stomach is again under control, he stands back up and leans against his horse for support.

"You okay?" Jiron asks.

"Better," he assures him, his speech only slightly affected.

"What happened to you?" Jiron asks, dismounting and coming over to him.

"Not really sure," he replies. "I remember you leaving and then things get kind of fuzzy after that. I remember being carried over your shoulder through town, or at least parts of it. But nothing really clear until a short time ago when I came to on the horse."

Jiron relates to James the events from when he returned to the camp and found him being loaded onto the wagon until now. "They must've done something to you," he states.

"I agree," he says. "Probably a drug of some kind."

"Think so?" Jiron asks.

"It would make sense," he replies. "A mage who's drugged wouldn't be able to focus clearly and do magic. Actually, it was quite effective." Holding his head, he looks to Jiron.

"I would say so," he agrees. "Can you do magic now?"

James concentrates, or tries to anyway and then shakes his head. "Not even if my life depended on it," he tells him. "Just have to wait until the effects wear off."

"Think they will?" Jiron asks.

"Don't know why they wouldn't," he says and then suddenly begins to panic as he grabs his shirt. "The medallion!" he cries out. "They took the medallion!"

Jiron reaches into the pouch hanging on his belt and removes the medallion, handing it back to James. "I grabbed it while I was getting you out of there," he tells him.

Sighing with relief, he takes it and places it once more around his neck. "Thank you," he says gratefully to Jiron.

"Thought you might want it when I saw it lying there," he says, grinning. "But we need to get going, if you think you can ride." He holds up the rope used to secure him to the saddle and asks, "Should I tie you to the saddle or can you make it on your own?"

"I think I'll be okay for now," James assures him. As he tries to get back in the saddle, he has a little difficulty with his coordination and balance. With a little help from Jiron he makes it up onto the horse. Once in the saddle, he's able to maintain his balance well enough despite continual spells of dizziness. With an eye on James, Jiron mounts up and they continue on into the desert.

The next morning when James wakes up, all effects of the drug have worn off. His head is clear and he once again is able to maintain his balance. While they prepare to ride, James realizes that his belt and slugs are gone.

"What's wrong?" Jiron asks him.

"My belt with the slugs is missing," he explains. "They must have taken it when they captured me."

Jiron takes the pouch off his belt and tosses it over to him, "Look in there." When James catches it and opens it up he continues, "I think all your stuff is in there. I quickly scraped everything off the table where they had placed your things."

James pulls out his belt and finds only five slugs remaining. He puts it back on and then looks through the pouch again. He pulls out a vial containing a clear liquid. Holding it up, he takes a close look at it as he says, "This might be the drug they used." He hands it over to Jiron who examines it.

"Didn't realize I had taken it," he tells him as he hands it back.

"It may come in useful," James says as he places it back in his pouch. *Yes, it may just come in useful.*

Before they mount, James pulls out his mirror and again finds Miko in the dark, picking away at the stone wall. "At least he's still alive," he says to Jiron.

"That's something, for sure," he replies.

James takes out the piece of cloth and casts his directional spell. It moves to indicate Miko lies off to the southwest, a little more west than south. "He's that way," he says to Jiron, pointing to the southwest before putting the cloth away.

Jiron sits for a second on his horse, contemplating how to say this, "You know, the noose is tightening. By now, soldiers are going to be swarming this entire area looking for us. And it's not just soldiers in the hunt, but mages too."

"What are you saying?" he asks him. "That we should give up? Leave him to his fate?" Shaking his head, he says, "No, I could never do that. If you feel you can't continue, I'll understand, but I need to try, or die doing it."

"It may well be impossible to reach him," he continues. "It may not be possible for us to even escape the Empire."

"Maybe not," agrees James, "but I've got to try."

"Don't worry about me abandoning you here," Jiron assures him, "I won't. I just wanted you to understand that things are getting more complicated."

"I know," he says. "I understand, we just need to be more alert and careful."

Jiron turns his horse to the southwest and asks, "Ready to go?"

Nodding, he says, "Yes."

As they ride, Jiron gets a notion and asks James, "Can your mirror locate enemies in the area? If we had that information, maybe we could avoid them and make better time."

"Possibly," he replies as he digs out his mirror. Handing his reins to Jiron, he concentrates as he stares into the mirror. The image blurs and then he sees a bird's eye view of them riding along. Expanding the view, he widens the scope to be able to see more of the surrounding desert than just themselves.

He's able to scroll the image for some distance in any direction. The further he scrolls the image away from their position, the greater the amount of magic needed to maintain the spell. He's also always able to come back and center the view on them with just a thought. "Yeah," he tells him, "I think I can manage that."

"Good," says Jiron. "Anyone in the vicinity?"

James scrolls the image and then shakes his head, saying, "No, there doesn't appear to be anyone ahead. Off to the north is a sizeable force but they're not coming our way."

"How far are we away from the coast?" he asks.

James tries scrolling the image, but fails to pick up the coast before the power drain becomes too severe. "I don't know," he replies. "I'm not able to see that far."

"Oh well, at least we know we're okay for awhile," he says, relieved. "Just check it often so we'll know when to detour."

"Alright," agrees James. He checks the area one last time and when he finds no one ahead, replaces the mirror back into his shaving kit.

They ride for several hours, James checking periodically for hostiles with his mirror. The second time he checked, he found a dozen riders coming their way and they had to swing to the south to avoid detection.

Continuing to detour around pockets of hostiles, they wind their way closer to the coast.

When night begins to fall, they stop for a short meal. All they have with them is what the riders had with them when Jiron appropriated their horses, which isn't much. "Think we should continue through the night?" Jiron asks him.

"I think the horses will be okay," he replies. "Besides, we're less likely to be discovered in the dark of night."

"I was hoping you'd say that," he tells him as he finishes his meal and mounts. James mounts as well and they continue their way toward the ocean.

Once night has fallen, the mirror becomes useless as everything is black. Now they have to depend on their senses to detect anyone approaching. A half moon rises later in the evening, giving them some light to see by. Sometime around midnight, they cross the main road going north and south. A short time after that, they begin to see the moon being reflected off of a body of water in the distance. The smell of salt in the air tells them they've reached the ocean's shore.

When they reach the shore, they pause a moment as Jiron asks, "Now where?"

Taking out his cloth, James again casts his directional spell and the cloth stiffens up and points out along the coast, almost due south. "Further south, it looks like," he tells Jiron as he puts away his cloth.

"Guess we follow the shoreline," he says to James.

Nodding in the dark, James replies, "That would seem to be the plan."

They follow the shoreline for another hour or two before running across what looks to be an old abandoned shack set up along the beach. It looks the worse for wear but it could hide them while they get a little sleep, they're both becoming quite tired. Jiron dismounts and goes up to the shack to look inside. He signals James to come on over when he finds it empty.

There's barely enough room inside for them and the horses, but leaving them outside would tell anyone passing by that someone's here. Bringing them in with them, they close the door and alternate between sleeping and keeping watch through the rest of the night.

The morning sun coming through the cracks of the shack awakens James. He sits up abruptly when he fails to see Jiron. His horse is here, but he's not.

Going to the door, he looks out and sees him outside walking along the shore, head down looking at the sand. Coming out, he asks, "What are you doing?"

Jiron holds up a conch shell and says, "I found this over by the water, incredible isn't it?"

Smiling, James replies, "Yeah, that's something alright."

With a last look around the sandy beach, Jiron joins James as he walks back to the shack. Once back inside, he puts the conch shell into one of his bags. "Going to give it to Tersa when we make it back," he explains.

"I'm sure she'll like it," he says.

They bring the horses out and mount, James checks the mirror before they leave and finds no enemy soldiers in the immediate vicinity or further to the south. He keeps the mirror out so he can check it periodically as they make their way along the shoreline.

After traveling for over an hour, James asks, "You got any water?"

Jiron shakes his head and says, "No, I used up the last of it this morning."

"We're going to need to find some soon, or we're not going to last long under this sun," he tells him.

"I know, my horse really could use some too," he says. "Can you find a source close by?"

"Maybe," he replies as he again gets out his mirror. After concentrating on water, the mirror opens up on a great expanse of water, "Think I may have found something." He expands the view and the edge of the water comes in and he sees two men on horseback riding along beside it. His excitement ends when he realizes that it's Jiron and him that he's seeing and that the body of water is the ocean.

Frustrated, he begins concentrating on 'fresh', drinking water. The image blurs and then focuses in on a small pool with several palm trees around the edge. "Got it!" he exclaims.

"Where?" asks Jiron.

Adjusting the view and scrolling the image, he determines it to be several miles off to the southeast.

"Anyone around?" he asks.

"Several people," he replies, "but no soldiers. They look to be just travelers stopping to get water."

Jiron nods his head, "We'll have to chance it." He turns his horse to the southeast and they soon cross the main road. One lone traveler sees them crossing but doesn't seem to be paying much attention to them.

As they ride, Jiron says, "That's a handy thing, your mirror."

"Yeah," replies James. "The more I use it, the easier it is to find what I want."

"Can you use anything?" he asks. "I mean, like a pool of water or something?"

"I would think so," replies James. "It would be the same principle, so yeah, I could."

About that time they begin to see palm trees coming into view on the horizon. They slow their approach when they see a dozen or so people around the water. "Must be a caravan of some sort," guesses James when he notices several wagons pulled up around the oasis. A road stretches in the distance on the other side of the oasis, going east to west.

"Looks like it," Jiron agrees. "Let's be careful, get in and out quickly."

"I'm with you on that," states James.

They approach the oasis, making a beeline straight for the water. When the others see them coming, they watch, but don't say anything.

Upon smelling the water, their horses quicken their pace, eager to reach the pool. While their horses begin drinking, they get down and fill their water bottles. Glancing over to the others who share the oasis with them, they notice that they've huddled together and are talking amongst themselves, occasionally peering over to them.

James also notices that a couple of the caravan guards have gone over to a wagon and are beginning to get out crossbows. "Jiron!" James cries out. "Time to leave!"

Jiron looks over and sees the guards preparing their crossbows and leaps into the saddle, James mounts quickly as well. As the guards are winding their crossbows, they turn their horses and head out of the oasis as fast as their horses will carry them. They turn to follow the road westward.

"Wonder what that was all about?" Jiron asks once they've put some distance between themselves and the oasis.

"Rumors must be circulating about us by now, I would imagine," James replies. "Two men, of obvious northern stock ride in out of the desert," he continues. "I'd be cautious too, maybe even be looking for a reward for taking us down."

Jiron laughs.

"What's so funny?" he asks.

"After all we've been through," he says, grinning, "escaping first Azzac and then Al-Kur. The thought of us being brought down by a bunch of caravan guards, it just seems funny."

"I suppose," replies James, not seeing the humor in it. He pulls out the mirror and checks for hostiles in the area, "Jiron, we got two approaching groups. A squad on foot to the northeast who're moving due south and a dozen riders on the road ahead of us, coming our way."

"To the south?" he asks.

James quickly checks and replies, "Doesn't look like anyone's in that direction."

Without hesitation, Jiron turns toward the south with James following suit. Kicking their horses into a gallop, they race off the road, hoping to remain unnoticed by the approaching horsemen.

James is sure they'll be seen, the amount of dust they're kicking up must be visible by the riders. Checking the mirror, he sees them continuing down the road toward the oasis, and the caravan there. They don't seem to see or care about the dust their horses are throwing into the air.

"They'll find out about us when they reach the oasis!" he hollers to Jiron.

"Then let's put as much distance between us as we can before they return." Jiron replies. They continue to gallop for a ways before bringing their speed down to a trot, saving their horses' strength for later.

Checking his mirror once more, James sees the riders have already reached the oasis and are there watering their horses, the people from the caravan are gathered around the riders, talking with them. As they ride, he continues watching the horsemen and then with dread, watches as they leave the oasis and begin moving to follow them, fast.

"They've left the oasis," he announces. When Jiron looks to him, he says, "And they're galloping our way."

"How far behind us are they?" he asks.

"It's hard to tell with this," he says, holding up the mirror. "But I wouldn't think much more than an hour."

"Great," Jiron says.

They make quick time, alternating between galloping and trotting to keep the horses strength up as best they can. Jiron looks over to James who is checking the mirror again and asks, "Well?"

"They're still behind us, though they're not gaining very fast," he replies. "To the south is another road, or rather a continuation of the coast road we followed previously. There doesn't appear to be any soldiers on it, just regular travelers."

"Wait!" he cries out.

"What?" asks Jiron.

"Oh man," he says. "A large force containing men and cavalry is coming from the south along the road, there must be over a thousand of them." He scans the mirror some more and says, "To the southeast is another band of horse coming in this direction too."

"You mean they've got us encircled?" Jiron asks.

"Yeah," he replies. "It looks like the only way to go is toward the coast but that's a dead end."

"Unless we find ourselves a boat!" states Jiron. "Is there a town to the west?"

"Let me check," he says as he scrolls the view further west. Excitedly, he exclaims, "Yes, there is and it looks like it's a port city."

"Any ships at the docks?" Jiron asks, hopefully.

"Four," he replies.

Turning his horse westward, Jiron says, "Then let's go get ourselves a boat."

"But," James says, "it's going to be broad daylight. How are we going to sneak aboard and take a boat?"

Giving James a slightly evil grin, Jiron replies, "Who said we were going to sneak!"

Chapter   Twenty Seven

Riding hard, they come to the road and move to follow it as it continues along the coast westward to the port city. Fellow travelers they pass along the road just stare at them as they fly by. Some holler words at them as they rush past but are soon left far behind.

Knowing they've not much time, James and Jiron race down the road weaving around those upon it, until the town begins to appear on the horizon ahead of them. The town appears rather large with no wall surrounding it, for which James is extremely grateful.

They slow down as they reach the outskirts of town so as not to attract undue attention. Heading straight down the main thoroughfare toward the docks, James fears that at anytime someone is going to challenge them.

But, acting like you belong is often the surest way of remaining unnoticed. Riding with a purpose, they make their way through the crowded streets and no one even gives them a second look. When they draw near to the docks, they stop in front of an inn and dismount, tying their horses to the post out front.

They quickly remove what they're going to need from their horses before continuing on foot. Before they reach the docks, Jiron motions for James to follow him into a side alley. Once within the alley he asks, "Can you see if any of our pursuers are getting close to the city?"

Taking out his mirror, James looks and after locating the armies approaching, shakes his head, saying, "It looks like they're all at least several miles away. We should have an hour, maybe more, before they arrive."

"Alright then," says Jiron, "let's go find us a boat."

They leave the alley and continue on their way toward the docks. When they get there, they see a dozen or more soldiers stationed in and around the dock area.

"Think they're there for us?" Jiron asks.

"Probably," replies James. "Looks like they're covering all their bases."

"Bases?" Jiron asks, confused at the term.

"Sorry," says James. "I just mean they're watching every avenue that we may take to get away."

"Oh," he says.

They pause near the entrance to the docks as they look at the ships tied there. One is a massive, deep sea cargo ship and the others are smaller, but all are clearly too big for their needs. Shaking his head, Jiron says, "I don't think these are going to help us any."

"I don't think so either," agrees James. Then he grabs Jiron's arm and directs his attention further down, away from the docks where a small, private ship is just pulling up to a small dock. "That will do fine, don't you think?" he asks.

"Perfect!" agrees Jiron.

They leave the dock area and head over toward the estate where the ship just docked. The estate has a protective wall around it and the gate is closed with a guard posted on the outside. They walk around the estate, doing their best not to attract attention as they look to see if there's another way in. The wall is high, too high to jump and grab the top. The only way in is through the gate.

They return to a spot near the gate and James asks, "Now what?"

"We gotta get through that gate," he replies. "I don't see any other way in."

The street passing in front of the estate is well traveled and any attempt to take out the guard will be readily seen by those passing by.

"We need a diversion so everyone will be looking away from the guard at the gate," he says as he looks to James.

"You want me to blow up the town again?" asks James, not entirely enthused with the idea.

"Not necessarily," he replies. "Just something that the people on the street will turn their attention to."

"Anything I do will announce that we're here," he says.

"They're going to know that soon enough anyway," Jiron explains. "As soon as those approaching forces meet up, they'll know we're here. A few minutes earlier really won't make that much of a difference."

"I suppose you're right," James says, resigned to the plan. "Let's go further into town and see what opportunity presents itself, I don't want to hurt innocents."

"Alright," says Jiron, understanding. "I'm sure there's something you can do that won't hurt anyone."

As they walk, James ponders different ideas, trying to come up with something that will distract but not hurt. "I think I have an idea," he tells Jiron after they've walked several blocks.

"What?" he asks.

"Well, you see…"

After getting everything ready, they return back to the gate. Jiron glances over at James where he's standing, silently counting. *Three…Two…One…*

From further into town, they begin to hear people screaming and running. The people on the street outside of the gate turn their attention toward the center of town and away from the gate to see what's going on.

"It's working," Jiron says as he begins edging slowly toward the gate.

James just nods in satisfaction with his solution and follows him.

When they near the gate, the guard is looking toward the center of town as well, fear evident on his face. James glances toward where he's looking and smiles when he sees the fifteen foot giant walking through town, a flaming sword gripped in its hand.

Jiron comes to the guard and places a knife to his throat as he says, "Open the gate!"

The guard suddenly realizes they're there and starts to draw his sword. Jiron presses the knife harder against his neck, "I wouldn't do that if I were you." When the guard relaxes his grip on his sword Jiron turns him so he's facing the gate. "Now, open it" he orders the man one more time. Despite the language barrier, the guard understands what Jiron is asking.

Shaken, the guard withdraws a key and places it in the lock, opening the gate. James looks at the passersby who are staring at the giant walking through town, many begin running for their lives.

"Come on, James!" urges Jiron.

Turning back to the gate, he sees that it's already open and follows Jiron and the guard inside. After the guard shuts and locks the gate, Jiron takes the key from him and says to James, "Let's get the boat and sail to Cardri as fast as we can." Then he hits the man in the head and knocks him out.

"What did you say that for?" he asks.

Grinning, Jiron replies, "When questioned, I'm hoping he'll tell them that we're going to Cardri so they'll look for us in that direction."

"Good idea, if he understood you," he says. Turning to the giant he created, he cancels the spell and it quickly dissipates back into nothing.

They run toward the estate and see someone run in through the front door just before it slams shut. Altering their course, they make for the front door. Jiron's the first to reach it and tries to open it only to find it locked. "It's locked," he tells James as he joins him at the door.

James puts his hand against it and lets loose the power. With a crack, the door flies open and smashes into the wall.

Jiron runs inside as he searches for whoever it was that had slammed the door shut, but is unable to locate anyone.

"The boat!" James says as he runs through the house to the back where the dock lies.

Jiron joins him and they race through the house and out the back door. Once outside, they find the man running toward the boat, intent on getting away. He turns and sees them leaving the house and bolts toward the boat, drawing a knife and cutting the lines as fast as he can. Giving the boat a shove, the man jumps aboard as the boat begins to drift away from the docks.

As they race onto the dock, the ship is now ten feet away and is beginning to pick up speed as the wind fills the hastily unfurled sails. Without even hesitating, Jiron runs to the edge and leaps across the distance, landing on the deck of the boat.

James stops on the dock and watches as Jiron draws his knives and advances on the man. With sword at the ready, the man engages him, but after a few quick exchanges, his sword drops to the deck and Jiron's knife is at his throat. He kicks the man's sword away and then points back to the dock where James is waiting.

Adjusting the sail and turning the tiller, the man maneuvers the boat back to the dock where James climbs on board. "Thank you," he says to Jiron.

Smiling back at him, he replies, "Not a problem."

James goes to the man and says, "Take us out to sea now, please."

The man just looks blankly back at James as if he doesn't understand. "Do you understand me?" he asks. Again, no response.

Jiron then says to James, "If he's not going to be any use to us, should I just slit his throat and toss his body over the side?"

The man visibly pales and says, "I can understand you."

"Thought you might," Jiron tells him. "Now, take us out to sea."

"What are you going to do with me?" the man asks, not making any move to comply with Jiron's demand.

"We merely wish to borrow you and your boat for a short time," he says. "If you're helpful, we might even pay you for your inconvenience." When the man still hasn't begun to get the boat underway, Jiron says, "Now, are you going to help or should I toss your lifeless body over the side?"

The man takes a moment, obviously deciding between flight and acquiescing. "If you jump in," Jiron tells him, "I'll jump in after you."

As if that's all he needed, the man turns and begins to get the sails in order. He then turns the tiller to angle the boat out to sea.

"Where is it we're going?" the man asks.

"Not exactly sure yet," James tells him. "Maybe you can help us with that."

"How can I be of any help?" the man asks, confused.

"We're searching for a friend of ours," he tells him. "He was taken as a slave and brought to this area. All we know now is that he's working underground somewhere, possibly in a mine."

"Then your friend is most likely at the Sorna Iron Mines," he tells them. "It's an island some miles off the coast to the south of here."

James nods his head and says, "That sounds right." He thinks for a moment as the ship sails further out to sea and away from the port. Coming to a decision, James says, "First, we want you to take us north for a ways and then swing west out to sea before heading to the island, understand?"

"No," he replies, "but I'll do it."

"Thank you," he says.

As the man turns the boat to follow the coast to the north, he asks, "Are you two the ones they're searching for?"

"Maybe," replies James. "Depends on who 'they' are, and who's doing the searching."

"There have been rumors that spies from the north have come to the Empire to sow dissension and destruction," he tells them. "One of them is a mage of some power, or so the rumor says."

James smiles at that, 'some power'. "What's your name?" he asks the man.

"Kristo," the man replies.

"Kristo?" Jiron say questioningly, "Doesn't sound like an empire name to me."

"It's not," Kristo replies. "My parents moved us here long ago from our home further to the south."

"Ah," replies Jiron.

They continue on up the coast for several miles and when they can no longer see anyone on the shoreline, they have him turn and head west, further out to sea.

James has always liked being out on the water, and with no one trying to immediately kill or capture him, he's able to sit back, relax and enjoy it. They continue on for another hour out to sea before turning to the south and the island.

By this time, the sun begins its descent toward the horizon. "How far is it to the island?" James asks Kristo.

"Not exactly sure," he says, "but probably several hours away." Glancing at the sun, he says, "Be dark by the time we get there."

"Will that be a problem?" James asks him.

"Definitely," he says. "I've never been there so don't know the waters or where the dangers are. We could just sail right into a reef or the side of the island before we were even aware it was there."

"Just sail until dark and then drop anchor," he tells him. "In the morning, we'll continue the rest of the way."

"Are you sure?" he asks. "This isn't a deep sea ship, just a coast hugger. If we're caught in a squall, we're going to go under."

James glances to the sky and at the clouds beginning to turn pink. "Pink at night, sailors' delight."

"What?" asks Jiron.

"Oh, just a saying from home," he says. "'Pink at night, sailor's delight. Pink in the morning, sailors take warning'." He gestures to the clouds overhead and says, "It just means if the clouds turn pink at sunset, then the sea should remain calm through the night."

"Is that true?" Jiron asks.

"Don't know," he replies with a shrug. "It's just a saying I picked up somewhere."

Kristo just shrugs as they look at him, "Don't ask me."

They continue sailing until dark and then Kristo drops the anchor as they await the coming of morning. James and Jiron take turns keeping watch on Kristo and the boat throughout the night, not wanting to take the chance that Kristo might do something.

When the sky starts to lighten with the dawn, they have Kristo raise anchor and lower the sails. The wind begins moving them and before too much longer, they're once more rapidly making their way across the water toward the island, hopefully where Miko is.

Using his mirror to locate other ships in the vicinity, James has Kristo steer around them, keeping a safe distance between them to avoid detection. "Jiron," James says after one such check.

"What?" he replies.

"We're coming up on the island," he tells him. "It should become visible pretty soon."

"And?" he asks.

"I've been searching the area and I think I've located where Miko would be," he says. "There's a compound on the northern section that looks to surround a mine entrance. To the south is a series of buildings with smoke coming from them. I think they may be processing whatever is coming out of the mines."

"Iron," interjects Kristo.

"What?" asks James.

"They're most likely iron smelters," he explains. "They mine iron ore on the island, it's one of the Empire's main sources of iron, or so I hear. Those buildings are most likely smelters where they extract the iron from the ore."

"Anyway," continues James, "there are two docks, one to the north and one closer to the smelting complex. They both have guards stationed there so we wouldn't be able to use them without notice."

Turning to Kristo, Jiron asks, "You have any ideas?"

Surprised at being asked, he says, "Me? Why would I help you? You break into my estate, kidnap me and steal my boat."

Shaking his head, Jiron says to James, "Any other place we might make landfall, far enough away to avoid notice?"

"I haven't examined the island that thoroughly yet, maybe," he says as he turns back to the mirror and begins a more precise examination of the island's coast.

After several minutes, he looks up and says, "There is an inlet on the southwestern side of the island, not very big. It would allow us to drop anchor near shore without being detected. A forest separates the inlet from the smelters."

"Perfect," Jiron says in satisfaction. "Can you direct him there?" he says, indicating Kristo.

"Definitely," he replies. Turning to Kristo, he says, "Steer us to a more westerly direction until I tell you to swing south."

With a slight movement of the tiller, Kristo steers in the desired direction. "That's good," says James when the boat is heading in the right direction.

They continue on the westerly heading until James determines the ship is at the proper position and then has Kristo swing due south. A half hour later, the island comes into view and James points out a large outcrop of the island and says, "The inlet is just to the right of there. You can't see it very well but it'll open up as you swing around it."

Sure enough, a small inlet extends some way past the outcrop. Kristo steers the boat around the outcrop and into a small, hidden cove. "Drop anchor," James tells him.

He furls the sails and drops anchor, bringing the boat to a stop.

James looks over to the shore, twenty feet away and says, "This will do nicely."

Jiron grabs some rope and comes toward Kristo. "What are you going to do?" he asks nervously as Jiron approaches.

"Tie you up so you won't take the boat and leave," he explains. "We'll need you to get us off the island."

Taking him over to the railing, he has him sit with his back to it and proceeds to secure him to it. When he's done, he tests the ropes to be sure Kristo won't be able to get free. Nodding satisfactorily, he says, "That should hold you until our return."

"What am I to do if you don't return?" he asks before Jiron places a gag in his mouth to prevent him from hollering for help.

"Just pray that we do," he tells him, receiving a glare in return.

Standing up, he turns to James and asks, "Ready?"

"Sure," he replies as he goes to the rail and stands up on it. Jumping off, he dives into the water, Jiron hitting the water just after him. They swim over to the shore and then climb out. James is shivering slightly from the coldness of the water.

"Now, let's go find your friend," Jiron says as they both enter the forest.

Chapter   Twenty Eight

After days of working in the mines, his hands have toughened up and the sores have begun to form calluses. A friendship has developed between Nate and him, each helping the other as needed. Even though the work is hard, he finds himself proud when his team achieves their quota for the day.

There are dozens of teams throughout the mines and a rough score is kept as far as how well each team consistently meets their quotas. His team, while at first having been low in the rankings due to the loss of men and the new ones joining, is now steadily climbing toward the lead team spot. Essin, though tough and strict, has been fair in his dealings with his men.

Since coming to join Essin's team, there have been two cave-ins, including the one that occurred on the first day. The second one, the team caught beneath the falling rocks hadn't been so lucky, they were crushed and killed. Miko's team wasn't the one sent to help dig out those poor souls, but had heard of it through the gossip channels later when leaving for the night.

Every other day or so, Black Tooth makes an appearance to give them their water and bread. His scowls have become so common now that Miko is no longer bothered by them. Lately, when they leave the mines at night, Black Tooth can be seen hanging around some of the supervisors, talking and joking with them. Whenever he sees Miko though, his smile fades from his face and hatred creeps into his features. He absently rubs his stump while looking at Miko, almost as if he's unconsciously reliving the day he lost his hand. But Miko no longer fears him. He's never far from his team and he knows they will stand by him should things ever get ugly between him and Black Tooth.

A day ago, during a break when bread and water was brought to them by someone other than Black Tooth, Miko had bitten into his bread and felt a sharp, jabbing sensation in his mouth. He reached in and pulled out a sharp rock, stained with blood from where it had punctured his tongue. If he would have swallowed it, it would've most likely torn apart his insides.

He had taken it to Essin who then proceeded to yell at the man who brought it. The man said he didn't know how it had made its way into the bread but that he would look into it when he got back. Later that day, when they were leaving the mines, Miko saw Black Tooth standing near the kitchen building talking to the one who had brought the bread down to them. He pointed them out to Nate who said, "Apparently, he's not through trying to get you, and he's enlisting aid."

"What can I do?" Miko asks him.

Shrugging, he says, "Nothing to do, just watch out until you have proof to bring to Essin."

Miko kept glancing over to Black Tooth until his team reached their room and went inside for the night.

The following morning after they reach their spot in the mines, all goes as usual and they are able to maintain their pace to achieve their quota for the day. The day passes uneventfully as they load wagon after wagon full of ore.

James and Jiron look out from the woods to where the smelting complex lies. Six buildings bellow smoke from tall smokestacks, wagons being unloaded into smaller carts which are then taken inside. Several other smaller auxiliary buildings surround them. Two wagons enter the complex from a road on the far side and make their way toward one of the smelters.

"That road must lead to where Miko is," states James.

"Let's work our way around to it," Jiron suggests.

Nodding, James makes to move when he's stopped by Jiron's hand on his shoulder. He glances back as Jiron indicates a group of workers walking along the side of a nearby building. Remaining motionless, they wait until the men move to the door in the side of the building and enter.

Working their way through the edge of the forest, they circumvent the smelting complex and come to the road. At the road they pause a moment as they look both ways. Not seeing anyone upon the road, they step out of the trees. James says, "Let's take the road. It'll be faster."

"Alright," he says. "But we better keep our eyes open."

They travel down the road for a hundred feet before Jiron suddenly takes him by the arm and whispers, "Someone's coming." Further up the road, movement can be seen.

James follows Jiron into the forest where they crouch down behind some bushes and trees to wait. Shortly, they begin to hear the unmistakable sound of a horse drawn wagon coming toward them down the road. When the wagon reaches them, they see that it's heaped full of ore from the mine, heading for the smelters. Aside from the driver, two guards with crossbows ride upon the wagon. After the wagon passes and has moved further down the road, they return to the road and continue down toward the mine.

An hour later finds them coming to the stockade wall that surrounds the mine. It appears out of the forest and then turns to run along the edge of the road. They enter the forest on the opposite side of the road from the wall before coming into view of the guards patrolling along the top. Keeping well within the woods, they make their way slowly alongside the road, all the while staying out of sight of the guards atop the walls. When they reach the area directly across from the gate, they stop and from a hidden location, watch the guards atop the gate.

The guards are fairly lax in their duty, most of their time is spent either engaged in conversation with the guard next to them or looking within the compound. Only occasionally does anyone glance around the outside along the road and into the forest.

"Looks like they're not too concerned about an attack from the outside," Jiron whispers to James.

"I think they are there more to keep people in than out," reasons James.

Jiron looks to him and nods, "That should make this all the easier, then."

"Let's hope so," he replies. Then he asks, "Can you get in?"

Shaking his head, he says, "Not with all those guards on the wall, they would spot me for sure. Let me go around the walls and see if there might be anyplace that would be less visible."

"Should I go with you?" James asks.

"No," he answers. "I can move a lot quieter and quicker if I'm by myself. Just stay here and keep an eye on the gate, see if you can determine some kind of routine for the guards."

"Alright," he says. "You be careful, this isn't like sneaking around a city."

"I will," he assures him and then begins moving along the road away from James, keeping in the trees to avoid detection. When he's gone far enough away beyond the point where the wall turns back into the forest, he quickly rushes across the road and enters the forest on the other side.

James catches his breath when he sees him crossing the road, sure that a guard on the wall will see him. He looks to the wall, but the guards are too engrossed with their conversation to have noticed. Hoping he finds a way in, James sits back against a tree and makes himself comfortable while waiting for his return.

Keeping a watch on the gate and the guards on the wall, he soon realizes there isn't any sort of routine or pattern. They simply stand there and converse among themselves, as well as others within the compound. One thing James has noticed is that there are always four guards walking the wall over the gate. Or rather, standing there talking to one another.

Jiron has been gone an hour when the gate opens and three wagons full of ore exit. The wagons turn south and begin rolling down the road toward the smelters. While the gate is open, James looks within but isn't able to see much more than some buildings scattered about. He does see other guards about the place, five others besides the ones on top of the wall. Once the last wagon has exited through the gate, the gate swings closed. With the gate closed, there's little for him to do other than sit back and wait for Jiron's return.

A hand touching his shoulder jolts him awake. Startled, he finds Jiron has returned and is shaking him. "Wake up," Jiron says with a smile as he sits next to him.

"What did you find?" James asks him.

"Just more of the same wall completely circling the entire encampment," he says. "Each wall has guards patrolling along the top which will make any attempt to gain entry difficult at best."

James gestures to the wall in front of them and says, "There are only four on patrol above the gate at any given time."

"That's about what it is on the others as well," he explains. "Most of them seem to be totally unconcerned with what goes on outside of the walls."

"I noticed that too," says James. "It feels like no one has ever tried to break in here before."

"Most likely," agrees Jiron. "Hopefully that will make our job that much easier."

"What's the plan?" he asks him.

Jiron sits and thinks for a minute before saying, "I really want to know what's on the other side of those walls. If I knew that, I would better know from where to attempt to gain entry."

"How about climbing a tree?" suggests James. "That should raise you high enough to see within the walls."

His eyes widen like he never even considered the option. Nodding, he says as he looks around the forest, "You may have something there." He gets to his feet and begins to look around for a suitable tree that's both tall enough and placed so he will be able to see over the walls without being observed.

When he finally locates one that appears to be acceptable, he says to James, "Be right back." Then he walks quietly through the trees until he comes to the one he spotted. The tree sits about thirty feet away from where the wall turns from the road back into the forest.

Jumping up, he grabs hold of one of the lower branches and swings himself up. James alternates between watching him climb and keeping an eye on the guards, all the while praying that he'll remain unobserved. The guards, totally oblivious to what's happening in the tree near them, continue talking among themselves.

James glances back to Jiron and sees that he's reached a height that will afford him a good view of the entire compound. He settles into the crook of a branch and stays up there quite awhile before beginning his descent back to the ground. Once down, he makes his way over to where James is waiting.

"Well?" he asks when Jiron approaches.

"They have a lot of guards within the walls," he says. "Thirty or more, I couldn't get an exact count. That of course, doesn't include any that are currently within the mine."

He takes a stick and begins drawing a diagram of the compound on the ground. He draws the wall and a large pit in the middle and large rectangles around the pit. "There's a large pit in the middle, most likely the entrance to the mines." Pointing to the rectangles around the pit he says, "These look to be quarters for the slaves and perhaps other auxiliary buildings, similar to the ones we saw back at the smelters."

"Did you see any of the slaves?" he asks.

"A few, but the majority must still be within the mine." He sits back and rests for a moment. "I'll go back up the tree and stay there till nightfall, just to see if things change. Then we can determine what we want to do."

"Alright," agrees James, anxious now that he's this close to getting Miko out.

Jiron reaches into his pouch and hands some dried beef to James as he says, "Here."

Taking the beef, James asks, "Where did you get this?"

"Found it on Kristo's boat," he says, grinning.

James tears off a bite and begins chewing, a little tough, but not bad. Jiron hands him another chunk and they have a quick meal before he returns to the tree to watch the compound. While they're eating, the gate opens and another five wagons leave the compound as they begin rolling south down the road to the smelters.

"They get a lot of iron from here, don't they?" he observes, a thoughtful look coming to him.

Nodding, James replies, "Yeah, I've been watching wagons leave all day. Why?"

"No reason," he replies. Finishing up, Jiron gets back to his feet and goes over to the tree where he again climbs up to keep an eye on what's going on inside the walls.

"Boys," Essin announces as the last wagon of the day rolls away, "I believe that puts us close to being the best team in the mines."

A cheer erupts from the men, Miko feels pride as Nate slaps him on the back and gives him a big grin. "Your hard efforts have not gone unnoticed and tonight you will not find the usual fare brought to your quarters. Tonight, you will have beef and wine."

A gasp escapes some of the men at the news. For those who've been here the longest, beef and wine is something they have all but forgotten. Miko's stomach begins to cramp and growl at the thought.

"If we can continue as we have," Essin tells them, "you can expect similar feasts in the future."

A shout erupts from the men as he turns and leads them from the mine.

Miko is happy. If this is to be his lot for the rest of his life, well, at least it could be much worse. A good crew to work with and an understanding boss, what more could a slave ask for. True, the work is hard and at times unforgiving, but the men he works with make it bearable.

As they continue through the mines, Essin turns his head back and says, "For the number one team, they'll give you women once a month as long as you keep being the best."

The men give out with another cheer and promises to be the best. As they leave the mine and head over to their quarters, Miko's jubilation is again dampened by the sight of Black Tooth carrying a water pail past on his way into the mines. But even his scowl isn't enough to wreck this day for him.

In the back of his mind, he wonders what James is doing, how he's getting along. He doesn't hold ill will to him, he knows that he's just a boy off the streets, not worth risking one's life for. He returns to the present as they enter their room and find the food already there for them.

The older guys snatch the jugs of wine first, but Miko doesn't care, his stomach cramps at the sight of the juicy, roasted beef sitting in heaping mounds on the platter. He grabs several thick slices and takes a big bite as he begins eating. The juices from the beef run down his chin, making tracks in the dust and dirt that coats his body.

For his crew of twelve, there are six jugs of wine, one of which has already been consumed by the others. Nate says to them, "Save some for Miko, he's earned it too."

"Sure thing," says Fez, one of the old timers. He goes over and slaps Miko on the back as he offers the jug to him, "Here you go, Miko me lad."

Miko takes the jug and has just a small drink before giving it back to Fez. He glances over to Nate who's giving him a grin. Nate's being moderate with the wine as well, taking only occasional sips of the wine as he concentrates mainly on the meat and loaves of bread.

When Miko finishes his fifth slice of bread, he begins to notice that Fez is behaving erratically. At first he assumes it's due to the large amount of wine he's consumed. But then he falls over and everyone starts laughing at his antics, thinking he has simply drunk too much.

Concerned, Miko goes over to him and tries to wake him up. "Fez," he says, shaking his shoulder.

"Leave him be," one of the others says. "He'll soon sleep it off."

But something just didn't feel right. Shaking him harder, he calls his name louder, "Fez!"

Turning to Nate, he says, "I think he's dead!"

As Nate goes over to him, another man cries out as he falls to the floor. Sudden pain rips through Miko's stomach as he watches Nate stumble and fall as his stomach, too, begins to cramp with pain.

"Poison!" Nate cries out, holding his stomach as the pain again rips through him.

Poison? thinks Miko as he comes over to where Nate has fallen. *Black Tooth!*

Chapter   Twenty Nine

James sits amidst the bushes in his spot across from the gate while Jiron keeps watch from his perch in the tree. As the sun begins to drop to the horizon, he notices Jiron perking up a little and begins gazing intently into the compound. A little after twilight, he comes down from the tree and back to where James is waiting for him.

"Looks like they have all the slaves come out of the mines at night," he informs him. Pointing to the diagram on the ground, he says, "These buildings here are where they keep the slaves for the night."

"You didn't see Miko did you?" he asks hopefully.

"I was too far away to make out more than vague features," he replies. "Can you determine which one of the buildings he's in with your mirror?"

Removing the mirror from his shaving kit, he says, "Possibly." In the fading light, it's actually easier to see the image coming into focus than in broad daylight. The image coalesces and they see Miko eating with the others.

"They sure feed them well here," comments Jiron when he sees the beef Miko is consuming.

Nodding, James expands the image and soon the exterior of the building comes into view. Once the image has zoomed far enough away to be able to see the entire compound, he points to the building where Miko is and then asks Jiron, "Recognize this?"

"Yeah, I know that one," he tells him. "It's on the opposite side of the pit from the gate. That one and the buildings next to it is where I saw the slaves being led."

Replacing the mirror back into his kit, he asks, "How do we get him out?"

"We could go around to where the wall is closest to him and try there," he says. "It's not much better than here, but there might be less scrutiny away from the gate."

"You may be right," agrees James. Getting up, he nods for Jiron to lead the way and then follows him as he moves through the forest away from the gate. At the point where the wall turns back into the forest, Jiron continues on until they've put sufficient distance between themselves and the men walking patrol atop the wall. Then with a quick glance atop the wall to make sure the guards aren't looking in their direction, they dart across the road quickly.

Jiron leads them deeper into the forest as they follow the wall from a distance, always keeping it in sight. He continues until the wall curves away from them and whispers to James that they're close to the building wherein they will find Miko.

Coming to a stop, he glances at James for a second, a question on his lips. He hesitates a moment before asking, "Can you destroy the mine when we leave?"

"What?" James replies in shock, taken off guard by the request. "Why?"

"You saw how much iron ore they've been removing," he says. "I was thinking that if they were no longer able to get iron from here it would seriously hurt their war machine." He turns and looks at James square in the eyes, "It might be enough to force them to leave Madoc, or at least hurt their attempts to take more of it."

"Possibly," he says. "But what about all the slaves here? I might kill them all!"

"Right now they're out and shouldn't be affected by whatever happens to the mine," he says.

"I'll see what I can do," he tells him. When he sees the look in Jiron's eye, he adds, "I understand what you're saying and the logic behind it. If I can, I will, okay? But not until we rescue Miko."

He nods his head, "Thanks."

"Now, what's the best way to get inside?" James asks.

Jiron points to an overhanging limb that comes close to the wall. "I can climb up there and swing over to the wall," he explains. "The only problem is the guards on watch up there." He looks to James and says, "I need you to take them out."

James gazes up at the wall and the guards walking there, considering the plan. He nods his head and says, "I think I can arrange that without alerting everyone to our presence."

"Good. Ready?" he asks.

"As ready as I'll ever be," replies James.

Jiron makes his way to the tree and begins to climb up to where the limb extends near the wall. As he climbs, he keeps as constant a watch on the guards as climbing will allow. Whenever they glance in his direction, he holds still until they once more turn away before continuing.

This section of the wall is not as long as the one by the gate so only has two guards. They're standing next to each other a couple yards from the tree Jiron is climbing, talking to each other. Contemplating what he's going to do, he watches Jiron as he climbs up to the limb that's extending over the wall and sees him give him a signal that he's ready.

James begins concentrating and then releases the magic. The two guards are suddenly pulled over the edge by an unseen force and plummet to the ground on the outside, just as if someone had grabbed them and pulled them off.

As they go over the edge, one of them cries out in startlement and then is silenced when he hits the ground. Running over to them, James finds that one has broken his neck and the other is unconscious. Tying and gagging the one still alive, he looks up to see Jiron lowering a rope down for him to climb the wall. "Hurry up!" can be heard as the rope reaches him.

He grabs the rope and tries to pull himself up but fails, his arms just not strong enough. In gym class, this is one of those things that kept causing him to almost fail every year. He was never able to get the hang of it. When Jiron realizes he's not going to be able to climb the rope, he whispers down, "Make a loop at the end for your foot and I'll pull you up!"

Waving back up to him, James bends down and ties the end in a loop. Putting his right foot in it, he gives two quick tugs on the rope and waves up to Jiron.

The tension in the rope suddenly increases and then the rope begins to rise. Gripping the rope tightly with both hands, he holds on until he's up to the top of the wall. He reaches out and takes hold of the ledge and begins pulling himself the rest of the way. Jiron releases the rope and helps him the last few feet. "Thanks," he says.

Jiron gives him a slight nod and says, "Just pretend you're a guard so if they look up here, all is normal."

"Alright," James says.

"What about those two down there?" Jiron asks him.

"One's dead," he tells him. "Broke his neck when he hit the ground, the other is tied and gagged."

Jiron shakes his head and says, "Should've just killed him."

"I can't do that," asserts James.

Shrugging, Jiron points over to a building twenty feet from the wall and says, "From what you showed me in the mirror, that should be where your friend is."

"How do we get down?" James asks.

Gesturing off to the right, he says, "There's a ladder over there we can use. Once we do though, it's only a matter of time before someone realizes there's no one up here and will come to investigate."

"We better hurry, then," James states as he makes for the ladder, Jiron right behind him. Jiron has him wait while he descends the ladder first to be able to deal with any trouble should it arise.

Just as Jiron reaches the bottom, a guard rounds the corner of a nearby building and walks up to them as he begins talking. His words cut off suddenly when he realizes he's not facing fellow guards but intruders. He turns to run as a cry begins to escape his lips just as Jiron tackles him. A quick strike with his knife and the guard is soon lying on the ground, choking as blood pours out of the wound in the side of his neck. In a moment, the guard is lying still and quiet.

A quick check to be sure no one heard the fight, they leave the dead guard behind and stay to the shadows as they work their way to the corner of the building. The side with the door to Miko's room is illuminated by a line of torches that shed light on the interior of the compound and the mine entrance.

"Don't think we can sneak in," Jiron tells him when he's assessed the situation. "But if we walk as if we belong here, we might make it before anyone realizes what's going on."

"Alright," he says nervously, "let's go."

They look around the corner to make sure the immediate area is clear before Jiron steps out as if he owns the place with James right behind. Going past the first three doors, they stop in front of the fourth where Jiron grabs the handle and pulls it open. The stench that wafts out from within catches him unexpectedly and his stomach tries to spew forth its contents. Keeping it under control, he steps into the room and sees bodies lying all over the floor.

James rushes past him and stops next to a boy with a man's head on his lap. "Miko," James says as he kneels on the floor next to him.

Miko's head comes up and as if he can't believe what he's seeing, asks, "James?"

James nods his head, tears coming to his eyes.

"I thought you had forgotten about me," Miko says.

"Never," he asserts. "We've come to get you out of here."

"I can't leave without Nate," he says indicating the man whose head he's cradling.

Closing the door, Jiron asks from where he stands just within the room, "What happened here?"

A look of anger overcomes Miko's features as he says, "A fellow slave I call Black Tooth slipped poison in the wine and now everyone's dead." Tears come to his eyes as he looks around at the friends he lost. Slaves though they were, they had been a team. *His team.*

"Why aren't you dead?" James asks.

Miko turns his red rimmed eyes to him and says, "I was too busy eating the meat and didn't drink that much of the wine." He motions to the man in his lap and says, "Nate here didn't drink much either, but he did have more than me."

Jiron comes over and checks Nate, finding him still alive but unconscious. "I don't know if we can take him with us," he says to James. "It's going to be hard enough to do it with just the three of us."

Miko gets a defiant look and says, "Then leave me here with him, I'd be dead by now without him. I can't leave him, he's my friend!"

Jiron glances to James who nods his head and says, "Then we take him with us."

He comes over to James and whispers, "Aren't we going to be a trifle conspicuous carrying an unconscious body around?"

"Be that as it may," James replies, "Miko's not leaving without him so he comes with us. Besides, if he has kept him alive all this time, then I owe him."

"Alright," he says, "but you're going to need to carry him, I'll be too busy fighting off the guards when they see us leave."

Nodding, James gets up and says, "Let me carry him Miko."

Miko removes his arms as James bends over to pick him up. As he slings him over his shoulder, Nate gives out with a slight groan but otherwise doesn't regain consciousness.

Jiron helps Miko to his feet and asks, "Are you alright?"

"Not really," he replies. "I did drink the wine, though just a little bit and it's causing no end of pain in my stomach."

As they make to leave, Miko looks around at the friends he's leaving behind. They were the best.

Jiron moves to the door and cracks it open, "Ready?" When he gets a nod from both of them, he says, "We'll make straight for the ladder and get over the wall. If anyone tries to stop us, they're dead."

Opening the door, they step out and hurry back the way they came. Suddenly a cry goes up and they look over to see a one handed slave looking in their direction as he lets out with another yell.

"Black Tooth!" Miko exclaims with hatred. "He's the one who poisoned us!"

From the door of an adjoining building, Black Tooth continues crying the alarm, as guards come running.

"To the wall," Jiron cries out as he begins running to the edge of the building. When he gets there, a man turns the corner and Jiron's knife flies into his hand and is suddenly tackled from behind by Miko. "He's a friend!" he yells at Jiron as they hit the ground.

"What's going on here?" Essin cries out when he sees Miko on the ground with a man wielding a knife. Eyes widen when he sees James standing there with Nate slung over his shoulder.

"Black Tooth poisoned the wine," Miko tells him as he extricates himself from Jiron. "The whole team is dead, except for Nate and me. We're leaving, come with us."

Jiron gets up off the ground and gives Miko a dirty look and says, "There's no time for talk, let's move!" He then turns the corner after giving Essin an annoyed look and heads for the wall.

A crossbow bolt strikes the building next to where Essin is standing and everyone turns to see the guards coming toward them.

Crumph!

The ground beneath the guards explodes upward. Essin gasps at the sight and then nods his head as he turns to follow Miko and the others to the wall.

"Get down!" James says to Jiron who is already several rungs up the ladder. Coming to the wall, he places his hand upon it and begins concentrating.

Jiron looks down to him, realizing what he's about to do and then jumps to the ground as far from the wall as he can. James releases the magic and a section of the wall fifteen feet across explodes outward, leaving them a clear exit from the compound. His knees begin to wobble and Essin comes to his side and says, "Let me carry Nate."

With relief, James hands the still unconscious Nate over to the man, who slings him over his shoulder and then follows the others. Once they've passed through the trees for a ways, James glances behind them and realizes none of the guards have followed them through the opening in the wall.

"Wait a second!" he hollers, bringing everyone to a halt. "Keep a watch out and I'll try to arrange a slight distraction for them." Sitting down he tries to relax as he calms himself as he summons the magic and begins to sink his senses down through the earth, to the depths where the magma flows.

Searching for fissures and cracks, he uses the magic to create a path up to the lowest level of the mines. Just like bringing the water up in the desert, he creates a pathway for the magma to travel. Widening the way here, closing off another route there, he continues to bring the magma up to the floor of the mines. The ground begins to shake violently from the pressure he's creating, causing those on their feet to lose their balance and fall to the ground.

Finally, his senses detect that the magma has broken through and has begun seeping into the mines. He is also able to sense a continued building of pressure as more magma presses to push through the path he made. Realizing an eruption may be imminent, he gets back to his feet as the shaking finally subsides. "We've got to move! NOW!" he shouts to the others. Essin again takes Nate and they race through the forest until they come to the road. Without even pausing, they burst out of the trees and run to the south to where their boat is waiting for them. As they race down the road, the ground begins to shake once more. With visions of volcano movies in his head, James gets ready to live his last moments on earth.

"What did you do?" Jiron shouts at him over the roar of the earthquake.

"Let nature loose!" he replies as they continue running, doing their best to remain upright as the tremors steadily increase in intensity.

Suddenly the ground stops shaking and all becomes unnervingly quiet. "Get down!" James yells. From behind them a massive explosion rips through the night as fire and lava burst from the ground and shoots up into the sky. The shockwave rolls over them, burning them as it goes. But just as soon as the burning starts, it stops. They get up, singed and feeling like they have just been roasted over a campfire. The smell of burnt hair permeates the air.

Looking back, they watch as lava balls are shot into the air and then come to land in the forest with terrible force. Fires begin to rage wherever one of them lands.

"You can't do anything halfway, can you?" Jiron yells at him.

James just gives him a look as he stands up. "I don't think it's over yet! Come on, we have to get off this island!"

They continue to race down the road as more lava balls are ejected from the mine. One arcs through the air toward them. "Watch out!" Miko cries out. Everyone pauses as they turn to watch the lava ball fly over their heads and strike the road a hundred feet ahead of them, entirely blocking the road with flame and setting the nearby trees on fire.

Immediately, Jiron leads them off the road in the direction of where they left Kristo and his boat. The sound of screams and yells come from all around as people flee the hot magma spilling out of the mine. Behind them, the sky is aglow from the numerous fires burning all across the island, the smell of sulfur infuses the air and begins causing them to cough.

Suddenly, three guards fleeing the eruption appear in the forest ahead of them, both sides surprised at seeing the others. One of the guards hollers something out and then all three draw their swords as they advance.

Jiron moves forward to meet them, both knives at the ready as one of James' stones sails past and takes one full in the chest, spraying gore upon the one behind. As the man in front of him falls, the gore covered guard stands there in shock and belatedly recognizes the threat Jiron poses as he approaches. Jiron is able to easily dispatch him and then steps around his lifeless body as he joins with the third guard.

This remaining guard, finally able to release his pent up anger and fear by all that has happened, comes at him with a vengeance. Crying a battle cry, he wields his sword in both hands as he slashes at Jiron.

With agility gained from hundreds of fights in the pits, Jiron maneuvers to avoid the sword and returns with a strike to the leg, drawing blood as his knife sinks an inch into the man's thigh.

Crying out in pain, the man brings his sword around for another attack which Jiron deflects with one knife while following through with the other, opening a four inch long cut along the man's left forearm.

The wound causes him to falter in his next swing, leaving him open to a thrust through the breastbone. Puncturing his heart, Jiron's knife becomes wedged between two ribs and is ripped out of his hands as the man falls to the ground. Bending down to retrieve his knife, Jiron has to place his foot on the man's lifeless body in order to pry the knife from where it's trapped.

Wiping the blood from his knives on the man's shirt he quickly gets his bearings and then continues to lead them through the forest toward the boat. The forest begins to fill with smoke as more and more of the trees catch fire, the roaring of the inferno behind them continues to grow with every passing second.

At last they come to the cove where they left Kristo and Jiron comes to a stop, cursing.

"What's wrong?" James asks as he comes to stand next to him. He looks out over the inlet and understands.

The boat is gone.

"I knew we should've killed him!" Jiron exclaims. "Now he's going to raise the alarm that the ones they were looking for on the mainland are now here." Behind them, another blast erupts into the night, throwing fire and lava in all directions. He looks to James and continues as he gestures behind them, "As if they wouldn't be able to figure it out with that going on."

"How are we to get off the island now?" Miko asks.

"There's still the dock over by the smelters," James replies. "It's further south a ways, but it's our only hope." The weight of impending doom seems to be dropping down upon him, "I don't think we have all that much time."

As they get moving though the forest, Essin asks, "Time for what?"

James glances back toward where the fire and lava shoots to the sky, "Before the entire island goes."

"Goes where?" Miko asks.

"**Kaboom!**" he shouts really loud, raising his arms into the air, "taking everything and everyone with it. Apparently, this area use to be volcanically active long ago, and I seem to have begun a series of events which are going to bring this area back alive again."

With renewed determination, everyone picks up speed as they crash through the underbrush, heading to the southern docks. James takes a turn at carrying the comatose Nate, giving Essen's arms a break.

When they come to the smelter area, there's a flurry of activity going on as the people there load what looks like long bars of iron onto wagons. Some wagons have already been loaded and are on their way to the southern docks.

"There must be a ship there," figures Jiron, "and they're trying to save as much of the iron as they can."

"Then we'll just have to convince them to take us along," James says as they remain in the forest and skirt around the buildings.

"Do you think they will?" asks Essin.

James just looks at him and shakes his head. "It'll end up being us or them," he says.

"Oh, right," he says.

Once around the camp and come to the road, they no longer try to avoid being seen as they race onto the road and make a break for it to the south. A cry goes up behind them from the drivers of the wagons currently on the road but they are slow and there are no guards with them. Not paying them any heed, they continue racing toward the docks and their only chance to make it alive off the island.

"How far is it?" Jiron asks.

"Not sure," James replies as he begins to get a stitch in his side, "maybe another mile or two." Then turning to Essin he says, "Here," as he hands the unconscious Nate back to Essin. "I may need my strength when we get to the docks."

Once Nate is back upon Essin's shoulder, James is better able to continue running. The ground begins to once more tremble as shockwaves ripple outward from the mine. "It's not going to be much longer!" he yells.

Suddenly, the road opens up on a clearing, the dock lies on the far side over a hundred yards away. Two wagons are being unloaded as a dozen people transfer the iron bars to the only ship docked there. A dozen guards stand watch.

When they enter the clearing and have covered half the distance to the docks, one of the workers sees them and gives the alarm. The twelve guards turn and draw their swords as they move to intercept them before they can reach the ship. Iron slugs begin flying toward the advancing guards, taking out five before they take a dozen strides. Using a tactic he saw in an old war movie, James takes out the ones in the rear to keep the advancing ones from realizing their number is decreasing.

Then he let's loose more of the power as the ground erupts, throwing another five into the air.

Jiron advances upon the remaining two, knives at the ready. The first one closes with him and he deflects the sword thrust with a knife as he follows through with the other. The guard dances back as his slice misses the guard's chest by bare inches.

The workers on the dock, having seen the guards taken out so readily, and the ground erupting before their eyes, turn to flee for their lives away from the wagons and the dock.

The ship's captain begins barking orders as he attempts to move his ship away from the dock before they have a chance to approach.

Essin lays Nate on the ground and grabs a nearby stick as he goes to aid Jiron. He comes up behind the second man Jiron is engaged with and strikes him in the back of the head. The man staggers a few steps before dropping to the ground.

Jiron glances over to Essin and gives him a slight nod as he continues the fight with the remaining guard.

Miko sees the boat begin to pull away and hollers over to James, "The boat is leaving!"

Looking over to the boat, James realizes it's already a good five feet from the dock and departing steadily. The magic surges out of him as he creates an invisible tether from the dock to the boat. The ship suddenly lurches to a stop, the captain shouting orders to his crew but nothing he does moves his ship one inch further. Beginning to pant with all the magical exertions, James begins to shorten the tether and the boat is slowly brought back to the dock. Spots dance before his eyes as he sinks to one knee from the effort of drawing the ship back to the dock. He glances over to Jiron and watches as the remaining guard falls to the ground.

After his remaining opponent falls, Jiron turns to find James at the edge of the dock on one knee. He runs to his side while Essin and Miko bring forward the unconscious Nate.

As the boat pulls up to the dock, James sees the captain and crew there with swords drawn ready to sell their lives dearly if they must. "Request permission to come aboard captain," James hollers to him.

"Why should I let you?" the captain yells back.

"Because your ship isn't going anywhere until we do," James tells him. "This island is about to erupt in a volcanic explosion of immense proportions and we all need to be as far away as possible."

As if to add credence to what James is saying, the ground begins to shake violently, dropping everyone to the ground. Trees in the forest are heard toppling over and from the mine area, another blast erupts into the sky.

When the ground once again calms, they return to their feet. The others gather around James as he stands there before the ship. When Essin and Miko bring Nate close, the captain sees him and says, "Nate?"

James looks over to Nate and then back to the captain, "You know him?"

"Aye," he replies, "he's my cousin." Turning to his men he signals for them to lower their weapons and then returns his own sword to the scabbard on his hip.

"Permission granted," he says, "hurry and come aboard."

As they begin moving toward the ship, a mob exits the forest behind them. Consisting of both slaves and guards from the compound, they swarm into the clearing, hell bent on reaching the ship and safety.

"Come on!" the captain yells and then begins barking out orders to his crew as they once more get the ship ready to sail.

Suddenly a hail of hot stones falls on the ship and those getting aboard from where they had been belched from the belly of the emerging volcano. One stone strikes James in the head, causing him to falter and fall to the ground. Jiron helps him to his feet and then half carries him across the gangplank to the ship's deck.

Miko turns and gasps when he sees one armed Black Tooth in the fore of the advancing mob. From somewhere he's acquired a sword and has it gripped in his remaining hand. When their eyes lock, an evil grin spreads across his face as he quickens his pace to reach Miko.

"Miko!" James yells from where he stands on the ship. "Hurry up!"

When Miko and Essin reach the gangplank, the captain is there and he takes Nate from them as they board the ship. Two crewmen pull in the gangplank as the wind fills the sails and the ship begins to back away from the dock now that James is no longer holding it captive.

Before the ship is able to put enough distance between them and the dock, a few of the people running toward them try jumping the distance between the dock and the ship. Most land in the water but a couple manages to reach the deck, Black Tooth is one of those to make the ship's deck.

Crying out as he lands on the deck, he turns toward Miko who's only a foot away and raises his sword to end his life. Miko looks up at death coming for him and then closes his eyes as he braces for the end.

As Black Tooth strikes down at Miko, he suddenly gasps and falters. Miko opens his eyes and sees a crossbow bolt sticking out of his chest, blood beginning to flow down the front of his body. Staggering to the side, he looks down at the bolt sticking out of him. With a cry of animal ferocity, he again lurches toward Miko, intent on killing him with his last ounce of strength.

Another bolt strikes him in the shoulder causing him to drop his sword. Coming forward with the crossbow still in his hands, Essin approaches and says, "This is for killing my crew!" Using his right foot, he kicks Black Tooth in the butt which causes him to stumble over the ship's rail. Leaning over the rail, Essin watches as he hits the water and proceeds to sink beneath the surface.

Only one of the others who made it to the ship still lives, another slave Essin knows and will vouch for his good behavior.

As they continue to pull away, the others remaining at the dock cry and plead for them to return, but the captain orders his men to make all speed to open water. "Put this god forsaken island behind us!"

"How is he?" the captain asks Miko as he comes over to see how his cousin Nate is doing.

"I don't know," replies Miko. "He was poisoned, the others who were poisoned are all dead, but he didn't drink as much as they had."

"Guess we'll know after awhile," states the captain. "Never thought to see him alive again."

James comes over to the captain and offers his hand. When the captain takes it, he says, "Appreciate you allowing us on, captain."

"Didn't do it for you," he says, "though after what you did to the guards I was of a mind to allow you on anyway. But when I saw Nate here, that clinched it."

"We appreciate it anyway," he assures him. Suddenly from the north end of the island, a gigantic explosion throws a tremendous volume of rocks and magma into the air. Several other spots on the island begin to erupt as well.

Steam rises from the ocean off the northern point of the island and soon, magma can be seen shooting upward through the water.

"Damn!" the captain exclaims at the sight.

"Full sails!" he hollers up to the men in the rigging. To the man at the wheel he shouts, "Straight away to open water!"

"Aye, aye captain," the man at the wheel replies as he alters the ship's course accordingly.

As the ship sails away, James can see several different areas where the magma is bursting through the surface of the sea. A whole chain of volcanoes is being created and the heat from them can be felt even from this distance. He feels bad, everyone that had been left on the island is most likely dead or will be. He can't conceive of anyone surviving what's happening.

He goes over to the captain and asks, "Where do you plan to take us?"

The captain looks at him for a second and then says, "To the city of Corillian, it's where Nate's family still resides. They should take you in and help you for saving his life."

Corillian, he ponders as he watches the volcanoes erupting in the distance.

Epilog

Standing there, staring out his window from the highest room of the tower, he again burns with anger at the destruction that has been wrought.

A day ago, smoke rose from the Iron Mines at Sorna just before it was engulfed by a series of erupting volcanoes. Shortly afterward, a great wall of water surged out of the sea and washed away a good portion of the dock area here at Tiru Stali.

Burning with impotent rage, unable to vent it upon the one that had brought this into being, he stands there. *A mage!* he rages within. *A single mage and so much destruction.* The last several days rumors have come to him of strange occurrences to the north, some hardly credible. A demon walks from an oasis which had dried earlier the same day and then water pours from the ground miles away.

Even here in Tiru Stali, a giant with a flaming sword supposedly went walking down the street. *Just what is going on!*

From everything he has been able to gather, these things have been occurring since the fall of the City of Light. He knew that venture had been ill fated, but his counsel hadn't been heeded.

A noise behind him causes him to turn and the sight both fills him with anticipation and dread. A small creature, only a foot in height sits on the table behind him. It's scaly, somewhat man-like form is bent over as if from carrying too much weight. Red eyes aglow with an inner light stare from its gnarled head at Abula-Mazki with cruel intelligence.

"A Hikuli!" Abula-Mazki exclaims aloud.

The Hikuli stares at him for a second longer before vanishing. Abula-Mazki instantly understands the significance of such a visit. Only one person on this world commands the Hikuli.

Looking back toward the destruction wrought under his dominion, he realizes there can be only one reason for him to be summoned to the High Temple.

With a thought, he summons one of his acolytes waiting in the adjoining room who immediately opens the door and enters. "A Hikuli has come," he tells the acolyte.

He can see the fear and uncertainty in the man's eyes. The acolyte nods his head in answer and then leaves, closing the door behind him.

Abula-Mazki turns back to the window, contemplating the summons until the door again opens. The acolyte returns with others bearing Abula-Mazki's armor and sword. He remains still as he allows them to put the heavy armor upon him and strap his sword belt around his waist. As his acolytes prepare him for his audience with the High Priest of Dmon-Li, he continues to stare out the window at the destruction.

When the last strap has been secured, they quietly turn and file out the door, leaving him once more alone.

Turning from the window, he walks over to a nearby wall and says "Hirun alib Mugana" and a section disappears, leaving a doorway open into an adjoining room.

No one but Abula-Mazki has ever been within this room, at least none living at this time. Stepping within, he walks to the center where a raised dais lies. Upon the dais is the symbol of the Warrior Priests of Dmon-Li, three dots forming the points of a triangle with connecting lines in between.

Stepping upon the dais, he activates the magic within and suddenly he's standing upon a matching one in the middle of a small, dark room. A solitary candle burns in a nearby wall niche doing its best to keep back the shadows of this grim place. The room is cold, cold to the skin and cold to the soul. A cowled figure stands waiting, and as soon as Abula-Mazki's eyes fall upon him, turns to leave without a word.

Without hesitation, Abula-Mazki steps off the dais and follows the cowled figure out of the room and down a long corridor.

He's passed this way several times before, but never with the dread filling him now. As he walks, more of the Hikuli pop in and out as they see who has come and then go to inform their master. None can walk the halls of Ith-Zirul without gaining their notice.

They finally come to the entrance to the Halls of Despair, the audience chamber of Ozgirath, High Priest of Dmon-Li. The cowled figure that had led him here waits until he passes into the room before he turns around and leaves.

If the rest of Ith-Zirul was cold, this room is absolutely frigid. Across the room from where he enters, lies a seat made entirely out of bones, some human, others not. On either side of the dark throne are two braziers burning with a purplish glow which seen to suck the warmth from Abula-Mazki as he approaches. Seated upon the throne is a dark figure. Glowing eyes, yellow and piercing, stare out at him from the shadows surrounding the throne as he approaches.

When he reaches the requisite distance, he falls to his knees and bows his head. "I have come, great one," he says in reverence to the figure before him.

"Arise," he hears Ozgirath's command, though it isn't so much a voice, as a thought.

Coming to his feet, he stands there in humility, waiting.

"The Star shines again," the voice says.

Gasping, Abula-Mazki lifts his head and looks directly at Ozgirath and says, "The Star of Morcyth?"

"Say not that name here," the voice commands.

"I plead forgiveness master," he says, again bowing his head.

"But, yes," the voice replies, "it again moves across the land."

"I had thought all were destroyed during the great purging," he says.

"No," Ozgirath replies, "they were not. Some escaped and have never been found."

Fear of being chastised for the destruction in his dominion begins to leave him. If he was here for that reason, they would hardly be having this conversation. "What would you have me do, master?" he asks.

"Hunt for the one wearing the Star," he replies.

Abula-Mazki raises his head and stares into the glowing eyes as Ozgirath says, "And bring him to me."

Made in the USA
Lexington, KY
30 December 2010